'[A   back

'Featu
    qu

'Step   horror stories. What the hell happened to the horror genre? It may have just received a life-saving jolt' undertowbooks.com

A
BOOK
of
HORRORS

Edited by
STEPHEN JONES

Jo Fletcher
BOOKS

First published in Great Britain in 2011 by Jo Fletcher Books
This edition published in 2012 by

Jo Fletcher Books
An imprint of Quercus
55 Baker Street
7th Floor, South Block
London
W1U 8EW

A
BOOK
of
HORRORS

Contents

Introduction

Whatever Happened to Horror?

WHAT THE HELL happened to the horror genre? Whatever happened to menacing monsters, vicious vampires, lethal lycanthropes, ghastly ghosts and monstrous mummies?

These days our bloodsuckers are more likely to show their romantic nature, werewolves work for covert government organisations, phantoms are private investigators and the walking dead can be found sipping tea amongst the polite society of a Jane Austen novel.

These are not the iconic figures of fear and wonder that we grew up with. These are not the Creatures of the Night that have scared multiple generations over the centuries and forced countless small children to hide under the bedclothes reading their books and comics by torchlight.

Today we are living in a world that is 'horror-lite'. This appalling appellation was coined by publishers to describe the type of fiction that is currently enjoying massive success under such genre categories as 'paranormal romance', 'urban fantasy', 'literary mash-up' or even 'steampunk'.

Although it cannot be denied that there is an audience for these types of fictions, for the most part these books are not aimed at readers of traditional horror stories. The audience for this type of fiction has no interest in being deliciously scared by what they read, or left thinking about a particularly disturbing tale long after they have finished a story and closed the book. And that would not be a problem if publishers and booksellers were not usurping the traditional horror market with an avalanche of disposable volumes aimed at the middle-of-the-road reader.

Well, the time has come to reclaim the horror genre for those who understand and appreciate the worth and impact of a scary story.

With *A Book of Horrors* we hope that we have lived up to that title and all that it implies.

As anybody who has ever read any of my other books knows, my own definition of what makes a superior horror story is pretty inclusive. Obviously not every tale is going to appeal to every reader, but what I have attempted to do is bring you a wide range of original stories, by some of the finest writers working in the field today, that explore the many monstrous facets of the genre that we like to call 'horror'.

That is not to say that there is no room for humour – check out Ramsey Campbell's grimly gruesome 'Getting it Wrong' and Robert Shearman's unsettling yet hilarious 'Alice Through the Plastic Sheet' – and our other horrors range from the more traditional monsters (Stephen King's 'The Little Green God of Agony' and Peter Crowther's 'Ghosts with Teeth') and the classic ghost story (John Ajvide Lindqvist's 'The Music of Bengt Karlsson, Murderer' and Reggie Oliver's 'A Child's Problem'), through the modern supernatural thriller (Lisa Tuttle's 'The Man in the Ditch' and Michael Marshall Smith's 'Sad, Dark Thing') and a pair of very different mythological menaces (Caitlín R. Kiernan's 'Charcloth, Firesteel and Flint' and Brian Hodge's 'Roots and All') to more lyrical and literary tales (Angela Slatter's 'The Coffin-Maker's Daughter', Dennis Etchison's 'Tell Me I'll See You Again' and Elizabeth Hand's remarkable novella 'Near Zennor'). Finally, we close with Richard

Christian Matheson's disturbingly dark epigram – the appropriately titled 'Last Words'.

Many of the contributors to this volume are experimenting with form and structure and length to bring the horror story bang up-to-date, while others are working in the age-old practice of presenting their terrors in the most straightforward – and effective – manner possible.

Whatever your fears, we hope that you will find them within these pages. This is what modern horror fiction is all about and, if you enjoy the stories assembled within these pages, then you can say that you were there when the fight back began.

Welcome to *A Book of Horrors* – it's time to let the nightmares begin . . .

—Stephen Jones
London, England
June 2011

The Little Green God of Agony

—STEPHEN KING—

'I WAS IN AN ACCIDENT,' Newsome said.

Katherine MacDonald, sitting beside the bed and attaching one of the four TENS units to his scrawny thigh just below the basketball shorts he now always wore, did not look up. Her face was carefully blank. She was a piece of human furniture in this big house – in this big bedroom where she now spent most of her working life – and that was the way she liked it. Attracting Mr Newsome's attention was usually a bad idea, as any of his employees knew. But her thoughts ran on, just the same. *Now you tell them that you actually caused the accident. Because you think taking responsibility makes you look like a hero.*

'Actually,' Newsome said, 'I caused the accident. Not so tight, Kat, please.'

She could have pointed out, as she did at the start, that the TENS lost their efficacy if they weren't tight to the outraged nerves they were supposed to soothe, but she was a fast learner. She loosened the Velcro strap a little, thinking: *The pilot told you there were thunderstorms in the Omaha area.*

'The pilot told me there were thunderstorms in the area,' Newsome continued. The two men listened closely. Jensen had heard it all before, of course, but you always listened closely when the man doing the talking was the sixth-richest man not just in America but in the world. Three of the other five mega-rich guys were dark-complected fellows who wore robes and drove places in armoured Mercedes-Benzes.

She thought: *But I told him it was imperative that I make that meeting.*

'But I told him it was imperative that I make that meeting,' Newsome carried on.

The man sitting next to Newsome's personal assistant was the one who interested her – in an anthropological sort of way. His name was Rideout. He was tall and very thin, maybe sixty, wearing plain grey pants and a white shirt buttoned all the way to his scrawny neck, which was red with overshaving. Kat supposed he'd wanted to get a close one before meeting the sixth-richest man in the world. Beneath his chair was the only item he'd carried into this meeting, a long black lunchbox with a curved top meant to hold a Thermos. A working man's lunchbox, although what he claimed to be was a minister. So far Rideout hadn't said a word, but she didn't need her ears to know what he was. The whiff of charlatan was strong about him. In fifteen years as a nurse specialising in pain patients, she had met her share. At least this one wasn't wearing any crystals.

Now tell them about your revelation, she thought as she carried her stool around to the other side of the bed. It was on casters, but Newsome didn't like the sound when she rolled on it. She might have told another patient that carrying the stool wasn't in her contract, but when you were being paid five thousand dollars a week for what were essentially human caretaking services, you kept your smart remarks to yourself. Nor did you tell the patient that emptying and washing out bedpans wasn't in your contract. Although lately her silent compliance was wearing a little thin. She felt it happening. Like the fabric of a shirt that had been worn and washed too many times.

Newsome was speaking primarily to the fellow in the farmer-goes-to-town get-up. 'As I lay on the runway in the rain among the burning pieces of a fourteen-million-dollar aircraft, most of the clothes torn off my body – that'll happen when you hit pavement and roll fifty or sixty feet – I had a revelation.'

Actually, two of them, Kat thought as she strapped a second TENS unit on his other wasted, flabby, scarred leg.

'Actually, two of them,' Newsome said. 'One was that it was very good to be alive, although I understood – even before the pain that's been my constant companion for the last two years started to eat through the shock – that I had been badly hurt. The second was that the word *imperative* is used very loosely by most people, including my former self. There are only two imperative things. One is life itself, the other is freedom from pain. Do you agree, Reverend Rideout?' And before Rideout could agree (for surely he would do nothing else), Newsome said in his waspy, hectoring, old man's voice: 'Not so goddam *tight*, Kat! How many times do I have to tell you?'

'Sorry,' she murmured, and loosened the strap. *Why do I even try?*

Melissa, the housekeeper, looking trim in a white blouse and high-waisted white slacks, came in with a coffee tray. Jensen accepted a cup, along with two packets of artificial sweetener. The new one, the bottom-of-the-barrel so-called reverend, only shook his head. Maybe he had some kind of holy coffee in his lunchbox Thermos. Kat didn't get an offer. When she took coffee, she took it in the kitchen with the rest of the help. Or in the summerhouse . . . only this wasn't summer. It was November, and wind-driven rain lashed the windows.

'Shall I turn you on, Mr Newsome, or would you prefer that I leave now?'

She didn't want to leave. She'd heard the whole story many times before – the imperative meeting, the crash, how Andrew Newsome had been ejected from the burning plane, about the broken bones, chipped spine and dislocated neck, most of all about the twenty-four months of unrelieved suffering, which he would soon get to – and it bored her. But Rideout didn't. Other charlatans would undoubtedly follow, now that all reputable relief resources had been exhausted, but Rideout was the first, and Kat was interested to see how the farmer-looking fellow would go about separating Andy Newsome from a large chunk of his cash. Or how he would try. Newsome hadn't amassed his obscene piles of cash by being stupid, but of course he wasn't the same man he had been, no matter how real his pain might be. On that subject, Kat had her own opinions, but this was the best job she'd ever had. At least in terms of money. And if Newsome wanted to continue suffering, wasn't that his choice?

'Go ahead, honey, turn me on.' He waggled his eyebrows at her. Once the lechery might have been real (Kat thought Melissa might have information on that subject), but now it was just a pair of shaggy eyebrows working on muscle memory.

Kat plugged the cords into the control unit and flicked the switch. Properly attached, the TENS units would have sent a weak electrical current into Newsome's muscles, a therapy that seemed to have some ameliorative effects . . . although no one could say exactly why, or if they were entirely of the placebo variety. Be that as it might, they would do nothing for Newsome tonight. Hooked up as loosely as they were, they had been reduced to the equivalent of joy-buzzers. Expensive ones.

'Shall I—?'

'Stay!' he said. 'Therapy!'

The lord wounded in battle commands, she thought, *and I obey*.

She bent over to pull her chest of goodies out from under the bed. It was filled with tools many of her past clients referred to as implements of torture. Jensen and Rideout paid no attention to her. They continued to look at Newsome, who might (or might not) have been granted revelations that had changed his priorities and outlook on life, but who still enjoyed holding court.

He told them about awakening in a cage of metal and mesh. There were steel gantries called fixators on both legs and one arm to immobilise joints that had been repaired with 'about a hundred' steel pins (actually seventeen; Kat had seen the X-rays). The fixators were anchored in the outraged and splintered femurs, tibiae, fibulae, humerus, radius, ulna. His back was encased in a kind of chain-mail girdle that went from his hips to the nape of his neck. He talked about sleepless nights that seemed to go on not for hours but for years. He talked about the crushing headaches. He told them about how even wiggling his toes caused pain all the way up to his jaw, and the shrieking agony that bit into his legs when the doctors insisted that he move them, fixators and all, so he wouldn't entirely lose their function. He told them about the bedsores, and how he bit back howls of hurt and outrage when the nurses attempted to roll him on his side so the sores could be flushed out.

'There have been another dozen operations in the last two years,' he said with a kind of dark pride. Actually, Kat knew, there had been five, two of those to remove the fixators when the bones were sufficiently healed. Unless you included the minor procedure to re-set his broken fingers, that was. Then you could say there were six, but she didn't consider surgical stuff necessitating no more than local anaesthetic to be 'operations'. If that were the case she'd had a dozen herself, most of them while listening to Muzak in a dentist's chair.

Now we get to the false promises, she thought as she placed a gel pad in the crook of Newsome's right knee and laced her hands together on the hanging hot-water bottles of muscle beneath his right thigh. *That comes next.*

'The doctors promised me the pain would abate,' Newsome said. 'That in six weeks I'd only need the narcotics before and after my physical therapy sessions with the Queen of Pain here. That I'd be walking again by the summer of 2010. *Last* summer.' He paused for effect. 'Reverend Rideout, those were false promises. I have almost no flexion in my knees at all, and the pain in my hips and back is beyond description. The doctors— *Ah! Oh! Stop, Kat, stop!*'

She had raised his right leg to a ten-degree angle, perhaps a little more. Not even enough to hold the cushioning pad in place.

'Let it go down! Let it *down*, goddammit!'

Kat relaxed her hold on his knee and the leg returned to the hospital bed. Ten degrees. Possibly twelve. Whoop-de-do. Sometimes she got it all the way to fifteen – and the left leg, which was a little better, to twenty degrees of flex – before he started hollering like a kid who sees a hypodermic needle in a school nurse's hand. The doctors guilty of false promises had not been guilty of false advertising; they had told him the pain was coming. Kat had been there as a silent onlooker during several of those consultations. They had told him he would swim in pain before those crucial tendons, shortened by the accident and frozen in place by the fixators, stretched out and once again became limber. He would have plenty of pain before he was able to get the bend in his knees back to ninety degrees. Before he would be able to sit in a chair or behind the wheel of a car, that was. The same was true of his back and his neck. The road to recovery led through the Land of Pain, that was all.

These were true promises Andrew Newsome had chosen not to hear. It was his belief – never stated baldly, in words of one syllable, but undoubtedly one of the stars he steered by – that the sixth-richest man in the world should not have to visit the Land of Pain under any circumstances, only the Costa del Sol of Full Recovery. Blaming the doctors followed as day follows night. And of course he blamed fate. Things like this were not supposed to happen to guys like him.

Melissa came back with cookies on a tray. Newsome waved a hand – twisted and scarred in the accident – at her irritably. 'No one's in the mood for baked goods, 'Lissa.'

Here was another thing Kat MacDonald had discovered about the mega-rich, those dollar-babies who had amassed assets beyond ordinary comprehension: they felt very confident about speaking for everyone in the room.

Melissa gave her little Mona Lisa smile, then turned (almost pirouetted) and left the room. *Glided* from the room. She had to be at least forty-five, but looked younger. She wasn't sexy; nothing so vulgar. Rather there was an ice-queen glamour about her that made Kat think of Ingrid Bergman. Icy or not, Kat supposed men would wonder how that chestnut hair would look freed from its clips, and lying all mussed up on a pillow. How her coral lipstick would look smeared on her teeth and up one cheek. Kat, who considered herself dumpy, told herself at least once a day that she wasn't jealous of that smooth, cool face. Or that heart-shaped bottom.

Kat returned to the other side of the bed and prepared to lift Newsome's left leg until he yelled at her again to stop, goddammit, did she want to kill him? *If you were another patient, I'd tell you the facts of life*, she thought. *I'd tell you to stop looking for short-cuts, because there are none. Not even for the sixth-richest man in the world. You have me – I'd help you if you'd let me – but as long as you keep looking for a way to pay yourself out of the shit, you're on your own.*

She placed the pad under his knee. Grasped the hanging bags that should have been turning back into muscle by now. Began to bend the leg. Waited for him to scream at her to stop. And she would. Because five thousand dollars a week added up to a cool quarter-mil a year. Did he know that part of what he was buying was her silence? How could he not?

Now tell them about the doctors – Geneva, London, Madrid, Mexico City, et cetera, et cetera.

'I've been to doctors all over the world,' he told them, speaking primarily to Rideout now. Rideout still hadn't said a word, just sat there with the red wattles, his overshaved neck hanging over his buttoned-to-the-neck country preacher shirt. He was wearing big yellow work boots. The heel of one almost touched his black lunchbox. 'Teleconferencing would be the easier way to go, given my condition, but of course that doesn't cut it in cases like mine. So I've gone in person, in spite of the pain it causes me. We've been everywhere, haven't we, Kat?'

'Indeed we have,' she said, very slowly continuing to bend the leg. On which he would have been walking by now, if he weren't such a child about the pain. Such a spoiled baby. On crutches, yes, but walking. And in another year, he would have been able to throw the crutches away. Only in another year he would still be here in this two-hundred-thousand-dollar state-of-the-art hospital bed. And she would still be with him. Still taking his hush-money. How much would be enough? Two million? She told herself that now, but she'd told herself half a million would be enough not so long ago, and had since moved the goalposts. Money was wretched that way.

'We've seen specialists in Mexico, Geneva, London, Rome, Paris . . . where else, Kat?'

'Vienna,' she said. 'And San Francisco, of course.'

Newsome snorted. 'Doctor there told me I was manufacturing my own pain. "To keep from doing the hard work of rehabilitation," he said. But he was a Paki. And a queer. A queer Paki, how's that for a combo?' He gave a brief bark of laughter, then peered at Rideout. 'I'm not offending you, am I, Reverend?'

Rideout rotated his head side-to-side in a negative gesture. Twice. Very slowly.

'Good, good. Stop, Kat, that's enough.'

'A little more,' she coaxed.

'Stop, I said. That's all I can take.'

She let the leg subside and began to manipulate his left arm. That he allowed. He often told people both of his arms had also been broken, but this wasn't true. The left one had only been sprained. He also told people he was lucky not to be in a wheelchair, but the all-the-bells-and-whistles hospital bed suggested strongly that this was luck he had no intention of capitalising on in the near future. The all-the-bells-and-whistles hospital bed *was* his wheelchair. It rolled. He had ridden all over the world in it.

Neuropathic pain, Kat thought. *It's a great mystery. Perhaps insoluble. The drugs no longer work.*

'The consensus is that I'm suffering from neuropathic pain.'

And cowardice.

'It's a great mystery.'

Also a good excuse.

'Perhaps insoluble.'

Especially when you don't try.

'The drugs no longer work and the doctors can't help me. That's why I've brought you here, Reverend Rideout. Your references in the matter of . . . er . . . healing . . . are very strong.'

Rideout stood up. Kat hadn't realised how tall he was. His shadow scared up behind him on the wall even higher. Almost to the ceiling. His eyes, sunken deep in their sockets, regarded Newsome solemnly. He had charisma, of that there could be no doubt. It didn't surprise her; the charlatans of the world couldn't get along without it, but she hadn't realised how much or how strong it was until he got to his feet and towered over them. Jensen was actually craning his neck to see him. There was movement in the corner of Kat's eye. She looked and saw Melissa standing in the doorway. So now they were all here except for Tonya, the cook.

Outside, the wind rose to a shriek. The glass in the windows rattled.

'I don't heal,' Rideout said. He was from Arkansas, Kat believed – that was where Newsome's latest Gulfstream IV had picked him up, at least – but his voice was accentless. And flat.

'No?' Newsome looked disappointed. Petulant. Maybe, Kat thought, a little scared. 'I sent a team of investigators, and they assure me that in many cases—'

'I *expel*.'

Up went the shaggy eyebrows. 'I beg your pardon?'

Rideout came to the bed and stood there with his long-fingered hands laced loosely together at the level of his flat crotch. His deep-set eyes looked sombrely down at the man in the bed. 'I exterminate the pest from the wounded body it's feeding on, just as a bug exterminator would exterminate pests – termites, for instance – feeding on a house.'

Now, Kat thought, *I have heard absolutely everything*. But Newsome was fascinated. *Like a kid watching a three-card monte expert on a street corner*, she thought.

'You've been possessed, sir.'

'Yes,' Newsome said. 'That's what it feels like. Especially at night. The nights are . . . very long.'

'Every man or woman who suffers pain is possessed, of course, but in some unfortunate people – you are one – the problem goes deeper. The possession isn't a transient thing but a permanent condition. One that worsens. Doctors don't believe, because they are men of science. But *you* believe, don't you? Because you're the one who's suffering.'

'You bet,' Newsome breathed. Kat, sitting beside him on her stool, had to restrain herself from rolling her eyes.

'In these unfortunates, pain opens the way for a demon god. It's small, but dangerous. It feeds on a special kind of hurt produced only by certain special people.'

Genius, Kat thought, *he's going to love that*.

'Once the god finds its way in, pain becomes agony. It feeds just as termites feed on wood. And it will eat until you are all used up. Then it will cast you aside, sir, and move on.'

Kat surprised herself by saying, 'What god would that be? Certainly not the one you preach about. That one is the God of love. Or so I grew up believing.'

Jensen was frowning at her and shaking his head. He clearly expected an explosion from the boss ... but a little smile had touched the corners of Newsome's lips. 'What do you say to that, Rev?'

'I say that there are many gods. The fact that our Lord, the Lord God of Hosts, rules them all – and on the Day of Judgment will *destroy* them all – does not change that. These little gods have been worshipped by people both ancient and modern. They have their powers, and our God sometimes allows those powers to be exercised.'

As a test, Kat thought.

'As a test of our strength and faith.' Then he turned to Newsome and said something that surprised her. Jensen, too; his mouth actually dropped open. 'You are a man of much strength and little faith.'

Newsome, although not used to hearing criticism, nevertheless smiled. 'I don't have much in the way of Christian faith, that's true, but I have faith in myself. I also have faith in money. How much do you want?'

Rideout returned the smile, exposing teeth that were little more than tiny eroded gravestones. If he had ever seen a dentist, it had been many moons ago. Also, he was a tobacco-chewer. Kat's father, who had died of mouth cancer, had had the same discoloured teeth.

'How much would you pay to be free of your pain, sir?'

'Ten million dollars,' Newsome replied promptly. Kat heard Melissa gasp. 'But I didn't get to where I am by being a sucker. If you do whatever it is you do – expelling, exterminating, exorcising, call it what you want – you get the money. In cash, if you don't mind spending the night. Fail, and you get nothing – except your first and only round trip on a private jet. For that there will be no charge. After all, *I* reached out to *you.*'

'No.' Rideout said it mildly, standing there beside the bed, close enough to Kat so she could smell the mothballs that had been recently keeping his dress pants (maybe his only pair, unless he had another to preach in) whole. She could also smell some strong soap.

'No?' Newsome looked frankly startled. 'You tell me no?' Then he began to smile again. This time it was the secretive and rather unpleasant smile he wore when he made his phone calls and did his deals. 'I get it. Now comes the curveball. I'm disappointed, Reverend Rideout. I really hoped you were on the level.' He turned to Kat, causing her to draw back a bit. 'You, of course, think I've lost my mind. But I haven't shared the investigators' reports with you, have I?'

'No,' she said.

'There's no curveball,' Rideout said. 'I haven't performed an expulsion in five years. Did your investigators tell you that?'

Newsome didn't reply. He was looking up at the thin, towering man with a certain unease.

Jensen said, 'Is it because you've lost your powers? If that's the case, why did you come?'

'It's God's power, sir, not mine, and I haven't lost it. But an expulsion takes great energy and great strength. Five years ago I suffered a major heart attack shortly after performing one on a young girl who had been in a terrible car accident. We were successful, she and I, but the cardiologist I consulted in Jonesboro told me that if I ever exerted myself in such a way again, I might suffer another attack. This one fatal.'

Newsome raised a gnarled hand – not without effort – to the side of his mouth and spoke to Kat and Melissa in a comic stage-whisper. 'I think he wants twenty million.'

'What I want, sir, is seven hundred and fifty thousand.'

Newsome just stared at him. It was Melissa who asked, 'Why?'

'I am pastor of a church in Titusville. The Church of Holy Faith, it's called. Only there's no church any more. We had a dry summer in my part of the world. There was a wildfire, probably started by campers. And probably drunk. That's usually the case. My church is now just a concrete footprint and a few charred beams. I and my parishioners have been worshipping in an abandoned gas station/convenience store on the Jonesboro Pike. It is not satisfactory during the winter months, and there are no homes large enough to accommodate us. We are many but poor.'

Kat listened with interest. As conman stories went, this was a good one. It had the right sympathy-hooks.

Jensen, who still had the body of a college athlete (he also served as Newsome's bodyguard) and the mind of a Harvard MBA, asked the obvious question. 'Insurance?'

Rideout once more shook his head in that deliberate way: left, right, left, right, back to centre. He still stood towering over Newsome's state-of-the-art bed like some country-ass guardian angel. 'We trust in God.'

'In this case, you might have been better off with Allstate,' Melissa said.

Newsome was smiling. Kat could tell from the stiff way he held his body that he was in serious discomfort – his pills were now half an hour overdue – but he was ignoring it because he was interested. That he *could* ignore it was something she'd known for quite a while now. He could battle the pain if he chose to. He had resources. She had thought she was merely irritated with this, but now, probably prompted by the appearance of the charlatan from Arkansas, she discovered she was actually infuriated. It was so *wasteful*.

'I have consulted with a local builder – not a member of my flock, but a man of good repute who has done repairs for me in the past and quotes a fair price – and he tells me that it will cost approximately six hundred and fifty thousand dollars to rebuild. I have taken the liberty of adding one hundred thousand dollars, just to be on the safe side.'

Uh-huh, Kat thought.

'We don't have such monetary resources, of course. But then, not even a week after speaking with Mr Kiernan, your letter came, along with the video-disc. Which I watched with great interest, by the way.'

I'll bet you did, Kat thought. *Especially the part where the doctor from San Francisco says the pain associated with his injuries can be greatly alleviated by physical therapy.* Stringent *physical therapy.*

It was true that nearly a dozen other doctors on the DVD had claimed themselves at a loss, but Kat believed Dr Dilawar was the only one with the guts to talk straight. She had been surprised that Newsome had allowed the disc to go out with that interview on it, but since his accident, the sixth-richest man in the world had slipped a few cogs.

'Will you pay me enough to rebuild my church, sir?'

Newsome studied him. Now there were small beads of sweat just below his receding hairline. Kat would give him his pills soon, whether he asked for them or not. The pain was real enough; it wasn't as though he were faking or anything, it was just . . .

'Would you agree not to ask for more? Gentleman's agreement. We don't need to sign anything.'

'Yes.' Rideout said it with no hesitation.

'Although if you're able to remove the pain – *expel* the pain – I might well make a contribution of some size. Some *considerable* size. What I believe you people call a love offering.'

'That would be your business, sir. Shall we begin?'

'No time like the present. Do you want everyone to leave?'

Rideout shook his head again: left to right, right to left, back to centre. 'I will need assistance.'

Magicians always do, Kat thought. *It's part of the show.*

Outside, the wind shrieked, rested, then shrieked again. The lights flickered. Behind the house, the generator (also state-of-the-art) burped to life, then stilled.

Rideout sat on the edge of the bed. 'Mr Jensen there, I think. He looks strong and quick.'

'He's both,' Newsome said. 'Played football in college. Running back. Hasn't lost a step since.'

'Well . . . a few,' Jensen said modestly.

Rideout leaned towards Newsome. His dark, deeply socketed eyes studied the billionaire's scarred face solemnly. 'Answer a question for me, sir. What colour is your pain?'

'Green,' Newsome replied. He was looking back at the preacher with fascination. 'My pain is green.'

Rideout nodded: up, down, up, down, back to centre. Eye-contact never lost. Kat was sure he would have nodded with exactly the same look of grave confirmation if Newsome had said his pain was blue, or as purple as the fabled Purple People-Eater. She thought, with a combination of dismay and real amusement: *I could lose my temper here. I really could. It would be the most expensive tantrum of my life, but still – I could.*

'And where is it?'

'Everywhere.' It was almost a moan. Melissa took a step forward, giving Jensen a look of concern. Kat saw him shake his head a little and motion her back to the doorway.

'Yes, it likes to give that impression,' Rideout said, 'but it's not so. Close your eyes, sir, and concentrate. Look for the pain. Look past the false shouts it gives – ignore the cheap ventriloquism – and locate it. You can do this. You *must* do it, if we're to have any success.'

Newsome closed his eyes. For a space of ninety seconds there was no sound but the wind and the rain spattering against the windows like handfuls of fine gravel. Kat's watch was the old-fashioned wind-up kind, a nursing school graduation present from her father many years ago, and when the wind lulled, the room was quiet enough for her to hear its self-important ticking. And something else: at the far end of the big house, elderly Tonya Andrews singing softly as she neatened up the kitchen at the end of another day: *Froggy went a-courtin' and he did ride, mmm-hm.*

At last Newsome said, 'It's in my chest. High in my chest. Or at the bottom of my throat, just below the windpipe.'

'Can you see it? Concentrate!'

Vertical lines appeared on Newsome's forehead. Scars from the skin that had been flayed open during the accident wavered through these grooves of concentration. 'I see it. It's pulsing in time to my heartbeat.' His lips pulled down in an expression of distaste. 'It's nasty.'

Rideout leaned closer. 'Is it a ball? It is, isn't it? A green ball.'

'Yes. Yes! A little green ball that *breathes*!'

Like the rigged-up tennis ball you undoubtedly have either up your sleeve or in that big black lunchbox of yours, Rev, she thought.

And, as if she were controlling him with her mind (instead of just deducing where this sloppy little playlet would go next), Rideout said: 'Mr Jensen, sir. There's a lunchbox under the chair I was sitting in. Get it and open it and stand next to me. You need to do no more than that for the moment. Just—'

Kat MacDonald snapped. It was a snap she actually heard in her head. It sounded like Roger Miller snapping his fingers during the intro to 'King of the Road'.

She stepped up beside Rideout and shouldered him aside. It was easy. He was taller, but she had been turning and lifting patients for nearly half her life, and she was stronger. 'Open your eyes, Andy. Open them right now. Look at me.'

Startled, Newsome did as she said. Melissa and Jensen (now with the lunchbox in his hands) looked alarmed. One of the facts of their working lives – and Kat's own, at least until now – was that you didn't command the boss. The boss commanded you. You most certainly did not startle him.

But she'd had quite enough, thank you. In another twenty minutes she might be crawling after her headlights along stormy roads to the only motel in the vicinity, a place that looked like the avatar of all roach-traps, but it didn't matter. She simply couldn't do this any longer.

'This is bullshit, Andy,' she said. 'Are you hearing me? Bullshit.'

'I think you better stop right there,' Newsome said, beginning to smile – he had several smiles, and this wasn't one of the good ones. 'If you want to keep your job, that is. There are plenty of other nurses in Vermont who specialise in pain therapy.'

She might have stopped there, but Rideout said, 'Let her speak, sir.' It was the gentleness in his tone that drove her over the edge.

She leaned forward, into his space, and the words spilled out in a torrent.

'For the last sixteen months – ever since your respiratory system improved enough to allow meaningful physiotherapy – I've watched you lie in this goddamned expensive bed and insult your own body. It makes me sick. Do you know how lucky you are to be alive, when everyone else on that airplane was killed? What a miracle it is that your spine wasn't severed, or your skull crushed into your brain, or your body burned – no, *baked*, baked like an apple – from head to toe? You would have lived four days, maybe even two weeks, in hellish agony. Instead you were thrown clear. You're not a vegetable. You're not a quadriplegic, although you choose to act like one. You won't do the work. You look for some easier way. You want to pay your way out of your situation. If you died and went to Hell, the first thing you'd do is look for a tollgate.'

Jensen and Melissa were staring at her in horror. Newsome's mouth hung open. If he had ever been talked to in such a fashion, it had been long ago. Only Rideout looked at ease. *He* was the one smiling now. The way a father would smile at his wayward four-year-old. It drove her crazy.

'You could have been *walking* by now. God knows I've tried to make you understand that, and God knows I've told you – over and over – the kind of work it would take to get you up out of that bed and back on your feet. Dr Dilawar in San Francisco had the guts to tell you – he was the only one – and you rewarded him by calling him a faggot.'

'He *was* a faggot,' Newsome said pettishly. His scarred hands had balled themselves into fists.

'You're in pain, yes. Of course you are. It's manageable, though. I've seen it managed, not once but many times. But not by a lazy rich man who tries to substitute his sense of entitlement for the plain old hard work and tears it takes to get better. You refuse. I've seen that, too, and I know what always happens next. The quacks and confidence men come, the way leeches come when a man with a cut leg wades into a stagnant pond. Sometimes the quacks have magic creams. Sometimes they have magic pills. The healers come with trumped-up claims about God's power, the way this one has. Usually the marks get partial relief. Why wouldn't they, when half the pain is in their heads, manufactured by lazy minds that only understand it will hurt to get better?'

She raised her voice to a wavering, childlike treble and bent close to him. 'Daddy, it *hurrr-rrrts*! But the relief never lasts long, because the muscles have no tone, the tendons are still slack, the bones haven't thickened enough to accommodate weight-bearing. And when you get this guy on the phone to tell him the pain's back – if you can – do you know what he'll say? That you didn't have *faith* enough. If you used your brains on this the way you did on your manufacturing plants and various investments, you'd know there's no little living tennis-ball sitting at the base of your throat. You're too fucking old to believe in Santa Claus, Andy.'

Tonya had come into the doorway and now stood beside Melissa, staring with wide eyes and a dishwiper hanging limp in one hand.

'You're fired,' Newsome said, almost genially.

'Yes,' Kat said. 'Of course I am. Although I must say that this is the best I've felt in almost a year.'

'Don't fire her,' Rideout said. 'If you do, I'll have to take my leave.'

Newsome's eyes rolled to the Reverend. His brow was knitted in perplexity. His hands now began to knead his hips and thighs, as they always did when his pain medication was overdue.

'She needs an education, praise God's Holy Name.' Rideout leaned towards Newsome, his own hands clasped behind his back. He reminded Kat of a picture she'd seen once of Washington Irving's schoolteacher, Ichabod Crane. 'She's had her say. Shall I have mine?'

Newsome was sweating more heavily, but he was smiling again. 'Have at her, Rideout. I believe I want to hear this.'

Kat faced him. Those dark, socketed eyes were unsettling, but she met them. 'So do I.'

Hands still clasped behind his back, pink skull shining mutedly through his thin hair, long face solemn, Rideout examined her. Then he said: 'You've never suffered yourself, have you, miss?'

Kat felt an urge to flinch at that, or look away, or both. She suppressed it. 'I fell out of a tree when I was eleven and broke my arm.'

Rideout rounded his thin lips and whistled: one tuneless, almost toneless note. 'Broke an *arm* while you were *eleven*. Yes, that must have been excruciating.'

She flushed. She felt it and hated it but couldn't stop the heat. 'Belittle me all you want. I based what I said on years of experience dealing with pain patients. It is a *medical* opinion.'

Now he'll tell me he's been expelling demons, or little green gods, or whatever they are, since I was in rompers.

But he didn't.

'I'm sure,' he soothed. 'And I'm sure you're good at what you do. I'm sure you've seen your share of fakers and posers. You know their kind. And I know yours, miss, because I've seen it many times before. They're usually not as pretty as you—' Finally a trace of accent, *pretty* coming out as *purty*. '—but their condescending attitude towards pain they have never felt themselves, pain they can't even conceive of, is always the same. They work in sickrooms, they work with patients who are in varying degrees of distress, from mild pain to deepest, searing agony. And after awhile, it all starts to look either overdone or outright fake to them, isn't that so?'

'That's not true at all,' Kat said. What was happening to her voice? All at once it was small.

'No? When you bend their legs and they scream at fifteen degrees – or even at ten – don't you think, first in the back of your mind, then more and more towards the front, that they are lollygagging? Refusing to do the hard work? Perhaps even fishing for sympathy? When you enter the room and their faces go pale, don't you think, 'Oh, now I have to deal with *this* lazy thing again?' Haven't you – who once fell from a tree and broke your *arm*, for the Lord's sake – become more and more disgusted when they beg to be put back into bed and be given more morphine or whatever?'

'That's so unfair,' Kat said . . . but now her voice was little more than a whisper.

'Once upon a time, when you were new at this, you knew agony when you saw it,' Rideout said. 'Once upon a time you would have believed in what you are going to see in just a few minutes, because you knew in your heart that malignant outsider god was there. I want you to stay so I can refresh your memory . . . and the sense of compassion that's gotten lost somewhere along the way.'

'Some of my patients *are* whiners,' Kat said, and looked defiantly at Rideout. 'I suppose that sounds cruel, but sometimes the truth *is* cruel. Some *are* malingerers. If you don't know that, you're blind. Or stupid. I don't think you're either.'

He bowed as if she had paid him a compliment – which, in a way, she supposed she had. 'Of course I know. But now, in your secret heart, you believe *all* of them are malingerers. You've become inured, like a soldier who's spent too long in battle. Mr Newsome here has been infested, I tell you, *invaded*. There's a demon inside him so strong it has become a god, and I want you to see it when it comes out. It will improve matters for you considerably, I think. Certainly it will change your outlook on pain.' To Newsome: 'Can she stay, sir?'

Newsome considered. 'If you want her to.'

'And if I choose to leave?' Kat challenged him.

Rideout smiled. 'No one will hold you here, Miss Nurse. Like all of God's creatures, you have free will. I would not ask others to constrain it, or constrain it myself. But I don't believe you're a coward, merely calloused. Case-hardened.'

'You're a fraud,' Kat said. She was furious, on the verge of tears.

'No,' Rideout said, once more speaking gently. 'When we leave this room – with you or without you – Mr Newsome will be relieved of the agony that's been feeding on him. There will still be pain, but once the agony is gone, he'll be able to deal with the pain. Perhaps even with your help, miss, once you've had the necessary lesson in humility. Do you still intend to leave?'

'I'll stay,' she said, then said: 'Give me the lunchbox.'

'But—' Jensen began.

'Give it over,' Rideout said. 'Let her inspect it, by all means. But no more talk. If I am meant to do this, it's time to begin.'

Jensen gave her the long black lunchbox. Kat opened it. Where a workman's wife might have packed her husband's sandwiches and a little Tupperware container of fruit, she saw an empty glass bottle with a wide mouth. Inside the domed lid, held by a wire clamp meant to secure a Thermos, was a green aerosol can. There was nothing else. Kat turned to Rideout. He nodded. She took the aerosol out and looked at the label, nonplussed. 'Pepper spray?'

'Pepper spray,' Rideout agreed. 'I don't know if it's legal in Vermont – probably not would be my guess – but where I come from, most hardware stores stock it.' He turned to Tonya. 'You are—?'

'Tonya Marsden. I cook for Mr Newsome.'

'Very nice to make your acquaintance, ma'am. I need one more thing before we begin. Do you have a baseball bat? Or any sort of club?'

Tonya shook her head. The wind gusted again; once more the lights flickered and the generator burped in its shed behind the house.

'What about a broom?'

'Oh, yes, sir.'

'Fetch it, please.'

Tonya left. There was silence except for the wind. Kat tried to think of something to say and couldn't. Droplets of clear perspiration were trickling down Newsome's narrow cheeks, which had also been scarred in the accident. He had rolled and rolled, while the wreckage of the Gulfstream burned in the rain behind him. *I never said he wasn't in pain*, she told herself. *Just that he could manage it, if he'd only muster half the will he showed during the years he spent building his empire.*

But what if she was wrong?

That still doesn't mean there's some sort of living tennis ball inside him, sucking his pain the way a vampire sucks blood.

There were no vampires, and no gods of agony . . . but when the wind blew hard enough to make the big house shiver in its bones, such ideas almost seemed plausible.

Tonya came back with a broom that looked like it had never swept so much as a single pile of floor-dirt into a dustpan. The bristles were bright blue nylon. The handle was painted wood, about four feet long. She held it up doubtfully. 'This what you want?'

'I think it will do,' Rideout said, although to Kat he didn't sound entirely sure. It occurred to her that Newsome might not be the only one in this room who had slipped a few cogs lately. 'I think you'd better give it to our sceptical nurse. No offence to you, Mrs Marsden, but younger folks have quicker reflexes.'

Looking not offended in the slightest – looking relieved, in fact – Tonya held out the broom. Melissa took it and handed it to Kat.

'What am I supposed to do with it?' Kat asked. 'Ride it?'

Rideout smiled, briefly showing the stained and eroded pegs of his teeth. 'You'll know when the time comes, if you've ever had a bat or raccoon in the room with you. Just remember: first the bristles. Then the stick.'

'To finish it off, I suppose. Then you put it in the specimen bottle.'

'As you say.'

'So you can put it on a shelf somewhere with the rest of your dead gods, I suppose.'

He smiled without humour. 'Hand the spray-can to Mr Jensen, please.'

Kat did so. Melissa asked, 'What do I do?'

'Watch. And pray, if you know how. On my behalf, as well as Mr Newsome's. For my heart to be strong.'

Kat, who saw a fake heart attack coming, said nothing. She simply moved away from the bed, holding the handle of the broom in both hands. Rideout sat down beside Newsome with a grimace. His knees popped like pistol-shots. 'You, Mr Jensen.'

'Yes?'

'You'll have time – it will be stunned – but be quick, just the same. As quick as you were on the football field, all right?'

'You want me to Mace it?'

Rideout once more flashed his brief smile, but now there was sweat on his brow as well as his client's. 'It's not Mace – that *is* illegal where I come from – but that's the idea, yes. Now I'd like silence, please.'

'Wait a minute.' Kat propped the broom against the bed and ran her hands first up Rideout's left arm, then his right. She felt only plain cotton cloth and the man's scrawny flesh beneath.

'Nothing up my sleeve, Miss Kat, I promise you.'

'Hurry *up*,' Newsome said. 'This is bad. It always is, but the goddam stormy weather makes it worse.'

'Hush,' Rideout said. 'All of you, hush.'

They hushed. Rideout closed his eyes. His lips moved silently. Twenty seconds ticked past on Kat's watch, then thirty. Her hands were damp with perspiration. She wiped them one at a time on her sweater, then took hold of the broom again. *We look like people gathered at a deathbed*, she thought.

Outside, the wind howled along the gutters.

Rideout said, 'For Jesus' sake I pray,' then opened his eyes and leaned close to Newsome.

'God, there is an evil outsider in this man. An outsider feeding on his flesh and bones. Help me cast it out, as Your Son cast out the demons from the possessed man of the Gadarenes. Help me speak to the little green god of agony inside Andrew Newsome in your own voice of command.'

He leaned closer. He curled the long fingers of one arthritis-swollen hand around the base of Newsome's throat, as if he intended to strangle him. He leaned closer still, and inserted the first two fingers of his other hand into the billionaire's mouth. He curled them, and pulled down the jaw.

'Come out,' he said. He had spoken of command, but his voice was soft. Silky. Almost cajoling. It made the skin on Kat's back and arms prickle. 'Come out in the name of Jesus. Come out in the names of all the saints and martyrs. Come out in the name of

God, who gave you leave to enter and now commands you to leave. Come out into the light. Leave off your meal and come out.'

There was nothing. He began again.

'Come out in the name of Jesus. Come out in the names of the saints and martyrs.' His hand flexed slightly, and Newsome's breath began to rasp. 'No, don't go deeper. You can't hide, thing of darkness. Come out into the light. Jesus commands you. The saints and martyrs command you. God commands you to leave your meal and come out.'

A cold hand gripped Kat's upper arm and she almost screamed. It was Melissa. Her eyes were huge. Her mouth hung open. In Kat's ear, the housekeeper's whisper was as harsh as bristles. '*Look.*'

A bulge like a goitre had appeared in Newsome's throat just above Rideout's loosely grasping hand. It began to move slowly mouthwards. Kat had never seen anything like it in her life.

'That's right,' Rideout almost crooned. His face was streaming with sweat; the collar of his shirt had gone limp and dark. 'Come out. Come out into the light. You've done your feeding, thing of darkness.'

The wind rose to a scream. Rain that was now half-sleet blasted the windows like shrapnel. The lights flickered and the house creaked.

'The God that let you in commands you to leave. Jesus commands you to leave. All the saints and martyrs—'

He let go of Newsome's mouth, pulling his hand back the way a man does when he's touched something hot. But Newsome's mouth stayed open. More: it began to widen, first into a gape and then into a soundless howl. His eyes rolled back in his head and his feet began to jitter. His urine let go and the sheet over his crotch went as dark as Rideout's collar.

'Stop,' Kat said, starting forward. 'He's having a seizure. You have to st—'

Jensen yanked her back. She turned to him and saw his normally ruddy face had gone as pale as a linen napkin.

Newsome's jaw had dropped all the way to his breastbone. The lower half of his face disappeared into a mighty yawn. Kat heard temporomandibular tendons creak as knee-tendons did during strenuous physical therapy: a sound like dirty hinges. The lights in the room stuttered off, on, off, then on again.

'Come out!' Rideout shouted. 'Come out!'

In the darkness behind Newsome's teeth, a bladderlike thing rose like water in a plugged drain. It was pulsing. There was a rending, splintering crash and the window across the room shattered. Coffee cups fell to the floor and broke. Suddenly there was a branch in the room with them. The lights went out. The generator started up again. No burp this time but a steady roar. When the lights came back, Rideout was lying on the bed with Newsome, his arms flung out and his face planted on the wet patch in the sheet. Something was oozing from Newsome's gaping mouth, his teeth dragging grooves in its shapeless body, which was stippled with stubby green spikelets.

Not a tennis ball, Kat thought. *More like one of those Kooshes the kids play with.*

Tonya saw it and fled back down the hall with her head hunched forward, her hands locked at the nape of her neck, and her forearms over her ears.

The green thing tumbled onto Newsome's chest.

'*Spray it!*' Kat screamed at Jensen. '*Spray it before it can get away!*' Yes. Then they would put it in the specimen bottle and screw the lid down tight. *Very* tight.

Jensen's eyes were huge and glassy. He looked like a sleepwalker. Wind blew through the room. It swirled his hair. A picture fell from the wall. Jensen pistoned out the hand holding the can of pepper spray and triggered the plastic nub. There was a hiss, then he leaped to his feet, screaming. He tried to turn, probably to flee after Tonya, but stumbled and fell to his knees. Although Kat felt too dumbfounded to move – to even stir a hand – part of her brain must still have been working, because she knew what had happened. He had gotten the can turned around. Instead of pepper-spraying the thing that was now oozing through the unconscious Reverend Rideout's hair, Jensen had sprayed himself.

'*Don't let it get me!*' Jensen shrieked. He began to crawl blindly away from the bed. '*I can't see, don't let it get me!*'

The wind gusted. Dead leaves lifted from the tree-branch that had come through the window and swirled around the room. The green thing dropped from the nape of Rideout's creased and sunburned neck onto the floor. Feeling like a woman underwater, Kat swiped at it with the bristle end of the broom. She missed. The thing disappeared under the bed, not rolling but slithering.

Jensen crawled headfirst into the wall beside the doorway. '*Where am I? I can't see!*'

Newsome was sitting up, looking bewildered. 'What's going on? What happened?' He pushed Rideout's head off him. The reverend slid bonelessly from the bed to the floor.

Melissa bent over him.

'*Don't do that!*' Kat shouted, but it was too late.

She didn't know if the thing was truly a god or just some weird kind of leech, but it was fast. It came out from under the bed, rolled along Rideout's shoulder, onto Melissa's hand, and up her arm. Melissa tried to shake it off and couldn't. *Some kind of sticky stuff on those stubby little spikes*, the part of Kat's brain that would still work told the part – the much larger part – that still wouldn't. *Like the glue on a fly's feet.*

Melissa had seen where the thing came from and even in her panic was wise enough to cover her own mouth with both hands. The thing skittered up her neck, over her cheek, and squatted on her left eye. The wind screamed and Melissa screamed with it. It was the cry of a woman drowning in the kind of pain the charts in the hospitals can never describe. The charts go from one to ten; Melissa's agony was well over one hundred – that of someone being boiled alive. She staggered backwards, clawing at the thing on her eye. It was pulsing faster now, and Kat could hear a low, liquid sound as the thing resumed feeding. It was a *slushy* sound.

It doesn't care who it eats, she thought, just as if this made sense. Kat realised she was walking towards the screaming, flailing woman, and observed this phenomenon with interest.

'Hold still! *Melissa, HOLD STILL!*'

Melissa paid no attention. She continued to back up. She struck the thick branch now visiting the room and went sprawling. Kat went to one knee beside her and brought the broom handle smartly down on Melissa's face. Down on the thing that was feeding on Melissa's eye.

There was a splatting sound, and suddenly the thing was sliding limply down the housekeeper's cheek, leaving a wet trail of slime behind. It moved across the leaf-littered floor, intending to hide under the branch the way it had hidden under the bed. Kat sprang to her feet and stepped on it. She felt it splatter beneath her sturdy New Balance walking shoe. Green stuff shot out in both directions, as if she had stepped on a small balloon filled with snot.

Kat went down again, this time on both knees, and took Melissa in her arms. At first Melissa struggled, and Kat felt a fist graze her ear. Then Melissa subsided, breathing harshly. 'Is it gone? Kat, is it gone?'

'I feel better,' Newsome said wonderingly from behind them, in some other world.

'Yes, it's gone,' Kat said. She peered into Melissa's face. The eye the thing had landed on was bloodshot, but otherwise it looked all right. 'Can you see?'

'Yes. It's blurry, but clearing. Kat . . . the pain . . . it was all through me. It was like the end of the world.'

'Somebody needs to flush my eyes!' Jensen yelled. He sounded indignant.

'Flush your own eyes,' Newsome said cheerily. 'You've got two good legs, don't you? I think I might, too, once Kat throws them back into gear. Somebody check on Rideout. I think the poor sonofabitch might be dead.'

Melissa was staring up at Kat, one eye blue, the other red and leaking tears. 'The pain . . . Kat, you have no idea of the pain.'

'Yes,' Kat said. 'Actually, I do. Now.' She left Melissa sitting by the branch and went to Rideout. She checked for a pulse and found nothing, not even the wild waver of a heart that is still trying its best. Rideout's pain, it seemed, was over.

The generator went out.

'Fuck,' Newsome said, still sounding cheery. 'I paid seventy thousand dollars for that Jap piece of shit.'

'*I need someone to flush my eyes!*' Jensen bellowed. '*Kat!*'

Kat opened her mouth to reply, then didn't. In the new darkness, something had crawled onto the back of her hand.

STEPHEN KING is the world's most famous and successful horror writer. His first novel, *Carrie*, appeared in 1974, and since then he has published a phenomenal string of bestsellers, including *Salem's Lot*, *The Shining*, *The Stand*, *Dead Zone*, *Firestarter*, *Cujo*, *Pet Sematary*, *Christine*, *It*, *Misery*, *The Dark Half*, *Needful Things*, *Rose Madder*, *The Green Mile*, *Bag of Bones*, *The Colorado Kid*, *Lisey's Story*, *Duma Key* and *Under the Dome*, to name only a few.

The author's short fiction and novellas have been collected in *Night Shift*, *Different Seasons*, *Skeleton Crew*, *Four Past Midnight*, *Nightmares and Dreamscapes*, *Hearts in Atlantis*, *Everything's Eventual*, *The Secretary of Dreams* (two volumes), *Just After Sunset: Stories* and *Stephen King Goes to the Movies*. *Full Dark, No Stars* is a recent collection of four novellas, and his latest novel is *11/22/63*, about a man who travels back in time to try to prevent the assassination of President John F. Kennedy.

The winner of numerous awards, including both the Horror Writers' Association and World Fantasy Lifetime Achievement Awards, and a Medal for Distinguished Contribution to American Letters from the National Book Foundation, King lives with his wife in Bangor, Maine.

'The Little Green God of Agony' is a tribute to the classic monster and old dark house stories. This is its first publication anywhere.

'Monsters are real,' says King, 'and ghosts are real too. They live inside us, and sometimes, they win.'

Charcloth, Firesteel and Flint

—CAITLÍN R. KIERNAN—

SHE DOESN'T KNOW HOW or where or why it began. She cannot even say when. These memories are as lost to her as is her own name. Sometimes, in the empty hours between burning, she has concocted scenarios, both elaborate and unadorned, mildly implausible and entirely outlandish, to explain how a woman might become the midwife of infernos. These fictitious consolations have numbered in the many tens of thousands, and most are soon forgotten. They rise from her like blackened bits of paper, glowing brightly about the edges and buoyed higher and higher by the updrafts of her singular desires. They are wafted away, to settle on unsuspecting rooftops and in patches of dry brittle grass, to lie smouldering in mountainous chaparral scrublands. In this way, they bear a great resemblance to the longings of all lonely persons.

'I am the daughter of Hephaestus and a mortal woman,' she whispers to the darkness. Or, 'I was born in the Valley of Hinnom, and am a child of Gehenna. The corpse of my pregnant mother was left there amid the rubbish and the dead, but I survived, however scarred.' Or she assures herself that she was only raped by a Catalan dragon, or that she is a salamander who was freed by a careless Arabian alchemist and thereafter assumed human form, so that she would not ever be found out.

'In the bright crucible of Earth's molten birth,' she says. 'I was conceived, a stray and conscious spark thrown from that accreting, protoplanetary disc. I swam seas of magma, and sank, and later slept long aeons beneath the cooling lithosphere, waiting to be born from some stratovolcanic convulsion.'

Of course, she *believes* none of her tales, not even for an instant. They are fancies, and nothing more. But without them, she would be lost. And were she lost, who would bear witness to the fires?

On a deserted stretch of Midwestern highway, half-an-hour past midnight on a hot summer night, a young man sees her in the glare of his headlights. She is not hitchhiking. She's not even walking, but merely standing alone in the breakdown lane, gazing up at the broad, star-freckled sky. When he pulls over, she lowers her gaze, meeting his through the windshield, and she smiles. It's a friendly, disarming smile, and he asks if she needs a ride, and tells her that he's going as far up I-29 as Sioux City, if she's headed that way.

'You're very kind,' she says, the words delivered in an accent he has never heard before and thinks might be from someplace in Europe. She opens the passenger-side door and slides in next to him. He thinks that he's never seen hair even half so black, though her skin is as pale as milk. She laughs and shakes his hand and, by the dashboard's glare, her eyes seem golden-brown, shot through with amber threads. Later, in a motel room on the outskirts of Onawa, he will see that her eyes are only hazel green.

When he asks her name, she decides on Aiden, as it's a name she hasn't used in a while (though Mackenzie, Tandy and Blaise also came immediately to mind). She doesn't volunteer a patronymic and the young man, whose name is only Billy, doesn't ask her for one. He notices that her unpolished nails are chewed down almost to the quick, and as she shuts the door and he shifts the car out of neutral, he catches the faintest whiff of woodsmoke. He doesn't ask where she's come from, or where she's bound, as it's no business of his; he keeps his eyes on the road, the broken white line rushing past on his left, while *she* talks.

'My father is a fireman,' she lies, though it's an old lie, worn smooth about its periphery. 'Well, not exactly a fireman, no. He's a certified fire investigator. He's the guy who decides whether or not it was arson, the fires, and if so, how the arsonists started them.'

She talks and Billy listens, and the indistinct smoky smell that seems to have entered the car with her comes and goes. Sometimes it's woodsmoke and sometimes the odour is almost sulphurous, as if someone has just struck a match. Sometimes it makes him think of the rusted-out old barrel his own father used for burning trash, the way the barrel smelled after a hard rain. He keeps waiting for her to light a cigarette, but she never does.

'Did you know,' she asks, 'that before gasoline was ever used to fuel internal combustion engines, it was sold in pretty little bottles to kill head lice? People sprayed it on their hair.' And no, he says, I didn't know that, and she smiles again and stares up at the stars, the wind through the open window whipping at her ebony hair. 'It wasn't called gasoline back then,' she says, 'Just petrol.'

'Wasn't that dangerous?' he asks her.

'Calling it petrol, instead of gasoline?'

'No,' he replies, only pretending to sound exasperated, 'folks putting gasoline in their hair.'

She laughs, and *when* she laughs, he thinks that the burnt smell grows slightly more pungent. 'Why do you think no one does it anymore?' she asks, but Billy doesn't answer. He drives on, shrouded by the west Iowa night, and she lets the wind blow through her hair and talks to keep him awake. He never mentions that he's sleepy, or that he's been on the road since just after dawn, but she sees it plainly enough on his face and hears it in his voice. He offers to turn on the radio, but says there's nothing out here except preaching and a few honky-tonk stations, and she tells him no, the night is fine without the radio, without music or disembodied voices threatening brimstone and damnation. It never once occurs to her that he might find it odd, how the topic of her conversation (which is really more a monologue, as he says very little) never strays far from matters of conflagration. She has too little understanding of thoughts other than her own to suspect, or even care, what anyone else might find peculiar. And in truth, he's so grateful for the company of this strange girl that her single-mindedness is an easy enough thing to overlook.

She recounts Algonquin, Creek and Ojibwa myths, and in all three, a rabbit or hare steals fire and gives it to humanity. She talks about Prometheus and the Book of Enoch and the relative temperatures of different regions and layers of the Sun. He has to interrupt and ask her to explain Kelvins, and when she converts the numbers to Celsius, he has to ask what that means in Fahrenheit.

'5,800 Kelvins,' she says, referring to the surface of the sun, and speaking without a hint of condescension or impatience in her voice, 'is roughly equal to 5,526 degrees Celsius, which comes to a little more than 9,980 degrees Fahrenheit. But you go deeper in, all the way down to the *core* of the sun, and it's very close to 13,600,000 degrees Kelvin, or almost 25,000,000 degrees Fahrenheit.' And then she informs him that, by comparison, the highest temperature ever recorded on the surface of the Earth was a mere 136 degrees Fahrenheit, in the deserts of El Azizia, Libya, on September 13th, 1922.

'That was sixty years before I was born,' he says, and tacks on, 'Libya. Now, that's in Africa, right?'

'Yes,' she replies, 'now, and in 1922, as well.'

He laughs, even though she'd not meant it as a joke. 'So, what's the hottest place in America?'

'North America?' she asks. 'Or do you mean the United States?'

'I mean the United States.'

She considers the question for only a few seconds, then tells him that sixty-nine years before he was born, a temperature of 134 degrees Fahrenheit was recorded in Death Valley, California, on July 10th, 1913. 'In fact, the hottest place in the US, or anywhere else in the Western Hemisphere, is Death Valley, which averages ninety-eight degrees in the summer.'

'Ninety-eight,' he says. 'That's not so hot.'

'No,' she agrees. 'It really isn't.'

'You learn all this stuff from your dad?' Billy asks her. 'A certified fire investigator, does he need to know all about Indian legends and how hot it gets on the sun?'

'My father is a fireworks manufacturer,' she says, as though unaware, or merely indifferent, that this lie contradicts the earlier one. 'He specialises in multi-break shells and time rain. He has factories in Taiwan and China.' And then, before Billy can object, she's already explaining how different chemical compounds produce different-coloured flames. 'Copper halides give you blue,' she says. 'Sodium nitrate, that makes a nice yellow. Cesium burns indigo.'

Billy flunked eleventh-grade chemistry, and none of this means much of anything to him. But he asks her how they get red anyway.

'Depends,' she sighs and leans back in her seat, pushing wind-blown strands of black hair from her face.

'On what?'

'What sort of red you're after. Lithium carbonate gives off a very nice moderate shade of red. But if you want something more intense, strontium carbonate's always your best bet.'

'And green?'

'Copper compounds, barium chloride.'

'And gold? What do you have to burn to get golden fireworks? The gold ones have always been my favourite. Especially the big starburst ones.' And he takes a hand off the wheel long enough to pantomime an exploding mortar and the gilded stream of sparks which follows.

She turns her head and watches him a moment, then says, 'Daddy uses lampblack for gold, usually.'

On his right, a reflective sign promises an exit, with motels, restaurants and a truck stop, only five miles farther along. He checks the gas gauge and sees that the red needle is hovering just above empty. 'I don't want to seem ignorant, but I have no idea what lampblack is,' he says to the woman calling herself Aiden.

'Lots of people don't,' she replies, and shuts her eyes. 'It's just an old word for soot, really. You know what soot is?'

'Yes,' Billy says. 'I *know* what soot is.'

'Well, lampblack is a very fine sort of soot, sometimes just called blacking, gathered from partially burned carbonaceous materials. It's been used as a pigment since prehistoric times, and is considered one of the least-reflective substances known to man.'

'I'm just gonna have to take your word for that,' he says, and she smiles her easy, disarming smile again and opens her eyes that only seem to be golden brown with glittering amber streaks. 'I'm also going to take the next exit, 'cause we need gas and I could use some coffee.'

'I have to pee,' she says, and briefly wishes she had a road map, because the positions of the stars and planets above the plains and cornfields can only tell her so much.

'You drink coffee?' Billy asks, and she nods her head.

'I drink coffee.'

'I'm guessing you drink it with milk, but no sugar.'

'I drink coffee,' she says again, as if perhaps she failed to make herself understood the first time. 'I drink it, though I've never much cared for the taste. It's bitter. I don't like bitter things.'

Billy only nods, because he doesn't much like the taste of coffee, either. And then they've reached the off-ramp and he cuts the wheel right, exiting the Interstate into the gaudy glimmer of convenience stores and gas stations. The exit for Onawa distinguishes itself in no way from most remote highway exits, just another oasis of electric light, parked automobiles and towering billboards touting everything from beer to a local strip club. The woman whose name is no more Aiden than it is McKenzie spots a McDonald's, a Dairy Queen and a Subway, and here and there, a few stunted, unexpected trees. Mostly this is farmland, and she suspects the fast-food places are more welcome than are the trees. Billy steers into the parking lot of a BP, not far from a motel; both lots are crowded with semis and pickup trucks.

'We could maybe get a room,' he says, as matter-of-factly as it's possible, considering he only met her a few hours before. 'We could get a room, grab a little sleep before driving into Sioux City.'

'We could get a room,' she replies, the words passing indifferently across her lips, hardly more than an echo. 'I need to pee,' she tells him again, changing the subject as though it's settled, and he stops the car beside the pumps, beneath the halogen shine of the station's aluminium canopy. When he's cut the ignition, she gets out and goes inside. The restrooms are in one corner, near an upright cooler filled with sodas and energy drinks. The women's room reeks of urine and cleaning products and sickly-sweet cakes of toilet deodoriser. But she's smelled much, much worse, times beyond counting.

When she's done, she goes back out to find him shutting the trunk. Though she doesn't ask, Billy hurriedly explains, 'Something was shifting around back there. Making a racket. Turns out, the lug wrench had come loose.' It's as good a story as any, and she doesn't dispute it.

'You heard it, yeah?' he asks.

'No,' she answers, and then gets back into the car.

He pulls his car from the BP's lot into the parking lot of a neighbouring Motel 6, and she waits alone while he goes into the lobby to register. Billy offers to pay for the room, since, after all, it was his idea, and she doesn't object. While she waits, she stares up at the night sky past the windshield, trying to pick out the stars through the orange-white haze of light pollution. But they've been blotted out, almost every one of them. Only the brightest and most determined are visible, even to her, and she knows the night sky better (as they say) than the back of her own hand. It occurs to her, in passing, that neither of them got coffee at the BP station.

When Billy returns, he has a small paper envelope with the motel's logo printed on it containing a plastic card, the sort with a magnetic strip on one side.

'I miss real keys,' she says, 'the old brass-coloured keys, attached to big diamond-shaped chunks of plastic with the room numbers stamped on them. You could steal them, those keys, and have a souvenir. But that,' and she pauses to point at the envelope, 'that doesn't make for a very interesting souvenir.'

'Where are you from?' he asks, squeezing the car into an empty space nearer their room. 'I don't recognise your accent.'

'Would it really matter?' she asks.

All he has for an answer is a shrug, and neither of them says much of anything after that. It may be they've passed the point where talk is necessary. That's what she would say, if the question were put to her. The night has gathered sufficient momentum it no longer needs to be propelled by small talk.

Inside, she goes to the sink and splashes her face and the back of her neck with icy-cold water. Billy switches on the television, to some channel that shows old movies 24/7, and he turns the volume down low. She doesn't recognise the film that's playing, but it's in black and white, which suits her fine. It helps to counter the garish, mismatched wallpaper and comforter, the ugly carpet and the uglier painting hung above the queen-sized bed.

'I was only fourteen, my first time—' he begins, but she places a wet finger to his lips, shushing him.

'It doesn't matter,' she says. 'Not to me, not to anyone.' And then he sits down at the end of the bed and watches her undress. She's thin, but not as thin as he'd expected. Her breasts are small, her belly flat. Her pubic hair is as black as the hair on her head, a sable 'V' there between her pale thighs. She folds her dingy, road-weary clothes neatly and sets them aside, which surprises him more than the crimson triangle tattooed between her shoulder blades. He asks her what it means, and she tells him that it's the alchemical symbol for fire, though it may mean many other things as well. He asks where she got it, and when, and she tells him, truthfully, that she doesn't remember.

'But it was a very long time ago,' she says, and then begins undressing him. She pulls the T-shirt off over his head, undoes his belt buckle, and then Billy takes it from there. The bed is soft and cool, and the white sheets are heavily perfumed with a floral-scented fabric softener. When he kisses her, she tastes like cinders, but he doesn't say anything. She climbs on top, and he enters her effortlessly. He comes almost immediately, but she doesn't seem to mind, and whispers soothing words in his left ear while she grinds her hips roughly against his. The thought occurs to him, then, that he might only be dreaming, because it all seems somehow so unlikely. He hasn't got off with anything but his own hands and tubes of KY in years. And because the words she's whispering are coalescing into such vivid pictures in his mind, images so clear he can't be entirely sure that he's not *seeing* them through his eyelids. She fucks him, and her teeth and tongue and spittle and palate taste of cinders, and the visions spill freely from her lips – dazzling, exquisite apparitions of holocaust – and he comes again. He opens his eyes and gasps loudly, and she smiles and kisses him again.

'Close your eyes,' she says, and there's a tone in her voice that's almost enmity. '*Keep* them closed. Close them as tightly as you can.'

Billy does as he's told, and he understands now that the bright visions are not so much what she *wants* him to see, but what he *needs* to see.

'That's a good boy,' she whispers and places a hand on either side of his head. The rhythm of their lovemaking has assumed a cadence, a force, that he will later describe, in the spiral-bound notebook he uses for a diary, as violent. *I almost thought that she was raping me*, he will write. *But it wasn't rape. It wasn't rape at all.* He will also write about how quiet she was, the unnerving, heavy silence of her orgasms. But mostly, he'll write about the fires.

He will write, *I think maybe she was Hawaiian. She was a Hawaiian woman, and her great, great grandmother made love to the goddess Pele.*

She fucks him, and the fire licks at his mind, at the inside of his eyelids and the chintzy wallpaper of the motel room.

'This is my gift,' she whispers. 'This is the only gift I have to offer.'

For half an instant, it is another summer night, July 18th, one thousand and forty-five years before the night he finds her standing at the side of an Iowa Interstate highway. And *he* stands on a Roman street, outside a cluster of shops near the Circus Maximus. It's two nights past the full moon, and the fire has already begun. It will burn for six days and seven nights, and Nero will accuse Christian arsonists of starting the blaze.

Billy can feel her hands on him, those short nails digging into his scalp and maybe even drawing blood. But he doesn't open his eyes, and he doesn't tell her to stop.

That half-instant passes, taking Rome away, taking century after century, until he finds himself on the banks of the Sumida River, looking out across the Japanese caste town of Edo. It is the second day of March 1657, and hurricane-force winds are sweeping down from the northeast, fanning the flames devouring the city of wood and paper houses, bamboo still tinder-dry from a drought the year before. But Billy hardly even feels the wind. It barely touches him. The sky overhead has been blotted out by smoke, underlit by the fire so that the grey-black billows glow as hellishly as anything

Dante or Milton will ever imagine. Over the next three days, more than a hundred thousand people will die.

And then he's sitting on a crowded wooden bleacher, beneath the big top of the Ringling Brothers and Barnum & Bailey Circus. It's a humid summer day in July of 1944, and far overhead, the Flying Wallendas have just begun their trapeze act. In only a few seconds, the tent will begin to burn. The canvas has been water-proofed with a mixture of paraffin and white gasoline. In less than eight minutes, the tent will be consumed, and the melting paraffin wax will drip down like a rain of napalm upon the heads of the 6,800 people trying to escape the fire. Near the end, Billy thinks he's hearing wild animals screaming, but no, she says, no, those are human voices. Not a single one of the cats or elephants or camels was killed that day.

'Enough,' he whispers, and tumbles from that day to another. But he doesn't tumble very far this time. Not so very far at all. Hardly more than a year, and it's August 6th, 1945, Hiroshima, and somehow Billy is not vaporised when the atomic bomb code-named 'Little Boy' detonates 1,900 feet overhead. The subsequent fireball reduces sand and glass to bubbling, viscous pools, and everything burns. Some of the 140,000 who die are so completely obliterated that they leave behind only shadows on bridges and the sides of buildings. Some leave even less than that.

And it does not matter how many times or how desperately he asks that she make it stop. He cries out and he screams and he sobs, and the immolations unfolding behind his eyelids, inside his skull, continue unabated.

'I was there,' she says. 'For every one, I was there. I carry the memories, and this is my gift to you.'

April 18th, 1906, and, in San Francisco, more than 3,000 perish in the earthquake and firestorm that proceeds it.

Dresden, Germany, a few minutes past midnight on the morning of February 14th, 1945, the holy day of Ash Wednesday, and hundreds of British bombers drop hundreds of tons of high explosives and incendiary devices on the seventh largest city of the Fatherland. Billy huddles in the largest of the public air-raid shelters, below the central train station, him and 60,000 others. Almost all of them will be dead soon. By sunrise, much of the city will be at the mercy of a fire whose temperatures will peak at more than 2,700 degrees Fahrenheit. He watches, unable to turn away, and is aware that the woman who calls herself Aiden is somewhere nearby. Near enough that he can hear her as she reads words a survivor will someday put to paper.

'We saw terrible things,' she reads, 'cremated adults shrunk to the size of small children, pieces of arms and legs, dead people, whole families burnt to death, burning people ran to and fro, burnt coaches filled with civilian refugees, dead rescuers and soldiers, many were calling and looking for their children and families, and fire everywhere, everywhere fire, and all the time the hot wind of the firestorm threw people back into the burning houses they were trying to escape from.'

'I do not know why you are showing me this,' he says, shouting to be heard above the cacophony of explosions and screams.

'Yes,' she whispers, and he hears her perfectly well. 'You know precisely why.'

And there is more, conflagrations beyond reckoning, though, later, he *will* try to write them all down: the burning of Atlanta, as ordered by Union General William Tecumseh Sherman. October 8th, 1871, and on the same day as the Great Chicago Fire, the town of Peshtigo Wisconsin, burns, along with the Michigan towns of Holland, Manistee and Port Huron. Hundreds die in Chicago, and in Peshtigo, men and women who try to seek refuge from the heat in the river that divides the town in two are boiled alive. The firestorm generates a tornado, flinging houses and boxcars into the air like incandescent toys . . .

'Open your eyes,' she says, and he does. And there's only the dingy motel room now, the murmur of the television and the naked girl straddling him. He's sobbing, and she watches him as one might watch some outlandish phenomenon that can never truly be understood. She climbs off him, and Billy sits weeping on the edge of the bed. Almost fifteen minutes pass before he says anything.

'I won't do it again,' he says. 'I promise. I won't ever fucking do it, not ever again.'

And she laughs, and it sounds like steam escaping a punctured pipe. A laugh like a thunder crack, that laugh, like lightning finding its mark.

'I didn't *come* to *stop* you, Billy. I came to be sure you'd *never* stop.'

His mouth tastes like cinders, and when he blinks and wipes his eyes, the air dances with the afterimages of a trillion embers sparkling against the backdrop of innumerable smoky skies.

'I didn't think I'd have to explain that part,' she says, remembering all the ones who have knelt at her feet and grovelled and, after she was done with them, begged for still *more* revelations.

'I was only fourteen the first time,' he says again.

'I know. You've done well, I think. You'll do great deeds before you're finished.'

And then she dresses, except for her shoes, which she carries, and leaves him alone in the room. No longer calling herself Aiden, the woman who doesn't know how or where or why it began, or even when, walks across the parking lot. She passes his car, and the homemade pipe bomb hidden in the trunk, packed snugly beneath the spare tyre, in its locked aluminium carrying case. She'll be in Sioux City when it goes off, of course. But right now, she needs to walk. The eastern horizon is going shades of pink and violet as the world rolls towards a new day, and by the time she reaches the northbound lane of the Interstate, she's begun telling herself a new story, about the phoenix that might have been her mother, and how she helped the great bird build a nest of frankincense and myrrh twigs. How she set the nest ablaze . . .

CAITLÍN R. KIERNAN is the author of several novels, including *Low Red Moon*, *Daughter of Hounds* and *The Red Tree*, which was nominated for both the Shirley Jackson and World Fantasy Awards. Her latest novel, *The Drowning Girl: A Memoir*, is published by Penguin.

Since 2000, her shorter tales of the weird, fantastic and macabre have been collected in several volumes, including *Tales of Pain and Wonder*, *From Weird and Distant Shores*, *To Charles Fort with Love*, *Alabaster*, *A is for Alien* and *The Ammonite Violin & Others*. Subterranean Press has recently released a retrospective of her early writing, *Two Worlds and In Between: The Best of Caitlín R. Kiernan (Volume One)*.

Kiernan lives in Providence, Rhode Island, with her partner Kathryn. She is currently working on her next two novels, *Blood Oranges* and *Blue Canary*.

'Almost always, it's hard for me to point to any single source of inspiration for any given story,' she reveals. 'I need to write a story. I sit down and write a story. I stare at the page, and something comes to me. Or, the vaguest germ of something occurs to me, and I sit down and make a story out of it. I find the story I need to write.

'In the case of "Charcloth, Firesteel and Flint" – which would make a fine name for a demonic law firm – I have nothing but a few faint inklings as to why I wrote this story when I wrote this story.

'I do know that, for many years, I've wanted to write a story about the 1871 Peshtigo Fire, which was really a very odd and terrible event, occurring at precisely the same time as the Great Chicago Fire *and* the Point Huron Fire, but so many miles apart. And this found its way into the story.

'How can we not be fascinated with fire, with its destructive capability when it's no longer under our control, or when it's used as a weapon? Many, many things in my head, writing this, all coalescing into the character of a woman who's drawn to fires before they occur.'

Ghosts with Teeth

—PETER CROWTHER—

*Horror of horrors! To remove the bones
and let the girls still live!*
—'The House of Horror'
by Seabury Quinn

'Boo!'
—Spooky, the Tuff Little Ghost

Prologue

HUGH WOKE UP to the sound of sirens and a pain between his temples that was to headaches what Hiroshima's 'Little Boy' was to Fourth of July firecrackers. The first thing he discovered was it was a good idea not to move anything – his head, his arms, his legs, his ass, his finger—

now why did just the thought of that, of moving a finger . . . why did it cause a sudden rush of anxiety?

—nothing. Even breathing was troublesome so he did it as slowly as he was able. He closed his eyes. That hurt, too.

The sirens stopped right outside – in fact, it sounded like they pulled up next to him . . . so maybe he was in the street. He opened his eyes again and slowly turned his head. Nope. He was in a room. The lights were on. He was lying on a carpet. It was his room, a room in his house.

His house?

His and *Angie's* house.

So he was face-down on the living-room floor of his own house. He shifted his head to an angle and saw that the sofa and a chair were tipped on their sides . . . and there was blood on the floor. His blood, he reckoned. There was no way on God's Earth that you could feel this much pain without there being blood. He moaned his wife's name. There was no answer. God, what was happening?

Someone thumped on his door.

'I can't move,' Hugh said, his voice croaky and soft.

'Police,' a stern voice proclaimed. 'Open up.'

He needed a drink. Something—

put on the pan said greedy nan, we'll sup before we go

—to take away the dryness in his mouth and throat.

'We're coming in,' the voice outside said.

'Angie,' Hugh whimpered.

And then it all started to come back.

I

The Previous Day.

Tuboise, ME – and that's *Tuh-bwah* and not *Two boys* – isn't a town, not as such. It's a bend in the road: a comma between words, a fart between stools . . . the middle film in a trilogy. A *bona fide* dalliance between pieces of real business, like Portland and Bangor, both a half-hour's drive away.

Tuboise: a seventeen-house community – just forty-one folks in what pretty much amounts to a dormitory – sitting astride Route 1 and barely a long spit on the coast-side of I-95, so close to the Atlantic you can sometimes see the ocean's white-caps and taste the salt on the sea breeze.

But they get rain here, and then some.

Hugh Ritter looked across at his wife, Angie, and gently rubbed her knee, the only part of her – aside from her forehead – that was exposed.

'Almost there, baby,' he said, his voice gentle. 'Almost home.'

Angie stretched and yawned, pulled her coat tighter as she emerged from beneath it and peered out the window.

'Whoa!' Hugh said. 'What's this?'

Just as they made to turn right, the familiar figure of Sheriff's Deputy Maude Angstrom tugged a ROAD CLOSED sawhorse into place.

Hugh rolled to a halt just in front of the sawhorse and the slick-ered deputy scooted around to his window.

'Hey, Maude,' Hugh said. 'What's up?'

'Hey, Hugh. Hey, Angie.'

'Hey yourself, Maudie. You aiming to Trick or Treat us?' Angie leaned so far over in order that she could see Maude Angstrom's expression that she was almost face down on her husband's lap and she felt her cheeks redden momentarily.

'I wish,' the deputy said, shouting above the rain and the wind as she pulled her slicker tighter around her neck. 'Road ahead's getting pretty washed out and we're gonna end up with vehicles in the ditch. Frank says to turn folks back here. I'm just getting myself set up. Only thing you can do is turn on back and make a left up to Wheeler's Point. Park your vehicle there and walk on across Archie Goodlowe's field into town.'

'Shoot!' Hugh shouted back at her. 'We got a trunk full of bags, Maude . . . all our clothes . . . other stuff.'

'You been away someplace, Hugh?'

Hugh nodded. 'Been staying with Angie's sister Nan and her boy other side of Boston. I just do not relish the idea of having to schlep a mile and then some carrying them all. There no way you can let us on through and put the sawhorses up when we're on our way?'

'Well, I don't know, Hugh. Frank was pretty firm about this.' Maude shrugged and looked first from Hugh to Angie and then back to Hugh. She smiled and, just for a moment, Hugh wished she hadn't. The smile was more of a rictus grin, the bottom lip pulling back and exposing teeth discoloured at the base and gums that were bruised a deep blue.

'We'd sure 'preciate that, Maudie,' Angie added for good measure.

'Oh, what the hell,' Maude Angstrom said, hitching up her pants through her slicker before wiping her face with her gloved hand. 'I'd kind of figured I was done, but two more won't hurt.' She hefted the sawhorses back out of the way. 'You go on – ain't like you're gonna be going anyplace once you get there.' She chuckled at that with a wheezy cough. 'Mind you drive careful, now,' she shouted as Hugh closed his window.

'We won't say anything to Frank if we see him,' Hugh shouted.

'Oh, he'll already know,' Maude Angstrom shouted after them. 'But I'll have to mention it to him anyways.'

When they were past Maude's cruiser, Hugh said, 'That's odd.'

'What's odd? Seems sensible to me. You go easy with that right foot of yours – we end up in a gully and Frank'll go ape-shit at us . . . and at Maudie for lettin' us through.'

'No, not that,' Hugh said, staring intently at his mirror. 'Where's she gone?'

Without answering, Angie pulled down her mirror. Hugh was right. The deputy had disappeared. 'Probably ducked into her cruiser, telling Frank she let us through.' Angie turned around in her seat. 'Come on, sweetie – when did she ever do anything without an okay from Frank?' And then, more to herself than to her husband, 'She can't have disappeared.'

Hugh slowed right down. 'Well, she's sure as hell not there.' He rolled to a stop and shifted into PARK. When he got out of the car and looked back, Hugh could see the sawhorses – all lined up like little soldiers, neat as all get-out – and there was Maude's cruiser. But no Maude.

Behind him, the car was beep-beeping.

'Push the door to, sweetie, we're gonna get washed out.'

Hugh closed the door and started back.

Angie shouted, 'Leave it be, sweetie. Maybe she went to the bathroom.'

'You mean for a pee, honey. If you mean she's taking a pee then say so.' But yeah, that could be it. She'd looked kind of anxious, now that he thought about it. And the last thing she would want him to do was stroll up while she had her pants down. He turned back and jogged to the car.

A few seconds later they were on their way ... though until they rounded the bend, Hugh couldn't stop staring at the mirror, half-expecting something – Maude Angstrom's cruiser, for a high-falutin' example – suddenly appearing on their tail.

II

As they pulled onto Main Street, Angie started sniggering.

'What?' Hugh slowed up to pass a Lincoln that someone had abandoned by the side of the road – in fact, checking his mirror, Hugh saw that the nearside front wheel was on the kerb. Even worse, the car had clearly continued forward and impacted on the wall of the old Maritime Museum. 'God, some people,' he said.

'Old Mrs Slater must have one of her daughters visiting.'

'And that's funny?'

The woman on the radio was speaking in a thick Maine accent, talking about ghosts as part of a Halloween special. Hugh reached over and turned it off.

'Well, she was – the daughter, not Mrs Slater – was standing almost glued up against the window—' Angie changed her voice to that of someone clearly distressed: '*Help, let me out of here for God's sake!*'

Hugh smiled. Across the street, on his right, the school bus was parked at the bus-stop, no driver to be seen anywhere.

'But then, when I looked back – I glanced away for like, a second – she'd gone. And I reckon she just ducked down when she saw me looking at her.'

Hugh had been about to remark that the street was remarkably quiet for the rush-hour, even though the rush-hour in Tuboise was neither fast-moving nor anywhere near as long as sixty minutes. The plain fact was there was nobody to be seen anywhere. But then, they were experiencing what, for the most part, was a rain-storm of almost Biblical proportions.

He sneaked a glance at the large windows of Maxell's Drugstore as they went by and was surprised to see it not only bereft of customers but also there was no sign of old Pop Maxell, generally to be seen on the front boards in that old wicker chair no matter what the weather.

Hugh leaned forward and looked up at the sky through the windshield. No witches to be seen anywhere, and barely an hour to go before Tricks and Treats would be the order of the day, with winter standing just around the corner of the curtains waiting for its cue to take to the stage.

He looked back at the road.

'Some woman staring out from the house next to Jerry's place.'

'The one that's been for sale for ages?' He sensed his wife nodding. 'Huh, I thought that place was empty.'

Well, what are *poltergeists?* the woman on the radio asked her studio guest, appropriately a writer of supernatural fiction.

Hugh looked down at the radio, frowning. 'I thought I'd turned that off?' he muttered.

Angie had turned around to keep watching. 'So did I,' she said. 'Thought it was empty, I mean.' Then she turned back and faced forward just in time for them to pull into their driveway.

'Well, I must say that I'm glad that's over,' Hugh declared. He turned off the engine and popped the CD/radio player cover from its mounting.

'Hugh—' Angie reached over and placed a hand on her husband's.

He looked up just in time to stare right into the face of Eleanor Ferguson, pressed up against the glass right next to his head. 'Jesus, Ellie, what—'

'Hugh? Angie? Is it you?'

Hugh popped his belt-clasp and opened the door. Eleanor stepped back, her hands up to the neck of her sweater, pulling it tight around her.

'Ellie, are you—?'

'They're here, Hugh,' she said, a sob stifled in her throat and quickly swallowed away. She turned her head and looked across the road. Joe McHendricks was standing in his drive, hoe in his hand, Red Sox ball cap pushed up and back off his forehead, sleeves turned up at the cuffs. He was watching them. Hugh gave a single wave and turned back to Ellie, but she had moved completely away and was now heading up the grassy roadside towards the beach, walking backwards, still pulling at her sweater and shaking her head, eyes as wide as saucers, her concentration shifting between Hugh and Angie and the straight-backed figure of Joe McHendricks. She waggled an index finger at Hugh admonishing – threatening? warning? – him.

Across the road, Mr McHendricks had stepped away from his driveway and was moving after the woman, his steps confident but unhurried, the hoe hanging in his hand like a tribesman's spear.

'Leave her be, sweetie,' Angie whispered.

'All of 'em!' Eleanor shouted, her voice dwindling now in the wind. 'They're *all* here.'

It was Halloween, a Saturday afternoon during what was already shaping up to be the wettest winter in Maine since 1973, when the Atlantic broke the barriers down at Sunny Hollow and came on up the Coast Road, just stopping short of Griggs' Mall. The rain was coming down near on horizontal now and Hugh and Angie were soaked . . . soaked but unable to move. The sky was darkening all around them, but cold and wet as he was, Hugh didn't feel all that comfortable going inside and leaving the old woman out there on the road.

'Mr McHendricks will get her,' shouted Angie, who had already got out of the car and was heading for the front door.

'What the hell's he doing,' Hugh muttered, 'gardening in the goddam rain?'

Watching the back of the striding figure of the man across the street, Hugh thought that was about right – McHendricks *would* get her. The idea of that just didn't fill him with optimism.

'Let's get inside,' Angie said. She turned around on the step and looked up at the sky.

Hugh moved to one side to look down the street just in time to see Mr McHendricks give a single wave and then disappear down the driveway of the old lumber mill road that led towards the pond. He shook his head and looked back at McHendricks's house.

'Hey, hold on there a—'

'What is it?'

Hugh pointed at the house. 'I just . . . Oh, he's gone now.'

'Who is? Hugh, can you get the damn key?'

'Oh, yeah, sorry.' He fumbled and pulled out the key. He unlocked the door. 'I thought I'd just seen McHendricks, that's all. In his house.'

'That doesn't seem so strange to me. It's his house, after all.' Angie pushed open the door – which set off the preliminary alarm – and walked across to the control panel to punch in the reset code.

'Hey,' Hugh said suddenly, 'the bedroom.'

'Damn!' Angie shielded her eyes to look up. 'Did I leave the window open again?' She came back outside and looked up to see the window firmly closed. She looked around at Hugh. 'This Trick or Treat or something?'

'It's *something*,' he said. 'I thought I saw someone at the window.' Hugh turned around and looked across at the McHendricks house. 'His place, too. McHendricks. Nobody there now,' he said.

'Trick of the light,' Angie said.

'Mmm. Maybe.'

'And where's Mr McHendricks?'

'He went after Ellie Ferguson.'

'So he couldn't be in his house?'

'Mmm. Maybe.'

'You know any other words?'

Hugh turned to her and his face broke into a grin. 'Mmm,' he said. 'Maybe.' And that was when Angie slapped his arm.

Hugh feigned pain and then looked down the street to the road to the lumber mill and then back at their own house.

'You want to cue me in on what's going on here?'

Hugh shrugged. 'Must just have been the rain and shadows is all.'

Angie looked up at the bedroom window. 'You think maybe we should call someone?'

Hugh opened the trunk and lifted out their two suitcases. 'Call someone?' He slammed it, pressed the automatic lock button on the key remote and ducked over beside his wife, who was straining her neck to see into the upstairs bedroom. 'Like who?'

'*Whom!*'

Hugh sighed. 'Like *whom*?'

'I was thinking maybe the Sheriff. I'm kind of scared to go in.'

Hugh shook his head. 'You just went in and turned off the alarm.'

Angie shrugged. 'Yes, well, you know what I mean.'

And he did. If the alarm wasn't picking up the presence of an intruder . . . 'The alarm would've gone off if someone had broken in,' he said, more for his own benefit than his wife's. 'Must have been the rain.'

Angie nodded. 'Yeah. And you're tired.' She put her head on one side and blinked at him. 'You are tired, aren't you, sweetie?'

'Well, it's a bit of a drive. Driving through Boston and all.'

'How's about I make you a coffee?'

'You bet,' Hugh said. 'But first I'm going to change my pants – I'm soaked . . . just from walking from the car.'

'Well, yes, and wandering around to see if Maude Angstrom was taking a pee and, just now, standing there in the downpour talking to Ellie,' Angie added. 'What did she mean – "they're all here"?'

Hugh shrugged.

'Who was she talking about?'

'I have no idea.'

Angie settled herself onto one of the counter-seats and started rubbing her hair with a towel. 'She didn't seem happy about it, that's for sure.'

The doorbell sounded hollow and Angie wasn't sure whether that was what startled her – the fact that it sounded as though the entire house was empty and—

listening to her, whispering about her, watching every move she . . .

—lonely, or wondering who was standing out there in the rain ringing their doorbell.

'Coming!' she shouted.

'What?' Hugh shouted from upstairs.

'Someone at the door,' Angie shouted back as she pulled it open.

'Yes, something at the door,' Frank Gozinsky said in an affected snarl. He removed his hat and smiled. 'You wanted me?'

'Did we?'

'Maude said.'

'She did?'

'Who is it, honey?'

Frank shifted his attention to the staircase and watched Hugh slowly appear, buttoning his shirt.

'Hey, Frank.'

Frank nodded – 'Hugh . . .' – blinked once and glanced sideways at Angie.

'Everything okay?'

'Frank says he thought we wanted him, sweetie. Apparently Maude told him.'

'Do we? Want him, I mean? What did Maude say exactly?'

'I just got it wrong. No big deal.'

'Give her a call,' Angie said. 'Could be she meant someone else.'

They waited for Frank to call her on the cell, but he just stood there.

'Hey, no problem.' Frank turned his hat around in his hands. 'Looks like I got the wrong end of the stick.' He waited and then he wagged a finger at them. 'She said she let you through, though. Naughty girl.'

'Yeah, my fault,' Hugh said. 'Don't get pissed at her.'

'Already did,' Frank said, and he made a clicking sound with his mouth.

'We just got home,' Angie said, deciding not to pursue the Maude connection.

'Uh huh?' Frank said. Rain was running off his forehead and pooling on the step.

'Boston,' Hugh offered.

'To see my sister,' Angie added.

'Nan,' Hugh said. 'Her name is Nan.'

'Hey, I remember Nan,' Frank said. 'I live here, remember.' He looked over at Hugh and laughed. 'Talking to me like I don't know her sister.'

Hugh chuckled and gave a *go figure* shrug.

Frank nodded. 'To bed, to bed, said Sleepyhead; tarry a while, said Slow; put on the pan, said Greedy Nan, we'll sup before we go.'

Nobody said anything for a few seconds (which seemed like an age to Angie) and then Hugh said, 'Children's rhyme?'

Frank's smile dropped from his face.

Angie took a step backwards without even thinking about it.

'No,' Frank said. 'It's a Wall Street saying.'

Hugh frowned and made to say something, but then Frank's face cracked into a chuckle and he slapped Hugh playfully with his hat. 'Naw, yeah . . . it's a kids' rhyme. From way back.'

They all laughed – Hugh and Angie a little dutifully, they both felt – and then Angie said, 'Oh, hey – I almost forgot.'

'Yeah? Forgot what?'

'Hugh saw someone in the house.'

'When we got back,' Hugh said, trying to sound dismissive.

'Yeah?' Frank said. 'You see who it was?'

Hugh shook his head and shot a glare at his wife. 'I'm not even sure . . . well, I think it was the rain.'

'It was raining in your house?' Frank's smile seemed to be lacking in humour and he stepped forward. For a few seconds, the Sheriff was standing almost nose to nose with Angie until she took another step back. *He's in the house*, a little voice whispered at the back of her head. *This isn't a good idea.*

'Maybe I should—?'

'Not a good idea,' Angie said in a daze.

'Not a good idea to check your house? When your husband says he's seen an intruder?'

'It wasn't an intruder,' Frank said.

'So you're saying it was someone you *allowed* in there?' The Sheriff looked over at Angie and then back at Hugh. 'I'm not too sure what—'

'The place is a mess,' Angie said.

She was immediately aware of how lame that explanation sounded but she couldn't think of anything further to say. So she took a small step forward. 'Once we get sorted out, we'll give the place a good going over . . .'

'And we'll give you a call, either way.'

'Unless you're dead,' Sheriff Frank Gozinsky said, his face deadpan. Then he chuckled and slapped Hugh with his hat again. 'Hey, I'm just pulling your tab here is all – you need to lighten up.'

The Sheriff turned around and pulled on his hat. As he stepped out of the doorway he said, 'But you do hear of some things. Why, a woman – local, as it turns out – was held captive for more'n a whole day,' he said without turning around. 'Her killer – went by the name of the Pain Man – opened her up and took out a lot of her insides . . . set 'em on—'

'Frank—' Hugh started.

'Jesus, so gross,' Angie whispered, more to herself than to anyone else.

'—set 'em out on plates right in front of her. And he clamped her head in a fixed position and clipped off her eyelids so she couldn't not see.'

'*Frank!*'

'And she was local?' Angie said.

'Ayuh,' Frank grunted.

'Never saw it in the papers. Or heard it on the news.'

'Didn't make it into the newspapers yet. Or on the TV. Will, though.'

'Well, we'll watch out,' Hugh said.

'Uh, huh. Took her near on twelve hours to die,' the Sheriff said, shaking his head. He looked up into the sky, shielding his eyes. 'Looks to me like it ain't ever gonna stop.' He turned around and gave a little salute. 'Be seeing you.' And he was gone, jogging through the rain to his cruiser.

As Angie watched him drive off, something felt wrong, but she couldn't say what it was. It didn't matter. It was already way too late.

III

Hugh pushed the door closed and started back upstairs.

'Where're you going, sweetie?'

'Thought I'd unpack.'

'I could do it later . . .'

Hugh shook his head. 'Might as well make a start.'

When he reached the top of the stairs, having turned from the first long flight onto the shorter second flight, Hugh couldn't help feeling just the slightest tug of anxiety. Maybe it was Ellie. Maybe it was the way Joe McHendricks had set off along the road. Or maybe—

all of 'em

—it was the slightly worrying feeling—

ain't like you're gonna be going anyplace once you get there

—that something was wrong. That there was somebody up here in the house . . . *with* him. Maybe he should have let the Sheriff take a look. He was alone, considerably removed from the normalcy of downstairs and the radio and the distant clunking of cupboard doors. It was like a different world, one he had stumbled into unbidden and unwanted.

He paused for a second, tilting his head to one side, and stared intently at the door to the front bedroom.

The sound of the radio drifted up behind him, a woman's voice saying, *It's not true that poltergeists are just mischievous, not at all.* Then a squawk of interference as the channel was changed led into the familiar strains of The Eagles' 'Hotel California'.

He went into the bedroom and turned on the radio, making sure it was tuned to the news channel, and opened wide the wardrobe doors. Behind him, a man's voice said *Imagine if you had a whole family of poltergeists.*

Sounds like something out of Casper the Friendly Ghost, a woman's voice chimed in. *With Spooky the Tuff Little Ghost, Wendy the Good Little Witch and the Ghostly Trio . . . all of them – 'ceptin' Casper and Wendy – just going around saying* Boo! *to folks.*

The audience laughed.

As he scanned the shirts on the rail, Hugh heard the unmistakable sound of someone turning over in bed.

'Hello?' Hugh said, his voice soft as he turned around. He didn't want Angie to hear him.

Was that a sigh?

It's a myth, the man was saying. *Poltergeists are not the kittens of the spectral plane, they're more the—* He paused, clearly trying to come up with the correct word.

'Hello?' Hugh said again. He walked out of the bedroom and onto the landing, looked over the banister. No sign of Angie, but he could hear the clanking of pans from the kitchen.

—Raptors, the man said.

Raptors? Like as in Jurassic Park?

Yeah, the man said. *Ghosts with teeth.*

Mmm, the woman said, *spooky.*

Dropping his pants onto the floor, Hugh sidled along the banister and then the adjoining wall all the way to the front-bedroom door. He craned his neck to see first through the open door – nothing sinister there: wardrobe, window showing the church clock next door, small pile of books and magazines on the floor – and then through the door jamb. That narrow little aperture didn't give much more – just the made-up bed, some clean sheets that Angie must have put there ready for the weekly change-over, and the right-hand edge of the window that Hugh had thought (and how silly he now felt that was) he had seen the vaguest impression of an intruder surveying the outside like he owned it. (*Was it a 'he'?* Hugh wasn't at all sure, though he fancied it was. Or *had been.*)

He moved forward slightly less gingerly now, until he was standing square-on with the doorway.

'You sure you want coffee? And not a cup of tea?' Angie shouted suddenly from downstairs.

Spinning around to face the door again, Hugh held his right hand to his chest and breathed out slowly. 'Either is fine.'

'Well, say which.'

'Okay, coffee.'

'Milk or cream?'

For God's sake, Angie— 'Cream,' Hugh said. 'Let's live dangerously.'

She moved away (she must have been immediately below him, in the hallway) and started humming.

Behind him, out on the street, a car engine made a noise like the phlegmy rattle of someone clearing his throat. Just for a second, Hugh thought about not turning but simply walking out of the room and then running down the stairs, taking them two or even three at a time until he reached the hallway. Instead, holding his breath, he turned around very slowly, his eyes leading the way, and fully prepared to cease the exercise if they encountered anything unpleasant.

There was nobody there.

'Of course there's nobody there,' Hugh said, spitting the words out as though they were tainted meat.

What do you say to all this, Hugh? The woman on the radio wanted to know. Hugh felt a seismic shift in the pit of his stomach, but then she added, *Are we likely to see any ghosts in the new series of* House – *either with teeth or without?*

Just scant minutes later, Hugh had found his favourite denims and a faded green collarless shirt and was jogging down the stairs . . . ignoring the way the wind had got up outside to the degree that it was blowing against the window and making it sound like small (and 'proper' – now where had he got *that* notion?) bony feet clumping along behind him.

IV

'I'll get it,' Hugh shouted, his mouth full of peanuts. 'Could be Frank again.'

'I hope not. And you're eating,' Angie snarled from the next floor, craning her head over the banister. 'No potatoes for you for supper tonight.'

Hugh put out his tongue, narrowly avoiding spitting a thick glob of half-chewed nuts onto the tiled floor, but Angie had already returned to her cleaning.

Hugh recognised the outline of Gary through the tinted glass of the front door. 'It's Gaz!' he shouted.

'Let me in!' Gary pleaded from the step. 'They're after me.'

Pulling back the door, Hugh held out his arms. 'Then come in, weary traveller.'

As he stepped into the hallway, Gary Aaronson said '"bout bloody time.'

'I came as soon as I heard the bell,' Hugh protested. 'Coffee? Or something stronger?'

'Coffee's fine. But only if you're having one.'

'We just had one . . . but I'll have another if you insist.'

'I insist. You know how I hate to drink alone.'

Hugh strode ahead through the living room to the kitchen.

'That's been my downfall at too many dinner parties,' he said, throwing the words over his shoulder.

'Well, you can always say no.'

'Yeah, right.' Hugh hit the switch on the Mr Coffee. 'And that would stop you pouring me another glass of wine?'

'Probably not. Talking of which, I may pop into the store on the way home and pick up a few bottles – place looks deserted and they've got an offer on for Oyster Bay . . . down to ten bucks a time.'

'Sounds like a bargain.'

Gary nodded emphatically. 'In fact,' he went on, 'pretty much the whole town is empty.'

'The weather,' Hugh said. 'People are sick of going out and—'

He stopped and thought back to what Maude had said:

ain't like you're gonna be going anyplace once you get there

'That's another thing,' Hugh said.

'Another thing? I think I might have blinked and missed the first thing.'

'Maude Angstrom is out at the turn-off on the Oguncuit road, off of I-95 and she's turning folks around.'

'Yeah?'

'Yeah.'

'And that's a thing, how?'

Hugh shook his head. 'Seems a little extreme. She says it's to stop folks driving off into the ditch.'

'Well, it surely is a bitch of a road.'

'Okay, it's a bad—'

'And the rain looks like it's set in for the duration, so the chances of slippin' and slidin' are gonna be lookin' pretty good.'

'Well, yeah, mayb—'

'And she didn't turn you around, right?'

'Hey you're not in court now, Mr Mason.'

Gary laughed.

Hugh took a sip of coffee. 'And another thing.'

'Hoo-eee, we're getting through these "things" thick and fast now, ain't we?'

'She said something.'

'Who? Angie?'

'No, Maude,' Hugh snapped. 'Stay with the goddam program, will you?'

'What'd she say?'

'She said, "It ain't like you're gonna be going anyplace once you get there".'

'Oh. Were you going out?'

'No . . . no, we weren't going out. But—'

'So she was right.'

'Yeah, but—'

'But you weren't going out.'

'No. We weren't going out.' Hugh sighed and rubbed his head. 'But she didn't mean that.'

'Didn't mean . . . that you weren't going out?'

Hugh waved a hand dismissively. 'And then there's Ellie Ferguson.'

'What did *she* do?'

'She said, "They're here . . . all of them".'

'All of who? Or should I say *whom*?'

'She didn't say. She said, "They're here, Hugh" . . . and then she said "all of them" . . . and then "they're all here".'

'You think somebody's going around sticking pods under folks' beds?'

'Oh, that's typical. Typical of you, Gaz.'

'What? What's typical?'

'You try to belittle people who are trying to discuss something.'

'You want to know what I think, amigo?'

'Not really, but you're going to tell me.'

'I am.'

After waiting a half-minute, Hugh said, 'Okay, so tell me.'

'I think you're getting too much sex.'

Hugh was incredulous. 'You think *what*?'

'I mean, Jesus Christ ... how long you two been married, anyway?'

'What do you mean?'

'What do I *mean*? Okay, let's do it slowly: How. Long. Have. Y—'

'No, idiot.' Hugh lifted the cookie jar out of the cupboard. 'I mean, what do you mean about us having—?'

'Hey, amigo, you're—'

'Will you not do that? Don't call me "amigo".'

Gaz put his head on one side and lowered his eyes.

'And don't do that, either.'

'What?'

'That hurt thing. That expression you use when you're trying to make out you've been wounded.'

Gary lifted a cookie to his mouth and crunched. Speaking around the crumbs, he said. 'I *saw* you – or Angela. Could have been Angela, but I reckon it was you.' He took another bite and munched happily, giving Hugh another wink.

'Gaz, you lost me here. You saw me when?'

'This morning.'

'In Boston?'

'Not in Boston – hey, these are *good*.' Gary took another cookie out of the jar and continued munching. 'I saw you *here*,' he mumbled, jerking his head upwards. 'In the front bedroom. That your little love-nest? I know you and Ange sleep in the ba—'

'Gaz, we were in Boston ... coming back from Nan's place.'

'Hey, how is she?'

'Good. Nan's good.'

'Excellent. I always had a soft—'

'When did you call round?'

Frowning now, seeing something in Hugh's own expression, Gary said, 'Around nine, nine-thirty. I'd just finished walking the dog.'

'We only got back a half-hour ago.'

Gary made a face and shrugged.

'And that's another thing.'

'Jesus Christ. More "things".'

'The Sheriff came round.'

'What did you do?'

'Nothing.'

Gary made a face. 'So he came around for—?'

'Maude told him we wanted to see him.'

'And you didn't?'

'Well, we didn't when we saw Maude, but then, when things got—'

'Them goddam "things" again.'

Hugh sighed deeply and rubbed his head. 'So you're telling me I was in the front bedroom . . . or rather this person was in the front bedroom?'

Gary nodded and then smiled. 'You ducked back when you saw me look up.'

'Gaz, I was out – O-U-T . . . what can't you understand about that?'

Gary held up his hands. 'Okay, okay, take it easy. You were out and not here at the house.'

Hugh watched his friend.

'That's fine. I'm happy for you.'

Neither of them said anything for a while.

At last, Gaz said, 'Angie not having coffee?'

'I doubt it. I'll check.'

Hugh walked back through into the hallway.

'Jeez, but these cookies are good. Where'd you get 'em?'

'Angie? Another cup?'

He waited.

'Better tell her to hurry if she wants a cookie,' Gary called from the kitchen.

Hugh held onto the newel post and leaned over so that he could look up to the spot where Angie usually leaned over. 'Angie?'

There was no answer.

'She got a radio on?' Gary asked, suddenly appearing behind Hugh with his cup in one hand and a chocolate chip cookie in the other.

Hugh didn't answer. He stepped onto the bottom stair and shouted up again. Then, when there was still no answer, he took another step, and then another.

'Angela?' Her Sunday-best name . . . the one he always used on the rare occasions that he was angry with her. *Or scared*, a voice whispered in Hugh's head.

'You want me to come up?' asked Gary.

Hugh didn't respond. Now he jogged the last few stairs two at a time. Gary stuck with him all the way.

'Angie?'

'Ange!' Gary shouted – he knew she hated that bastardisation of her name and was thus sure to comment. But there was nothing. 'Come on, Angie . . . quit fooling around.'

Hugh went and checked the bathroom, then their bedroom – nothing.

In the bedroom, a man with a European accent – German? Swedish? Hugh couldn't make out which – was saying *There are many well-documented cases of let's say spiritual infestation down the years but, for the most part, they're just one ghost. Imagine if there were more than one.*

What, the woman said, *like two or maybe three?*

Oh, I'm thinking more than that. I'm thinking many more than that.

Gary placed his cup on the little table next to the *chaise longue*, leaned into the small stairway up to the top floor – the guest-floor, as Hugh and Angie called it – and shouted, but there was still no response. He jogged up the stairs and Hugh heard him moving from room to room, calling Angie's name ... and now *he* was using her Sunday-best, too.

V

When Gary came back down, he said, 'She's not there, is she?'

Gary shook his head some more. 'No. Not there.'

Hugh turned to the door of the front bedroom.

'Have you been in there?' Gary asked.

His voice barely above the sound of air moving out between his teeth, Hugh said, 'I daren't.'

Gary moved past his friend and went into the room. He stepped back immediately. He didn't have to say anything. Instead, Gary said, 'Could she have stepped out?'

'Why would she step out? I mean, without *telling* me?'

'No,' he said, the word seeming at once both tired and inadequate.

'Hold on,' Hugh said.

Gary's face lightened.

'She *must* have gone out,' he said.

Gary nodded, but the smile of anticipation at what was coming – *she told me she was nipping out to the store*, or something – was quickly fading. 'Of course,' he said. Then he added, 'What was she doing up here?'

Hugh shrugged. His stomach was starting to knot and he suddenly felt like a good sit-down on the toilet might be a good idea. 'Tidying? Sorting stuff out ... that kind of thing.'

Gary looked at the front bedroom door. 'Looks like she was having a nap, state of the bedclothes.' He winked. 'You sure you two weren't—?'

Hugh didn't wait for the rest of it. He almost lurched forward into the bedroom and stopped dead just inside the doorway. The bedclothes were indeed rumpled – in fact, they were a mess.

'Gaz,' Hugh said, 'something's wrong.'

You talk about ghosts as being infestations.

Yes, I think that is a reasonable description.

How do you know if you've got them? I mean, an early sign.

Like ghost droppings? Hugh Laurie suggested.

The audience laughed.

'Let me turn off that fucking radio,' Hugh said. And he did.

Following him into the bedroom, Gary didn't say anything but looked down at his hand. The chocolate chips had melted over his fingers. He lifted the cookie and popped it into his mouth, licking the fingers one by one as he watched Hugh, searching his friend's face.

At last Gary said, 'You didn't— didn't have a fight, did you?'

'A fight?'

'You know . . . a difference of opinion, let's say.' He pointed at the bedclothes.

'You're asking me if we had an argument over *sex*?'

'Well, not exac—'

'Jesus Christ, Gaz.'

'No, I—'

'I mean, Jesus fucking *Christ*, Gary!'

Gary didn't say anything.

They stood like that in silence for what felt like an age.

Then Hugh said, 'Where *is* she, Gaz?'

'I don't know.'

'It's like she's just gone' – and Hugh snapped his fingers – '*poof!*'

Gary didn't comment. Well, Hugh reasoned, what *could* he comment? Instead, he just stared at the sheets. Then he stepped out into the hallway and picked up the phone.

VI

'Here we all are again,' Frank said when Hugh opened the door. 'Hey, Gary,' he said as he stepped into the hallway, hat in hand.

'You're having quite a day of it,' Gary said.

Frank shrugged. 'We don't usually bother with missing person reports until twenty-four hours have gone by but . . . under these circumstances,' he added. Hugh refrained from asking exactly how these circumstances differed from any other missing person report, but he reasoned that coming across as a smart-ass probably wouldn't be constructive.

He had known Frank and his brother Gordy for most of his life – Gordy was a District Detective Supervisor over in Boston – and he was all too well aware they were serious about their jobs . . . perhaps more particularly Frank, despite the fact that Tuboise was a far cry from Boston.

Gary had called home and asked Sarah to come round. She was in the kitchen now, making coffee, and toast with peanut butter and raspberry jelly. The last thing Hugh wanted to do was eat, but he knew he should build up some energy. He felt totally exhausted.

'This is just a formality,' Frank said. His face was tight and his mouth tight-shut. When he talked to Hugh, he stared into Hugh's eyes, reading every response and every answer. 'You ask me, we're wasting our time.' He smiled and rolled his eyes. 'Most often,' he added, lowering his voice and glancing at the door that Sarah had just peered around, 'they've just had a bit of a mood and gone walkabout. She might even be back before I've finished my report.'

'She's never just walked out like this,' Hugh said.

'Sometimes wives behave out of character,' Gary said softly.

The Sheriff nodded. 'Okay, your wife's age, Hugh?'

'Forty-six.'

'And her full name?'

'Angela Rose.'

'Okay, so tell me about the man you say you saw in your room?'

'Nothing much to say really. We—'

'I saw him, too,' Gary said, resuming his place in the chair by the piano.

'In the same room?' Frank jerked his head upwards. 'The front bedroom?'

'I thought it was Hugh,' Gary said. 'He stepped back when he saw me.'

'And this wasn't you, Hugh?'

'No, we – Angie and me – we were coming back from Boston. Like I told you before.'

'And you have an alarm?'

'Yes, we do.'

'Yes. I thought I'd seen a keypad in the kitchen.' Frank wrote some more and then looked up in the middle of a sentence.

'Yeah?'

Frank frowned. 'Yeah?'

'The keypad in the kitchen?'

'Yeah, I've seen it.'

'When was that?'

'When did I see the keypad?'

'Mm hmm.'

'Some other time, I guess.'

Hugh was quiet.

'That a problem?'

'It's not a problem.'

Frank waved his hands around, palms up. 'It's just you make it sound like it's—'

'It's not a problem, Frank. I just don't recall you ever being in the kitchen is all.'

The Sheriff gave a little laugh and looked at Gary.

Gary gave a little laugh in response and looked at Hugh.

Hugh gave a little laugh and jiggled his head from side to side. 'Have you had any trouble with it?'

'With the alarm?' When Frank nodded, Hugh said, 'No, no trouble at all. A few power cuts, but they have a seventy-two-hour battery back-up. We had to call them once for the whole system to be reset, but no problems as such.'

'It didn't go off, though. I mean, when you saw the person when you got in and—' He turned to Gary. '—when you saw him this morning. Is that correct?'

'I'm not sure what you're asking me, Frank.'

'I'm saying, Gary, that the alarm was not going off when you saw Hugh here – sorry, when you *thought* you saw Hugh – in his bedroom this morning. Is that correct?'

Gary looked at Hugh. Returning his attention to the Sheriff, he said, 'Yes, that's correct.'

'Correct that the alarm was not going off?'

'Yes. There was no alarm.'

'And no alarm when *we* got back,' Hugh said.

'And the alarm had been activated while you were out?'

'Yes. All the time we were away, in fact.'

'So it would also have been activated when Gary saw this person in your bedroom?'

'Yes, it was the same time. Well, the same session . . . if that's what they call it.'

'But you haven't had any problems with the alarm? It's a SuperSafe, I believe, yes?'

'Yes, SuperSafe. They're in Boston.'

'Yes, we're familiar with them.'

'"Familiar with them" as in you've had problems with them before?'

'No, no problems.' Frank shrugged. 'We just know about them.'

'Funny thing, though,' Hugh said.

Frank shifted his attention from one man to the other and then back again. He pursed his lips. 'Okay, I think that's about it for now. Let's see if Angie turns up and then take it from there.'

The Sheriff closed his notebook and slipped the pen into his pocket. 'Okay, Frank. We'll leave it at that for now.' He slapped Frank on the shoulder. 'You'll see her again,' he said. 'Don't worry.'

Hugh and Gary stood at the door until the cruiser had disappeared. Closing the door, Hugh said, 'That was an odd thing for him to say.'

'Telling you not to worry? I don't think—'

'No, saying I'd see Angie again.'

'Well, you will.'

'But where *is* she, Gaz?'

VII

Gary wanted Hugh to go round to their place but Hugh said no. 'I want to be here when she comes back.'

Sarah said she understood that. But there was nothing else they could do for him, she explained. They would come and stay here with him, Sarah said, but they were having the principal and his wife around for dinner – Gary said they could cancel it (though Hugh didn't feel Sarah's look indicated that was a good idea), but Hugh wouldn't have any of it.

'I'll be fine,' he told them at the door, with the first telltale sign of a winter evening draining the light from the sky. In the park across the street, a sea fog was spindling misty fingers amidst the tree branches.

'You sure?'

'I'm sure.'

The quick glance between Hugh's friends would have been lost on anyone else, but not Hugh. It was the kind of exchange you only ever see between people who are totally comfortable and have known each other for many years. Perhaps Sarah gave the most imperceptible of nods and perhaps she did not, but she turned around, shrugged on her coat and, removing the car keys from her pocket, announced that she would get the car started.

'Okay,' Gary said. He turned to face Hugh and scanned his friend's face. 'You okay?'

Hugh nodded. 'I already said.'

'I know, I know.' Gary's eyes narrowed as though physically piercing the protective barrier that Hugh had erected. The car engine started with a loud *clunk* and then quickly settled into a gentle idle.

As he watched it go, listening to the sound of the tyres on the gravel, Hugh felt a momentary panic. He wanted to run after them and tell them he had changed his mind . . . that yes, he would like them to stay: would like them to make it all okay again and laugh about things. Maybe even produce Angie, who had just 'had a turn' as Hugh's mother had liked to say way back when.

He stayed his ground, but he did see the expression of profound sadness on Gary's face. But it looked as though Sarah was saying something to cheer up her husband, because her face was smiling, bathed in the greenish glow of the dashboard instruments. With the car already being consumed by the fog, Hugh turned to the house and with a heavy heart took the first step back.

The silence that washed around him as he closed the door and threw the deadbolt was profound – in fact, it was as though he had been suddenly struck deaf. So when the telephone rang, the noise was shrill and almost physical.

Grimacing and praying for it to cease, Hugh lurched unevenly into the sitting room. Perhaps this was Angie, calling to explain what had happened and where she was. *I'm afraid I just needed to get away for a while, sweetie,* he imagined her voice saying to him through the ear-piece as he lifted it clear of the cradle and said, 'Hello?'

At first, the crackle seemed to be all there was until a man's voice said, 'Mr Ritter?'

It sounded a bit like Gary and for the most fleeting of seconds, Hugh thought perhaps Gary and Sarah had got back home to find Angie sitting on their stoop. But, no, they wouldn't be home yet – they lived barely a mile away, but they had been gone only a couple of minutes. He turned around quickly – perhaps rather too quickly – just in time to see someone standing outside the high windows of the sitting room.

Just as he wondered what they were doing talking on a telephone out there – with the fog now thickening against the glass to such a degree that the hedge was hard to make out – he realised that it was his own reflection. 'Yes,' he said at last, wondering if the fog were affecting the lines in some way, so as to make the voice sound strangely speeded up and slowed down at the same time.

'Mr Ritter?' the voice said again.

'Yes, this is Hugh Ritter.'

'Did you say goodbye to your friends, Mr Ritter?'

'Excuse me?'

'And the Sheriff? You say goodbye to him?'

'Who is—?'

'Oh, we are multitudes, Mr Ritter – or may I call you Hugh?' the Sheriff's voice intoned lazily. 'First we are this,' Angie's voice added, 'and then we are that,' Gary's voice continued, 'and then we are someone or something completely different.' The last one was Sarah Aaronson, who went on to say, in a squawky voice that belonged to Maude Angstrom and was filled with good-natured chuckles, 'And we're gonna have ourselves some fun. After all, ain't like you're gonna be going anyplace.'

The line went dead.

'Hello?'

The line remained dead.

He had always wondered how he would cope in such a situation, in a moment of profound and senseless chaos and confusion. Okay, what had always figured in his mind was Angie dying on him. But he reasoned that in such a situation he would have time to acclimatise. And as horrific as the scenario might be, it would make sense. The events of the day he had just lived through made no sense at all.

Hugh moved the handset away from his ear and looked at it accusingly, immediately annoyed with himself for descending so quickly into cliché. Whatever was the point of *looking* at the handset? There *wasn't* a point. The handset's countenance could offer no explanation for the caller ringing off – or was it callers? Could all those voices have been the one person? If so, it was one hell of a trick. But maybe he/they hadn't rung off. Perhaps he had simply been *cut* off. That made much more sense, particularly with the fog and all.

Hugh looked up at the window and saw his reflection standing watching him. Was it his imagination or did the window-Hugh's hand – the one holding the telephone – continue to move after the real Hugh had kept his own hand stationary?

Preposterous.

'Preposterous,' Hugh exclaimed.

He looked back at the handset and immediately pressed *69. A rather informal-sounding woman's voice told him that a caller had dialled in at 7:02 p.m. The only problem was that the number she gave was—

'That's *my* number,' Hugh said. 'How can I be calling myself on *my* number?'

He hit *69 again. The line was busy. He was about to ask aloud how it could ever be busy when he realised that the repeated beep-tone did not signify that the person at that number was already dealing with a call. Rather, it informed him that someone else had picked up one of the other handsets somewhere in the house.

He pressed the button to get the dial tone and said 'Hello?'

Maybe it was the wind buffeting the eaves of the house and exploring the chimneys, but he couldn't shake the feeling that he could hear breathing – not the in-out, in-out sigh of a sleeper but the cautious surveillance of a watcher.

'Hello? Is someone there?'

The phone clicked in his ear and almost immediately began to ring.

'Hello?'

'Mr Ritter?'

'What the hell do you want?'

The caller – a man – sounded genuinely surprised. 'Pardon me?'

'Did you just call? A few minutes ago?'

There was a short silence that suggested the caller was shaking his head, though, to be safe, he said, 'No. I called just now.'

'For the first time?'

'Yes, for the first time.'

Hugh waited for a few seconds to regain his composure and then said, 'I'm so sorry for that outburst. It's my wife. It's been—'

'It's about your wife I'm calling, Mr Ritter.'

'Do you know where she is?'

'It's not too late is it, Mr Ritter? To call you, I mean?'

'What? Oh, no . . . no, it's not too late. You said—'

'This is Shelley Mitford, with the Sheriff's office here in Tuboise? The Sheriff asked me to give you a call.'

'About my wife?' *Who the hell is Shelley Mitford?* Hugh thought. He had never heard of him. 'Do you—?'

'It's about the alarm, sir.'

'The alarm?'

'We've been in touch with the people at SuperSafe – the alarm people?'

'Yes?'

'And the Sheriff needs me to ask you if it's possible that you didn't set the alarm before you went out today.'

'Didn't set the alarm?'

'Yes, sir.'

'Well, it's always possible that I might forget but— No – when Angie and I—' Hugh suddenly felt like sitting down and weeping, '—when we got back home, Angie cancelled the alarm code as we walked into the house.'

There was a pause. 'Who else knows the code, sir?'

'Who else knows the code?' Hugh was beginning to feel like a parrot. 'Gary ... Gary Aaronson. He was round here with the Sheriff this afternoon – and I suppose that means Sarah will know it, too. Er ...'

'Sarah, sir?'

'Sarah Aaronson. That's – I mean "*she's*" – Gary's wife.'

'Anyone else, sir?'

Hugh thought for a minute, then said, 'I think maybe Angie's friend.'

'And she is?'

'Florence. Florence Gilliard.'

'Could you spell that for me, sir?'

Hugh spelled it out.

'And she lives locally?'

Not much point in her having a fucking key if she didn't live locally, Hugh thought. 'Yes,' he said, and he gave the address.

'Thank you.'

'Before you ring off—'

'Yes sir?'

'What did they say? The alarm people, I mean. You said you'd been in contact with them?'

'They said it wasn't possible for someone to be moving around inside the house while the alarm was active.'

Hugh waited for more but there wasn't any.

'What does that mean?' Hugh asked.

'It means that someone who knew the alarm code was in the house or—'

'Or?'

'Or you've made a mistake in one or more parts of your story.'

'A mistake?'

'Yes, sir.'

'You mean "or I lied".'

'I didn't—'

'That's what you meant, isn't it?'

'We have to keep all options open, sir.' After a few more seconds, the policeman added, 'You might even have a poltergeist.' He coughed and cleared his throat, making a noise that sounded like *goeswithseeth* and Hugh said, 'I'm sorry, what did you say?'

'Sir? I said we have to keep all—'

'No, after that.'

'I didn't say anything after that, sir.'

The fog must have affected the phone lines because it sounded as though, just for a few moments, the man was stifling amusement.

'Have a good night, sir.'

Hugh hung up.

He went out to the kitchen and started to key in the alarm code, but then thought better of it. What if Angie came back home? She would have her key – wouldn't she? Hugh went to the little rack of hooks and checked. Her house key was not there . . . but, of course, that didn't mean anything.

Ghosts with teeth, a voice said at the back of Hugh's head. *That's what he said, the guy on the phone. Ghosts with teeth.*

VIII

'Is that the door?'

Gary Aaronson dropped his jacket onto the kitchen table and pocketed the house keys. 'What time did you tell them?'

'Eight,' Sarah shouted. 'The fire's not even lit.'

Gary reached the front door. Through the frosted glass he could see only one figure and it looked to be too tall for the principal. 'Won't take me a minute,' he shouted to Sarah. The figure on the step was wreathed in shadow and for a moment Gary couldn't make it out, though it looked familiar.

'Hurry up and close the—' Sarah started as she came up behind her husband. And then, 'Oh.'

The figure stepped forward, smiling.

'Did you forget something?' Gary asked the Sheriff.

'Have you found her?' Sarah interjected.

'Let's close the door, shall we,' the Sheriff said and, as he stepped into the house, the screen door clattered to and the inner door slowly closed itself.

'How . . . how do you do that?' Gary asked.

'Let's talk about poltergeists,' Frank Gozinsky said. And when he turned around, Gary saw that there were other people standing with the Sheriff, but slightly to one side, peeping cheerfully around Frank's shoulders as though to surprise an infant. One by one they sidled out into full view. It looked as though they had come to do some kind of repair work, for they carried all manner of tools – saws, hammers and drills, plus coils of twine.

'Gary?' Sara said.

Gary felt an almost indescribable urge to turn and flee . . . to get out of the house, back into the wind and rain. But this feeling did not translate to his face or his arms and legs. There was a calm about his exterior that was not replicated inside, where his stomach churned and his heart thudded like a racehorse running the final straight.

The radio came on and a voice said, *Hello Gary and Sarah. Welcome to Halloween. Your guests are here to entertain you. Say hello.*

Gary felt himself smiling as he gave a little wave. Out of the corner of his eye, he saw Sarah do the same and he whimpered, 'Sarah,' but he didn't think she had heard him. There were now six people standing between them and the door.

Gary turned fully to look at Sarah and she turned to look at him. She mouthed his name, but no sounds emerged. Was that a tear just hovering at the corner of her right eye?

Say hello, folks. Come on . . . be nice.

'Hello,' Gary said.

'Hello,' said Sarah.

'We have a busy night ahead,' Frank said, 'so best get started. Trick or Treat?'

IX

It sounded like the sea, at first. Hugh was dreaming. He was on a boat – Angie was there, doing something with the rigging, smiling at him. The way he was watching her was as though he was watching a film taken of her. When he moved closer towards her – he saw his arms stretching out in front of himself – he noticed that she was crying.

Oh, sweetie, she said. Her lips moved in sync to the words, but there was no sound . . . just the internal sound of his brain processing them, the same as his brain's interpretation of the sound of the sea all around them. *I'm so sorry,* Angie said.

What are you sorry for? he thought at her.

The boat cleaved the water, proudly lifting and then dropping into the waves. *Shhh!* it whispered.

Angie turned to her right, both expectantly and fearfully, her eyes wide, her mouth slightly agape. *It's coming,* she said. As he started to turn his head, something very big and very black rose up like a thick curtain in front of him and a loud crashing sound made him open his eyes.

Hugh was lying on his bed – no, not his bed; the bed he shared with his wife. It was *their* bed.

Not any more, sweetie, the remnants of Angie's voice whispered in his head, growing fainter and fainter.

He glanced at the clock: 1:37.

The light was still on.

He looked at the crumpled ball of Angie's nightdress and then reached out and pulled it towards him, buried his face in it and breathed in.

Shhh!

'Hello?'

Someone was moving around on the landing. Hugh let the nightdress fall to the pillow as he slid from the bed. 'Angie?'

The movement stopped right outside the bedroom door and Hugh felt a wave of energy coming at him as though he were walking into a gale-force wind. His heart pounded in his chest and his forehead . . . and that was somehow worse because it drowned out the sounds that whatever was on the other side of the door was making – drowned them out, but deep down, Hugh knew those sounds were there.

The door – which had not been fully closed, just pushed to – started to move inwards and Hugh watched it with a kind of detached fascination. It had gone perhaps two inches, maybe three, when it stopped. There was silence, but it was not a good silence, not a calm or quiet silence. Rather than it being simply nothing – just a quietness with nothing added – this felt like a quietness with its very soul removed. Hugh wanted to say his wife's name, whisper it, over and over, but that first syllable – '*An—*', drawn out like soft nougat – lodged in his throat and just wouldn't move. What the hell was he doing? he thought.

Hugh strode across the floor and yanked the door wide.

'Ah,' said Sheriff Frank Gozinsky, 'there you are!'

'Where did you think I'd be?' Hugh asked. 'I live here.'

'Indeed you do, Hugh.'

'How'd you get in?'

'The front door, Hugh. You didn't mind me coming right in, did you, Hugh?'

'I locked it.'

The Sheriff's brow furrowed as he turned around to start down the stairs. 'You can't have done, Hugh,' he said, throwing the words over his shoulder, 'because I'm here.'

'I did lock it,' Hugh repeated. 'I did call out. But you didn't answer.'

They walked down the stairs slowly and in silence.

X

When they reached the bottom of the stairs, the telephone rang.

'Telephone,' said the Sheriff.

Hugh fought off the urge to give a sarcastic *Oh, thanks . . . I didn't hear it,* and lifted the receiver. 'Hello?'

'Hello, Hugh.'

'Nan? Everything okay?'

'Everything's fine, Hugh. How are things with you?'

'Nan, it's so late.' Hugh checked his watch. 'Christ, not just *late* . . . it's almost two o'clock. You should be in bed.'

'Oh, "To bed, to bed," said Sleepy Head: "tarry a while," said Slow.'

'Nan?'

'"Put on the pan," said Greedy Nan, "we'll sup before we go."'

Hugh stood in silence, gawping through the sitting room and trying to figure out where the Sheriff had disappeared to.

'That's what she used to call me, Hugh – Greedy Nan.'

'Nan, is your sister with you? Is that why you're calling? Is Angie there?' How could she be there, though? Nan lived in Boston . . .

There was a slight pause and then Nan said, 'Angie's with *you*, Hugh.'

'Well, the fact is—'

'She's with *you*, Hugh.'

Hugh heard a clattering in the kitchen and he leaned over to see what was happening, but he couldn't see anything. Then the Sheriff shouted, 'Where do you keep your knives, Hugh? Ah, okay . . . I got them.'

'Nan, Angie has—'

'Would *you* like a pot of something, Hugh?' Nan asked. Her voice was lower somehow, and it sounded menacing.

Menacing? This was Angie's kid sister he was talking to. But what on earth was she doing – or why was she doing it, more like – ringing him at two in the morning?

'Well, do you?' the Sheriff called.

Very softly, Hugh said, 'Nan? Are you still there?' But the line was dead.

He hit *69. It was as he expected – the call had come from his own telephone number. Which was, of course, impossible.

He dialled Nan Brannigan's number and stepped back from the sitting room doorway as he listened to it ringing through the earpiece.

'Bit late isn't it?' the Sheriff said, his voice getting louder.

Hugh took another step backwards and fell against the stairs as Frank emerged from the room with a cup of tea in one hand and his cell phone in the other, pressed up against his ear. 'I could have been asleep,' he muttered into the phone. He put the cup of tea on the floor beside Hugh, then turned around and went back into the sitting room. 'Any developments?'

A sleepy voice said 'Hello?' in Hugh's ear. 'Who is this?'

'Nan? It's me.'

'Hugh? What's up? Is everything okay? Is Angie okay? It's very late.'

'I know. I'm sorry.' He backed up the stairs, holding the phone away from his ear so that he could hear the policeman muttering in the sitting room. 'Nan, Angie's gone.'

'Gone? Gone where?'

'I don't know. I should have called you earlier.'

'Did you have a fight?'

'No, we didn't have a fight.' He waited for Nan to say something but when she didn't, he said, 'We never fight. You know that.'

'Nobody *never* fights, Hugh.'

'Well, you know what I mean.'

Something clattered to the floor upstairs.

'What was that?'

Hugh stared at the front door – someone walked up the pavement outside the house and disappeared behind the bushes. 'What was what, Nan?'

'The noise. Something fell over,' Nan said, whispering.

Hugh heard a doorbell chime from the earpiece. Someone was at Angie's sister's door at 2:00 a.m. in the morning, ringing her bell.

'Oh my,' Nan said, 'someone at the door. I'll just—'

'Nan!' Hugh snapped, 'don't answer it.'

'—swer it. Did you say something, Hugh?'

'Nan, don't answer the door.'

'Don't answer the door? Whatever for?'

'It's—'

What? What was it exactly? Halloween? The Bogeyman? A gen-

you-whine 'thing' from someplace where there were no lights and no smiles, no love and no softness, only pain and grief and sadness, loss and regret ... something that could lift a foot to take a step from rainy Tuboise and put that very same foot down at a front door in far-off Boston in the blink of an eye? All of the above, even?

Hugh heard the sound of the telephone being put down on the little mahogany table in Nan's hallway.

'Hold on a second!' he heard Nan shouting.

Bing bong, went the doorbell.

'Nan!' Hugh shouted.

A wind whistled down the wire and Hugh heard Nan say, 'Yes?'

Then he heard the Sheriff's distant voice say, 'Trick or Treat, ma'am?'

'Oh, Nan,' Hugh said.

'"To bed, to bed," said Sleepy Head; "No, tarry—"'

Hugh disconnected the call and stood up, just in time to hear the squeak of the garden gate. An indistinct figure marched up the path, reached out an arm and pressed the bell.

'Door,' the Sheriff shouted.

Hugh trotted down the last few steps, walked across and opened the door.

'Hey,' Sheriff Gozinsky said from the front step. 'Boo! You think maybe I should Trick or Treatcha?'

'What's going on Sheriff? How'd you get—? How can you be out there and' – he turned and pointed to the living room and the kitchen beyond it – 'in there,' Hugh finished.

'You mean, both at the same time?'

Hugh nodded.

'Because I'm a Sheriff. An upholder of the law.' He gave a big grin and then frowned, his tongue exploring the blackened bottom teeth at the front of his mouth. He pushed at one of them a couple times and then reached up and just pulled it out, then turned around and tossed it into the yard.

'I don't know what's—'

'Going on?' Gozinsky rolled his eyes theatrically and put on a voice. 'Hey, man . . . wha's happenin', man?'

'Farmer?'

'Yep, in one. The local freak. Watch.'

The Sheriff stepped through the doorway and, kicking the door closed, he ran the flat of his right hand over his face. When the hand got to his chin, he wasn't the Sheriff any more. He was Moss Farmer, who lived in a shack overlooking Angel Rocks.

'The late Moss Farmer, may he rest in piece,' Gozinsky said. He removed his hat and feigned sadness. 'Or pieces,' he added with a chuckle.

'Now watch.' He ran his hand over his face again and then dropped it by his side . . . only it was her side now. 'You go on – ain't like you're gonna be going anyplace once you get there,' Maude Angstrom said in her unmistakable sing-song voice.

'Maude?' Hugh said.

'Ker-rect,' said the Maude thing. 'Hey, a puzzle for you.' She ran her small-boned hand over her face and the Sheriff reappeared.

Hugh glanced at the closed door.

'Hey, forget it.' He waggled the serrated knife at Hugh and shook his head. 'I'll get you before you take a second stride.'

Sheriff Frank took a deep breath and smiled. He looked tired.

'My friends and me, we've been educating,' he said at last. 'And I think it's fair to say that our students have been fascinated with what we had to show them.' He nodded. 'Yes indeedy. Oh, they've occasionally been surprised and . . . well, often they've been a mite uncomfortable. But, you know what they say: "knowledge is power. And strength".' He cocked his head on one said. 'They do say that, don't they, Hugh.'

'I have no idea what you're talking about,' Hugh said. 'And I have no—'

'Did you know that the small intestine is twenty-two feet long?'

'What?'

'The small intestine. Twenty-two feet. I didn't know that. And your wife's sister didn't know it either. Believe me. Oh, but you know,' he said, clapping his hands together theatrically, 'it does so make for a swell wall display.' The Sheriff leaned against the wall and looked into the far distance. '"Swell" . . . that's a grand word, ain't it? Doesn't get used anywhere near enough. I was sorry when that went out of fashion.'

Hugh looked around for something that he might use as a weapon.

'Who are you?'

'Well, I guess it's safe for us all to assume I'm not the Sheriff.' He pushed the knife through the palm of his left hand, looked at it with his head on one side, and then removed the blade. There seemed to be no loss of blood.

'You're crazy. Mad. Insane,' Hugh said. Then he shook his head. 'No, maybe it's me. Maybe I'm the one who—'

'You, dear Hugh? Oh, there's nothing wrong with you.' He chuckled and glanced down at the knife in his hand. 'Not yet, anyways.' He shrugged and blinked three times in rapid succession. 'I will readily admit to there being some kind of imbalance up here' – he knocked the side of his head with his knuckles – 'but I would plead to there being extenuating circumstances.'

'Why here? Why us?' Hugh said, his voice barely above a whisper.

The Sheriff sat down on one of the counter chairs and slumped his arms on the bar. 'Why is it everyone asks that? "Why me?"' he whined shrilly. '"What did *I* do?"' He pointed to one of the chairs and said simply, 'Sit – or should I maybe say, "Tarry a while"?'

Hugh sat, and in doing so realised that he was unable to move his feet or arms. He could do only those things that the Sheriff allowed.

Frank, or whatever it was in Frank's guise – Hugh was now totally convinced that this entity in his kitchen was not Frank

Gozinsky – got to his feet and started moving around the kitchen, opening cupboard doors and drawers and then closing them, all the time talking.

'The mistake you all make is that you think *here* and *me* pack some kind of emotional currency . . . that they're somehow special. Well, I'm sorry to say, they're not. You're not special, dear Hugh. And neither is – or *was* – Maude Angstrom. Or your dear friend Gary. Or his wife Sarah. Or Mrs Slater, or Eleanor, or Pop Maxell, or Ellie, or Joe McHendricks, or Archie Goodlowe, or Jerry Fettinger, or Nan, or' – Frank tapped each one off on his fingers and then, as he pulled open the large drawer next to the oven hob, he clapped his hands loudly once – 'or your own wonderful wife.' He turned around and smiled at Hugh, reaching into the drawer and lifting out a handful of knives. 'The tools of my trade,' he said, and he set all the knives out in a line next to each other.

Hugh could feel his heart pounding. When he tried to swallow it was as though his throat had been sandpapered.

'Scared, Hugh?'

Hugh nodded. 'What are you going to do?'

'I'm still debating it.' The Frank-thing thought for a few seconds and then said, 'Was your wife a good timekeeper, Hugh?'

'What?'

'Because she's late now.' He laughed. 'Get it? "Late"?'

'What have you—?'

'I killed her, Hugh. There'll be no cavalry in this oater, no flashing lights seen through the window and some fat slob with a bullhorn trying to talk me out because—' He swaggered clumsily and put one circle-shaped hand to his mouth. '"Come on out now, Sheriff – we've got you surrounded."' He put a finger to his mouth feigning a surprise discovery. 'Only, oops! I'm not the Sheriff, am I?'

Hugh stared at his hand and tried to will the fingers to move. It wasn't working.

'And I don't respond to the things you would expect a thinking, caring, person would respond to. What do they call it? Sociopathic tendencies? Something like that, I think. The thing is, the things I do I don't do simply because I enjoy doing them – though, to be fair about this, I do – but rather I do them because I *have* to do them. Does that make sense?'

Hugh's left index finger was slowly lifting itself from his knees, where both of his hands were laying flat. He nodded, and then he shook his head, relaxing the finger. 'No . . . no, it doesn't make sense.'

'Oh, come on now . . . one or the other, Hughie.' The Gozinsky-thing lifted a serrated bread-knife and walked across to Hugh, crouching down next to him. 'You're trying to multi-task here, aren't you?'

Hugh frowned. 'What—?'

The Sheriff nodded at Hugh's hands. 'You're trying to keep me occupied talking – because I surely do like to talk and that's a fact – while you try to free yourself from my . . . my *mind control*.' He said the last two words in a deep wavering voice.

The Sheriff rested the bread-knife on Hugh's knee, right next to his left hand. 'I'm wondering, see . . . wondering if maybe we should' – he tapped the finger with the knife – 'if maybe we should just chop it right off so that it doesn't distract us from our little conversation. What do you think about that, Hughie? Good idea?'

'No.'

'What? I don't seem to be able to hear you. Did you say, "Yes, sure, go right ahead, Sheriff, and chop off that naughty old finger!" Did you say that, Hugh?'

Hugh shook his head.

'Hugh, let's pretend I can't see you and can't tell you're shaking your head. Let's pretend I can only hear your voice . . . and that if I don't get a good answer, then I'll just go right ahead and chop off that finger.' He made a tutting sound with his mouth. 'And what you need to worry about then is where do I stop. You understand that, Hugh?'

'Yes. Yes, I understand.'

'Because I am one of the Pain People, Hugh. In fact, I am *the* Pain Man.' Frank clapped his hands. '*Koo koo ka-chew.* Delivered to your very door, agonies beyond belief. Beyond even your most fevered imagination.' He leaned in closer, his nose and beady pig-eyes right up against Hugh's face, and said, 'It's what I do, Hugh. You understand that? It's my job. What was it they said on the radio? Ghosts with teeth? I like that.' He chuckled and shook his head. 'I do like that.'

'Causing pain is what you do,' Hugh said.

The Sheriff nodded. 'Causing pain,' he said, the edge now gone from the tone of his voice. 'Let's go downstairs,' he said. 'To the cellar.'

'Downstairs?'

Frank nodded again, but, for a second, it wasn't Frank. It was Maudie Angstrom taking a hold of Hugh's hand, lifting it up so that Hugh would follow after it and walk with her. 'Hold on,' she said as she scooped up all the knives. 'Mustn't forget my tools. Ain't no way I'm gonna get any work done if'n I don't take muh tools. Ayuh, and that is a fact.'

'I don't want to go downstairs,' Hugh said.

Maude was now Pop Maxell. 'Hell, boy, I kin unnerstand that sho'nuff, yessiree. Trouble is, we cain't allas do what we want now, kin we?'

'I don't want to go—'

'Shh, hush now,' Pop said soothingly. 'You're gonna get me all lathered up so's I cain't think straight. And when I cain't think straight, why . . . I just has to do me some cutting, and some clipping. Maybe a little sawing and some prising. No need for that, I'm thinking. Is that what you're thinking, too?'

Pop had morphed into Angie's sister, Nan, and was picking

up one of cordless house-phones. 'Gonna need this,' Nan said.

'Nan?'

'Oh, dear . . . no, it's not *me*, Hugh.'

'Are you going . . . are you going to kill me?'

'Here we go – mind that first step now.' Nan hit the rocker switch at the top of the stairs.

'Oh no,' Hugh said.

'Hold your nose,' said the thing in front of him, now a curious amalgam of Maude Angstrom and Pop Maxell, skin rippling, hair frizzing in a series of small undulations.

'Oh, Christ, no,' Hugh said.

'Oh, He has no jurisdiction here, young fella,' Maude said in Pop's baritone voice. 'This here's *my* domain.'

Hugh covered his face with one hand and still held tightly onto Pop's with the other. 'What have you *done*?'

'I bin bizzy, young fella,' Pop announced proudly, just as they reached the final few steps and the full Technicolor majesty of the cellar lay before them.

Each of the 'guests' had their own special position. Some of them were on chairs, some were hanging – both regular way and upside-down – and a few were lying down. Hugh saw two – he was almost certain one was Joe McHendricks – were thick piles of flesh from which all the bones appeared to have been removed. The smell was rank, a mixture of shit, vomit and old food left too long in the sun.

Maude/Pop was now Sheriff Frank and he gave Hugh a big smile. 'Welcome, my friend, to the show that never ends,' he said, adding, 'I seen this in a movie one time,' as he reached up and set the hanging light-shades to swinging, bathing the whole vista in a swirling miasma of light and shadow and making it look like the poor unfortunates were still alive and moving. But they weren't. Not for a long time. 'Just needed some screeching violins.'

'Angie—' Hugh said.

Angela Ritter, her eyelids clipped away so that her eyes remained fiercely open, was tied to a chain hanging from one of the cellar beams. Her arms and legs had been broken in several places and strapped to her sides, so that thick brown tape wrapped around her head at mouth level secured her feet to her ears. She was naked.

Sheriff Frank – the real one – lay on the floor in a thick stain. His feet had been removed and his eyes gouged out.

Hugh glanced at the others – even recognised a couple of them – and then looked away.

He felt a strange calm come over him, like a wave over his feet while paddling on the beach at Oguncuit or Wells. He lifted his hands and looked at them. Every fibre of his being, every cell in his brain, was crying out for him to avenge the deaths of these people . . . but he couldn't move – at least not aggressively. It was as though he had been paralysed.

The Frank-thing reached down and took hold of the real Sheriff's collar, pulled him across the floor. 'You have civic duties to perform, Sheriff,' he said. 'A telephone call and some finger-printing, for example. But first, you have to administer a near miss.' He pulled out his revolver.

'Turn around,' he said to Hugh.

'You sick bas—'

'Just turn around.'

Hugh did as he was told.

The Frank-thing rested the barrel of the revolver against Hugh's forehead and fired.

Blammmmm!

XI

Hugh woke up to the sound of sirens and a pain between his temples that was to headaches what Hiroshima's 'Little Boy' was to Fourth of July firecrackers. The first thing he discovered was it was a good idea not to move anything – his head, his arms, his legs, his ass, his finger—

now why did just the thought of that, of moving a finger . . . why did it cause a sudden rush of anxiety?

—nothing. Even breathing was troublesome so he did it as slowly as he was able. He closed his eyes. That hurt, too.

The sirens stopped right outside – in fact, it sounded like they pulled up next to him . . . so maybe he was in the street. He opened his eyes again and slowly turned his head. Nope. He was in a room. The lights were on. He was lying on a carpet. It was his room, a room in his house.

His house?

His and *Angie's* house.

So he was face down on the living room floor of his own house. He shifted his head to an angle and saw that the sofa and a chair were tipped on their sides . . . and there was blood on the floor. His blood, he reckoned. There was no way on God's earth that you could feel this much pain without there being blood. He moaned his wife's name. There was no answer. God, what was happening?

Someone thumped on his door.

'I can't move,' Hugh said, his voice croaky and soft.

'Police,' a stern voice proclaimed. 'Open up.'

He needed a drink. Something—

put on the pan said greedy nan, we'll sup before we go

—to take away the dryness in his mouth and throat.

'We're coming in,' the voice outside said.

'Angie,' Hugh whimpered.

The door bounced open, splinters of wood raining onto the tiled hallway floor. Barked orders flooded Hugh's head—

oh, Christ, no, he recalled saying

—in a bizarre jumble of meaningless words and phrases, melding into the loud clatter of feet working their way to him, moving from the tiled floor into the carpeted living room where he lay.

Hugh pulled his arms back so that he might rest on them in order to lift his head and torso but a loud voice—

welcome my friend to the show that never ends

—screeched at him to lay still. 'Sir, do not move. Place your hands out in front of you.' As Hugh did as he was told, and stretched out his hands, he discovered a bread-knife under the palm of his right hand, with the end of it snapped clean off. He wondered what on earth it was doing there.

Feet ran past him heading for—

angie . . .

—the cellar. 'No,' he barely managed to say, a single faint word lost in the chaos and confusion.

Footsteps clattered up the carpeted stairs, going from the hallway and down the wooden steps leading to—

i bin bizzy, young fella

—leading to . . . leading to . . .

Somewhere a phone rang.

'Oh my fucking hell!' a voice exclaimed.

Someone else said, 'Jesus H. Christ!'

Footsteps slowed, didn't stop . . . just wound down.

'Angie,' Hugh Ritter whimpered.

He heard muttering from the top of the cellar stairs.

'How many?' someone asked.

'Motherfucker,' a voice said.

Someone threw up noisily.

Rough hands pulled his arms behind his back and clamped cuffs on his wrists. Then the same hands lifted him to his feet. His head felt like it had been hit with a baseball bat. He caught sight of himself in the mirror – his forehead was a red gash with black edges, a flap of skin hung down from his hairline almost to his left eye.

'I want . . . I want to see her,' Hugh croaked.

'Who? Who do you want to see, you sick fuck?' a voice said.

'Easy, Mike,' someone said to Hugh's right.

'My wife. I want to see my wife.'

A phone rang and was quickly answered.

'Ten, fifteen . . . no way of knowing,' someone else said, his voice hushed.

'Removed their bones,' another voice said, the words oozing incredulity.

'Clipped her eyelids.' Another.

'Every single tooth—' One more.

'Fingernails. Toenails . . .'

Hugh's vision was swimming, but very slowly, shapes were becoming clearer. A policeman had hold of his right arm, pulling it upwards all the time so that Hugh had to lean to his left. This must be Mike.

'Take him up,' the other voice said. 'Read him his rights.'

Mike turned and pulled him towards the cellar steps.

The policeman hoisted him higher and forced him further forward as they stumbled down the stairs, narrowly avoiding a pile of vomit splashed over two steps.

Upstairs, the doorbell rang.

'I didn't do this,' Hugh said as the full impact of the cellar pulled into view. He remembered it now, remembered seeing it before. 'I didn't do any of this.'

'Sure you didn't,' Mike said and, just for a moment, Hugh was taken in by what sounded like it just might be compassion in the voice . . . until he turned and saw the hatred and disgust in the policeman's face.

A man in a white coverall clapped his hands and spoke loudly. 'I want everyone back upstairs please. Nobody down here at all unless you're wearing a white overall.'

Mike started to turn Hugh around, but Hugh faltered and wrenched his arm free. He had seen Angie. The sound from his throat stopped everything and Hugh could barely believe that he was making it. He couldn't form any actual words, could only howl in pain.

'He's fucking good,' someone said, edging past Hugh and Mike to get to the stairs.

'Come on,' Mike said.

Hugh turned around, his mouth wide open in a soundless scream. On the floor at the bottom of the stairs lay Sheriff Frank Gozinsky. His feet had been sawn off. In his right hand he still clasped a revolver. In his left, a telephone handset. A snapped-off serrated blade protruded from his right eye-socket.

'I don't know how he did that,' a young man with a heavy Massachusetts accent was saying. 'Must have had balls of steel. Just think . . . making a phone-call with a knife in your eye.'

Hugh snapped his head around and pushed forward towards the young man, who visibly flinched backwards. 'He didn't do that,' Hugh said. 'He was dead before that. It was . . . it was—'

Who was it? Hugh thought. Or more to the point, *what* was it that did this deed?

It was a shape-shifter whut done it, Muskie, a Deputy Dawg voice whispered in the back of Hugh's head. *It wuz some kinda Hellspawn demon with a penchant for torture whut killed these folks.*

But would they believe him?

'I didn't do it,' Hugh said, fighting to keep his voice quiet and emotion-free. 'I didn't do any of it. Hey, hey . . . hear me out,' he whined as the policeman started tugging him up the steps. 'Look . . . just look at it, for Christ's sake.'

The cop stopped and looked down, then back at Hugh. 'He's got a gun in the one hand – that he shot at me with, right?' Hugh wiggled his face and particularly his forehead in front of Mike the policeman. 'Around that same time – either just before or just after – I stabbed him in the eye-socket with a bread-knife and then snapped the blade, leaving part of it sticking out of his head.

'I then staggered upstairs – without finishing the job, incidentally and still holding the handle-end of the bread-knife – only to collapse in the sitting room, still holding the fucking bread-knife yet. Meanwhile, the Sheriff keeps a hold of the gun, valiantly ignores the knife in his eye and the fact that I have sawn off his feet and calmly dials you folks in . . . in where?'

'Portland,' Mike said.

'Calls you in Portland and then dies before you get here. That about it?'

Mike nodded. 'I guess that's about it, yeah.'

Hugh joined in on the nodding.

Two of the guys in white coveralls started lifting bodies away from the steps and placing them side by side against the far wall. A third was talking into a hand-held recorder.

Hugh pointed down at the Sheriff with his elbow. 'Okay, fuckwit, how did he dial? Answer me that. There he is, a knife in his eye, his feet sawn off, and his corpse has a gun clamped in one hand and a phone clamped in the other. So he dialled, how?'

Mike looked puzzled. Then he said, 'So if it didn't happen that way – and you didn't do it – who did?'

'I told you. It was hard enough to tell you the first time, but it's harder to repeat it. It was some kind of . . . some kind of entity that has the ability to—'

The cop dropped his pen.

Hugh watched it fall.

Then he watched Mike smile at him, turn around to check on the forensics cops, then bend down to retrieve the pen. Just before he picked it up, the cop took hold of the gun and pulled it. It was difficult at first – the Sheriff must have really had it clamped – but at last it came well free of his hand. The cop retrieved the pen and stood up straight again.

Hugh stared at him.

The cop smiled and slipped the pen into his tunic pocket. 'Good spot,' he said, his face momentarily shifting into the familiar lines of Angela Ritter, '*sweetie.*'

Hugh staggered back and fell against the steps.

The policeman's features returned and Angie disappeared again.

'I think this one is one of my favourites,' he said softly, yanking on the cuffs behind Hugh's back and turning him to start back up the stairs. 'All the rest – the breakings, the eyelids, the removal of internal organs and hands and feet and stuff – all that is routine. I'm talking in torture terms here, right?'

Hugh did not respond. Instead, he looked around for some way to escape – some means of getting out, someone to talk to, to explain himself . . . maybe to reason with. Perhaps there would be a way to measure times of death on the bodies? That way, they could show that the Sheriff couldn't have called them.

The cop-thing was still talking as they reached the kitchen.

'But this is . . . how shall we say – psychological. We all know about making bars of soap and lampshades out of the flesh of young children – it's gross, sure. But the kind of *mental* cruelty – *mental torture* – that asks the victim to choose between which of their kids gets it, well . . . that's special, isn't it? It's a change from the basic stuff . . . more cerebral.'

A senior policeman was walking over to them as Mike-the-cop-who-wasn't-a-cop stopped, still holding onto Hugh's cuffs.

Suddenly Hugh lurched to one side and knocked Mike sprawling. The senior policeman pulled his nightstick free and lifted his arm back.

'Nononononono,' Hugh cried, 'before you do that, hear me out.' The room was already full of cops, and the three forensics guys appeared at top of the cellar stairs.

Then Hugh told them about the Sheriff.

And the phone.

And the gun.

And the bread-knife.

The whole nine yards.

And then he told them all about Mike, the cop-who-was-not-a-cop – about him pulling free the Sheriff's gun, and leaving his fingerprints on it.

'Check it out,' Hugh pleaded, his voice almost hoarse. 'Take his prints and check the gun. That'll prove it.'

'Mike?' the senior policeman said. 'Did you do what he says? Did you pull the gun free?'

Mike nodded. His face serious.

'So the fingerprints would bear out what he says?'

Another nod.

The senior policeman took a deep sigh. 'Fuck,' he said.

He turned and smiled at the others.

The other uniformed cops pulled out their nightsticks.

Mike pushed Hugh onto the floor and lifted free his own baton.

'To bed, to bed,' Mike began.

'Said Sleepyhead,' said the senior officer.

'Tarry a while,' continued another.

'Said Slow,' said a fourth.

'Put on the pan,' said the young rookie from Massachusetts.

'Said Greedy Nan,' added Mike.

'We'll sup . . . before we go,' finished the senior officer.

Then someone turned off the lights.

And a voice said '*Party time!*' as the room was filled with a symphony of splintering bone.

PETER CROWTHER is the recipient of numerous awards for his writing, his editing and, as publisher, for the hugely successful PS Publishing (now including the Stanza Press poetry subsidiary and PS Art Books, a specialist imprint dedicated to the comics field).

As well as being widely translated, his short stories have been adapted for TV on both sides of the Atlantic and collected in *The Longest Single Note*, *Lonesome Roads*, *Songs of Leaving*, *Cold Comforts*, *The Spaces Between the Lines*, *The Land at the End of the Working Day* and the upcoming *Jewels in the Dust*. He is the co-author (with James Lovegrove) of *Escardy Gap* and *The Hand That Feeds*, and has also written *By Wizard Oak* and the *Forever Twilight* SF/horror cycle.

He lives and works with his wife and business partner, Nicky Crowther, on England's Yorkshire coast.

'I rarely go to the *Nasty Place* in my fiction,' admits Crowther, 'that old cerebral cellar where it's cold and dank and it smells of rotten vegetables, ratshit and long-dead bodies left to ripen in the dark.

'I know the way there – heck, I pass the door a time or two on every tale I write – but I tend to stop my hand whenever it reaches for the handle and instead, I duck off into one of the upstairs rooms where there are windows and I can stir at least *some* light into whatever I'm working on.

'But every now and again I think, *Oh, to hell with it* . . . and I grasp that cellar door-handle full on, turn it around, pull it open and stride forward into the gloom, heart thumping and throat threatening to upchuck with every step I take downwards.

'Those visits are never what one might term "enjoyable", and the tale you've just read (unless you're cheating, of course, and sneaking a look at what I have to say about it first) is a classic example. But my idea was that maybe the old chestnut about poltergeists being little more than *Casper the Friendly Ghost* is a long ways off of the truth.

'Thus the ghosts in my tale don't just move ornaments around and empty drawers onto the floor . . . no sirree. The ghosts in my tale have teeth. And they bite.'

The Coffin-Maker's Daughter

—ANGELA SLATTER—

THE DOOR is a rich red wood, heavily carved with improving scenes from the trials of Job. An angel's head, cast in brass, serves as the knocker and when I let it go to rest back in its groove, the eyes fly open, indignant, and watch me with suspicion. Behind me is the tangle of garden – cataracts of flowering vines, lovers' nooks, secluded reading benches – that gives this house its affluent privacy.

The dead man's daughter opens the door.

She is pink and peach and creamy. I want to lick at her skin and see if she tastes the way she looks.

'Hepsibah Ballantyne! Slattern! Concentrate, this is business.' My father slaps at me, much as he did in life. Nowadays his fists pass through me, causing nothing more than a sense of cold ebbing in my veins. I do not miss the bruises.

The girl doesn't recognise me although I worked in this house for nigh on a year – but that is because it was only me watching her and not she me. When my mother finally left us it became apparent she would not provide Hector with any more children, let alone a son who might take over from him. He decided I should learn his craft and the sign above the entrance to the workshop was changed – not to BALLANTYNE & DAUGHTER, though. BALLANTYNE & OTHER.

'Speak, you idiot,' Father hisses, as though it's important he whisper. No one has heard Hector Ballantyne these last eight months, not since what appeared to be an unseasonal cold carried him off.

The blue eyes, red-rimmed from crying, should look ugly in the lovely oval face, but grief becomes Lucette D'Aguillar. Everything becomes her, from the black mourning gown to the severe, scraped back coiffure that is the heritage of the bereaved, because she is that rare thing: born lucky.

'Yes?' she asks, as if I have no right to interrupt the grieving house.

I slip the cap from my head, feel the mess it makes of my hair, and hold it in front of me like a shield. My nails are broken and my hands scarred and stained from the tints and varnish I use on the wood. I curl my fingers under the fabric of the cap to hide them as much as I can.

'I'm here about the coffin,' I say. 'It's Hepsibah. Hepsibah Ballantyne.'

Her stare remains blank, but she steps aside and lets me in. By rights, I should have gone to the back door, the servants' entrance. Hector would have – he did so all his life – but I provide a valuable service. If they trust me to create a death-bed for their nearest and dearest, they can let me in the front door. Everyone knows there's been a death – it's impossible to hide in the big houses – and I will not creep in as though my calling is shameful. Hector grumbled the first few times I presented myself in this manner – or rather shrieked, subsided to a grumble afterwards – but as I said to him, what were they going to do?

I'm the only coffin-maker in the city. They let me in.

I follow Lucette to a parlour washed with tasteful shades of grey and hung with white lace curtains so fine they must be made by spinners with eight legs. She takes note of herself in the large mirror above the mantel. Her mother is seated on a chaise; she too regards her own reflection, making sure she still exists. Lucette joins her and they look askance at me. Father makes sounds of disgust and he is right to do so. He will stay quiet here; even though no one can hear him but me, he will not distract me. He will not interrupt *business*.

'Your mirror should be covered,' I say as I sit, uninvited, in a fine armchair that hugs me like a gentle, sleepy bear. I arrange the skirts of my brown mourning meetings dress and rest my hands on the arms of the chair, then remember how unsightly they are and clasp them in my lap. Black ribbons alone decorate the mirror's edges, a fashionable nod to custom, but not much protection. 'All of your mirrors. To be safe. Until the body is removed.'

They exchange a glance, affronted.

'The choice is yours, of course. I'm given to understand that some families are delighted to have a remnant of the deceased take up residence in their mirrors. They enjoy the sensation of being watched constantly. It makes them feel not so alone.' I smile as if I am kind. 'And the dead seem to like it, especially the unexpectedly dead. Without time to prepare themselves, they tend to cling to the ones they loved. Did you suspect your husband's heart was weak, or was it a terrible surprise?'

Madame D'Aguillar hands her black shawl to Lucette, who covers the mirror with it then rejoins her mother.

'You have kept the body wrapped?' I ask, and they nod. I nod in return, to tell them they've done only just enough. That they are foolish, vain women who put their own reflections ahead of keeping a soul in a body. 'Good. Now, how may I be of assistance?'

This puts them on the back foot once again, makes them my supplicants. They must *ask* for what they want. Both look put out, and it gives me the meanest little thrill, to see them thus. I smile again: *Let me help you.*

'A coffin is what we need. Why else would *you* be here?' snipes Madame.

Lucette puts a hand on the woman's arm. 'We need your services, Hepsibah.' My heart skips to hear my name on her lips. 'We need your help.'

Yes, they do. They need a coffin-maker. They need a death-bed to keep the deceased *in*, to make sure he doesn't haunt the lives they want to live from this point on. They need my *art*.

'I would recommend an ebony-wood coffin, lined with the finest silk padding stuffed with lavender to put the soul to rest. Gold fittings will ensure strength of binding. And I would affix three golden locks on the casket, to make sure. Three is safest, strongest.' Then I name a price – down to the quarter-gold, to make the sum seem considered – one that would cause honest women to baulk, to shout, to accuse me of the extortion I'm committing.

Madame D'Aguillar simply says, 'Lucette, take Miss Ballantyne to the study and give her the down-payment.'

Oh, how they must want him kept under!

I rise and make a slight curtsey before I follow Lucette's gracefully swaying skirts to the back of the house.

I politely look away as she fumbles with the lockbox in the third drawer of the enormous oak desk her father recently occupied. When she hands me the small leather pouch of gold pieces her fingers touch my palm and I think I see a spark in her eyes. I believe she feels it, too, and I colour to be so naked before her. I slide my gaze to the portrait of her dearly departed, but she grasps my hand and holds it tight.

Oh!

'Please, Hepsibah, please make his coffin well. Keep him *beneath*. Keep us – keep *me* – safe.' She presses her lips to my palm; they are damp, slightly parted and ever so soft! My breath escapes me, my lungs feel bereft. She trails her slim pink cat's tongue along my life-line, down to my wrist where the pulse beats blue and hard and gives me away. There is a noise outside in the hall, the scuttling of a servant. Lucette smiles and steps back, dropping my hand reluctantly.

I remember to breathe, dip my head, made subservient by my desire. Hector has been silent all this time. I see him standing behind her, gnarled fingers trying desperately to caress her swan's neck but failing, passing through her. I feel a rage shake me, but I control myself. I nod again, forcing confidence into my motions, meeting her eyes, bold as brass, reading a promise there.

'I need to see the body, take my measurements, make preparations. I must do this alone.'

'Stupid little harlot.' Hector has more than broken his silence, again and again, since we returned to the workshop. I have not answered him because I sense in his tone *envy*.

'How hard for you, Father, to have no more strength than a fart, all noise and wind.'

If he were able, he would throw anything he could find around the space, chisels and planes and whetstones, with no thought for the damage to implements expensive to replace: the tools of our trade inherited from forefathers too many to number. The pieces of wood have been purchased at great expense and treated with eldritch care to keep the dead *below*.

I ignore his huffing and puffing and continue with Master D'Aguillar's casket. It is now the required shape and dimensions, held together with sturdy iron nails and the stinking adhesive made of human marrow and boiled bones I'm carefully applying to the place where one plank meets another to ensure there are no gaps through which something ephemeral might escape. On the furthest bench, far enough away to keep it safe from the stains and paints and tints, lies the pale lilac silk sack that I've stuffed with goose down and lavender flowers. This evening, I will quilt it with tiny, precise stitches then fit it into the casket, this time using a sweet-smelling glue to hold it in place and cover the stink of the marrow sealant.

We may inflate the charge for our services, certainly, but the Ballantynes never offer anything but their finest work.

I make the holes for the handles and hinges, boring them with a hand-drill engraved with Hector's initials – not long before his death, the drill that had been passed down for nearly one hundred years broke, the turning handle shearing off in his hand and tearing open his palm. He had another made at great expense. It is almost new; I can pretend the initials are mine, that the shiny thing is mine alone.

'Did you get it?' asks Hector, tired of his sulk.

I nod, screwing the first hinge into place; the dull golden glow looks almost dirty in the dim light of the workshop. Soon I will illuminate the lamps so I can work through the night; that way I will be able to see Lucette again tomorrow without appearing too eager, without having to manufacture some excuse to cross her threshold once more.

'Show me.'

I straighten with ill grace and stretch. In the pocket of my skirt, next to a compact set of pliers, is a small tin, once used for Hector's cheap snuff. It rattles as I open it. Inside: a tooth, black and rotten at its centre and stinking more than it should. There is a sizeable chunk of flesh still attached to the root and under-neath the scent of decay is a telltale hint of foxglove. Master D'Aguillar shall enter the earth before his time, and I have some-thing to add to our collection of contagions that will not be recognised or questioned.

'Ah, lovely!' says Hector. 'Subtle. You could have learned some-thing from them. Cold in a teacup – it wasn't very inventive, was it? I expected a better death, y'know.'

'It wasn't a cold in a teacup, Father.' I hold up the new hand-drill. 'It was the old one, the handle was impregnated with apple-seed poison and I filed away the pinion to weaken everything. All it needed was a tiny open wound. Inventive enough for you, Hector?'

He looks put out, circles back to his new favourite torment. 'That girl, she doesn't want you.'

I breathe deeply. 'Events say otherwise.'

'Fool. Desperate sad little fool. How did I raise such an idiot child? Didn't I teach you to look through people? Anyone could see you're not good enough for the likes of Miss Lucette D'Aguillar.' He laughs. 'Will you dream of her, Hepsibah?'

I throw the hand-drill at him; it passes through his lean outline and hits the wall with an almighty metallic sound.

'I kept you wrapped! I covered the mirrors! I made your casket myself and sealed it tight – how can you still be here?' I yell.

Hector smiles. 'Perhaps I'm not. Perhaps you're so lonely, Daughter, that you thought me back.'

'If I were lonely I can think of better company to conjure.' But there may be something in what he says, though it makes me hurt.

'Ah, there's none like your own family, your dear old Da who loves your very skin.'

'When I have her,' I say quietly, 'I won't need *you*.'

Ghost or fervid imagining, it stops him – he sees his true end – and he has no reply but spite. 'Why would anyone want you?'

'You did, Father, or has death dimmed your memory?'

Shame will silence even the dead and he dissolves, leaving me alone for a while at least.

I breathe deeply to steady my hands and begin to measure for the placement of the locks.

'The casket is ready,' I say, keeping the disappointment from my voice as best I can. Lucette is nowhere in evidence. An upstairs maid answered my knock and brought me to the parlour once more where the widow receives me reluctantly. The door angel did not even open its eyes.

Madame nods. 'I shall send grooms with a dray this afternoon, if that will suffice.' But she does not frame it as a question.

'That is acceptable. My payment?'

'Will be made on the day of the funeral – which will be tomorrow. Will you call again?' She smiles with all the charm of the rictus of the dead. 'I would not wish to waste your time.'

I return her smile. 'My customers have no choice but to wait upon my convenience.' I rise. 'I will see myself out. Until tomorrow.'

Outside in the mid-morning sun I make my way down the stone front steps that are set a little too far apart. This morning I combed my hair, pinched colour into my cheeks and stained my lips with a tinted wax that had once belonged to my mother; all for naught. I am about to set foot on the neatly swept path when a hand snakes out from the bushes to the right and I'm pulled under hanging branches, behind a screen of sickly-strong jasmine.

Lucette darts her tongue between my lips, giving me a taste of her, but pulling back when I try to explore the honeyed cave of her mouth in turn. She giggles breathlessly, chest rising and falling, as if this is nothing more than an adventure. She does not quake as I do; she is a silly little girl playing at lust. I know this; I know this but it does not make me hesitate. It does not make my hope die.

I reach out and grasp her forearms, drawing her roughly in. She falls against me and I show her what a kiss is. I show her what longing is. I let my yearning burn into her, hoping that she will be branded by the tip of my tongue, the tips of my fingers, the tips of my breasts. I will have her here, under the parlour window where her mother sits and waits. I will tumble her and bury my mouth where it will make her moan and shake, here on the grass where we might be found at any moment. And I will make her mine if through no other means than shame; her shame will bind us, and make her *mine*.

'Whore,' says Hector in my ear, making his first appearance since yesterday. Timed perfectly, it stops me cold and in that moment when I hesitate, Lucette remembers herself and struggles. She steps away again, breathing hard, laughing through a fractured, uncertain smile.

'When he is *beneath*,' she tells me. A promise, a vow, a hint, a tease.

'When he is *beneath*,' I repeat, mouthing it like a prayer, then take my unsteady steps home.

I stood in the churchyard this morning, hidden away, and watched them bury Master D'Aguillar. Professional pride for the most part. Hector stood beside me, nodding with more approval than he'd ever shown in life, a truce mutually agreed for the moment.

'Hepsibah, you've done us proud. It's beautiful work.'

And it was. The ebony-wood and the gold caught the sun and shone as if surrounded by a halo of light. No one could have complained about the effect the theatrics added to the interment. I noticed the admiring glances of the family's friends, neighbours and acquaintances as the entrance to the D'Aguillar crypt was opened and four husky men of the household carried the casket down into the darkness.

And I watched Lucette. Watched her weep and support her mother; watched them both perform their grief like mummers. When the crowds thinned and there were just the two of them and their retainers to make their way to the black coach and four plumed horses, Lucette seemed to sense herself observed. Her eyes found me standing beside a white stone cross that tilted where the earth had sunk. She gave a strange little smile and inclined her head, just so.

'Beautiful girl,' said Hector, his tone rueful.

'Yes,' I answered, tensing for a new battle, but nothing came. We waited in the shade until the funeral party dispersed.

'When will you go to collect?' he asked.

'This afternoon, when the wake is done.'

He nodded, and kept his thoughts to himself.

*

Lucette brings a black lacquered tray, balancing a teapot, two cups and saucers, a creamer, sugar boat and silver cutlery. There are two delicate almond biscuits perched on a ridiculously small plate. The servants have been given the afternoon off. Her mother is upstairs, resting.

'The house has been so full of people,' she says, placing the tray on the parquetry table between us. I want to grab at her, bury my fingers in her hair and kiss her breath away, but broken china might not be the ideal start. I hold my hands in my lap. I wonder if she notices that I filed back my nails, made them neat? That the stains on my skin are lighter than they were, after hours of scrubbing with lye soap?

She reaches into the pocket of her black dress and pulls forth a leather pouch, twin to the one she gave me barely two days ago. She holds it out and smiles. As soon as my hand touches it, she relinquishes the strings so our fingers do not meet.

'There! Our business is at an end.' She turns the teapot five times clockwise with one hand and arranges the spoons on the saucers to her satisfaction.

'At an end?' I ask.

Her look is pitying, then she laughs. 'I thought for a while there I might actually have to let you tumble me! Still and all, it would have been worth it, to have him safely away.' She sighs. 'You did such beautiful work, Hepsibah, I am grateful for that. Don't ever think I'm not.'

I am not stupid enough to protest, to weep, to beg, to ask if she is joking, playing with my heart. But when she passes me a cup, my hand shakes so badly that the tea shudders over the rim. Some pools in the saucer, more splashes onto my hand and scalds me. I manage to put the mess down as she fusses, calling for a maid, then realises no one will come.

'I won't be a moment,' she says, and leaves to make her way to the kitchen and cleaning cloths.

I rub my shaking hands down my skirts and feel a hard lump. Buried deep in the right hand pocket is the tin. It makes a sad, promising sound as I tap on the lid before I open it. I tip the contents into her empty cup, then pour tea over it, letting the poisoned tooth steep until I hear her bustling back along the corridor. I fish it out with a spoon, careful not to touch it with my bare hands and put it away. I add a little cream to her cup.

She wipes my red-hot flesh with a cool wet cloth, then wraps the limb kindly. Lucette sits opposite me and I hand her the cup of tea and give a fond smile for her, and for Hector who has appeared at her shoulder.

'Thank you, Hepsibah.'

'You are most welcome, Miss D'Aguillar.'

I watch her lift the fine china to her pink, pink lips and drink deeply.

It will be enough, slow-acting, but sufficient. This house will be bereft again.

When I am called upon to ply my trade a second time I will bring a mirror with me. In the quiet room when we two are alone, I will unwrap Lucette and run my fingers across her skin and find all the secret places she denied me, and she will be mine and mine alone, whether she wishes it or no.

I take my leave and wish her well.

'Repeat business,' says Father gleefully as he falls into step beside me. 'Not too much, not enough to draw attention to us, but enough to keep bread on the table.'

In a day or two, I shall knock once more on the Widow D'Aguillar's front door.

ANGELA SLATTER is the author of two short story collections: *Sourdough and Other Stories* (Tartarus Press, UK), and *The Girl with No Hands and Other Tales* (Ticonderoga Publications, Australia), both published in 2010. *The Girl with No Hands* won the Aurealis Award for Best Collection in 2011 and her story with Lisa L. Hannett, 'The February Dragon', won the Aurealis Award for Best Fantasy Short Story the same year.

Her short stories have appeared in the anthologies *The Mammoth Book of Best New Horror Volume Twenty-Two*, Jack Dann's *Dreaming Again*, Tartarus Press's *Strange Tales II* and *III* and Twelfth Planet Press's *2012*, as well as such journals as *Lady Churchill's Rosebud Wristlet* and *Shimmer*.

In 2012 she will have another collection of short stories published by Ticonderoga, *Midnight and Moonshine*, a collaboration with friend and writing-partner-in-crime, Lisa Hannett.

Slatter is a graduate of Clarion South 2009 and the Tin House Summer Writers Workshop 2006.

'When the editor emailed me, asking for a submission for this anthology that needed to be "more horror than fantasy", I was casting about for ideas with a bit of personal terror,' recalls the author. 'I don't really think of myself as a horror writer. My first effort was deemed "Good, but I think you can do better". After some fist-shaking and howling (on my part), I went back to work. I was listening to Florence and the Machine's *Lungs* for the first time . . . when "My Boy Builds Coffins" came on, I started to think about a society that regarded coffin-making not simply as a necessary service, but also as an art form. On top of that, it was an eldritch art form required to keep the dead beneath the earth. I wanted a story that had layers of unspoken secrets.

'When I heard "Girl with One Eye", I got a picture of Hepsibah in my mind's eye – this thin girl standing in front of a heavy door, with a short gamine haircut that had started to grow out and curl a bit because she wasn't overly given to worrying about her appearance. She was wearing a brown woollen dress, a bit Jane Eyre-like, with long sleeves, buttons up the front and long skirts, and she had on a kind of baker boy's cap. At her shoulder was the ghost of her father, and Hector is a nasty piece of work. I could hear his voice and knew how adversarial their relationship was; but that no matter how much Hepsibah hated her father, she shared some characteristics with him and that's why he was still hanging around. The society was a kind of Victorian setting, but mixed with some elements similar to the world of *Sourdough and Other Stories*.

'Hepsibah is one of my favourite characters – she's a terrible mess of a human, but really fascinating.'

Roots and All

—BRIAN HODGE—

T HE WAY IN was almost nothing like we remembered, miles off the main road, and Gina and me with one half-decent sense of direction between us. *Do you need us to draw you a map,* our parents had asked, hers and mine both, once at the funeral home and again over the Continental breakfast at the motel. *No, no, no,* we'd told them. *Of course we remember how to get to Grandma's.* Indignant, the way adults get when their parents treat them like nine-year-olds.

Three wrong turns and fifteen extra minutes of meandering later, we were in the driveway, old gravel over ancestral dirt. Gina and I looked at each other, a resurgence of some old telepathy between cousins.

'Right,' I said. 'We never speak of this again.'

She'd insisted on driving my car, proving . . . something . . . and yanked the keys from the ignition. 'I don't even want to speak about it now.'

If everything had still been just the way it used to be, maybe we would've been guided by landmarks we hadn't even realised we'd internalised. But it wasn't the same, and I don't think I was just recalling some idealised version of this upstate county that had never actually existed.

I remembered the drive as a thing of excruciating boredom, an interminable landscape of fields and farmhouses, and the thing I'd dreaded most as a boy was finding ourselves behind a tractor rumbling down a road too narrow for us to pass. But once we were here, it got better, because my grandfather had never been without a couple of hunting dogs, and there were more copses of trees and tracts of deep woodland than the most determined pack of kids could explore in an entire summer.

Now, though . . .

'The way here,' I said. 'It wasn't always this dismal, was it?'

Gina shook her head. 'Definitely not.'

I was thinking of the trailers we'd passed, and the forests of junk that had grown up around them, and it seemed like there'd been a time when, if someone had a vehicle that obviously didn't run, they kept it out of sight inside a barn until it did. They didn't set it out like a trophy. I was thinking, too, of riding in my grandfather's car, meeting another going the opposite direction, his and the other driver's hands going up at the same moment in a friendly wave. Ask him who it was, and as often as not he wouldn't know. They all waved just the same. Bygone days, apparently. About all the greeting we'd gotten were sullen stares.

We stood outside the car as if we needed to reassure ourselves that we were really here. Like that maple tree next to the driveway, whose scarlet-leafed shade we parked in, like our grandfather always had – it had to have grown, but then so had I, so it no longer seemed like the beanstalk into the clouds it once was. Yet it had to be the same tree, because hanging from the lowest limbs were a couple of old dried gourds, each hollowed out, with a hole the size of a silver dollar bored into the side. There would be a bunch more hanging around behind the house – although they couldn't have been the same gourds. It pleased me to think of Grandma Evvie doing this right up until the end, her life measured by the generations of gourds she'd turned into birdhouses, one of many scales of time.

How long since we've been here, Gina?

Ohhh . . . gotta be . . . four or five gourds ago, at least.

Really. That long.

Yeah. Shame on us.

It was the same old clapboard farmhouse, white, always white, always peeling. I'd never seen it freshly painted, but never peeled all the way down to naked weathered wood, either, and you had to wonder if the paint didn't somehow peel straight from the can.

We let ourselves in through the side door off the kitchen – I could hardly remember ever using the front door – and it was like stepping into a time capsule, everything preserved, even the smell, a complex blend of morning coffee and delicately fried foods.

We stopped in the living room by her chair, the last place she'd ever sat. The chair was so thoroughly our grandmother's that even as kids we'd felt wrong sitting in it, although she'd never chased us out. It was old beyond reckoning, as upholstered chairs went, the cushions flattened by decades of gentle pressure, with armrests as wide as cutting boards. She'd done her sewing there, threaded needles always stuck along the edge.

'If you have to die, and don't we all,' Gina said, 'that's the way to do it.'

Her chair was by the window, with a view of her nearest neighbour, who'd been the one to find her. She'd been reading, apparently. Her book lay closed on one armrest, her glasses folded and resting atop it, and she was just sitting there, her head drooping but otherwise still upright. The neighbour, Mrs Tepovich, had thought she was asleep.

'It's like she decided it was time,' I said. 'You know? She waited until she'd finished her book, then decided it was time.'

'It must've been a damn good book. I mean . . . if she decided nothing else was ever going to top it.' Totally deadpan. That was Gina.

I spewed a time-delayed laugh. 'You're going to Hell.'

Then she got serious and knelt by the chair, running her hand along the knobbly old fabric. 'What's going to happen to this? Nobody'd want it. There's nobody else in the world it even fits with. It was *hers*. But to just throw it out . . . ?'

She was right. I couldn't stand the thought of it joining a landfill.

'Maybe Mrs Tepovich could use it.' I peered through the window, towards her house. 'We should go over and say hi. See if there's anything here she'd like.'

This neighbourly feeling seemed as natural here as it would've been foreign back home. The old woman in that distant house . . . I'd not seen her in more than a decade, but it still felt like I knew her better than any of the twenty or more people within a five-minute walk of my own door.

It was easy to forget: really, Gina and I were just one generation out of this place, and whether directly or indirectly, it had to have left things buried in us that we didn't even suspect.

If the road were a city block, we would've started at one end, and Mrs Tepovich would've been nearly at the other. We tramped along wherever walking was easiest, a good part of it over ground that gave no hint of having been a strawberry field once, where people came from miles around to pick by the quart.

But Mrs Tepovich, at least, hadn't changed, or not noticeably so. She'd seemed old before and was merely older now, less a shock to our systems than we were to hers. Even though she'd seen us as teenagers she still couldn't believe how we'd grown, and maybe it was just that Gina and I looked like it had been a long time since we'd had sunburns and scabs.

'Was it a good funeral?' she wanted to know.

'Nobody complained,' Gina said.

'I stopped going to funerals after Dean's.'

Her husband. My best memory of him was from when the strawberries came in red and ripe, and his inhuman patience as he smoked roll-your-own cigarettes and hand-cranked a shiny cylinder of homemade ice cream in a bath of rock salt and ice. The more we pleaded, the slyer he grinned and the slower he cranked.

'I've got one more funeral left in me,' Mrs Tepovich said, 'and that's the one they'll have to drag me to.'

It should've been sad, this little sun-cured widow with hair like white wool rambling around her house and tending her gardens alone, having just lost her neighbour and friend – a fixture in her life that had been there half-a-century, one of the last remaining pillars of her past now gone.

It should've been sad, but wasn't. Her eyes were too bright, too expectant, and it made me feel better than I had since I'd got the news days ago. *This was what Grandma Evvie was like, right up to the end. How do you justify mourning a thing like that? It should've been celebrated.*

But no, she'd got the usual dirge-like send-off, and I was tempted to think she would've hated it.

'So you've come to sort out the house?' Mrs Tepovich said.

'Only before our parents do the real job,' Gina told her. 'They said if there was anything of Grandma's that we wanted, now would be the time to pick it out.'

'So we're here for a long weekend,' I said.

'Just you two? None of the others?'

More cousins, she meant. All together, we numbered nine. Ten once, but now nine, and no, none of the others would be coming, although my cousin Lindsay hadn't been shy about asking me to send her a cell phone video of a walkthrough, so she could see if there was anything she wanted. I was already planning on telling her sorry, I couldn't get a signal up here.

'Well, you were her favourites, you know.' Mrs Tepovich got still, her eyes, mired in a mass of crinkles, going far away. 'And Shae,' she added softly. 'Shae should've been here. She wouldn't have missed it.'

Gina and I nodded. She was right on both counts. There were a lot of places my sister should've been over the past eight years, instead of . . . wherever. Shae should've been a lot of places, been a lot of things, instead of a riddle and a wound that had never quite healed.

'We were wondering,' Gina went on, 'if there was anything from over there that you would like.'

'Some of that winter squash from her garden would be nice, if it's ready to pick. She always did grow the best Delicata. And you've got to eat that up quick, because it doesn't keep as long as the other kinds.'

We were looking at each other on two different wavelengths.

'Well, it doesn't,' she said. 'The skin's too thin.'

'Of course you're welcome to anything from the garden that you want,' Gina said. 'But that's not exactly what we meant. We thought you might like to have something from *inside* the house.'

'Like her chair,' I said, pretending to be helpful. 'Would you want her chair?'

Had Mrs Tepovich bitten into the tartest lemon ever grown, she still wouldn't have made a more sour face. 'That old eyesore? What would I need with that?' She gave her head a stern shake. 'No. Take that thing out back and burn it, is what you should do. I've got eyesores of my own, I don't need to take on anyone else's.'

We stayed awhile longer, and it was hard to leave. Harder for us than for her. She was fine with our going, unlike so many people her age I'd been around, who did everything but grab your ankle to keep you a few more minutes. I guessed that's the way it was in a place where there was always something more that needed to be done.

Just this, on our way out the door:

'I don't know if you've got anything else planned for while you're here,' she said, and seemed to be directing this at me, 'but don't you go poking your noses anywhere much off the roads. Those meth people that've made such a dump of the place, I hear they don't mess around.'

Evening came on differently out here than it did at home, seeming to rise up from the ground and spill from the woods and overflow the ditches that ran alongside the road. I'd forgotten this. Forgotten, too, how night seemed to spread outward from the chicken coop and creep from behind the barn and pool in the hog wallow and gather inside the low, tin-roofed shack that had sheltered the pigs and, miraculously, was still standing after years of disuse. Night was always present here, it seemed. It just hid for a while and then slipped its leash again.

I never remembered a time when it hadn't felt better being next to somebody when night came on. We watched it from the porch, plates in our laps as we ate a supper thrown together from garden pickings and surviving leftovers from the fridge.

When she got to it, finally, Gina started in gently. 'What Mrs Tepovich said . . . about having anything else planned this weekend . . . meaning Shae, she couldn't have been talking about anything else . . . she wasn't onto something there, was she? That's not on your mind, is it, Dylan?'

'I can't come up here and *not* have it on my mind,' I said. 'But doing something, no. What's there to do that wouldn't be one kind of mistake or another?'

Not that it wasn't tempting, in concept. Find some reprobate and put the squeeze on, and if he didn't know anything, which he almost certainly wouldn't, then have him point to someone who might.

'Good,' she said, then sat with it long enough to get angry. We'd never lost the anger, because it had never had a definite target. 'But . . . if you did . . . you could handle yourself all right. It's what you do every day, isn't it.'

'Yeah, but strength in numbers. And snipers in the towers when the cons are out in the yard.'

She looked across at me and smiled, this tight, sad smile, childhood dimples replaced by curved lines. Her hair was as light as it used to get during summers, but helped by a bottle now, I suspected, and her face narrower, her cheeks thinner. When they were plump, Gina was the first girl I ever kissed, in that fumbling way of cousins ignorant of what comes next.

There was no innocence in her look now, though, like she wished it were a more lawless world, just this once, so I could put together a private army and come back up here and we'd sweep through from one side of the county to the other until we finally got to the bottom of it.

Shae was one of the ones you see headlines about, if something about their disappearance catches the news editors' eyes: MISSING GIRL LAST SEEN MONDAY NIGHT. FAMILY OF MISSING COLLEGE STUDENT MAKE TEARFUL APPEAL. Like that, until a search team gets lucky or some jogger's dog stands in a patch of weeds and won't stop barking.

Except we'd never had even that much resolution. Shae was one of the ones who never turned up. The sweetest girl you could ever hope to meet, at nineteen still visiting her grandmother, like a Red Riding Hood who trusted that all the wolves were gone, and this was all that was found: a single, bloodied scrap of a blouse hanging from the brambles about half a mile from where our mother had grown up. The rest of her, I'd always feared, was at the bottom of a mineshaft or sunk weighted into the muck of a pond or in a grave so deep in the woods there was no chance of finding her now.

I'd had three tours of duty to erode my confidence about any innate sense of decency in the human race, and if that weren't enough, signing on with the Department of Corrections had finished off the rest. For Shae, I'd always feared the worst, in too much detail, because I knew too well what people were capable of, even the good guys, even myself.

We made little progress that first evening, getting lost on a detour into some photo albums, then after an animated phone conversation with her pair of grade-schoolers, Gina went to bed early. But I stayed up with the night, listening to it awhile from Grandma Evvie's chair, until listening wasn't enough and I had to go outside to join it.

There was no cable TV out this far, and Grandma hadn't cared enough about it for a satellite dish, so she'd made do with an ancient antenna grafted to one side of the house. The rotor had always groaned in the wind, like a weathervane denied its true purpose, the sound carrying down into the house, a ghostly grinding while you tried to fall asleep on breezy nights. Now I used it as a ladder, scaling it onto the roof and climbing the shingles to straddle the peak.

Now and again I'd see a light in the distance, the September wind parting the trees long enough to see the porch bulb of a distant neighbour, a streak of headlights on one of the farther roads, but the blackest nights I'd ever known were out here, alone with the moon and the scattershot field of stars.

So I listened, and I opened.

The memory had never left, among the clearest from those days of long summer visits – two weeks, three weeks, a month. We would sleep four and five to a room, when my cousins and sister and I were all here at once, and Grandma would settle us in and tell us bedtime stories, sometimes about animals, sometimes about Indians, sometimes about boys and girls like ourselves.

I don't remember any of them.

But there was one she returned to every now and then, and that one stuck with me. The rest were just stories, made up on the spot or reworked versions of tales she already knew, and there was nothing lingering about them. I knew that animals didn't talk; the good Indians were too foreign to me to really identify with, and I wasn't afraid the bad ones would come to get us; and as for the normal boys and girls, well, what of them when we had real adventures of our own, every day.

The stories about the Woodwalker, though ... those were different.

That's just my name for it. My own grandmother's name for it, she admitted to us. *It's so big and old it's got no name. Like rain. The rain doesn't know it's rain. It just falls.*

It was always on the move, she told us, from one side of the county to the other. It never slept, but sometimes it settled down in the woods or the fields to rest. It could be vast, she told us, tall enough that clouds sometimes got tangled in its hair – when you saw clouds skimming along so quickly you could track their progress, that's when you knew – but it could be small, too, small enough to curl inside an acorn if the acorn needed reminding of how to grow.

You wouldn't see it, even if you looked for it every day for a thousand years, she promised us, but there were times you could see evidence of its passing by. Like during a dry spell when the dust rose up from the fields – that was the Woodwalker breathing it in, seeing if it was dry enough yet to send for some rain – and in the woods, too, its true home, when the trees seemed to be swaying opposite the direction the wind was blowing.

You couldn't see it, no, but you could feel it, down deep, brushing the edges of your soul. Hardly ever during the day, not because it wasn't there, but because if you were the right sort of person, you were too busy while the sun was up. Too busy working, or learning, or visiting, or too busy playing and wilding and having fun. But at night, though, that was different. Nights were when a body slowed down. Nights were for noticing the rest.

What's the Woodwalker do? we'd ask. *What's it for?*

It loves most of what grows and hates waste and I guess you could say it pays us back, she'd tell us. *And makes sure we don't get forgetful and too full of ourselves.*

What happens then, if you do? Somebody always wanted to know that.

Awful things, she'd say. *Awful, awful things.* Which wasn't enough, because we'd beg to know more, but she'd say we were too young to hear about them, and promise to tell us when we were older, but she never did.

You're just talking about God, right? one of my cousins said once. *Aren't you?*

But Grandma never answered that either, at least not in any way we would've understood at the time. I still remember the look, though . . . not quite a 'no', definitely not a 'yes', and the wisdom to know that we'd either understand on our own someday, or never have to.

I saw the Woodwalker once, Shae piped up, quiet and awestruck. *One weekend last fall. He was looking at two dead deer.* None of us believed her, because we believed in hunters a lot more than we believed in anything called the Woodwalker. But, little as she was, Shae wouldn't back down. Hunters, she argued, didn't stand deer on their feet again and send them on their way.

I'd never forgotten that.

And so, as the night blustered on the wings of bats and barn owls, I listened and watched and took another tiny step towards believing.

'Any time,' I whispered to whatever might speak up or show itself. 'Any time.'

The milk had gone bad and the bacon with it, and we needed a few other things to get us through the weekend, so that next morning I volunteered to make the run back to the store near the turn-off on the main road. I decided to take the long way, setting off in the opposite direction, because it had been years and I wanted to see more of the county, and even if I made more wrong turns than right, there were worse things than getting lost on a September Saturday morning.

Mile after mile, I drove past many worse things.

You can't remember such a place from before it got this way, can't remember the people who'd proudly called it home, without wondering what they would think of it now. Would *they* have let their homes fall to ruin with such helpless apathy? Would they have sat back and watched the fields fill with weeds? Would they have ridden two wheels, three wheels, four, until they'd ripped the low hills full of gouges and scars? Not the people I remembered.

It made me feel old, not in the body but in the heart, old in a way you always say you never want to be. It was the kind of old that in a city yells at kids to get off the lawn, but here it went past annoyance and plunged into disdain. Here, they'd done real harm. They'd trampled on memories and tradition, souring so much of what I'd decided had been good about the place, and one of them, I could never forget, had snatched my sister from the face of the earth.

Who were the people who lived here now, I wondered. They couldn't all have come from somewhere else. Most, I imagined, had been raised here and never left, which made their neglect even more egregious.

But the worst of it was in the west of the county, where the coal once was. The underground mines had been tapped out when we were children, and while that's when I'd first heard the term strip-mining, I hadn't known what it meant, either as a process or its consequences.

It was plain enough now, though, all the near-surface coal gone too, and silent wastelands left in its wake, horizon-wide lacerations of barren land pocked with mounds of topsoil, the ground still so acidic that nothing wanted to grow there.

No matter how urgently the Woodwalker might remind the seeds what to do.

It was the wrong frame of mind to have gotten in before circling back to the store. I left my sunglasses on inside, the same way I'd wear them on cloudy days while watching the inmates in the yard, and for the same reasons, too: as armour, something to protect us both, because there was no good to come from locking eyes, from letting some people see what you think of their choices and what they'd thrown away.

The place was crowded with Saturday morning shoppers, and there was no missing the sickness here. *Those meth people that've made such a dump of the place, I hear they don't mess around,* Mrs Tepovich had said, and for that matter, neither did the meth. I knew the look – some of the inmates still had it when they transferred from local lockups to hard time – and while it wasn't on every face in the market, it was on more than enough to make me fear it was only going to get worse here. A body half-covered with leprosy doesn't have a lot of hope for the rest of it.

The worst of them had been using for years, obviously, their faces scabbed and their bones filed sharp. With teeth like crumbling gravel, they looked like they'd been sipping tonics of sulphuric acid, and it was eating through from the inside. The rest of them, as jumpy and watchful as rats, would get there. All they needed to know about tomorrow was written in the skins of their neighbours.

It had an unexpected levelling effect.

From what I remembered of when we visited as children, the men nearly always died first here, often by a wide margin. They might go along fine for decades, as tough as buzzards in a desert, but then something caught up with them and they fell hard. They'd gone into the mines and come out with black spots on their lungs, or they'd broken their backs slowly, one sunrise-to-sunset day at a time, or had stubbornly ignored some small symptom for ten years too many. The women, though, cured like leather and carried on without them. It was something you could count on.

No longer.

The race to the grave looked like anybody's to win.

When I got back to the house, I discovered we had a visitor, a surprise since there was no car in the drive. As I came in through the kitchen, Gina, over his shoulder, gave me a where-were-you-all-this-time look that she could've stolen from my ex. They were sitting at the kitchen table with empty coffee mugs, and Gina looked like the statute of limitations on her patience had expired twenty minutes earlier.

I couldn't place him, but whoever he was, he probably hadn't had the same fierce black beard, lantern jaw, and giant belly when we were kids.

'You remember Ray Sinclair,' she said, then jabbed her finger at the door and it came back in a rush: Mrs Tepovich's great-nephew. He used to come over and play with us on those rare days that weren't already taken up with chores, and he'd been a good guide through the woods – knew where to find all the wild berries, at their peak of ripeness, and the best secluded swimming holes where the creeks widened. We shook hands, and it was like trying to grip a baseball glove.

'I was dropping some venison off at Aunt Pol's. She told me you two were over here,' he said. 'My condolences on Evvie. Aunt Pol thought the world of her.'

I put away the milk and bacon and the rest, while Gina excused herself and slipped past, keeping an overdue appointment with some room or closet as Ray and I cleared the obligatory small talk.

'What have you got your eye on?' he asked then. 'For a keepsake, I mean.'

'I don't know yet,' I said. 'Maybe my granddad's shotgun, if it turns up.'

'You do much hunting?'

'Not since he used to take me out. And after I got back from the army . . . let's just say I wasn't any too eager to aim at something alive and pull a trigger again.' I'd done fine with my qualifications for the job, although that was just targets, nothing that screamed and bled and tried to belly-crawl away. 'But I'm thinking if I had an old gun that I had some history with, maybe . . .' I shrugged. 'I guess I could've asked for it after Granddad died, but it wouldn't have seemed right. Not that Grandma went hunting, but left alone out here, she needed it more than I did.'

He nodded. 'Especially after your sister.'

I looked at him without being obvious about it, then realised I hadn't taken off my sunglasses yet, just like at the market. *It could've been you*, I thought. No reason to think so, but when a killing is never solved, a body never found, it can't *not* cross your mind when you look at some people, the ones with proximity and access and history. The ones you really don't know anything about any more. If Ray had known where to find berries, he'd know where to bury a girl.

'Especially then,' I said.

'Did I say something wrong?' he asked. 'My apologies if I did.'

He sounded sincere, but I'd been hearing sincere for years. *Naw, boss, I don't know who hid that shank in my bunk. Not me, boss, I didn't have nothing to do with that bag of pruno.* They were all sincere down to the rot at their core.

The other COs had warned me early on: *There'll come a time when you look at everybody like they're guilty of something.*

I'd refused to believe this: *No, I know how to leave work at work.*

Now it was me telling the new COs the same thing.

I took off the shades. 'You didn't say anything wrong. A thing like that, you never really get over it. Time doesn't heal the wounds, it just thickens up the scars.' I moved to the screen door and looked outside, smelled the autumn day, a golden scent of sun-warmed leaves. 'It's not like it used to be around here, is it?'

He shrugged. 'Where is?'

I had him follow me outside and turned my face to the sun, shutting my eyes and just listening, thinking that it at least sounded the way it had. That expansive, quiet sound of birds and wide-open spaces.

'When I was at the market, I would've needed at least two hands to count the people I'd be willing to bet will be dead in five years,' I said. 'How'd this get started?'

Ray eyed me hard. I knew it even with my eyes closed. I'd felt it as sure as if he'd poked me with two fingers. When I opened my eyes, he looked exactly like I knew he would.

'You're some kind of narc now, aren't you, Dylan?' he said.

'Corrections officer. I don't put anybody in prison, I just try to keep the peace once they're there.'

He stuffed his hands in his pockets and rocked back and forth, his gaze on far distances. 'Well . . . the way anything starts, I guess. A little at a time. It's a space issue, mostly. Space, privacy. We got plenty of both here. And time. Got plenty of that, too.'

His great-uncle hadn't, not to my recollection. Mr Tepovich had always had just enough, barely, to do what needed doing. The same as my grandfather. I wondered where all that time had come from.

'How many meth labs are there around here, I wonder,' I said.

'I couldn't tell you anything. All I know's what I hear, and I don't hear much.'

Can't help you, boss. I don't know nothing about that.

'But if you were to get lucky and ask the right person,' Ray went on, 'I expect he might tell you something like it was the only thing he was ever good at. The only thing that ever worked out for him.'

The trees murmured and leaves whisked against the birdhouse gourds.

'He might even take the position that it's a blessed endeavour.'
I hadn't expected this. 'Blessed by who?'

His hesitation here, his uncertainty, looked like the first genuine expression since we'd started down this path. 'Powers that be, I guess. Not government, not those kinds of powers. Something . . . higher.' He tipped his head back, jammed his big jaw and bristly beard forward, scowling at the sky. 'Say there's a place in the woods, deep, where nobody's likely to go by accident. Not big, but not well hid, either. Now say there's a team from the sheriff's department taking themselves a hike. Fifteen, twenty feet away, and they don't see it. Now say the same thing happens with a group of fellows got on jackets that say "DEA". They all just walk on by like nothing's there.'

He was after something, but I wasn't sure what. Maybe Ray didn't know either. They say if you stick around a prison long enough, you'll see some strange things that are almost impossible to explain, and even if I hadn't, I'd heard some stories. Maybe Ray had heard that as well, and was looking for . . . what, someone who understood?

'I don't know what else you'd call that,' he said, 'other than blessed.'

'For a man who doesn't hear much, you have some surprising insights.'

His gaze returned to earth and the mask went back on. 'Maybe I keep my ear to the ground a little more than I let on.' He began to sidle away towards his aunt's. 'You take care, Dylan. Again, sorry about Evvie.'

'Hey Ray? Silly question, but . . .' I said. 'Your Aunt Polly, your own grandma, your mom, anybody . . . when you were a kid, did any of them ever tell you stories about something called the Woodwalker?'

He shook his head. 'Nope. Seen my share of wood*peckers*, though.' He got a few more steps away before he stopped again, something seeming to rise up that he hadn't thought of in twenty years. 'Now that you mention it, I remember one from Aunt Pol about what she called Old Hickory Bones. It didn't make a lot of sense. "Tall as the clouds, small as a nut", that sort of nonsense. You know old women and their stories.'

'Right.'

He looked like he was piecing together memories from fragments. 'The part that scared us most, she'd swear up and down it was true, from when she was a girl. That there was this crew of moonshiners got liquored up on their own supply and let the still fire get out of hand. Burned a few acres of woods, and some crops and a couple of homes with it. Her story went that they were found in a row with their arms and legs all smashed up and run through with hickory sticks . . . like scarecrows, kind of. And that's how Old Hickory Bones got his name. I always thought she just meant to scare us into making sure we didn't forget about our chores.'

'That would do it for me,' I said.

He laughed. 'Those cows didn't have to wait on me for very many morning milkings, I'll tell you what.' He turned serious, one big hand scrubbing at his beard. 'Why do you come to ask about a thing like that?'

I gestured at the house. 'You know how it is going through a place this way. Everything you turn over, there's another memory crawling out from underneath it.'

Later, I kept going back to what I'd said when Gina and I had first walked in and looked at Grandma's chair: that it seemed like she'd finished her book and set it aside and peacefully resolved it was a good day to die. It's the kind of invention that gives you comfort, but maybe she really had. She kept up on us, her children and grandchildren, even though we were scattered far and wide. She knew I had a vacation coming up, knew that it overlapped with Gina's.

And we were her favourites. Even Mrs Tepovich knew that.

So I'm tempted to think Grandma trusted that, with the right timing, Gina and I would be first to go through the house. She couldn't have wanted my mother to do it. Couldn't have wanted my father to be the first up in the attic. Some things are too cruel, no matter how much love underlies them.

Maybe she'd thought we would be more likely to understand and accept. Because we were her favourites, and even though my mother had grown up here, and my aunts and uncles too, they were so much longer out of the woods than we, her grandchildren, were.

It broke the agreeable calm of Saturday afternoon, Gina and I in different parts of the house. I was in the pantry, looking through last season's preserves, and had discovered an ancient Mason jar full of coins when a warbling cry drifted down. I thought she'd come across a dead racoon, a nest of dried-out squirrels . . . the kind of things that sometimes turn up in country attics.

But when Gina came and got me, her face was pale and her voice had been reduced to such a small thing I could barely hear it. *Shae,* she was saying, or trying to. *Shae.* Over and over, with effort and an unfocused look in her eyes. *Shae.*

I didn't believe her while climbing the folding attic ladder; still didn't while crossing the rough, creaking boards, hunched beneath the slope of the roof in the gloom and cobwebs and a smell like a century of dust. But after five or twenty minutes on my knees, I believed, all right, even if nothing made sense any more.

There was light, a little, coming through a few small, triangular windows at the peaks. And there was air, slatted vents at either end allowing some circulation. And there was my sister's body, on a cot between a battered steamer trunk and a stack of cardboard boxes, covered by a sheet that had been drawn down as far as her chest.

The sheet wasn't dusty or discoloured. It was clean, white, recently laundered. Eight years of washing her dead grand-daughter's sheets – my head had trouble grasping that, and my heart just wanted to stop.

Gradually it dawned on me: With Shae eight years dead, we shouldn't have been able to recognise her. At best, she would've mummified in the dry heat, shrivelled into a husk. At worst, all that was left would be scraps and bones, and the strawberry blonde silk of her hair. Instead, the most I could say was that she looked very, very thin, and when I touched her cheek, her skin was smooth and stiff but pliable, like freshly worked clay. I touched her cheek and almost expected her eyes to open.

She'd been nineteen then, was nineteen now. She'd spent the last eight years being nineteen. Nineteen and dead, only not decayed. She lay on a blanket and a bed of herbs. They were beneath her, alongside her. Sprigs and bundles had been stuffed inside the strips of another sheet that had been loosely wound around her like a shroud. The scent of them, a pungent and spicy smell of fields and trees, settled in my nose.

'Do you think Grandma did this?' Gina was behind me, pressing close. 'Not *this* this, that's obvious, but . . . killed her, I mean. Not on purpose, but by accident, and she just couldn't face the rest of us?'

'Right now I don't know what to think.'

I shoved some junk out of the way to let more light at her. Her skin was white as a china plate, and dull, without the lustre of life. Her far cheek and jaw were traced with a few pale bluish lines like scratches that had never healed. Gently, as if it were still possible to hurt her, I turned her head from side to side, feeling her neck, the back of her skull. There were no obvious wounds, although while the skin of her neck was white as well, it was a more mottled white.

'Do me a favour,' I said. 'Check the rest of her.'

Gina's eyes popped. 'Me? Why me? You're the hard-ass prison guard.'

It was then I knew everything was real, because when tragedy is real, silly things cross your mind at the wrong times. *Corrections Officer*, I wanted to tell her. *We don't like the G-word.*

'She's my sister. She's still a teenager,' I said instead. 'I shouldn't be . . . she wouldn't want me to.'

Gina moved in and I moved aside and turned my back, listening to the rustle of cotton sheets and the crackle of dried herbs. My gaze roved and I spotted mousetraps, one set, one sprung, and if there were two, there were probably others. Grandma had done this, too. Set traps to keep the field mice away from her.

'She's, uh . . .' Gina's voice was shaky. 'Her back, her bottom, the backs of her legs, it's all purple-black.'

'That's where the blood pooled. That's normal.' At least it didn't look like she'd bled to death. 'It's the only normal thing about this.'

'What am I looking for, Dylan?'

'Injuries, wounds . . . is it obvious how she was hurt?'

'There's a pretty deep gash across her hipbone. And her legs are all scratched up. And her belly. There are these lines across it, like, I don't know . . . rope burns, maybe?'

Everything in me tightened. 'Was she assaulted? Her privates?'

'They . . . look okay to me.'

'All right. Cover her up decent again.'

I inspected Shae's hands and fingertips. A few of her nails were ragged, with traces of dirt. Her toenails were mismatched, clean on one foot, the other with the same rims of dirt, as if she'd lost a shoe somewhere between life and death. Grandma had cleaned her up, that was plain to see, but hadn't scraped too deeply with the tip of the nail file. Maybe it just came down to how well she could see.

I returned to Shae's neck, the mottling there. Connect the dots and you could call it lines. If her skin weren't so ashen, it might look worse, ringed with livid bruises.

'If I had to guess, I'd say she was strangled,' I told Gina. 'And maybe not just her throat, but around the middle, too.' Someone treating her like a python treats prey, wrapping and squeezing until it can't breathe.

We tucked her in again and covered her the rest of the way, to keep off the dust and let her return to her long, strange sleep.

'What do you want to do?' Gina said, and when I didn't answer: 'The kindest thing we could do is bury her ourselves. Let it be our secret. Nobody else has to know. What good would it do if they did?'

For the first minute or two, that sounded good. Until it didn't. 'You don't think Grandma knew that too? It's not that she couldn't have. If she was strong enough to work the soil in her garden, and to get Shae up the ladder, then she was strong enough to dig a grave. And there's not one time in the last eight years I heard her say anything that made me think her mind was off track. You?'

Gina shook her head. 'No.'

'Then she was keeping Shae up here for a reason.'

We backed off towards the ladder because another night, another day, wasn't going to do Shae any harm.

And that's when we found the envelope that Gina must have sent flying when she first drew back the sheet.

'*How you react to what I got to say depends on who's done the finding,*' our Grandma Evvie had written.

> *I have my hopes for who it is, and if it hasn't gone that way I won't insult the rest by spelling it out, but I think you know who you are.*
>
> *First off, I know how this looks, but how things look and how things are don't always match up.*

Know this much to be true: It wasn't any man or woman that took Shae's life. The easiest thing would've been to turn her over and let folks think so and see her buried and maybe see some local boy brought up on charges because the sheriff decides he's got to put it on somebody. I won't let that happen. There's plenty to pay for around here, and maybe the place would be better off even if some of them did get sent away for something they didn't do, but I can't help put a thing like that in motion without knowing whose head it would fall on.

If I was to tell you Shae was done in by what I always called the Woodwalker, some of you might believe me and most of you probably wouldn't. Believing doesn't make a thing any more or less true, it just points you towards what you have to do next.

If I was to tell you you could have Shae back again, would you believe it enough to try?

In the kitchen that evening, across the red oilcloth spread over the table, Gina and I argued. We argued for a long time. It comes naturally to brothers and sisters, but cousins can be pretty good at it too.

We argued over what was true. We argued over what couldn't possibly be real. We weren't arguing with each other so much as with ourselves, and with what fate had shoved into our faces.

Mostly, though, we argued over how far is too far, when it's for family.

Living with this has been no easy task. What happened to Shae was not a just thing. Folks here once knew that whatever we called it, there really is something alive in the woods and fields, as old as time and only halfway to civilised, even if few were ever lucky or cursed enough to see it. We always trusted that if we did right by it, it would do right by us. But poor Shae paid for other folks' wrongs.

She meant well, I know. It's no secret there's a plague here and it's run through one side of this county to the other. So when Shae found a trailer in the woods where they cook up that poison, nothing would do but that she draw a map and report it.

Till the day I die I won't ever forget the one summer when all the grandchildren were here and the night little Shae spoke up to say she'd seen the Woodwalker. I don't know why she was allowed at that age to see what most folks never do in a lifetime, but not once did I think she was making it up. I believed her.

The only thing I can fathom is this: Once she decided to report that trailer and what was going on there, the Woodwalker knew her heart, and resolved to put a stop to her intentions.

I spent half of Sunday out by myself, trying to find what Shae had found, but all I had to go by was the map she'd drawn. There was no knowing how accurate it was when it was new, and like the living things they are, woods never stop changing over time. Trees grow and fall, streams divert, brambles close off paths that were once as clear as sidewalks.

And whoever had put the trailer there had had eight years to move it. What it sounded like they'd never had, though, was a reason.

I had the map, and a bundle of sticks across my back, and like any hunter I had a shotgun – not my granddad's, since that one had yet to turn up, and it's just as well I went for the one in my trunk, carried out of habit for the job – but sometimes hunters come home empty-handed.

At least I came back with a good idea of what else I needed before going out to try again.

I don't want to say what I saw, but it was enough to know that it was no man using all those vines to drag her off towards the hog wallow, faster than I could chase after them. By the time I caught up, it had choked the life from her.

It didn't do this because it wanted to protect those men for their own sakes. I think it's because it wants the plague to continue until it finishes clearing away everybody who's got it, and there's nobody left in this county but folks who will treat the place right again.

These days you'll hear how the men who've brought this plague think they're beyond the reach of the law, because their hideaways can't be found. Well, I say it's only because the Woodwalker has a harsher plan than any lawman, and blinds the eyes of those who come from outside to look.

But Shae always did see those woods with different eyes.

'Remember what Grandma used to call her?' Gina asked. I was ashamed to admit I didn't. '"Our little wood-elf",' she said, then, maybe to make me feel better, 'That's not something a boy would've remembered. That's one for the girls.'

'Maybe so,' I said, and peeled the blanket open one more time to check my sister's face. I'd spent the last hours terrified that there had been some magic about our grandmother's attic, and that once she was carried back to the outside world again, the eight years of decay Shae had eluded would find her at last.

One more time, I wouldn't have known she wasn't just dreaming.

Instead, the magic had come with her. Or maybe the Woodwalker, spying us with the burden we'd shared through miles of woodland, knew our hearts now, too, and opened the veil for our eyes to see. Either way, I'd again followed where the old map led, and this time Shae had proven to be the key.

'Do you think it goes the other way?' Gina asked.

'What do you mean?'

'If we stood up and whoever's in there looked out, would they see us now? Or would they look straight at us and just see more trees?'

'I really don't want to put that to the test.'

The trailer was small enough to hitch behind a truck, large enough for two or three people to spend a day inside without tripping over each other too badly. It sat nestled into the scooped-out hollow of a rise, painted with a fading camouflage pattern of green and brown. At one time its keepers had strung nets of nylon mesh over and around it, to weave with branches and vines, but it looked like it had been a long time since they'd bothered, and they were sagging here, collapsed there. It had a generator for electricity, propane for gas. From the trailer's roof jutted a couple of pipes that had, ever since we'd come upon it, been venting steam that had long since discouraged anything from growing too close to it.

Eventually the steam stopped and a few minutes later came the sound of locks from the other side of the trailer door. It swung open and out stepped two men. They took a few steps away before they stripped off the gas masks they'd been wearing and let them dangle. They looked glad to breathe the cool autumn air.

I whispered for Gina to stay put, stay low, then stepped out from our hiding place and went striding towards the clearing in-between, and maybe it did take the pair of them longer to notice than it should've. They each wore a pistol at the hip but seemed to lack the instinct to go for them.

And the trees shuddered high overhead, even though I couldn't feel or hear a breeze.

'Hi, Ray,' I called, levelling the shotgun at them from the waist.

'Dylan,' he said, with a tone of weary disgust. 'And here I believed you when you said you weren't no narc.'

For a while I'd been wondering if he'd simply dropped by while visiting his great-aunt and Shae had suspected him for what he was and followed him here, righteous and foolhardy thing that she could be.

I glanced at the gangly, buzz-cut fellow at his side. 'Who's that you're with?'

'Him? Andy Ellerby.'

'Any more still inside?'

Ray's fearsome beard seemed to flare. 'You probably know as

well as I do, cooking is a two-man job at most.' He scuffed at the ground. 'Come on, Dylan, your roots are here. You don't do this. What say we see what we can work out, huh?'

I looked at his partner. Like Ray, the edges of his face and the top of his forehead were red-rimmed where the gas mask had pressed tight, and he gave me a sullen glare. 'Andy Ellerby, did I know you when we were kids?'

He turned his head to spit. 'What's it matter if you did or didn't, if you can't remember my name?'

'Good,' I said. 'That makes this a little easier.'

I snapped the riot gun to my shoulder and found that, when something mattered this much, I could again aim at something alive and pull the trigger. The range was enough for the twelve-gauge load to spread out into a pattern as wide as a pie tin. Andy took it in the chest and it flung him back against the trailer so hard he left a dent.

I'd loaded it with three more of the same, but didn't need them, so I racked the slide to eject the spent shell, then the next three. Ray looked confused as the unfired shells hit the forest floor and his hand got twitchy as he remembered the holster on his belt, but by then I was at the fifth load and put it just beneath his breastbone, where his belly started to slope.

He looked up at me from the ground, trying to breathe with a reedy wheeze, groping where I'd shot him and not comprehending his clean, unbloodied hands.

'A beanbag round,' I told him. 'We use them for riot control. You can't just massacre a bunch of guys with homemade knives, even if they are a pack of savages.'

I knelt beside him and plucked the pistol from his belt before he remembered it, tossed it aside. Behind me, Gina had crept out of hiding with her arms wrapped around herself, peering at us with the most awful combination of hope and dread I'd ever seen.

'I know you didn't mean to, and I know you don't even know you did it, but you're still the reason my little sister never got to turn twenty.' I sighed, and tipped my head a moment to look at the dimming sky and listened to the sound of every living thing, seen and unseen. 'Well . . . maybe next year.'

I drew the hunting knife from my belt while he gasped; called for Gina to bring me the bundle of hickory sticks that my grandmother must have sharpened years ago, and the mallet with a cast-iron head, taken down from the barn wall. It would've been easier with Granddad's chainsaw, but some things shouldn't come easy, and there are times the old ways are still the best.

I patted Ray's shoulder and remembered the stocky boy who'd taken us to the fattest tadpoles we'd ever seen, the juiciest berries we'd ever tasted. 'For what it's worth, I really was hoping it wouldn't be you coming out that door.'

If the family is to have Shae back again, there's some things that need doing, and I warn you, they're ugly business.

Dylan, if you're reading this, know that it was only you that I ever believed had the kind of love and fortitude in you to take care of it and not flinch from it. Whether you still had the faith in what your summers here put inside you was another matter. I figured that was a bridge we'd cross when it was time.

But then you came back from war, and whatever you'd seen and done there, you weren't right, and I knew it wasn't the time to ask. Somehow the time never did seem right. So if I was to tell you that I got used to having Shae around, even as she was, maybe you can understand that, and I hope forgive me for it.

It never seemed like all of her was gone.

The Woodwalker could've done much worse to her body, and I think it's held on to her soul. What I believe is that it didn't end her life for good, but took it to hold onto awhile.

Why else would the Woodwalker have bothered to bring her back to the house?

*

My sister saw the Woodwalker once, so she'd claimed, looking at two dead deer, and the reason she'd known it was no hunter was because hunters don't help dead deer back to their feet and send them on their way.

There's give and there's take. There's balance in everything. It was the one law none of us could hide from. Even life for life sometimes, but if Shae really did see what she thought she had, I wondered what she *hadn't* seen – what life the Woodwalker had deemed forfeit for the deer's.

As I went about the ugliest business of my life, I thought of the moonshiners from the tale Mrs Tepovich had told Ray as a boy – how they'd burned out a stretch of woodland and fields, and the grotesque fate they'd all met. But Grandma Evvie, as it turned out, had a different take on what had happened, and why the woods and crops rebounded so quickly after the fire.

'That story about Old Hickory Bones your Aunt Pol told you?' This was the last thing I said to Ray. 'It's basically true, except she was wrong about one thing. Or maybe she wanted to give you the lesson but spare you the worst. But the part about replacing the bones with hickory sticks? That's not something the Woodwalker does . . . that's the gift it expects us to give it.'

Whatever else was true and wasn't, I knew this much: Grandma Evvie would never have lied about my grandfather taking part in such a grim judgement when he was a very young man, able to swing a cast-iron mallet with ease.

Just as he must've done, I cut and sliced, pounded and pushed, hurrying to get it finished before the last of the golden autumn light left the sky, until what I'd made looked something like a crucified scarecrow. It glistened and dripped, and for as terrible a sight as it was, I'd still seen worse in war. When I stood back to take it in, wrapped in the enormous roar of woodland silence, I realised that my grandmother's faith in me to do such a thing wasn't entirely a compliment.

Gina hadn't watched, hadn't even been able to listen, so she'd spent the time singing to Shae, any song she could think of, as she prepared my sister's body. She curled her among the roots of a great oak, resting on a bed of leaves and draped with a blanket of creepers and vines. How much was instruction and how much was instinct grew blurred, but it seemed right. She shivered beneath Shae's real blanket after she was done, and after I'd cleaned myself up inside the trailer I held her awhile as she cried for any of a hundred good reasons. Then I built a fire and we waited.

You let yourself hope but explain things away. No telling why that pile of leaves rustled, why that vine twitched – anything could've done it. Flames flickered and shadows danced, while something watched us in the night – something tall enough to tangle clouds in its hair, small enough to hide in an acorn – and the forest ebbed and flowed with the magnitude of its slow, contemplative breath.

A hand first, or maybe it was a foot . . . something moved, too deliberate, too human, to explain away as anything else. Eight years since I'd heard her voice, but I recognised it instantly in the cough that came from beneath the shadows and vines. Gina and I dug and we pulled and scraped away leaves, and in the tangled heart of it all there was life, and now only one reason to cry. Shae coughed a long time, scrambling in a panic across the forest floor, her limbs too weak to stand, her voice too weak to scream, and I wondered if she was back at that moment eight years gone, reliving what it was like to die.

We held her until, I hoped, she thought it was just another dream.

I cupped her face, her cheeks still cold, but the fire gave them a flush of life. 'Do you know me?'

Her voice was a dry rasp. 'You look like my brother . . . only older.'

She had so painfully much to learn. I wondered if the kindest thing wouldn't be to keep her at the house until we'd taught each other everything about where we'd been the last eight years, and the one thing I hadn't considered until now was what if she wasn't right, in ways we could never fix, in ways beyond wrong, and it seemed like the best thing for everybody would be to send her back again.

For now, though, I had too much to learn myself.

'Take her back to the house,' I told Gina. 'I'll catch up when I can.'

They both looked at me like I was sending them out among the wolves. But somebody, somewhere, was expecting what had just been cooked up in the trailer.

'And tell them not to put the place up for sale. I'll need it myself.'

It was Shae, with the wisdom of the dead, who intuited it first, with a look on her face that asked *What did you do, Dylan, what did you do?*

I kissed them both on their cold cheeks and turned towards the trailer before I could turn weak and renege on the harshest terms of the trade.

Because there's give and there's take. There are balances to be kept. And there's a time in everyone's life when we realise we've become what we hate the most.

I was the bringer of plague now. There could be no other way.

And though I knew it would be a blessed endeavour, they still couldn't die fast enough.

BRIAN HODGE lives in Boulder, Colorado, where he also dabbles in music, sound design and photography. He loves everything about organic gardening except the thieving squirrels, and trains in Krav Maga and Brazilian Jiu-Jitsu, which are of no use at all against the squirrels.

Hodge is the author of ten novels, more than a hundred short stories, novelettes and novellas, and four collections, the first of which, *The Convulsion Factory*, was listed by critic Stanley Wiater as one of the 113 best books of modern horror. The capstone of his second collection, the novella 'As Above, So Below', was selected for inclusion in the massive *Century's Best Horror* anthology. His most recent book is his latest collection, *Picking the Bones*, which received a starred review in *Publishers Weekly*.

By the time this sees print, he should be done with his next novel, while another recent project has been completing the conversion of his backlist titles into e-books. Also forthcoming is a hardcover edition of his early epic novel, *Dark Advent*.

'Even though I had no idea what the story would be, "Roots and All" is something I wanted to write for a long time,' reveals Hodge. 'My father, who went on to become a respected and beloved educator and administrator, came from just such a place as in this story.

'Its seed was planted before my move to Colorado, when, some time after my grandmother's death, I was on the jury in a trial over a stabbing that had occurred in her community. Upon getting a glimpse of how that area was changing, I felt an unexpectedly strong sorrow. The need was rekindled after a recent visit, when I learned from an uncle that it has since degenerated into a meth haven.'

Tell Me I'll See You Again

—DENNIS ETCHISON—

S AY IT HAPPENED like this:

All the lawns were dry and white that day. Cars hunkered in driveways or shimmered like heat mirages at the curb. Last summer the four of them had tried to fry an egg on the sidewalk. This year it might work. As she walked past Mrs Shaede's rosebush she noticed a cricket perched on the bleached yellow petals. When she stopped for a closer look the insect dropped off and fell at her feet. She studied it, the papery body and thin, ratcheted legs, but it did not move again. So she reached down, picked it up and slipped it carefully into her shirt pocket.

At that moment there was a rumbling in the distance.

She knew the sound. Mr Donohue's truck had a bad muffler. She glanced up in time to see it pass at the end of the street. A few seconds later a bicycle raced across the intersection, trying to catch the truck. The spokes flashed and the tyres snaked over the hot pavement.

'David!' she shouted, and waved, but he pedalled away.

The muffler faded as the pickup headed for the boulevard. Then she heard a faint metallic clatter somewhere on the next block. It could have been a bicycle crashing to the ground.

She hurried for the corner.

Vincent came out of his house, drinking a Dr Pepper. 'Where you going?' he said.

'Did you hear that?'

'Hear what?'

Now there was only the buzzing of bees, the raspy bark of a dog in a backyard.

'I think it was David.'

'What about him?'

'He's in trouble,' she said, and hurried on.

Vincent followed at a casual pace. By the time he caught up she was squinting along the cross-street.

'What happened?'

'I don't know!'

'Don't worry about it.' He showed her the can of soda. 'Want one? I got some more in the basement.'

'Not now!'

'Aw, he's all right.'

'No, he's not. Look.'

A couple of hundred feet down, before the turn onto Charter Way, the bicycle lay on its side in the grass, the front wheel pointing at the sky and the spokes still spinning. David was twisted under the frame, the handlebars across his chest.

She ran the rest of the way, stopped and waited for him to move.

'Not bad.' Vincent walked around the crash scene. 'I give him a seven.'

'This isn't a game.' She studied the boy on the ground, the angle of his neck. She watched his eyelids. They remained shut.

'Sure it is,' said Vincent. 'We used to play it last summer. Remember?'

She got down on her knees and pressed her ear to his chest. There was no heartbeat. She unbuttoned his shirt to be sure. Then she moved her head up until her cheek almost touched his lips.

No air came out of his nose or mouth. This time he was not breathing at all.

'Help me,' she said.

'I don't see any blood.'

Vincent was right about that. And the bike seemed to be undamaged, as if it had simply fallen over.

'David? Can you hear me?'

'It looks pretty real, though. The way he's got his tennis shoe in the chain . . .'

'Are you going to help or not?'

Vincent raised the bike while she worked the foot free. She slipped her arm under David's shoulders and tried to sit him up. 'David,' she whispered. 'Tell me you're all right.'

'Okay, okay,' Vincent said, 'I'll give him an eight.'

She lowered David back down, dug her fingers into his hair and tapped his head against the ground. Then she did it again, harder. Finally his chest heaved as he began to breathe. His eyelids opened.

'I knew he was faking,' Vincent said.

'You take the bike,' she told him.

'Eric used to do it better, though.'

'Shut up.'

Vincent started to wheel the bike onto the sidewalk. He had to turn the handlebars so he did not run over a small mound on the grass.

'What the hell is that?' he said. 'A dead racoon?'

'Leave it.'

'I hate those things.' Vincent raised his foot, ready to kick it like a football.

'It's a possum. I said *leave it*.'

She got up quickly, walked over, took hold of the animal by the fur and tapped it against the ground. Once was enough. The frightened creature sprang to life, wriggled free and scurried off.

'Faker!' said Vincent.

'Take the bike, I told you. We'll meet at his house.'

She went back to David and held out her hand.

'Come on. I'll walk you home.'

David blinked, trying to focus. 'Is my dad there?'

'I didn't know you went out,' said his grandmother from the porch.

'Sorry,' said David.

'You should always tell someone.'

'Do you know where my dad went?'

'To get some kind of tool.'

'Oh.'

'Come in the house. You don't look so good. Would your friends like a cold drink?'

'Not me,' said Vincent.

'No, thank you,' said the girl.

'Is he coming back?'

'Why, of course he is, Davey. Now come in before you get heat stroke.'

'I have to put my bike away.'

'Well, don't be long.' She opened the screen door and went inside.

'I gotta go, anyway,' Vincent said. He started out of the front yard. 'Wanna come over to my place?'

'Not right now,' said David.

'We can play anything you want.'

David was not listening. His eyes moved nervously from the driveway to the end of the block and back again. The girl moved over and stood next to him.

'Maybe later,' she said.

'Okay. Well, see ya.'

She sat down on the porch as Vincent walked away.

'Are you sure you're all right?'

'Yeah.'

'I thought you got hit by a car or something.'

'Naw.'

'What do you remember?'

'Nothing.'

'You never do. But that's okay. We'll figure it out.'

There was the rumbling of the muffler again, at the end of the block. David stood by the driveway until the pickup truck rounded the corner and turned in. His father got out, carrying a bag.

'Hey, champ,' he said.

'Where were you?'

'At the Home Depot.'

'Why didn't you take me?'

'Did you want to go?'

'I always do.'

'Next time, I promise. Hello, there. Charlene, isn't it?'

'Sherron. Hi, Mr Donohue.'

'Of course. You're David's friend from school. How have you been?'

'Fine.'

'You knew Eric, didn't you? David's brother?'

'Yes,' she said in a low voice.

'Dad . . .'

'I have an idea. Why don't you stay for lunch? Would you like that?'

Something moved in her chest, or at least in the pocket of her shirt, trying to get out. The cricket from the rosebush had come back to life. 'I would. I mean, I do. But I sort of have to get home. My mom's expecting me. She's making something special.'

'Another time, then.'

'I was wondering,' she said carefully. 'Could David come, too? She said it was all right.'

'Why, I think that's a fine invitation. Don't you, son?'

David considered. 'Are you leaving again?'

'Not today. I've got plenty to do in the garage.'

'Please?' she said to David. 'I need you to help me with something.'

'Well . . .'

'My science project. It's really cool.'

'I'll bet it is,' said the man. 'You know, my wife was interested in science. Do you remember David's mother?'

'Yes,' she said, looking at her shoes.

'Eileen was doing research when I met her, at college. We got married right after graduation . . .'

'Dad, please.'

'She was a very nice lady,' said the girl.

'Yes. She was.' His father took a deep breath and closed his eyes for a second. 'Anyway, you two have a great time. And don't be such a stranger, Sherron. You're always welcome here.'

'Thanks, Mr Donohue.'

'Then – I'll see you later, Dad.'

His father winked. 'You can count on it.'

'Are you going to tell my dad?'

'Not if you don't want me to.'

They walked around the corner to the next street. The pavement smelled like melting asphalt. Somewhere a sprinkler hissed, beating steam into the air. Her house had trees that kept the sun away from the roof and the windows, so when they went inside it was hard to see for a minute. No one was home. She poured two glasses of sweet tea from the refrigerator and led him to her room.

As soon as she closed the door she took the cricket out of her pocket. Before it could hop away she put it in a Mason jar. A grasshopper and a beetle crawled along a leaf at the bottom. As soon as she touched the jar they stopped moving. She screwed the wire lid back on.

'Your folks let you keep those?'

'I told them it's for school.'

'What do you need them for?'

'My project. If I get a fish tank, I can have frogs, too. And one of these.' She opened a book to a picture of a small snake.

'Why?'

'I found it on the Internet.'

'But *why*?'

She turned her computer on and showed him a page from a university website. There was an article called *Thanatosis: Nature's Way of Survival*, with close-ups of insects, a possum, a leopard shark and a hog-nosed snake. He read the first paragraph. It explained how some creatures protect themselves when afraid by pretending to be dead.

'You think I'm like them?'

'I don't know yet. But I'm going to find out.'

'Well, you're wrong.'

She noticed that his eyes were now focused on the bulletin board by the computer, and the headline of the newspaper clipping she had pinned there months ago: LOCAL WOMAN, SON DIE IN FIERY CRASH. She snatched it down and put it in the drawer.

'Oh, David. I'm really sorry.'

'I better go.'

'But I need you to help me.'

'You think I'm faking it.'

'No, I don't. I was there this time.'

'Then you know I'm a freak,' he said. 'Like one of those animals. Like a bug.'

'You're *not*.'

'What's the difference?'

'They just – freeze up when they get scared. But you weren't even *breathing*. Your *heart* stopped.'

'So what am I scared of?'

'It's okay to say it. David, I saw you chasing the truck. Every time he leaves – well, you're afraid he won't come back either. Aren't you?'

He made a sound like a laugh. 'You don't know anything.'

'Don't I?'

The laugh stopped. 'If he doesn't, it means I got a second chance and I blew it.'

'What are you talking about?'

'Don't you get it? She was going to take me, but I was off playing that stupid game. She wasn't supposed to take Eric. It was supposed to be me.'

Her mouth stayed open while she tried to find words.

'I have to go now,' he said.

Once he was out from under the trees the sky was fierce again. Leaves curled, flowers turned away from the sun and the asphalt began to glisten. He heard footsteps on the sidewalk that were not his own.

'You're right. I don't know anything.'

'Forget it, Sher.'

They passed rosebushes, the yellow petals now almost white. It was half a block before she spoke again.

'Can I ask one question?'

'Go ahead.'

'How does it feel?'

'I told you, I don't remember.'

'Can you at least try?'

He kept walking, stepping over cracks. Mrs Shaede's rainbird sprinkler came on and a silver mist rose into the air.

'Wilson's Market,' he said under his breath.

'What?'

'Nothing.'

'The one on Charter Way? What about it?'

'We used to go there, when I was little.'

'We did, too.'

'There was this one time,' he said slowly, as they neared the end of the block, 'I was four or five, I guess. Eric wasn't born yet. She was wearing her long coat.'

'The grey one? I remember that.'

'Anyway, we went like always, just the two of us. And we got a shopping cart and she let me push it, so I could help. You know, put the milk and the groceries in for her. I stopped to look at the cereal, and I was going to tell her what kind to get, but when I looked up she was way ahead. I could only see the back of her coat. And you know what? There was another cart behind her, and another little boy was pushing it, and she was handing *him* the cans. I didn't understand. I thought they were going to drive off and leave me there. So I started to cry. I yelled, 'Mama, that isn't me!' And when she turned around, it wasn't my mother. It was another lady with the same kind of coat. But before she turned, that was the feeling. If you want to know.'

Her eyes were bright as diamonds and she had to look away. And then she did something she had never done before. She hooked her arm through his and reached down and lifted his wrist and laced her fingers between his fingers and held his hand very tightly. He let her do that.

After a while she said, 'You know, they have better nurses at middle school. Maybe they can give you pills to make it stop.'

'I don't care.'

'I do.'

'Maybe I *was* dead. So what? Next time, I hope I don't wake up! What do you think of that? Huh?'

When she did not answer he looked around for her.

If she was not there she should have been.

The next school year was a crazy one, say like landing behind enemy lines and fighting your way out, and the next one was even worse, so he saw less of her, even before his father learned the truth and started driving him to the Institute for tests. By then it did not happen very often but at least David was with him. The only time he was not was when Dad's heart gave out suddenly during senior year. She broke up with Vincent when her family moved and people said she went away to college to study pre-med, but no one knew exactly where. If you ever meet her, you might tell her this: just that life goes on, and her project – say his name was David – finally figured out that there are so many small dyings along the way it hardly matters which one of them is Death.

(for Kenneth Patchen)

DENNIS ETCHISON is a three-time winner of both the British Fantasy and World Fantasy Awards. His short stories have been collected in *The Dark Country*, *Red Dreams*, *The Blood Kiss*, *The Death Artist*, *Talking in the Dark*, *Fine Cuts* and *Got To Kill Them All & Other Stories*.

He is also the author of the novels *Darkside*, *Shadowman*, *California Gothic*, *Double Edge*, *The Fog*, *Halloween II*, *Halloween III* and *Videodrome*, and editor of the anthologies *Cutting Edge*, *Masters of Darkness I-III*, *MetaHorror*, *The Museum of Horrors* and (with Ramsey Campbell and Jack Dann) *Gathering the Bones*.

He has written extensively for film, television and radio, including hundreds of scripts for *The Twilight Zone Radio Dramas*, *Fangoria Magazine*'s *Dreadtime Stories* and Christopher Lee's *Mystery Theater*.

His next book is a much-anticipated collection of new stories.

'When I was a boy,' recalls Etchison, 'some grotesque tales would not die. They were always recounted as absolutely true ("It happened to my cousin's best friend, I swear to God!") and eventually they acquired the weight of Known Facts, like Mick Jagger's search for a lost Mars Bar or Richard Gere's problem with a misplaced gerbil.

'Years later I learned that the Vanishing Hitchhiker, the Hook, the Killer in the Backseat and many more classics had been told throughout the land until they became Urban Legends. This made me question whether other strange events, which I knew to be true because they had happened to me, were really so strange after all.

'For example, we used to play at staging the most realistic accident scenes possible, usually involving a bicycle, to create the illusion that one of us had just been killed. We struck extreme poses and took turns holding our breath and voted on whose death was the most convincing. Looking back, this seemed a truly odd and morbid game – until recently, when I did a reality check. My friend

Mike Lester, who grew up in a distant state, admitted that he and his childhood pals had done exactly the same thing, but next to the busiest roadways they could find, in hopes of freaking out passing motorists.

'Now the writer in me was hooked. Add a metafictional interest in the authorial voice (who is actually telling this, and why?), plus the metaphysical spell of *Prelude to a Kiss*, the film version of Craig Lucas's superb play, and inspiration as always from Kenneth Patchen's emotional courage and control ... and presto, a new short story.

'Of course the larger question remains: Why did these particular elements, and not others, come together in my unconscious? I honestly can't say, which may be the real mystery. I only play what I hear, even when I don't understand where the music is coming from.'

The Music of Bengt Karlsson, Murderer

—JOHN AJVIDE LINDQVIST—

Translated by Marlaine Delargy

I'M ASHAMED to admit it, but I bribed my son to get him to start learning to play the piano.

The idea came to me one night when I heard him sitting plinking and plonking away on the toy synthesiser he'd been given for his birthday two years earlier. He'd actually taken a break from playing computer games – imagine that. So I went into his room and asked if he'd like piano lessons.

No, he would not. No way. I hinted that an increase in his pocket money might well be on the cards if he agreed. Eighty kronor a week instead of fifty. Robin must have realised how desperate I was, because he refused even to come and look at the community music school unless we were talking about doubling the amount. A hundred kronor a week.

I gave in. What else could I do? Something had to change. My son was sliding towards unreality, and if a piano lesson now and again could bring him back to the IRL-world to some extent, then one hundred kronor a week was a cheap price to pay.

IRL. In real life. I don't know what the other world is called, but that was where Robin spent almost all of his waking hours when he wasn't in school. Online. Wearing a headset and with a control in his hands, he had surfed away to a coastline where I could no longer reach him.

Not too much of a problem, you might think. Completely normal, the youth of today *etc*. Well yes. But he was only eleven years old. It just can't be healthy to sit there locked inside an electronic fantasy world for five, six, seven hours a day at that age. So I bribed him.

And what would an eleven-year-old do with the hundred kronor a week he had managed to extort from a father who was completely at a loss? What do you think? *Buy new games*, of course. But I couldn't work out what else to do. Anything that could divert him from slaying monsters and conversing with invisible friends felt like progress.

Now I know better. Now I wish I'd spent the money on a faster Internet connection, a cordless headset, a new computer, anything at all. Perhaps then the darkness wouldn't have got hold of me. I'll never know.

It started well. Robin turned out to have a natural inclination for playing the piano, and after spending a few weeks playing 'Frère Jacques' and 'Mary Had a Little Lamb' with one finger, he had grasped the basic principles of the notes and was able to play his first chord. His achievement was all the more praiseworthy because there was no help to be had from his father.

I am completely useless when it comes to music. I've never sung, nor played any instrument. Robin must have inherited that gene from his mother, and she should have been the one sitting beside him on the piano stool. But one of the few things we have left of her is her piano. Perhaps that was why I insisted on Robin playing that particular instrument. To maintain some form of . . . contact.

When Robin started piano lessons it was almost two years to the day since Annelie got in the car and never came back. An icy road, a bus coming from the opposite direction . . . only a month later they erected a central barrier separating the two carriageways.

About bloody time. I came to hate that barrier, its wire structure like a wound across my field of vision every time I drove past the spot. Because it hadn't been there *then*.

Six months after Annelie's death, we moved. There were too many rooms in the old house, rooms meant for more children, for Annelie's loom. Rooms just standing there like empty memorials to a life that might have been. Rooms where I could get trapped, sitting there hour after hour. And on top of all that: rooms which together made up a house that was far too big and far too expensive to run on one income.

I decided to try to come to terms with all the dreams that had died, and got a job 300 kilometres away in Norrtälje. We moved from the house in Linköping to an eighty-square-metre wind-blown shack in the forest. The house was five kilometres from the town, where I didn't know a soul. The property was surrounded by coniferous forest on three sides, and in the winter you hardly ever caught a glimpse of the sun.

But it was cheap. Extremely cheap.

I carried out the move in a state of agitation. After six months, during which my grief had taken on a physical form and squeezed my throat at night, tangled me up in the sheets and thrown me out of bed, I saw the chance to breathe in at least a little light. I would start afresh in a new place – for Robin's sake, if nothing else. It wasn't good for him, living with a father whose only companion in bed was death, and who never slept for longer than an hour at a time.

So I cleared the place out. Anything we didn't need for our new life on the edge of the forest went into a skip: Annelie's clothes, her hand-woven rugs, piece after piece of furniture that belonged to a life for two, and carried its own memories. Out. I smashed up the loom with an axe and took it out in bits.

The night after the skip had been taken away, I slept well for the first time in six months, only to wake up in absolute terror.

What had I done?

In my feverish enthusiasm I had thrown away not only things that Robin and I could have made use of (but I just couldn't keep the kitchen table where she still sat with her cup of coffee, or the lamp that still illuminated her face, casting dead shadows), but also things that I would have liked to keep. The cushion she used to hug to her stomach. Her hair slides, with a few strands of hair still attached. The odd talisman. But everything had been crushed to bits at some rubbish dump.

The only thing that remained was the piano. The lads who came to pick up the skip had refused to touch it, and I couldn't manage to drag it out on my own. So it stayed where it was, with her fingerprints still lingering on the keys.

That morning . . . oh, that morning. If it hadn't been for the piano I might have lost my mind completely, and Robin would have ended up calling the emergency services instead of being driven to school to say goodbye to his classmates. It's a paradox, but that's just how it was: that piano kept me from sinking.

And so it came with us to our new home, and the only place we could find enough space was in Robin's bedroom, and that's how it came about that Robin started to play the piano, and after six weeks was able to try out his first hesitant chord.

I can't say he practised much, but enough to get by. He liked his piano teacher, a guy who was a few years younger than me but had already settled for a cardigan and Birkenstocks. Robin wanted to please his teacher, so he did his exercises, which meant at least an hour or two away from the games.

Since I had nothing to offer in musical terms, Robin didn't want me in the room when he was practising. Instead I would sit at the kitchen table reading the paper, listening as his plinking became more assured each time he went through 'Twinkle, Twinkle Little Star'.

Then the roars and explosions of *Halo* or *Gears of War* took over again, and I would move into the living room and the TV, pleased with how things had turned out in spite of everything.

If I remember rightly, it happened in the eighth week. I had just driven Robin home from his piano lesson and settled down at the kitchen table with a cup of coffee and the newspaper, while he started practising in his room.

Since I had got used to the sound, I was able to concentrate on my reading without being distracted. But after a while I began to feel uneasy, for some reason. I looked up from the paper and listened.

Robin was playing the piano. But what was he playing?

I listened more carefully and tried to pick out a melody, something I recognised. From time to time I heard a sequence of notes which at a push could be linked to an existing tune, only to fall apart again. I assumed Robin was just messing around on the keyboard, and I should have been pleased that he'd reached this point. If it hadn't been for that strange sense of unease.

The only way I can explain it is to say that I thought I recognised the notes, in spite of the fact that I had no idea what it was, and in spite of the fact that it didn't sound like a melody. It was like knowing that you know something, but at the same time being incapable of expressing it. That feeling. That sense of unease.

I gritted my teeth, put my hands over my ears and tried to concentrate on the newspaper. I knew I ought to welcome this new development, and it would be completely wrong to go and ask Robin to stop. So I tried to concentrate on an article about the expansion of wind power, but failed to read a single word. The only thing that went into my head was the faint sound of those notes vibrating through the palms of my hands.

I was on the point of getting up and going to knock on Robin's door after all when there was a short pause, followed by a halting version of 'Jingle Bells'. I let out a long breath and returned to my reading.

That night I had a horrible dream. I was in a forest, a dense coniferous forest. Only a glimmer of moonlight penetrated down among the dark tree trunks. I could hear singing coming from somewhere, and I stood there motionless as a weight dragged me towards the ground. When I looked down I could just make out a crowbar. A heavy iron crowbar, which I was holding in my hands. The singing turned into a scream, and I woke up with the taste of rust in my mouth.

Even though it was the end of November, we still hadn't had any snow. Robin was practising for the Christmas concert – songs about happy little snowflakes and sleigh rides – while the temperature refused to drop below zero. Dark mornings with the smell of rotting leaves in the damp air, long evenings with the pine trees around the house swaying and creaking in the strong winds.

One evening I was sitting at the table in the living room with my MacBook, trying to write a job application. I was in charge of the greengrocery department at the ICA hypermarket, but for a long time I had dreamed of being in charge of a smaller shop. Such a position had just come up. The work itself would be more varied, plus my journey would be five kilometres shorter each day.

So I polished up my set phrases and tried to present myself in as responsible and creative a light as possible, while the wind howled in the television aerial and Robin began to play the piano.

My fingers stopped, hovering over the keys. It was those notes again. Despite the wind which was making the windows creak and the wooden joints whimper, I could hear the notes as clearly as if the piano had been in the same room.

Dum, di-dum, dum . . .

I couldn't remember whether the notes were exactly the same as the last time, but I always knew exactly which note would come next, even though there was nothing recognisable or logical about the melody. My fingers extended and moved in time with the music as my thoughts drifted off into space.

I was woken by the sound I made closing the computer. The clock showed that half an hour had passed, half an hour of which I had no memory whatsoever.

Robin had stopped playing the piano, and from his room I could hear the low murmur of conversation as he spoke to some friend on Skype or Live. As usual I wondered what they actually talked about, given that they had no real lives, if you'll pardon the expression.

I sat down at the kitchen table with a cup of coffee and stared out at the swaying trees; I could vaguely make out the shapes in the glow of the outside light. No real lives. But then again, what would people say about my own life?

My empire during the day was a space measuring some two hundred square metres, where my role was to satisfy people's need for fruit and vegetables in a way that pleased the eye: no empty shelves, fresh goods on display, arranging the trays in combinations that were dictated by head office, teaching assistants the correct way to handle mushrooms.

On one occasion when we were running a promotion I had improvised slightly and placed a battery-driven monkey among the bananas. Naturally it had frightened a child so much that the kid burst into tears, and I had received a reprimand from up above, instructing me to stick to the manual issued by head office. It's like working in an East European dictatorship, but with brighter colours.

I was sitting at the kitchen table thinking about all this when the fir trees and pine trees suddenly disappeared. All the tiny electronic sounds of equipment on standby were gone, and the house was completely silent.

A power cut. I sat for a while in the darkness, listening to the silence. As I was just about to get up and find some candles and oil lamps, I heard something that made me stop dead.

The electricity was off and nothing was working. So how come Robin was still talking away in his bedroom? I turned my head towards the sound of his voice and tried to listen more closely. What I heard made me shudder. Of course it was only a phenomenon created by the movement of the wind through and around the house, but I really thought I could hear one or more voices in addition to Robin's.

It's hardly a father's job to come up with imaginary friends for his son, but I still couldn't help sitting with my head tilted to one side, trying to make out what those voices were saying. Faint, almost inaudible utterances, and then Robin's replies, which I couldn't make out either. I chewed my nails. Robin wasn't in the habit of talking to himself, as far as I knew. Perhaps he'd nodded off, and was talking in his sleep?

I groped my way over to the side of the room to get out the torch. Just as I pulled open the drawer the power came back on and I let out a little scream as all the everyday objects jumped out of the darkness. The voices in Robin's room fell silent, and the fridge shuddered as it started up again.

When I knocked on Robin's door it was a couple of seconds before I heard 'Mmm?' from inside. I looked in and saw him sitting on the piano stool, his body turned away from the instrument.

'Hi,' I said.

I was expecting the usual expression of listless amazement at the fact that I was disturbing him yet again, but the look he gave me was that of someone trying to place a face which is vaguely familiar. He said: 'Hi?' as if he were speaking to a stranger.

'There was a power cut,' I said, unable to help myself from

glancing around his room to see if I could spot the people who had been talking. The scruffy, peeling wallpaper I hadn't had the time or energy to change, the vinyl flooring with its gloomy '70s pattern.

'Yes,' said Robin. 'I noticed.'

I nodded, my eyes still flicking from the bed to the desk, the wardrobe. The wardrobe.

'Were you talking to somebody just now?'

Robin shrugged his shoulders. 'Yeah, what about it? On Skype.'

'But . . . when we had the power cut.'

'When we had the power cut?'

I could hear how stupid it sounded. But I had heard *something*. My gaze was drawn to the wardrobe. It was a basic, recently purchased IKEA wardrobe in white laminate, but I thought there were an unusual number of grubby marks around the doorknob.

'So you weren't talking to anybody then?'

'No.'

Before I could stop myself I had taken three strides into the room and pulled open the wardrobe door. Robin's clothes had been shoved carelessly into the wire baskets, with odd tops and shirts that he never wore arranged on hangers. Apart from that, the wardrobe was empty.

'What are you doing?' he asked.

'Just checking that . . . you've got clean T-shirts and stuff.'

I couldn't come up with anything better, even though I'd folded and put away the clean laundry that very afternoon. As I pretended to check the stock of underwear I felt a cold draught. The window was slightly ajar, with both catches open.

'Why is the window open?'

Robin rolled his eyes. 'Because I forgot to close it, maybe?'

'But why did you open it? It's really windy out there.'

Robin was now back to himself, and gave me the look that means: *Have you got any more amazingly interesting questions?* Even I didn't understand what I was getting at, so I closed the window, flicked the catches down and left the room. As I was closing the door I saw Robin start up the computer, and a few minutes later I could hear the one-sided mumbling as he communicated via Skype. I placed a pan on the hob to make our bedtime hot chocolate.

It was a bad habit I couldn't bring myself to give up, that hot chocolate. Because Robin spent so much time sitting still it had begun to show on his body; he had a little belly protruding above the waistband of his trousers. But I still made hot chocolate every night, and we had three pastries each along with it.

Because that's what we used to do when he was little. Ever since he was four years old it had been a little ritual every night: the three of us would gather around the kitchen table before it was time for Robin to go to bed, and we would drink hot chocolate and chat.

I couldn't bring myself to let go, even though there were only two cups on the table and we frequently ended up sitting in mutual silence. At least we were sitting there. When Annelie was alive we used to have a lit candle in the middle of the table, but I decided to skip that particular detail after trying it once following her death. It had felt like keeping vigil beside a corpse.

When the chocolate was ready I placed six pastries in the microwave and shouted for Robin. We munched our way through the pastries and drank our chocolate without saying anything while the wind continued to squeeze the house and nudge its way in through the cracks. I was picking up bits of sugar by pressing my finger down on them when Robin suddenly said: 'Did you know a murderer used to live here?'

I stopped with my finger halfway to my mouth. 'What are you talking about? A murderer?'

'Yes. His bed used to be where mine is now.'

'Who is this murderer, and who's he supposed to have murdered?'

'Children. He murdered children. And his bed used to be where mine is now.'

'Where did you get this from?'

Robin finished off his chocolate and an impotent wave of tenderness swept through me as I noticed that he had a chocolate moustache. When I pointed to it he rubbed it off and said: 'I heard it.'

'Who from?'

Robin gave his trademark shrug and got up from the table, then went and placed his cup in the sink.

'Hang on,' I said. 'Where are you going with all this?'

'Nowhere. That's just the way it is.'

'I don't understand . . . do you want to move your bed or something?'

Robin considered this for a moment with a frown. Then he said: 'No, it's fine. He's dead,' at which point he left me alone with my empty cup and the wind. I sat there for a long time staring at the streaks of chocolate in the bottom of the cup, as if there were something to be interpreted from the pattern they formed.

He murdered children. His bed used to be where mine is now.

The television aerial began to sing, as it sometimes does when the wind is coming from a certain direction. It sounded as if the house itself was moaning or crying out for help.

I found it difficult to sleep that night. The aerial's lament combined with Robin's strange assertion kept me awake, and I lay tossing and turning in my narrow bed.

The double bed from the years with Annelie had been the first thing I dragged outside for disposal when I was getting ready to move. Night after night I had lain awake in that bed, tormented by the phantom pains of grief just below my collarbone where she used to rest her head when we settled down to go to sleep.

The new single bed went some way towards helping me cope

with her searing absence, but I still sometimes reached out to touch her when I was half-asleep, only to find myself fumbling in the empty space beyond the edge of the bed.

'Annelie,' I whispered, 'what shall I do?'

No reply. Outside the bedroom window sleet had begun to fall; the wind was driving it against the pane, and it sounded like little wet feet scrabbling across the glass. I crawled out of bed and pulled on my dressing gown with the idea of sitting down at the computer and idly surfing the net until I felt tired enough to sleep.

When I opened the screen I was confronted by the document I had left half-finished in the afternoon. I read through the account of my responsibilities in the greengrocery department, my experience in negotiating with suppliers and with quality control, my social skills and—

What the hell?

I had no recollection whatsoever of writing the final section, and it sat badly with the rest of the text, to say the least. I read the whole passage once again.

During my three years in charge of the fruit and vegetable section my areas of responsibility have included among other things the dead speak through the notes, but how can a person bear it?

There was a cold draught blowing through the house and I shivered as I sat there in my thin dressing gown, staring at the words I had written. *The dead speak through the notes.* I understood which notes it was referring to, of course, but where had I got such an idea?

I'm losing the plot. Soon I'll be singing along with the TV aerial.

I felt a strong desire to smash the computer to pieces, but I pulled myself together and deleted the whole passage instead, then settled down to rewrite it.

*

The next morning, the previous afternoon and evening felt like a bad dream. The wind had abated and the sun was peeping through gaps in the cloud cover. When I drove Robin to school he allowed himself a big hug before he got out of the car. On the way to work I switched the radio on and was rewarded with 'Viva la Vida' by Coldplay.

I drummed along with the beat on the steering wheel and managed to convince myself that it was loneliness, grief and my anxiety about Robin that made it feel as if reality was slipping through my fingers. That I just needed to pull myself together. Life *could* work if I could just manage to slough off the old skin and accept things as they were. From now on I would make it work.

I spent the morning inspecting the fruit counters and making some adjustments to Thursday's order, as well as putting up posters announcing this week's promotion: fifty kronor to fill a plastic bucket with your choice of fruit, and you get to keep the bucket into the bargain.

Kalle Granqvist from the deli counter took his lunch break at the same time as me, and we sat in the staff room talking about this and that. Kalle is a permanent fixture at the store; he's been there since it opened in '89, and is due to retire next year. Since he's also something of a local historian I took the opportunity to tackle the issue that was niggling away at me.

Over coffee I asked: 'Apropos of nothing, do you have any idea who used to live in our house? Before, I mean.'

Kalle stroked his short grey beard and said: 'Benke Karlsson.'

'Benke Karlsson?'

'Yes.'

He said the name in the way you might say 'Olof Palme' or 'Jussi Björling': a person everybody is expected to know, with no further explanation needed. Kalle assumed that everyone was as well up on the recent history and characters of the area as he was.

'Should I have heard of Benke Karlsson?' I asked, relieved at the everyday sound of the name.

'I don't know,' said Kalle. 'I mean, it's a while since he was up to his tricks.'

'Up to his tricks? What does that mean, *up to his tricks*?'

Kalle grinned. 'Why are you looking so worried? He was a musician. He used to play at parties and such like, until . . .' Kalle jerked his head a few times, which could have meant just about anything.

'Until what?'

'Oh, you don't want to go poking into all that.'

'What happened?'

'Well, his wife died. And he took it badly. After a few years he killed himself. That's all it was.'

Kalle gathered up his dishes, rinsed them and placed them in the dishwasher. I knew I shouldn't ask, that it was probably better not to know, but I couldn't help myself: 'How did he kill himself? And where?'

Kalle sighed and looked at me with a somewhat sorrowful expression. He seemed to be searching for a more sympathetic way of putting it, but the only thing he could come up with was: 'He hanged himself. At home.'

'In the house where we live now?'

Kalle scratched his beard. 'Yes. I assume that's why you got it so cheap. Shall we go?'

I didn't believe in ghost stories, which was just as well, I thought as I tidied up after lunch. But still I felt a tinge of unease and my hands were shaking slightly as I drank a glass of water. I thought I had an idea where Benke Karlsson had chosen to leave this earthly life.

What I called my bedroom was in fact just a part of the living room. Fixed to the ceiling in the centre of the room was a substantial hook that had probably supported a heavy lamp. I went through the rest of the house in my mind and couldn't find any other fixture on a ceiling that would bear the weight of a grown man's body. Benke Karlsson had hanged himself two metres from the spot where I slept.

A suicide, then. That was an unpleasant enough idea. But where had Robin got the idea that Benke Karlsson had also murdered children? And that his bed had stood where Robin's was now?

Regardless of what you believe or don't believe, it was an uncomfortable image. I had cleared out my own past and instead moved straight into another man's dark history. Fortunately there are no direct links between the present and the past, except in our minds.

That's what I thought at the time. Now I think differently.

I could hear the notes as soon as I got out of the car.

It was half-past five and I was worn out after a day at work, during which I had had to make a real effort to concentrate on the task in hand and to stop my thoughts drifting off to the former owner of our house. The outside light was switched off, and apart from the faint glow from Robin's room where he sat playing, only the moonlight made it possible to see my way.

I slammed the car door and the tinkling of the piano stopped. I stood there taking deep breaths as my eyes grew accustomed to the darkness. Then it occurred to me that I ought to go to the tool shed. There was something in there I needed to look at.

As I groped my way towards the blacker darkness that was the old shed, I caught a movement out of the corner of my eye. The light from Robin's room had illuminated something moving on the ground outside his window. I would have investigated the matter if it hadn't seemed more important at the time to go and look at what was in the shed.

Dum, di-dum.

The notes Robin had played were still echoing in my head as I lifted the hasp on the door of the shed, which I hadn't cleared out after the previous owner. Benke Karlsson. *He took it badly*.

The darkness inside was dense and I couldn't see a thing. However, some time ago I had left a box of matches just inside the door for situations such as this. I stepped into the shed, found the half-full box and struck a match.

Shelves cluttered with extension leads, folded tarpaulins, screws and nails. A carpenter's bench where my own tools lay in a higgledy-piggledy heap with things that had already been there when we moved in. But I was looking for something else. What I wanted to see was right at the back.

I crouched down, blew out the match which was starting to burn my fingers, and struck another. Leaning against the wall was a spade with a wooden handle and a heavy iron crowbar. I gazed at the two objects. Spade and crowbar. Crowbar and spade.

Dum, di-dum, dum. Di-di-dum.

By the time I had finished looking there was only one match left in the box. I put it back in the right place and stepped out into the pale moonlight. As I lowered the hasp I couldn't understand what I had been doing in the shed. I had a bag full of groceries in the car, I was on my way indoors to cook dinner for Robin and me. What was this detour all about?

Annelie used to say that if there was a complicated way of doing things, I would find it. I smiled to myself, hearing her voice inside me as I walked over to the car. When I had put the key in the lock of the boot, I stopped.

I *had* heard her voice, hadn't I? Just recently, somewhere. I looked around as if I was expecting to see her standing next to the car, her hands pushed down in the pockets of that duffel coat she'd found at a flea market.

But I had shoved the duffel coat into a rubbish bag myself. It had been incinerated at some dump, and no Annelie would ever put it on again. I was overwhelmed with a sense of loss so strong and physical that I had to lean on the boot for support to stop myself from falling as my knees gave way. Why is the world constructed in such a way that people can be taken away from one another?

Then I picked up the bag of groceries and went inside to make dinner.

As I was boiling the potatoes for mash and frying the sausages, I could hear Robin mumbling into his headset, along with the roar of futuristic weapons and the groans of vanquished enemies. I wondered what Annelie would have said about it all.

She would probably have come up with a way of limiting the amount of time Robin spent gaming, thought of alternatives. I couldn't do that.

Can two people converse or hang out together when they live on different planets? Here was I, frying sausages and adding nutmeg to my mashed potatoes, while Robin battled against mutants with a flame-thrower. If you looked at it like that, could we ever really meet?

I knocked on Robin's door and told him dinner was ready. He asked for five more minutes to finish off the session. I sat down at the kitchen table with my hands resting on my knee, listening to the sounds of the slaughter. I looked at the dish of steaming mashed potato and felt so unbearably lonely.

Robin emerged after five minutes. As we were eating I asked what kind of a day he'd had in school, and he said 'Good' with no further comment. I asked how the gaming was going and that was good too. Everything was good. The mash grew in my mouth and I felt as if my throat was closing up. I had to make a real effort in order to swallow.

When we'd finished I asked Robin if he fancied a game of Monopoly. He looked at me as if I'd made a bad joke, then disappeared into his room. I tackled the washing up.

I had just put the last plate in the drying rack when I heard those notes again. I listened more carefully, and thought they reminded me of voices. Had I been mistaken the previous evening, during the power cut? Was it in fact the piano I had heard? There was something about the rise and fall of the notes that sounded like voices. Terrified voices.

My arms dropped, but before I disappeared into the same state as before, I got a grip, strode over to Robin's door and pushed it open.

Robin was sitting at the piano with tears pouring down his cheeks. On the music stand I saw a piece of paper, stained and yellowed. The last note he had played died away and he looked at me wide-eyed.

'What are you doing?' I asked. 'What's that you're playing?'

Robin's eyes were drawn to the piece of paper, which flickered as a gust of wind blew in through the half-open window. When I went over to close it I noticed bits of soil on the windowsill. Behind me Robin played a couple more notes and I yelled: 'Stop it! Stop playing!'

He lifted his hands from the keyboard and I slammed the lid shut. Robin jumped and the sharp crash as wood met wood vibrated through my breastbone, through the walls. Robin's eyes met mine. They were the eyes of a child, pure and clear. He whispered: 'I don't want to play, Dad. I don't want to play.'

I sank to my knees and he fell into my arms, still whispering through his tears: 'I don't want to play, Dad. Fix it so I don't have to play any more, Dad.'

Over his shaking shoulders I could see the piece of paper on the music stand. It was covered in hand-written notes. Here and there things had been crossed out and something new added; dark brown patches caused by damp made some of the notes illegible. It must have been written over a fairly long period, because several different writing implements – a pencil, a ballpoint pen, a fountain pen – had been used.

I stroked Robin's head and sat with him until he had calmed

down. Then I took his head between my hands and looked him in the eye. 'Robin, my darling boy. Where did you get that piece of paper?'

His voice was muffled from all the tears and he glanced over at his bed. 'I found it. Behind the wallpaper.'

The wallpaper next to his bed was coming away from the wall and was ripped in a couple of places; Robin had made it worse by lying there picking at it. I nodded in the direction of the torn patch and asked: 'There?'

'Yes. He wrote the notes.'

'Who?'

'The murderer. Can we have some hot chocolate?'

We didn't bother with the pastries as it wasn't long since we'd eaten. As we sat at the table with our cups, Robin's gaze was more open than it had been for months. He looked me in the eye and didn't waver. This was so unusual that I didn't know what to say; in the midst of everything I was just so happy to feel that contact between us. I sat and revelled in it for a while, but eventually we had to talk about what had happened.

'This murderer,' I said. 'Do you know his name?'

Robin shook his head.

'So how do you know he was a murderer, then?'

Robin sat there chewing his lips, as if he were considering whether what he wanted to say was permitted or not. With a glance in the direction of his room he whispered, 'The children told me.'

'Children? What children?'

'The children he murdered.'

This was the point at which I should have said: 'What on earth are you talking about, that's nonsense' or: 'Now you see what happens if you spend too much time playing computer games', but that wasn't what I said because

The dead speak through the notes

because I knew that something was going on in our house that wasn't covered in the *Good Advice for Parents* handbook. Instead I looked at Robin in a way that I hoped would indicate that I was taking him seriously and asked: 'Tell me about these children. How many of them are there?'

'Two. Quite small.'

'What do they look like?'

'Don't know.'

'But you've seen them, haven't you?'

Robin shook his head again and stared down at the table as he said, 'You're not allowed to look at them. If you do, they take your eyes.' He glanced anxiously at his room. 'I don't know if you're allowed to talk about them either.'

'But they talk to you?'

'Mm. Can I sleep in your room tonight?'

'Of course you can. But there's something we're going to do first of all.'

I went into Robin's room and picked up the hand-written sheet of music from the piano. A horrible feeling had settled in my chest after what Robin had said, and as I stood there with the piece of paper in my hand I had the impression that something was radiating from it. I ran my eyes over the messy notes, the damp patches and the creases and I saw that it was *evil*.

As I said, I can't read music, so it must have been something in the way the notes were written, the hand that had guided the pen, the pens. Or perhaps there is a language that transcends the barriers of reason and goes straight in without passing through the intellect.

Whatever the case may be, there was only one sensible thing to do. I took the piece of paper into the kitchen, screwed it up and dropped it in the stove. Robin sat watching from his chair as I struck a match and brought it towards the paper.

I have to admit that my hand was shaking slightly. My sense of the inherent evil in the piece of paper had been so strong that I was afraid something terrible would happen when I set fire to it. But it began to burn just like any other piece of paper. A little yellow flame took hold, flared up, and after ten seconds all that remained were black flakes, torn apart by the draught from the chimney.

I gave a snort of relief and shook my head at my own fantasies. What had I expected – blue flashes, or a demon flying out of the fireplace and running amok in the kitchen? I flung my hands wide like a magician demonstrating that an object really has disappeared.

'There,' I said. 'Now you don't have to play those notes any more.'

I looked at Robin, but the relief I had hoped to see on his face wasn't there. Instead his eyes filled with tears and he tapped his temples with his fingertips as he whispered: 'But I can remember them, Dad. I can *remember* them.'

If there's one expression I can't stand, it's *Every cloud has a silver lining*. Take Annelie's death. I can think until my ears bleed without coming up with a single good thing it has brought us. The atomic bombs that were dropped on Japan? They led to Japan's dominance of the electronics market through a complex pattern of cause and effect, but tell that to those who were blown to bits, wave the stock market prices under the noses of the children mutilated as a result of radiation. Good luck with that.

I'm rambling. What I wanted to say was that for once there was a grain of truth in that ugly expression. Later in the evening Robin and I actually played Monopoly. He didn't want to go back to his room; he preferred to sit beneath the safe circle of the kitchen lamp, moving his little car along the unfamiliar streets of Stockholm.

The wind was whistling around the house and I had lit a fire. The roll of the dice across the board, the soft rustle of well-worn bank notes changing hands, our murmured comments or cries of triumph or disappointment. They were good hours, pleasant hours.

It was half-past ten by the time I found myself bankrupt as a result of Robin's ownership of Centrum and Norrmalmstorg, with the requisite hotels. As we gathered up the plastic pieces and various bits of paper, Robin said with amazement in his voice, 'That was quite good fun!'

I made myself a bed on a mattress on the floor so that Robin could have my bed. I set the alarm for seven as usual and turned off all the lights apart from the lava lamp; I lay there for a long time watching the viscous, billowing shapes until my eyelids began to feel heavy. Then I heard Robin's voice from the bed.

'Dad?'

I sat up, leaning on my elbow so that I could see him. His eyes were open and in the soft, red light he looked like a small child.

'Yes?'

'I don't want to play the piano any more.'

'No. I understand.'

'And I don't want us to keep the piano.'

'Okay. We'll get rid of it then.'

Robin nodded and curled up, closing his eyes. I lay down on my side and looked at my son. For the second time that day the feeling struck me again: things could all work out, in spite of everything. It might all be okay.

The feeling didn't diminish when Robin half-opened his eyes and mumbled sleepily, 'We can play Monopoly or something. Or cards. So I don't spend as much time playing computer games.'

'We certainly can,' I said. 'Now go to sleep.'

Robin muttered something and after a moment his breathing was deeper. I lay there looking at him, listening to the wind and waiting for it to increase in strength and make the aerial sing. It happened just as my consciousness was about to drift away, and a single long note followed me down into sleep.

*

Annelie came to me that night.

If it had been a dream, the setting should have been one of the many places where we had actually slept and made love. But she came to me there on the mattress next to the bed. She crept naked under the narrow spare duvet and one thigh slid over mine as she burrowed her nose in the hollow at the base of my throat.

I could smell the scent of her hair as she whispered, 'Sorry I went away,' and her dry palm caressed my chest. I pulled her close and held her tight. If I had doubted that this was really happening, my doubts dispersed when she said: 'Hey, steady!' because I was squeezing her as hard as I could to prevent her from disappearing again.

'I've missed you so much,' I murmured, moving one arm so that I could stroke her belly, her breasts, her face. It really was Annelie. The particular curve of her hips, the birthmark beneath her left breast, all the tiny details imprinted on my mind. Only now did I understand how intense the actual physical longing for this woman had been, this woman whose skin I knew better than my own.

She moved her fingers over my lips and said, 'I know. I know. But I'm here now.'

One part of my body had been sure ever since her thigh slid over mine. I was so hard I felt as if I might burst. I pressed her body to mine and as I pushed inside her I couldn't tell whether the throbbing beats pulsating through me were mine or hers. I followed their rhythm, and the rhythm turned into notes which became a melody that I recognised, and I couldn't hold back. My body contracted in a convulsion so powerful that I slipped out of her and my seed shot out all over the sheets in a single spasm.

I opened my eyes wide.

I was alone on the mattress. My penis was stiff and I could feel the warm stickiness of my ejaculation, the faint aroma of sperm beneath the covers. But that wasn't all. Annelie's scent still lingered in the room. The shampoo she always used, the moisturiser from the Body Shop perfumed with oranges and cinnamon, the one she called her 'Christmas moisturiser'. Plus the scent of her own body, but I have no words to describe that. They were there in the room. All of them.

I was so preoccupied with trying to drink in that smell and to remain in the moment that it was a long time before I grasped that the notes were real. That they were being played in the house.

I propped myself up on one elbow and saw that the bed was empty. Robin had got up and gone to the piano.

Something moved in my peripheral vision. A faint, swaying movement. Annelie's scent was superseded by another – sweaty feet. Horrible, stinking, sweaty feet. I turned my head slowly to the side and saw a bare foot swinging to and fro next to me. As my gaze travelled upwards I saw that the foot belonged to an equally naked body. A hairy pot belly and flaccid testicles. A head on a broken neck, eyes staring into mine. The hanged man opened his mouth and said:

'Without her . . . nothing. That's true, isn't it? You can get her back. I did. I am happy now.'

I squeezed my eyes tight shut and pressed my wrists against my eyelids so hard that my eyeballs were pushed into my skull and I saw a shower of red stars. I counted to ten, and while I was counting the piano stopped playing. I heard voices coming from Robin's room. And a faint creaking sound.

I opened my eyes. A long, dirty toenail was swaying to and fro centimetres from my face, and from above I heard the gurgling, muffled voice saying, 'The door is open. You just have to—'

A strong impulse made me want to curl up, put my hands over my ears and wait until the madness went away. Perhaps I might even have done it if I hadn't heard Robin. In a tearful voice he suddenly yelled: 'I can't! I can't!'

I rolled off the mattress, away from the visitation above my head. I got to my feet and ran to Robin's room without looking back.

The window was wide-open and the room was freezing cold. Robin was standing by the window dressed only in his underpants, leaning out. When I put my arms around him to pull him inside I saw movement on the lawn outside. Two small, hunched bodies dressed in rags were running erratically towards the forest.

The door is open.

In my despair I pulled too hard and Robin lost his balance. I fell over backwards and he landed on top of me without making a sound.

'Robin? Robin? Are you all right?'

I sat up, holding him in my arms. His expression was distant and he was looking straight through me. I shook him gently.

'Robin? What happened?'

His head moved feebly from side to side, and when I checked him over I saw four long scratches on one forearm, scratches made by fingernails.

I picked him up and carried him into the kitchen. As I approached the door of the living room I let out a sob and held onto him more tightly. I inched forward two steps and peered in through the doorway. Above my mattress and the stained duvet cover there was nothing but an empty hook on the ceiling.

'Robin? It's okay now. They've gone.' It was as if another voice was speaking through my mouth as I added, 'The door is closed.'

Robin didn't respond as I gently laid him down on my bed and tucked him in. His wide-open eyes were staring at the hook. Could he see something I couldn't? The stale smell of sweaty feet still lingered in the room, and had completely obliterated the scent of Annelie. I looked at the hook with loathing. *Couldn't the bastard have showered before he hanged himself?*

'Dad . . .'

I stroked Robin's hair, his cheeks. 'Yes, son?'

'Dad, get rid of it. Get rid of it.'

I nodded and licked my lips. They had a sour taste, like sweaty feet. When I got up from the bed I realised I was still naked. I pulled on my dressing gown, went into the kitchen, rummaged in the drawer where I kept tools for indoor use and dug out a pair of heavy pliers.

The first thing I did was to unscrew the hook from the ceiling. I didn't know if it would help, but I didn't want the accursed thing in the house. When I opened the living room window Robin whispered, 'No, no, don't open it.' I hurled the hook as far as I could, closed the window and said: 'It's fine'.

'Get rid of it, Dad. You have to get rid of it. I can't.'

'What do you mean, son?'

'The piano. Get rid of it. I don't want to.'

I was on the point of saying that it would have to wait until tomorrow because I hadn't the strength to carry or even drag the piano on my own, but then I realised there might be a simpler solution.

When I stood in front of the open lid looking at the keyboard, the notes were playing inside my head. By now I had heard them so many times I knew them by heart. I was able to make out a melody, and what's more, when I looked at the keys it was as if some of them glowed, flashed as the notes passed through my mind. *I can play, if I want to.* My hands were irresistibly drawn towards the piano.

Dum, di-dum, daa.

Just once. Or twice. Or as many times as necessary.

When I placed my right hand on the keyboard to begin playing, there was something in the way. A pair of pliers. I was holding a pair of pliers in my hand. A pair of pliers. I worked the handles and saw the sharp jaws opening and closing. *Bite through it. Snip snip.*

I blinked a couple of times and pushed the notes out of my head, concentrating on the pliers. Then I opened the top of the piano and whispered, 'Sorry, Annelie.'

It took me ten minutes to snip through every single string inside the piano, and when I hit a key to check, the hammer thudded against empty space and the note didn't play. The piano was dead.

Finally I fetched a roll of duct tape and wound it round and round the window catches so that it would be impossible to open them without tools. When I turned away the piano was staring at me; the notes popped into my head and my fingers itched.

I laughed out loud, sat down at the piano and played through the entire melody, but the only sound was the soft, dull thud of the hammers.

'Try that, you bastard,' I said, without any idea of who the bastard in question was.

Robin was still awake when I went back into the living room. When I told him what I'd done he nodded and said, 'But I don't want to sleep in there.'

'You don't have to,' I said, lying down beside him on the narrow bed. 'You can sleep here for as long as you like.'

He reached for my hand and tucked my arm around his chest. I held him and rested my forehead against the back of his head. When five minutes had passed and he still hadn't relaxed, I said: 'Do you want to tell me what happened?'

Robin mumbled something into the pillow, but I couldn't make any sense of it. 'What did you say?'

Robin turned his head a fraction to the side; his voice was so faint that I had to put my ear right next to his mouth in order to pick up the words. 'Those children came. They want me to find them. He killed them.'

I glanced up at the hole in the ceiling and shuddered as I thought about the pale, shapeless face that had been hanging there. Puffy cheeks covered with stubble. I had no doubt whatsoever that it was the murderer I had seen. The murderer who had spoken to me. Bengt Karlsson. *He took it badly.*

'I don't want to do it, Dad.'

'Of course you're not going to do any such thing. How could you?'

'Because they told me. Where they are.'

Bearing in mind the insanity in which my son and I found ourselves, perhaps it won't sound too strange if I say that it was a relief to think that here at least was something to hold onto, something I recognised.

While Annelie was still alive we had watched all the *Emil in Lönneberga* films. Robin had been frightened by Krösa-Maja's talk of mylings, the ghosts of murdered children who have not been given a proper burial.

Mylings. If someone had told me a week ago . . . but never mind. I took it seriously. I accepted that this was what we were dealing with, and so I was relieved that it had a name. Something that has a proper designation can probably be dealt with.

I asked: 'So where are they, then?'

Robin whispered, 'In the forest.'

'Did he bury them in the forest?' Robin shook his head. 'So what did he do?'

Robin carried on shaking his head as he buried his face in the pillow.

I tugged gently at his shoulder. 'Robin? You have to tell me. I don't know what we can do, but . . . you have to tell me. I believe you.'

Suddenly he curled himself into a ball with his bottom sticking up in the air, just like he used to do when he was asleep when he was very small. Then he yelled into the pillow, 'It's so horrible!'

I stroked his back and said: 'I know. I know it's horrible.'

Robin shook his head violently and shouted: 'You haven't a clue how horrible it is!' He was breathing hard through the pillow, in and out, in and out, and his body kept on heaving those deep, convulsive breaths as I helplessly carried on stroking his back.

I was afraid he was actually going over the edge in some way. It would hardly be surprising. I too felt that I was very close to the edge in terms of what my mind could cope with.

Suddenly Robin's body grew still and he rolled over onto his back. In a thin, expressionless but perfectly clear voice he addressed the ceiling: 'The man found a rock. A big rock. He dug a hole next to the rock. Then he tied up the child so that it couldn't move. Then he carried the child to the hole. He had one of those iron bar things. He had it with him so that he could roll the rock down into the hole. On top of the child. But the child's head was sticking out so that the man could listen to the child screaming. And the child screamed because it hurt so much. Lots of bones got broken when the rock rolled on top of the child. The man sat and listened to the child screaming. He sat and listened right up until it died. It might have taken all night. Then he dug a little more and moved the rock so that the child disappeared.'

When Robin had uttered the final words he pulled the covers over his head and rolled himself into a secure cocoon. I lay there beside him with his story crawling around inside my head like a mutilated child.

His bed used to be where mine is now.

The man who had done these things had slept in Robin's room. How had he been able to sleep? He had made his coffee on our stove and drunk it in our kitchen. He had looked out of the same windows as us, walked on the same floors, heard the same creaking floorboard just inside the door. And he had hanged himself next to my bed.

My eyes were drawn to the dark spot on the ceiling where the hook had been.

I am happy now.

*

I lay there looking at the black hole for so long that it started to take on the qualities of its astronomical namesake. Everything in the room was being drawn towards it, waiting to be sucked in; my thoughts moved around it like defenceless planets, orbiting in ever-decreasing circles on their way to destruction. And all the time I could hear the music. Round and round the music went, twelve notes in an incomplete melody.

Incomplete?

If you hum: 'Baa baa black sheep, have you any wool, Yes sir, yes sir, three—' and stop there, then you know some notes are missing, even if you've never heard the tune before. It was equally clear to me that notes were missing from the melody which was now so much a part of me that I couldn't get it out of my head. I lay in bed staring at the hole and trying to catch hold of the missing notes.

The pile of bedding next to me had started to move up and down with deep, regular breaths, and I managed to free Robin's sweaty head without waking him up before tucking him in properly. Then I got up and put my clothes on, barely aware of what I was doing, because the notes absorbed all of my attention.

Dum, di-dum, daa.

I sat down at the piano and played the entire melody. The notes were so clear to my inner ear that I had played it twice before I realised there was no sound. I banged a couple of the notes really hard as if violence was the way to entice them out. It was only then I remembered. The pliers. The strings.

I looked around the room, unsure what to do, and I caught sight of the box under Robin's bed. Among cast-off cuddly toys and plastic figures I found the Casio toy synthesiser. It covered only three octaves, but that was enough.

I played the twelve notes, and a dark serenity came over me. Yes, dark serenity. I can't find a better way to express it. It was like getting stuck in the mud and slowly sinking. The moment when you realise it's pointless to struggle, that there is no help to be had, and that the mud is going to win. I imagine you reach a point when you give up, and that this brings with it a certain serenity.

Over and over again I played the twelve notes, trying out different instruments in the synthesiser's repertoire to make them sound good; in the end I settled for 'harpsichord'. I think it's called *cembalo* in Swedish, and the imitation of its metallic tone was quite convincing.

Dum, di-dum, daa . . .

I went into the hallway, put on my jacket, found the head-torch, switched it on and fastened it around my head. The synthesiser had a strap, which meant I could hang it around my neck. Fully equipped, I opened the front door and set out for the forest.

A mist hung in the air, and although the head-torch was powerful, the light reached no further than about ten metres. As I set off among the damp tree trunks it was like walking through an underground vault where the trunks were pillars, carrying their crowns like a single, immense roof. There wasn't a sound apart from the soft rustle as drops of water fell from the branches onto last year's dead grass.

I hadn't played for several minutes, and the blind determination that had driven me on had begun to falter when I reached the place.

This had to be the spot. I had walked in a straight line from the house; I might even have followed an overgrown path, come to think of it. On the way I had passed the odd rock, but none of them would have been suitable for the purpose Robin had described.

In front of me lay a number of large rocks which sprang up out of the darkness when the beam of the head-torch swept over them. When I examined the area more closely I found something in the region of fifty large and small erratic blocks strewn by the inland ice across the ground where pines and fir trees would one day grow. Even without the knowledge I possessed, it didn't take much imagination to compare this place with a graveyard.

With two inhabitants. Two children. Beneath the rocks.

I wandered around aimlessly, directing the beam of the torch at the base of the rocks in the hope of finding some sign that the ground had been disturbed. But everything was overgrown, and every rock looked the same as every other rock. I wrapped my arms around my body and shivered.

What was to say that there weren't dead people, dead children under every single rock? What was to say things would be better if I found the two who had sought out Robin to ask for help, to ask him to find them?

We have to move away from here!

The idea was so obvious I couldn't understand why I hadn't thought of it before. There was nothing to tie me or my son to this haunted place, with its gloomy coniferous forest and its brooding rocks. Nothing. It wasn't my responsibility to drive away the ghosts of evil deeds committed in the past.

I breathed out and switched off the head-torch, closed my eyes and listened to the silence, relaxed. When I had been standing like that for a little while, a faint awareness came over me. It grew into a certainty: diagonally in front of me to the left. Something was drifting towards me from that direction, faint as the draught caused by a fly's wings against the skin, and blacker than the night. When I opened my eyes it was gone.

The darkness felt almost solid, and the only light came from the diode indicating that the toy synthesiser around my neck was on. I switched on the torch and studied the keyboard. Then I played a note. Then another. The twelve notes echoed from the plastic speakers and were swallowed up by the darkness and the mist. I edged forward a few steps and played the melody again.

Something moved in front of me and I glimpsed a figure disappearing behind a rock. I went over and leaned my back against the rough surface, then crouched down and played the melody once more. When I took my fingers off the keys I could hear scrabbling, the sound of small feet flitting across the moss and needles on the other side of the rock.

You're not allowed to look at them. If you do, they take your eyes.

I directed the beam of the head-torch at the trunk of a fir tree five metres in front of me and spoke out into the air: 'I am here now.'

Feet moved across the ground, rustling, squelching as they came closer. Nails scraped down the rock just a metre or so away, and I closed my eyes so that I wouldn't be tempted to look over my shoulder. Then I said it again: 'I am here now. What shall I do?'

At first I thought it was a noise originating from the forest. A broken branch creaking in a gust of wind, or the distant cry of an injured animal. But it was a voice. The faint, mournful voice of an unhappy old man who has lost everything but his memories, who cries at the sight of semolina pudding because it reminds him of his childhood and makes him talk in the voice of a child:

'Find us,' said the voice behind my shoulder.

Without opening my eyes I replied, 'I have found you. What shall I do now?'

'Fetch us.'

I had somehow known that this was my task right from the start, from the moment I stood in front of the spade and crowbar in the tool shed. To find, to fetch, to . . . *conclude.*

'Why?' I whispered. 'Why did he do this to you?'

The only response was the slow breathing of the forest. I pressed my back against the stone, suddenly conscious of its terrible weight and solidity. To have that weight on top of you, to be slowly crushed to pieces beneath its impervious hardness. To be a child.

When the voice spoke again the tone had changed; perhaps it

wasn't the same voice. Cutting through the old man's growl there was something that told me this was a younger child.

'The old man had a piece of paper,' said the voice. 'He was writing.'

'What do you mean, writing?' I asked. 'When?'

'When I was dying. I screamed. Because it hurt so much. Then he wrote on the piece of paper. He said I would scream a lot. And I screamed. Because it hurt so much.'

The voice was faint as it uttered the final words, and I felt the presence behind me disappear. I bent my head so that the beam of the torch shone on the keyboard. Thirty-six innocent pieces of black and white plastic. Now I understood how I had mistaken the notes for terrified voices.

Bengt Karlsson, the musician who *took it badly*, had made musical notes out of the most horrific sound imaginable, the tortured screams of a dying child. And these notes . . . opened the door.

How can a person bear it?

I struggled to my feet and pressed my knuckles against my temples as I staggered among the rocks. How can a person bear it? The dampness, the mist, the dark tree trunks, the evil contained within the very warp and weft of existence. How? I watched myself strike the rough surface of a rock with the palms of my hands until the blood flowed.

The pain woke me up. I gazed at my bleeding hands. Then I glanced up. All the rocks looked the same, and I no longer knew where the dead children were.

When I played the first note on the synthesiser, my finger left a dark streak on the white plastic. By the time I had played the whole melody, the keys were soiled with blood and a few of them resisted when I pressed them. Soon it would be impossible to play.

I found the button that said REC and pushed it down, then I played the whole melody again and pressed REC STOP. Then PLAY.

I laughed out loud as the toy synthesiser carried on playing the melody all by itself, over and over again.

Dum, di-dum, daa . . .

I slipped the instrument round to the side so that I was comfortable, and it went on playing the melody as I set off for home and the tool shed.

A dirty grey dawn had found its tentative way among the tree trunks by the time my work was finished. The blood from my hands had been absorbed by the spade's wooden handle, spread itself over the dark iron of the crowbar. The synthesiser's batteries were running out, and the sound of the melody was growing ever fainter as I walked back from the forest, opened the front door and went into the hallway.

I picked up the duct tape which was still lying on the piano. The notes from the synthesiser were now so weak that they were drowned out by the creaking of the kitchen floor as I crossed the threshold. But the incomplete melody playing inside my head was all the stronger, and I noticed without surprise that Bengt Karlsson was sitting at the kitchen table with his hands neatly folded on top of one another.

The black line around his neck became visible when he nodded to me, and I nodded back in mutual understanding. We were men who knew what must be done. He had been unable to bear it. Now it was time for me to take over.

Robin didn't wake up until I had secured his hands behind his back with the tape, and I placed a strip over his mouth before he had time to start yelling. I would have to remove it later, of course, but at the moment it would be troublesome to have him screaming. I held his legs firmly so that I could secure his ankles, then slipped my arm beneath the back of his knees and heaved him up over my shoulder.

The melody continued to play as I carried him through the kitchen, softly, softly as a whisper it played, and I hummed along. My body was aching with a feverish longing for the missing notes, desperate to hear the completed melody.

Robin twisted and turned over my shoulder, and his underpants rubbed against my ear as I carried him across the lawn. The skin on his bare legs turned to gooseflesh in the chill of the winter dawn. I could hear him panting and snuffling behind my back as snot spurted out of his nose, and from the muffled sounds he was making I guessed that he was crying. It didn't matter. Soon it would be over. Concluded.

The pale light of dawn made the tree trunks step forward out of the mist like dark silhouettes, a silently observing group of spectators with no knowledge of right or wrong, good or evil. Only the blind laws of nature and the circle of life and death, life and death. And the door between them.

I laid Robin down in the hollow I had dug next to a rock. I no longer knew whether the music I could hear existed only inside my head. Robin twitched and jerked, his fair skin in sharp contrast to the dark earth. His head moved from side to side and his eyes were wide open as he tried to scream through the duct tape.

'Hush,' I said. 'Hush . . .'

I ripped off the gag, and without paying attention to his pleading sobs I concentrated on the crowbar which I had driven into the ground on the other side of the rock. I calculated that it would take just one decent push forwards to make the rock tip over into the hollow. I rubbed my hands, which were covered in flakes of coagulated blood, and set to work.

As I grabbed hold of the crowbar I was aware of a movement out of the corner of my eye. Instinctively I looked over and saw a child. Its age was difficult to determine, because the face was so sunken that the cheekbones stood out. It was dressed in the remains of silky red pyjamas patterned with yellow teddy bears, and its chest was visible through the torn material. A number of ribs were crushed, and sharp fragments of bone had pierced the skin in several places.

The child raised its hands to its face. The nails were long and broken from scratching at rocks. And behind the fingers, the eyes. I looked into those eyes and they were not eyes at all, but black wells of hatred and pain.

Only then did I realise what I had done.

Before I had time to close my eyes or grab hold of the crowbar again, another small body hurled itself onto my back. I bent over and the child in pyjamas leapt up and seized me around the neck, burying its fingers just above my shoulder blades.

The body on my back ran its hands over my forehead, and then I felt jagged nails moving over my eyelids. I screamed as the sharp edges penetrated the skin on either side of the top of my nose, and blood ran down into my mouth. The child let out a single sharp hiss, then jerked its hands outwards.

Both my eyeballs were ripped out of my skull, and the last thing I heard before I lost consciousness was the viscous, moist sound of the optical nerves tearing, then a grunting, smacking noise as the children chewed on my eyes.

I don't know how long I was out. When I came round I could no longer see any light, and I had no idea of the sun's progress across the sky. There were empty holes in my head where my eyes had been, and my cheeks were sticky with the remains of my eyelids and optical nerves. The pain was like a series of nails being hammered into my face.

I pulled myself up onto my knees. Total darkness. And silence. The synthesiser's batteries had given up. I fumbled around and found the crowbar, traced the surface of the rock until I reached the edge of the hollow, and was rewarded with the only sound that was of any importance now.

'Dad . . . Dad . . .'

I crawled down to Robin. I bit through the tape around his wrists and ankles. I tore off my jacket and shirt and wrapped them around him. I wept without being able to shed any tears, and I fumbled in the darkness until he took my hand and led me back to the house.

Then he made a call. I couldn't use the phone, and had forgotten every number. I was frightened when he spoke to someone whose voice I couldn't hear. I groped my way to bed and sought refuge beneath the covers. That's where they found me.

They say I'm on the road to recovery. I will never regain my sight, but my sanity has begun to return. They say I will be allowed out of here. That I will learn to adapt.

Robin comes to see me less and less often. He says he's happy with his foster family. He says they're nice. He says he doesn't spend so much time playing games these days. He's stopped talking about how things will be when I get out.

And I don't think I will get out, because I don't want to leave.

Food at fixed times and a bed that is made every day. I move blindly through the stations of each day. I have my routines, and the days pass. No, I shouldn't be let out.

Because when I sit in the silence of my room or lie in my bed at night, I can hear the notes. My fingers extend in empty space, moving over an invisible keyboard, and I dream of playing.

Of replaying everything. Getting Annelie to visit me again and embracing her in the darkness, paying no heed to which doors are open or what might emerge through them.

There are no musical instruments in the unit.

JOHN AJVIDE LINDQVIST was born 1968 and is probably the only Swedish person who makes his living from writing horror. His first novel, *Let the Right One In*, has sold over half a million copies in a country with nine million inhabitants. The book has been published in thirty countries and been made into two movies, one Swedish and one American (under the title *Let Me In*).

His other novels include *Handling the Undead* and *Harbour*, both of which are in the process of being turned into films. His most recent book, *Little Star*, was recently published by Quercus.

The following novella is the author's first story written specifically for an English-language market and, as Lindqvist explains: 'The idea for "The Music of Bengt Karlsson, Murderer" came to me four years ago, when my son was ten years old and started taking piano lessons.

'The disjointed, unharmonic notes coming from his room gave me the thought, *What if he would accidentally hit on a series of notes that . . . summoned something?* I wrote down the idea and waited for that critical second idea that could turn it into a story. It never came by itself, so the original idea just lay slumbering in that special file on my computer.

'When the editor asked me for a contribution to this anthology, I opened the file, shook life into the notes-that-summon-idea and examined it more closely. Originally I had a vague plan of some Cthulhuesque monster being attracted by the music, but that didn't work out. Then the idea of a father and son being alone and isolated clicked together with the image of *mylingar*, the ghosts of murdered children . . . and the rest was the usual sweat and tears to forge those images into a story.

'It might be the one story I have written that has scared me the most. It plays deeply on my own fears of losing all I love. Especially towards the end, I wrote on in a state of mild but constant horror.

'It was a relief when it was over.'

Getting it Wrong

—RAMSEY CAMPBELL—

EDGEWORTH WAS LISTENING to a reminiscence of the bus ride in Hitchcock's *Lucky Jim* when the phone rang. He switched off the deluxe anniversary special collector's edition of *Family Plot* and raised the back of his armchair to vertical. As he grabbed the receiver he saw the time on his watch jerk even closer to midnight. 'Hello?' he said and in less than a second 'Hello?'

'Is this Mr Edgeworth?'

He didn't recognise the woman's voice, not that he knew any women he could imagine ringing him. 'That's who you've got,' he said.

'Mr Eric Edgeworth?'

'You're not wrong yet.'

'Have you a few minutes, Mr Edgeworth?'

'I don't want anybody fixing my computer. I haven't had an accident at work or anywhere else either. I'm not buying anything and I'm not going to tell you where I shop or what I shop for. My politics are my affair and so's the rest of what I think right now. I've never won a competition, so don't bother saying I have. I don't go on holiday abroad, so you needn't try to sell me anything over there. I don't go away here either, not that it's any of your business. Anything else you want to know?'

'That isn't why we're calling, Mr Edgeworth.' In the same brisk efficient tone she said 'Will you be a friend of Mary Barton?'

At first Edgeworth couldn't place the name, and then it brought him an image from work – a woman heaping cardboard tubs of popcorn while she kept up a smile no doubt designed to look bright but more symptomatic of bravery. 'I wouldn't go that far,' he said, although the call had engaged his interest now: it might be the police. 'Is she in trouble?'

'She's in inquisition.' This might well have meant yes until the woman added 'She'd like you to be her expert friend.'

'Never heard of it.' Having deduced that they were talking about a quiz show, Edgeworth said 'Why me?'

'She says she's never met anyone who knows so much about films.'

'I don't suppose she has at that.' All the same, he was growing suspicious. Could this be a joke played by some of his workmates? 'When's she going to want me?' Edgeworth said.

'Immediately, if you're agreeable.'

'Pretty late for a quiz, isn't it?'

'It's not a show for children, Mr Edgeworth.'

'Aren't I supposed to be asked first?'

'We're doing that now.'

If all this was indeed a joke, he'd turn it on them. 'Fair enough, put her on,' he said as he stood up, retrieving his dinner container and its equally plastic fork from beside the chair.

'Please stay on the line.'

As Edgeworth used his elbow to switch on the light in the boxy kitchen off the main room of the apartment, a man spoke in his ear. 'Eric? Good to have you on. Terry Rice of *Inquisition* here.'

He sounded smug and amused, and Edgeworth had no doubt he was a fake. The kitchen bin released a stagnant tang of last night's Chinese takeaway while Edgeworth shoved the new container down hard enough to splinter it and snap the fork in half. 'Mary's hoping you'll give her an edge,' the man said. 'Do you know the rules?'

'Remind me.'

'There's only one you should bother about. You're allowed to get three answers wrong.'

'If we're talking about films I'm not bothered at all.'

'You don't need any more from me, then. Mary, talk to your friend.'

'Eric? I'm sorry to trouble you like this so late. I couldn't think of anybody else.'

That was a laugh when she'd hardly ever spoken to him. It was the first time she'd even used his name, at least to him. From her tone he could tell she was wearing her plucky smile. 'What channel are you on?' he said.

He was hoping to throw her, but she barely hesitated. 'Night Owl.'

The hoaxers must have thought this up in advance. Edgeworth would have asked how he could watch the channel, but he didn't want to end the game too soon. He'd begun to enjoy pretending to be fooled, and so he said 'What have you brought me on for?'

'Because I don't know what a film is.'

He thought this was true of just about all his workmates – a good film, at any rate. He'd imagined a job in a cinema would mean working with people who loved films as much as he did. Had she tried to put a tremble in her voice just now? She'd got that wrong; contestants on quiz shows weren't supposed to sound like that. 'Give me a go, then,' he said.

'What's the film where James Dean has a milkshake?'

Edgeworth waited, but that was all. She ought to be telling him how little time he had, and shouldn't there be some kind of urgent music? '*East of Eden*,' he said.

'That's a twist,' said whoever was calling himself Terry Rice.

'Mr Rice is saying you're not right, Eric.'

It was a funny way of saying so, even by the standards of a prank. Perhaps that was why she sounded nervous. 'Then it'll be *Rebel without a Cause*,' Edgeworth said with a grin but no mirth.

'That's another.'

'Mr Rice says that's not right either.'

She sounded close to desperation. However far they took the pretence, Edgeworth could go further. 'It's *Giant* for sure, then,' he said. 'They're the only films he starred in.'

'That's one more.'

Did Edgeworth hear a faint suppressed shriek? Perhaps one of Mary Barton's accomplices had poked her to prompt her to speak. 'That can't be right, Eric,' she said high enough to irritate his ear.

'Give up,' the supposed quizmaster said or asked, though Edgeworth wasn't sure who was being addressed. 'Eric can't have heard of *Has Anybody Seen My Gal?*'

'Of course I have. I've seen it. James Dean has a milkshake at the soda fountain.' In case this failed to restore his own reputation Edgeworth added 'I knew it was the answer.'

'Were you fancying a bit of fun? You should play seriously even if you think it's just a game.' To Edgeworth's disbelief, this sounded like a rebuke. 'I expect your friend has something to say about it,' the man said.

'She's not my friend and none of you are.' Edgeworth confined himself to mouthing this, if only to hear what comment she would have to manufacture. He heard her draw an unsteady breath and say 'Thanks for coming on, Eric. I wish—'

'No point in wishing here. You know that isn't how we play. Thank you for entering into the spirit, Eric,' the man said and, along with Mary and the girl who'd called, was gone.

Surely his last words contradicted his rebuke, which had to mean he couldn't even keep the hoax up. Of course the number he'd called from had been withheld. It was too late for Edgeworth to go back to the commentary on the disc, and he returned the film to the shelf before tramping to the bathroom and then to bed.

With all his films he didn't need to dream. In the morning he ate off a tray in front of *Third Time Sucky*, a Stooges short just the right length for breakfast. 'I wish I knew what to wish for.' 'I wish I had one of your wishes.' 'I wish you two would shut up,' Moe retorted, the effects of which made Edgeworth splutter a mouthful of Sticky Rotters over his dressing-gown. He showered and donned his uniform, which said Frugotomovies on the sweater, and headed for the Frugoplex.

The cinema was an extensive concrete block that resembled the one where he lived. The February sky was just as flat and white. He'd chosen the apartment because he could walk to the cinema, but there were increasingly fewer new films that he wanted to watch; he hardly used his free pass any more. At least he didn't have to enthuse about them to the public. He was gazing with disfavour at the titles outside when the manager let him in. 'Any problem?' Mr Gittins said, and his plump smooth face displayed a smile too swift and sketchy to be identified as such. 'I hope you can leave it at home.'

Rather than retort that some of his workmates were to blame, Edgeworth made for the anonymous concrete staffroom. Soon the rest of the staff began to show up, some of them not far from late. Without exception they were decades younger than he was. As he took his place behind a ticket desk Larry Rivers came over. 'What were you watching last night, Eric?' Larry said with a grin as scrawny as his face.

Had he called himself Terry Rice last night? His name was similar, and he liked quizzing Edgeworth, who said 'I was listening.'

'What were you listening to, Eric?'

He was using the name like a quizmaster. Edgeworth was tempted to confront him, but perhaps that was exactly what he and the rest of them wanted. 'The man who wrote *North by Northwest*,' Edgeworth said.

'Don't know it. Is it a film?'

Edgeworth suspected this wasn't even meant as a joke. 'Cary Grant,' he said. 'James Mason.'

'Don't know them either.'

'Hitch, for heaven's sake.'

'Is that the film with Will Smith?' one of the girls seemed to feel it would be helpful to suggest.

'Hitchcock, love.'

'Sounds a bit mucky to me.'

'Sounds a bit like sexual harassment,' another girl warned Edgeworth.

'Alfred Hitchcock,' he said in desperation. '*Psycho*.'

'Was that the one with Vince Vaughn?' Larry said.

Did they all think the past – anything older than them – was a joke? No wonder Timeless Video had failed when there were so many people like them. Edgeworth had lost all the money he'd sunk in the video library, which was why he'd been glad of the job at the Frugoplex. Some old things wouldn't go away, not least him. He was about to say at least some of this when Mr Gittins opened the door once again. 'Only just in time,' he said like a head teacher at a school gate.

Mary Barton ducked as if her apologetic smile had dragged her head down. Did she glance at Edgeworth or just towards all the staff around the ticket counter? She seemed wary of being seen to look. She hurried to the staffroom and scampered back to the lobby as Mr Gittins addressed the staff. 'Let's keep the public happy and coming back for more.'

Edgeworth might have wished to be a projectionist if the job wouldn't have involved watching too many films that bored him if not worse. He was reduced to noticing which film attracted the most customers, a dispiriting observation. Today it was the latest 3-D film, *Get Outta My Face*. Whenever there was a lull he watched Mary Barton at the refreshments counter opposite. Had her left little finger been bandaged yesterday? It looked significantly bigger than its twin. Her smile was if possible braver than ever, especially if she caught him watching, though then he stared at her until her eyes flinched aside. At times he thought her thin prematurely lined face was trying to look even older than it was, almost as old as him. He wasn't going to accuse her and give everyone a chance to scoff at him; he wouldn't put it past them to accuse him of harassing her. Instead he made sure she never had an opportunity to speak to him away from the public – she clearly didn't have the courage or the gall to approach him in front of anyone who wasn't privy to last night's witless joke.

When he left for home she was besieged by a queue, but as she filled a popcorn tub that she was holding gingerly with her left hand she sent him an apologetic look. If they'd been alone it might well have goaded him to respond. He had to be content with stalking next door to Pieca Pizza, where he bought a Massive Mighty Meat that would do for tomorrow's dinner as well.

He downed two slices in the kitchen and took another three into the main room, one for each version of *Touch of Evil*. He was halfway through Orson Welles' preferred cut when the phone rang. He paused the manic gangling hotel clerk and prepared to say a very few short words to the uninvited caller. 'It's that time again, Eric,' said a voice he could hardly believe he was hearing.

'My God, you're worse than a joke.' Edgeworth almost cut him off, but he wanted to learn how long they could keep up the pretence. 'Can't you even get your own rules right?' he jeered.

'Which rules are those, Eric?'

'Three mistakes and I was supposed to be out of your game.'

'You haven't quite got it, my friend. Last night was just one question you couldn't answer.'

'Trust me, I could. I was having a laugh just like you.'

'Please don't, Eric.'

Mary Barton sounded so apologetic it was painful, which he

hoped it was for her. He could almost have thought she'd been forced against her will to participate in the hoax, but any sympathy he might have felt she lost by adding 'Don't make any more mistakes. It's serious.'

'He sounds it.'

'We get this problem sometimes.' The man's amusement was still plain. 'Listen to your friend,' he said. 'See how she sounds.'

'I'm truly sorry to be pestering you again, Eric. Hand on heart, you're my only hope.'

Edgeworth didn't know which of them angered him more. Her pathetic attempt to convince him she was desperate made her sound as though she was trying to suppress the emotion, and he was provoked to demand 'Where are you on the television? I want to watch.'

'We're on the radio.' With a giggle all the more unpleasant because it had to be affected the man said 'You wouldn't want to, trust me.'

Edgeworth agreed, having left out the comma. What radio show would have inflicted this kind of conversation on its audience? All that interested him now, though not much, was learning what question they'd come up with this time. They must have been reading a film guide to have thought of last night's. 'Go on then, Mr Terry Rice,' he said, baring his teeth in a substitute for a grin. 'Terrorise me again.'

'Do your best, Mary.'

'What's the Alfred Hitchcock film where you see him miss a bus?'

Someone stupider than Edgeworth might have imagined she was pleading with him. Did they genuinely expect him not to realise they were mocking what he'd said today to Larry Rivers? '*Strangers on a Train*,' he said at once.

'Have a closer look.'

He didn't know if this was meant for him or the Barton woman, but her voice grew shrill and not entirely firm. 'Not that one, Eric.'

'Must have been *The Birds*, then.'

'Closer.'

'Please, Eric,' Mary Barton blurted, and he was disgusted to hear her attempting to sound close to tears. 'You must know. It's your kind of thing.'

'I know,' Edgeworth said with a vicious grin. 'I'll give it to you. *Rope.*'

'Not close enough yet.'

'Please!'

Edgeworth jerked the receiver away from his aching ear. 'What are you supposed to be doing?'

'It's my eye.'

Was he also meant to hear a stifled sob? 'That's what my grandma used to say,' he retorted. 'She'd say it to anyone talking rubbish.' Nevertheless he wasn't going to seem ignorant. 'Here's your answer since you're making such a fuss about it, as if you didn't know. It's—'

'Too late, Eric,' the man said without concealing his delight. 'You've had your second chance.'

'Please . . .'

Edgeworth could only just hear Mary Barton's voice, as if it was no longer directed at him. He was right to hold the phone at arm's length to protect his eardrum from any surprises they had in mind, because he heard a shrill metallic sound before the line went dead. It was ridiculous even to think of searching the airwaves for Night Owl. He did his best to pick up the Welles film where he'd left off, but the twitching maniac in charge of the motel disturbed him more than he liked. He put the film back in its place among the dozens of Ts before tramping angrily to bed.

He lurched awake so often, imagining he'd heard the phone, that not just his eyes were prickly with irritation by the time he had to get up for work. He was going to let Mary Barton know he'd had more than enough, and he wouldn't give the rest of them the chance to enjoy the show. 'Eager to get going?' the manager said by way of greeting.

'I'm eager all right,' Eric said and grinned as well.

He clocked on and hurried to the ticket counter, hoping Mary Barton would be first to arrive so that he could follow her to the staffroom. She'd been warned yesterday about timekeeping, after all. He watched the manager let in their workmates and grew more frustrated every time the newcomer wasn't her. Larry Rivers was among the last to join Edgeworth at the counter. 'What were you up to last night, Eric?' he said.

Edgeworth almost turned on him, but he could play too. 'Nothing you've ever seemed interested in.'

Somebody more gullible than Edgeworth might have thought the fellow felt rebuffed. No doubt he was disappointed that Edgeworth hadn't taken the bait, and some of their audience looked as if they were. There was still no sign of Mary Barton by opening time. 'Meet the public with a smile,' Mr Gittins said.

Perhaps the woman had stayed home because she was too embarrassed to face Edgeworth, unless it was her day off. 'Isn't Mary Barton coming in?' he said before he knew he meant to.

'She's called in sick.' Mr Gittins seemed surprised if not disapproving that Edgeworth felt entitled to ask. As he made for the doors he added 'Some trouble with her eye.'

Edgeworth struggled to think of a question. 'She'll have had it for a while, won't she?'

'She's never said so.' Mr Gittins stopped short of the doors to say 'Her mother hasn't either.'

'What's she got to do with anything?'

'She's looking after Mary's children while Mary's at the hospital. Happy now, Eric? Then I hope we can crack on with the job.'

As Mr Gittins let the public in, one of the girls alongside Edgeworth murmured 'You'll have to send her a Valentine, Eric. She isn't married any longer.'

'Keep your gossiping tongues to yourselves.' He glared at her and her friends who'd giggled, and then past them at Rivers. 'I'm putting you on your honour,' he said as his grandmother often had. 'You and your friends have been ringing me up at night, haven't you?'

'What?' Once Rivers finished the laugh that underlined the word he said 'We get more of you here than we want as it is, Eric.'

After that nobody except the public spoke to Edgeworth, and he couldn't even interest himself in which films they were unwise enough to pay for. Of course there was no reason to believe Rivers was as ignorant as he'd pretended – not about the late-night calls, at any rate. Edgeworth felt as if the long slow uneventful day were a curtain that would soon be raised on a performance he had no appetite for. At last he was able to leave behind everyone's contemptuous amusement, which felt like a threat of worse to come. When he shut himself in his apartment he found that he hoped he was waiting for nothing at all.

The pizza tasted stale and stodgy, an unsuccessful attempt to live up to itself. He tried watching classic comedies, but even his favourites seemed unbearably forced, like jokes cracked in the midst of a disaster or anticipating one. They hardly even passed the time, never mind distracting him from it. He was gazing in undefined dismay at the collapse of a dinosaur skeleton under Cary Grant and Katherine Hepburn when the phone went off like an alarm.

He killed the film and stared at the blank screen while the phone rang and rang again. He left it unanswered until a surge of irrational guilt made him grab it. 'What is it now?' he demanded.

'Someone was scared you weren't playing any more, Eric.'

'I thought your friend was meant to be in hospital,' Edgeworth said in triumph.

'She's your friend, Eric, only yours. You're the only one she can turn to about films.'

'Can't she even speak for herself now?'

'I'm here, Eric.' Mary Barton's voice had lost some strength or was designed to sound as feeble as the prank. 'They've fixed me up for now,' she said. 'I had to come back tonight or I'd have lost everything.'

'Trying to make a bit extra for your children, are you?'

'I'm trying to win as much as we need.'

Was she too preoccupied to notice his sarcasm, or wouldn't that fit in with her game? Could she really be so heartless that she would use her children to prolong a spiteful joke? His grandmother never would have – not even his mother, though she'd had plenty to say about any of Edgeworth's shortcomings that reminded her of his unidentified father. 'Ready to help?' the man with Mary Barton said.

'What will you do if I don't?'

Edgeworth heard a suppressed moan that must be meant to sound as terrified as pained. 'Up to you if you want to find out,' the man said.

'Go on then, do your worst.' At once Edgeworth was overtaken by more panic than he understood. 'I mean,' he said hastily, 'ask me about films.'

'Be careful, Mary. See he understands.'

The man seemed more amused than ever. Did he plan to ask about some detail in the kind of recent film they knew Edgeworth never watched? Edgeworth was ready with a furious rejoinder by the time Mary Barton faltered 'Which was the film where Elisha Cook played a gangster?'

There were three possibilities; that was the trick. If she and Rivers hoped to make Edgeworth nervous of giving the wrong answer, they had no chance. '*The Maltese Falcon,*' he said.

'Wider, Mary.'

'That's not right, Eric.'

Her voice had grown shriller and shakier too, and Edgeworth was enraged to find this disturbed him. 'He was a gangster in that,' he objected.

'It isn't what they want.'

'Then I expect they're thinking of *The Killing*.'

'Wider again,' the man said as if he could hardly bear to put off the end of the joke.

'No, Eric, no.'

It occurred to Edgeworth that the actor had played a criminal rather than a gangster in the Kubrick film. The piercing harshness of the woman's ragged voice made it hard for him to think. 'Just one left, eh?' he said.

'Please, Eric. Please be right this time.'

She might almost have been praying. Far from winning Edgeworth over, it embarrassed him, but he wasn't going to give a wrong answer. 'No question,' he said. 'It's *Baby Face Nelson*.'

'Wider still.'

'What are you playing at?' Edgeworth protested. 'He was a gangster in that.'

'No, it was his son,' the man said. 'It was Elisha Cook Junior.'

'That's what you've been working up to all along, is it?' Edgeworth wiped his mouth, having inadvertently spat with rage. 'What a stupid trick,' he said, 'even for you.' He would have added a great deal if Mary Barton hadn't cried 'No.'

It was scarcely a word. It went on for some time with interruptions and rose considerably higher. Before it had to pause for breath Edgeworth shouted 'What are you doing?'

'It's a good thing we aren't on television.' By the sound of it, the man had moved the phone away from her. 'We couldn't show it,' he said gleefully, 'and I don't think you'd want to see.'

'Stop it,' Edgeworth yelled but failed to drown out the cry.

'Relax, Eric. That's all for you for now,' Terry Rice said and left silence aching in Edgeworth's ear.

The number was withheld again. Edgeworth thought of calling the police, but what could that achieve? Perhaps it would just prove he'd fallen for a joke after all. Perhaps everything had been recorded for his workmates to hear. He grabbed the remote control and set about searching the audio channels on the television. He thought he'd scanned through every available radio station, since the identifications on the screen had run out, when a voice he very much wished he couldn't recognise came out of the blank monitor. 'This is Night Owl signing off,' Terry Rice said, and Edgeworth thought he heard a muffled sobbing. 'Another night, another game.'

Edgeworth gazed at the silent screen until he seemed to glimpse a vague pale movement like a frantic attempt to escape. He turned off the set, nearly breaking the switch in his haste, and sought refuge in bed. Very occasionally his thoughts grew so exhausted that they almost let him doze. He did without breakfast – he couldn't have borne to watch a film. Once the shower had made him as clean as he had any chance of feeling he dressed and hurried to work.

He had to ring the bell twice at length to bring Mr Gittins out of his office. The manager's plump smooth face set not much less hard than marble as he saw Edgeworth. He was plainly unimpressed by Edgeworth's timeliness; perhaps he thought it was a ruse to gain his favour. 'I hope you'll be doing your best to get on with your colleagues,' he said.

'Why, who's said what?'

Mr Gittins didn't deign to answer. He was turning away until Edgeworth blurted 'Do we know if Mary Barton's coming in today?'

'What concern is it of yours?' Having gazed at Edgeworth, Mr Gittins said 'She won't be in for some time. I'm told she can't walk.'

Edgeworth swallowed, but his voice still emerged as a croak. 'Do we know why?'

'It really isn't something I'm prepared to discuss further.'

Mr Gittins looked disgusted by Edgeworth's interest and whatever it revived in his mind. Edgeworth gave him a grimace that felt nothing like apologetic and dashed to the staffroom. For once the list of staff and their phone numbers on the notice board was of some use. He keyed Mary Barton's number on his mobile and made the call before he had time to grow any more fearful. Well ahead of any preparation he could make for it a woman's tightened weary voice said 'Hello, yes?'

'I'm one of Mary's friends at work. I was wondering how she is.' With more of an effort he managed to add 'Just wondering what's wrong with her.'

'Has it got something to do with you?'

The woman's voice was loud and harsh enough to start two children crying, and Edgeworth felt as if the sounds were impaling his brain. 'I wouldn't say it has exactly, but—'

'If I thought you were the man who did that to Mary I'd find you and make sure you never went near a woman again. Just you tell me your name or I'll—'

Edgeworth jabbed the key to terminate the call and shoved the mobile in his pocket. As soon as it began to ring he switched it off. He couldn't loiter in the staffroom in case Mr Gittins wondered why, and so he ventured into the lobby, where a stray lump of popcorn squeaked piteously underfoot and then splintered like an insect. He'd hardly reached the ticket counter when the phones on it began to ring in chorus. 'See who it is,' Mr Gittins said.

Edgeworth clutched at the nearest receiver and hoisted it towards his face. 'Frugoplex Cinemas,' he said, trying not to sound like himself.

When he heard the woman's voice he turned his back on the manager. While she wasn't the caller he'd been afraid to hear or the one he might have hoped for, she was all too familiar. 'Congratulations, Eric,' she said. 'Three wrong means you're our next contestant. Someone will pick you up tonight.'

He dropped the phone, not quite missing its holder, and turned to find Mr Gittins frowning at him. 'Was that a personal call?'

'It was wrong. Wrong number,' Edgeworth said and wished he

could believe. Mr Gittins frowned again before making for the doors as some of Edgeworth's workmates gathered outside. Edgeworth searched their faces through the glass and struggled to think what he could say to them. Just a few words were repeating themselves in his head like a silent prayer. 'You're my friend, aren't you?' he would have to say to someone. 'Be my friend.'

RAMSEY CAMPBELL was born in Liverpool, where he still lives with his wife Jenny. His first book, a collection of stories entitled *The Inhabitant of the Lake and Less Welcome Tenants*, was published by August Derleth's legendary Arkham House imprint in 1964, since when his novels have included *The Doll Who Ate His Mother, The Face That Must Die, The Nameless, Incarnate, The Hungry Moon, Ancient Images, The Count of Eleven, The Long Lost, Pact of the Fathers, The Darkest Part of the Woods, The Grin of the Dark, Thieving Fear, Creatures of the Pool, The Seven Days of Cain* and the movie tie-in *Solomon Kane*.

His short fiction has been collected in such volumes as *Demons by Daylight, The Height of the Scream, Dark Companions, Scared Stiff, Waking Nightmares, Cold Print, Alone with the Horrors, Ghosts and Grisly Things, Told by the Dead,* and *Just Behind You*. He has also edited a number of anthologies, including *New Terrors, New Tales of the Cthulhu Mythos, Fine Frights: Stories That Scared Me, Uncanny Banquet, Meddling with Ghosts,* and *Gathering the Bones: Original Stories from the World's Masters of Horror* (with Dennis Etchison and Jack Dann).

PS Publishing recently issued the novel *Ghosts Know*, and the definitive edition of *Inhabitant of the Lake*, which included all the first drafts of the stories. Forthcoming is another novel, *The Black Pilgrimage*.

Ramsey Campbell has won multiple World Fantasy, British Fantasy and Bram Stoker Awards, and is a recipient of the World Horror Convention Grand Master Award, the Horror Writers' Association Lifetime Achievement Award, the Howie Award of the H.P. Lovecraft Film Festival for Lifetime Achievement, and the International Horror Guild's Living Legend Award. For many years he reviewed films for BBC Radio Merseyside and he is also

President of both the British Fantasy Society and the Society of Fantastic Films.

'This is one of many tales that spring from some everyday element that I've taken for granted for years and suddenly don't,' explains the author. 'In this case, quiz shows where contestants can phone a friend. I think I may also have had at the back of my mind one of our friend John Probert's wickeder delights.

'Oddly enough, after finishing the tale I discovered that there could have been another answer to the Elisha Cook, Jr. question, since he also plays a criminal in the Mickey Spillane film *I, the Jury*. Though he has two major scenes, he isn't credited. Let's assume my characters didn't know that any more than I did.'

Alice Through the Plastic Sheet

—ROBERT SHEARMAN—

A LAN AND ALICE liked Barbara and Eric. Barbara and Eric were good neighbours. Barbara and Eric were quiet. Barbara and Eric never threw parties – or, at least, not *proper* parties, not the sort of parties with music and loud noise; they'd had a dinner party once, and Alan and Alice knew that because they'd been invited beforehand, inviting them had been such a good neighbourly thing for Barbara and Eric to do. And Alan and Alice had thanked Barbara and Eric, and said that it was a very nice gesture, but they wouldn't accept, all the same – they gave some polite reason or other, probably something about needing a babysitter for Bobby (although Bobby was a good boy, he didn't need a babysitter).

But the real reason they didn't go was that they didn't *know* Barbara and Eric. They liked them, they liked them perfectly fine. They were good neighbours. But they didn't want them to be *friends*. As good neighbours, they worked. Good neighbours was good.

Barbara and Eric had a dog, but it was a quiet dog, it was just as quiet as Alan and Alice's own. They had two children, but they were grown-up children, and the three times a year the grown-up children visited Barbara and Eric (Christmas, both parent birthdays) they did so without fuss or upheaval. Some weekends Alan would see Eric, out clearing leaves from the front garden, out mowing the lawn, and Alan might be out tending to his own lawn, and the two of them would recognise the mild coincidence of that, Eric might raise a hand in simple greeting over the fence and Alan would do the same in return; for her part, Alice might smile at Barbara in the supermarket. And when Barbara put the house up for sale, Alan and Alice didn't know why.

'Hello!' said Alice cheerily one day when she saw Barbara at the checkout queue, 'So, where are you off to then?' And Barbara had told her that Eric was dead, Eric had had a heart attack, Eric was *dead* – months ago now, and she couldn't bear the loneliness any longer, she worried quite honestly that the loneliness would drive her mad. And she'd broken down in tears right there in front of Alice. Shrill, with lots of noise; it wasn't like Barbara at all. And Alice said she was sorry, she offered Barbara her condolences, she offered Barbara her handkerchief, she said she and Alan had had no idea, 'how dreadful!' and 'we had no idea!' And later she told Alan she'd felt a bit embarrassed, how *could* they have had no idea? How could all that death and suffering have been going on not thirty feet away without their knowing? She supposed they hadn't been especially good neighbours after all.

'We're going to miss them,' said Alice, as the family gathered around – Alice, Alan, little Bobby, even the dog got in on the act – and peered through the curtains to watch the removal men take the last pieces of Barbara's life away.

'I suppose we will,' said Alan. And let the curtains twitch back.

'They're never going to sell it like that,' said Alan one night at dinner. Alan worked in sales, he was an expert on sales. He was pretty much Head of Sales really, or would have been had Old Man Ellis not nominally still been in charge, but Alan was pretty much *de facto* Head of Sales, even Ellis had said so, pretty much everyone accepted that. 'The first rule of sales,' said Alan, 'is you have to let the consumers know you've something to sell in the first place. There's no point in being coy about it.'

There was a FOR SALE sign stuck into the lawn of the house they all still thought of as Barbara and Eric's, but, as Alan said, it wasn't well displayed. It was positioned right beside the largest of the trees so it was permanently obscured by shadow; from the road you could barely see it at all. 'It'll never sell,' said Alan, and sliced into his potatoes with an air of smug finality – and it did the trick, this was certainly where the conversation ended, as neither Alice nor Bobby nor the dog showed any inclination to contradict him.

Later that evening, Alan was giving Bobby a game of Super Champion Golf Masters IV on the Xbox, and Bobby was playing as Tiger Woods and Alan was playing as Jack Nicklaus but frankly would rather have played as Tiger Woods, but Bobby had been a good boy and had done his homework promptly and done the washing-up without being asked and was in consequence allowed first pick – and as all this was going on, Bobby said he had an idea.

Alan said, well, champ, I'm all ears. And Bobby suggested that maybe he and his Daddy could move the FOR SALE sign away from the tree and into a more prominent position. That would help everybody, wouldn't it? Though he didn't use the word 'prominent'. And Alan thought about it as he made Jack Nicklaus putt, and then said that they really shouldn't bother; after all, wasn't it quite nice that they didn't have any neighbours, wasn't it nice that it was all so quiet? Wouldn't it be nice if no one moved in ever, couldn't it be their little secret?

And Bobby shrugged, and said okay, and made par. Bobby was really a very kind and considerate child; Alan had been warned by his friends at work that children could start getting snippy when they got older, and Alan was watching out for it, but here was Bobby eight years old already and there was no sign of it so far. Bobby would say that playing golf with his father on the Xbox was the best part of his day, and Alan would like that, sometimes Alan was touched. What did his friends at work know anyway? Maybe Bobby would always be like this. Right then Alan decided he liked Bobby as a person, not just as a son but a Person in his own right – one day, when he was older, he looked forward to sharing a pint with him in a pub, men together, he'd be so much better company than his friends at work, he didn't like his friends much. He looked forward to playing golf with Bobby for real.

Anyway, Alan was wrong. The house was sold within the week.

The van arrived early in the morning, before Alan went to work, and stout uniformed men began unloading boxes and furniture on to the next-door lawn. When Alan returned home nine hours later they were still at it; and Alice was *still* watching it all from behind the curtains. 'You haven't been here all day, have you?' asked Alan.

And Alice said, 'Of course not!', and looked a bit cross. 'Alan,' she said, 'there's so much *stuff*, how do they have so much stuff? How are they going to fit it all in the house?'

'I'm hungry,' said Bobby, and he sounded unusually plaintive – and the dog began to yip for food as well.

'It's all right, champ,' said Alan, 'let's go and see what's in the fridge, shall we?'

After supper Alan went back to join Alice at the window. 'They'll have to stop soon,' said Alice. 'It's getting dark. You can't go moving stuff in the dark. That makes no sense, does it? You won't be able to see what the stuff is.'

Now the removal men were offloading from the van a green Chesterfield sofa. It was large and heavy, and the men struggled with it in the summer evening clamminess. At last it was out, and down – and joined three other sofas on the lawn, just as big and cumbersome, all in different colours – one was black, one was burgundy, one was a beige so lurid it could hardly be called beige at all. All four of them were still covered in their protective plastic sheets, not a single sofa had ever been used.

'It's all been brand-new,' said Alice. 'All the televisions, the washing machines, the hi-fi system. All still in their packaging. Isn't that peculiar?'

'I expect so,' said Alan, 'if you like. And what of our new neighbours themselves? What do they look like?'

'I haven't seen them yet,' said Alice. 'I keep on looking, but there's been no sign. I might,' she admitted ruefully, 'have missed them,' and she turned to Alan for the first time since he'd come home, her eyes so full of apology as if she'd let him down somehow. Then she started, she realised she'd taken her eyes off the game, and back whirled her head towards the chink of opened curtain.

'Maybe,' said Alice suddenly, 'I should go over there.'

'Why?'

'Maybe,' Alice said, 'I should take them a cup of sugar.'

'What for?'

'It'd be the neighbourly thing to do.'

'They probably have sugar,' said Alan. 'They have four sofas and, look, three widescreen TVs. Look.'

'I'll take them some sugar,' said Alice, and she tore herself away from the window and hurried to the kitchen. Alan followed her. She poured the sugar into a cup – not one of the best cups – she wasn't offering them the cup to keep, the cup was merely a receptacle for the sugar, she wanted the cup back – but she didn't want any awkwardness, if the cup were to be accidentally sacrificed in the spirit of good neighbourliness then it was going to be a cup she didn't like all that much. And then, now appropriately armed, she went outside and up the driveway to the next-door house.

Alan watched her from the window. He was surprised to see that in the little time it had taken Alice to fetch the sugar that the removal van had gone; the lawn was bare; the garden was deserted;

night had fallen. Alan saw Alice knock at the door. He saw Alice pause, then knock harder. He saw her bite her lip and chew it, it was what she always did when she couldn't make up her mind. Then she set the cup down gently, carefully, upon the welcome mat; she stood up, waited expectantly, as if that very act alone might have attracted the neighbours' attention.

'Can we play golf, Daddy?'

'Isn't it a bit late?'

'Please, Daddy.'

'All right. Just for a little while.'

'Can I be Tiger Woods again?'

At last Alice came home. 'They weren't in,' she said.

'So I gathered.'

'I waited a bit, though.'

'So I gathered.'

She frowned. 'Who are you tonight, Alan?'

'I'm Jack Nicklaus,' said Alan.

'And I'm Tiger Woods,' said Bobby.

Alice drifted back to the window. She gave a little cry of surprise that caused Alan to miss his stroke. 'What?' he said.

'The cup,' she said. 'It's gone.'

'Right,' said Alan.

'They must have been in after all,' said Alice. 'How very rude. I wonder,' she went on, and she pressed her hands hard against the window, as if she could force her way through it, be that tiny bit nearer, 'I wonder what they're *like*.'

Alan said, 'I just wonder why you care.'

They said no more about it, and when they went to bed Alice undressed silently, and went to sleep without saying goodnight. Alan wondered whether she was in a mood or not – but it was so hard to tell, she was usually pretty quiet in the bedroom, it had never been a place for noise or chat.

*

Theirs had never been a relationship based upon romance. Not even at the start, not even on that first date. And for the first few years this had nagged at Alan a little, he suspected he was doing something wrong, missing out on something nice all his friends at work got. So he would take to giving Alice boxes of chocolates, sending her the odd bouquet of flowers every now and again. And Alice would eat the chocolates, and she'd put the flowers in a vase, and she'd do both readily enough, but never with any especial gratitude; indeed, sometimes she'd give him a look, *that* look, as if to say, 'What do I want these for?' So he stopped.

Alan hadn't wanted a date anyway, not after Sandra, not after what Sandra had done to him and (he supposed) what he had done to her. But Tony had said to him one day, 'You could do with a girlfriend, feller,' and Alan respected Tony, Tony was very senior in sales, at that time Tony was pretty much the *de facto* head. Alan thought at first this was typical Tony banter, and Alan laughed along, but Tony assured him he was being very serious. 'It shows stability of character, feller,' he said. 'It shows us you're somebody we can rely upon.' And he recommended Alan try someone he knew, he recommended Alice, and so Alan gave Alice a call, and Alice suggested they meet for dinner that very Friday.

Alan could come and pick her up, early would be best, there was an Italian restaurant she liked around the corner, close enough that if the date wasn't working to either of their advantages they could skip dessert and she could be back home without wasting the entire evening.

Alan dressed up for the date. He took a second set of clothes with him to the office, and at five o'clock got changed in the toilet. Alice had dressed up too; when she opened the door to him Alan noticed right away how immaculate her make-up was, nothing too much, nothing garish or extreme – and it took him a few long seconds to recover and look through the shininess and see the woman underneath.

She looked him up and down. She nodded. She gave him a polite smile, and he gave one back, just as polite. He told her his name was Alan. She nodded again, fetched her coat.

As they were walking down the street to the restaurant, Alice suddenly stopped. It caught Alan up short, right in the middle of some smart observation he'd been making about the weather.

'Have you forgotten something?' he asked.

'Yes. No. Oh,' she said, 'oh.' And looked him up and down again, and chewed at her lip. She looked quite distressed for a moment, and Alan felt a sudden desire to protect her, to assure her that everything would be okay. 'Please don't take this the wrong way,' she said.

'No, no . . .'

'But. Your tie.'

'My tie?'

'It's just wrong. It doesn't go with that jacket at all.'

'Oh,' he said. And then, somewhat lamely, 'It's my best tie.'

'Would you mind?' she asked. 'I'm sorry. Would you mind if? We went back? I have ties. I have a better tie for you.'

'Oh. Well. If you'd prefer.'

'I would.'

'If it means that much to you.'

'It does.'

'All right then.' And they turned around and walked back to the house. Alan resumed his weather remark from where he'd left off, but he soon stopped, his heart really wasn't in it.

'You wait down here,' Alice said. 'Make yourself at home. I won't be a moment.' And she went upstairs. Alan looked around the sitting room. It was pretty. The wallpaper was a woman's wallpaper, but quite nice. Everything was clean and ordered and well vacuumed, and there was the smell of recent polish, and Alan thought to himself that he could get used to that.

'Here,' said Alice. And she was smiling, and it was proper smiling this time, there was a warmth to it. 'Try this one.' She held out to him a tie, quite formally, draped over her arm. It was pure black. Alan put it on, taking off his own tie with stripes. Alice gave him an inspection.

'Yes,' she said. 'Yes. Oh. Oh. Just wait,' and then she went back upstairs. This time she came down with a jacket, and a shirt, and some shoes. 'Try these,' she said, 'these will go with the tie.' And she was smiling all over now, her face was one big beaming smile, and Alan couldn't help but beam back, and he did as he was told.

'Why do you have all these clothes?' he asked, and she stopped smiling, and gave a sort of shrug.

She didn't smile again for the rest of the evening. The moment had been lost. He had lasagne, she fettuccini. The lasagne took longer to cook than the fettuccini, and that kept her waiting and he felt a bit guilty. She didn't respond to his conversation; his small talk was too small, he realised, and he longed suddenly for Sharon with whom he could have talked about *anything*, even if there sometimes had been shouting and swearing included, and though the restaurant was quite busy and the tables squashed too close together Alan felt desperately lonely. He didn't expect Alice would want dessert. She did. She ordered tiramisu. Alan was so surprised that he ordered tiramisu as well, even though he didn't like tiramisu.

And when she had devoured the tiramisu, after she had consumed it deliberately and precisely, Alice laid down her dessert spoon and examined Alan quite intently. She chewed her lip. 'I cannot decide,' she said, at last. 'Whether we're going to be friends or not. I can't work you out.'

And Alan said something about how he hoped they'd be friends, and she laughed at that, shook her head.

He paid for the meal; she let him. He walked her home, and neither of them said a word. He pretended they were both enjoying the still of the night. 'You'd better come in,' she said. He supposed this was so he could retrieve his own clothes. But as soon as the front door was closed behind them she tore into him, she ripped off his tie, his jacket, began to unbutton his shirt. Then she grabbed at the trousers, and Alan suddenly thought, the trousers are *mine*, she's at last touching something that's *me*.

And he knew then that she would look after him. That she'd make sure he looked good for the office and wore the right things, that she cared, she actually *cared* about him, that somebody out in the whole wide world was prepared to do that.

She proposed to him on their fourth date, and he could see no reason to refuse. He asked Tony to be his best man, and Tony said yes, and although asking Tony was a good career move it wasn't just that, Alan genuinely felt quite grateful his boss had played matchmaker. It was during the best man speech that Tony announced Alan's promotion.

Alan and Alice had a son called Bobby, and the way he was conceived wasn't especially romantic either, but Alan admired the way Alice took all those vitamins and boosters to facilitate the chances of pregnancy once she'd decided it was time they had a baby. And they all moved to a bigger house, and the neighbours were nice and quiet and elderly. And Bobby was bought a dog when he was deemed old enough to take care of it. And the sex between Alan and Alice swiftly became more sober, more manageable, and ultimately more for special occasions, and that was a good thing, a Good Thing, and Alan only very rarely thought of Sandra at all. And Tony, Tony was long dead, Tony had died years ago, Alan took his job and the power that went with it, Alan very rarely now thought of Tony either.

By the time Alan got home from work he was already in a bad mood. Sales were down, and that of course was a nonsense; there were more and more people in the world, and people needed more and more Stuff, and Stuff just happened to be what they were selling. Impressing upon his workers the logic of this had exhausted him. As *de facto* head, he felt responsible for their incompetence.

'They're having a party,' said Alice, the moment he closed the door.

'Who's having a party?'

'The neighbours. Housewarming, I bet. And they didn't invite us.'

Alan began to reply to that, but Alice shushed him. She raised a finger for silence. 'Listen,' she mouthed. So he did. And yes, he supposed it was true, he could hear the beat of distant music.

'Why would they invite us? They don't know us.'

'That's right, Alan, take their side. All I know is . . . that what they're doing is *invasive*. I feel *invaded*. How long's this music going on for? What if we can't sleep?'

'It isn't very loud,' said Alan.

'What if Bobby can't sleep?'

'I'll be able to sleep,' said Bobby, cheerfully.

'It's like an *invasion*,' said Alice. 'And I think you should go over there, and ask them to turn it down.'

'It's still early,' said Alan. 'If the music is still playing later. Then. Then we'll see.'

The family ate their dinner in silence. Silence, except for the bass thumping from next door. Alice deliberately didn't mention it, but Alan was annoyed to hear she was right, it *was* getting louder, and it *was* invasive. There was a snatch of something familiar about the music, but he couldn't place it, the melody was smothered by the thump.

Alan tried to talk, he hoped that some dinner conversation would drown out the neighbours, or at the very least distract him a bit. He would have liked to have told his family about his day, about the slump in sales, but he knew they wouldn't be interested.

'What did you learn at school today, Bobby?' he asked at last. 'Give me one fact you learned,' and Bobby promptly gave him the date for the Battle of Naseby. There wasn't much to add to that. 'Hey, good boy,' said Alan, relieved to see the dog slouch past the open doorway, 'hey, come here, come here, boy.' The dog trotted closer, but when he saw that Alan had no intention of feeding him anything, turned right around and trotted away again.

'I bet the music will be off by nine o'clock,' said Alan. 'That's the watershed. Everyone knows that.'

Bobby did the washing-up, and so as a treat was allowed to be Tiger Woods until bedtime. Alan enjoyed concentrating on golf for a while; he almost persuaded himself he couldn't hear the beat of music getting louder and thicker and uglier, couldn't hear the pointed sighs of despair from his wife.

'It's gone nine o'clock,' Alice said at last. 'You said they'd have stopped by now.'

'I said they might have.'

'Bobby has to go to bed. Bobby, will you need ear plugs?'

'I don't need ear plugs,' said Bobby. 'I'm fine. I kind of like it. Night, Mummy. Night, Daddy.'

Alan and Alice watched television for a while.

'There's a child here trying to sleep!' Alice suddenly cried, and she didn't even wait for a commercial break. 'That's what I don't understand! How they can just ignore that!'

'They don't know we've got a child,' said Alan.

'They didn't bother to ask. It's gone ten o'clock.'

'I know.'

'Next, it'll be eleven. Eleven!'

'Yes, I know.'

The music never stopped. There was never a pause when one song ended, and another waited to begin. Alan idly wondered how they managed to do that. Was it just lots of little songs mashed into one unending paste, or were his neighbours simply playing the longest song in the world?

At last Alan and Alice went to bed. Alice used the bathroom first. Alan got undressed in the bedroom. At first he thought the music was quieter in the bedroom, and that was good, that was a relief. But then he realised it wasn't quieter, it was just different – and this different, if anything, was louder. He heard Alice spit out her toothpaste, and she really spat, she really went for it.

They swapped positions, bedroom out, bathroom in, and he brushed his teeth as well. He thought he saw the mirror reverberate to the sound of the beat, but he had to really stare at it to check, and he wasn't sure whether it was just the effect of his head moving as he breathed. He got into bed beside Alice. She had her eyes screwed up tight, not wanting to look at him, not wanting to let in the world. He turned off the light.

As soon as the red neon of the clock radio turned midnight, that very second, Alice said, 'That's enough.'

'Yes.'

'You have to do something now.'

'All right.' Alan turned on the bedside lamp. He put on his dressing gown, his slippers.

'Tell me what you're going to say to them,' said Alice.

'Um. Please turn the music down?'

'Ask them to turn the music *off.*'

'I will.'

'Down isn't good enough.'

'All right.'

'And be firm.'

'Yes.' He went towards the door.

'You can't go out like that,' she said. 'Not in your pyjamas.'

'But I've just been woken up . . .'

'It sends entirely the wrong message,' said Alice. 'It robs you of any authority. You should look smart, formal even. Wait. Wait.' She got up, looked through the wardrobe. She handed him a jacket, a freshly ironed shirt. 'This will do,' she said. She smiled as he put the clothes on, she was enjoying this. 'Now, go. And whilst you're there, get me my cup back.'

He stepped outside into the night. The air was still so clammy, but there was a welcome breeze to it and Alan closed his eyes and drank it in and *enjoyed* it; he wished he was still wearing his pyjamas, he'd have loved to have felt it properly against his skin. He could feel the sweat already beginning to pool behind the layers of his suit, and rebelliously he loosened his tie . . .

. . . and listened. Because he could now hear what the music was, and it wasn't aggressive, it posed no threat, it was charming, *charming*. And he felt the urge to go back inside, go and fetch Alice – yes, and Bobby too, wake him up, wake him and the dog, bring them all out for this.

How much we take it for granted, thought Alan, when it plays on every television ad, when it's pumped into every department store, when it's allowed to define just one little month of the year, when it sells *stuff* – you get sick of it, or you screen it out – but now, *here*, in the middle of a July heat-wave, how incongruous it sounds, how *nostalgic*. Memories of days long ago, when he was a child, when his mother was still alive, when his father still talked to him – and he felt his eyes pricking with happy tears, he should rush inside, get his family whilst the music lasted, this was a treat.

But he didn't go back inside. He didn't want his family there. He didn't want them, and the thought of that surprised him and hurt him a bit, and somehow made him lighter too. And he stood on his porch, and listened, and basked in the little breeze he could feel, basked in the sound of 'Hark the Herald Angels Sing' as it segued seamlessly into 'Santa Claus is Coming to Town'.

But he knew Alice would be watching him. She'd be watching from behind the curtains. Watching and waiting. So he set his face into the proper authoritative pose, he straightened his tie again.

And he marched down the garden path, out on to the pavement, through the next-door gate, into strangers' territory.

There was no light visible from the house. All the curtains were closed. It looked as if everyone had gone to bed – no, more than that, it looked as if the house were deserted, as if it had been long ago abandoned and no one had lived in there for years and no one ever would again. It looked like a dead place. And he nearly turned back – not out of fear, good God, no – but because it was ridiculous to think that such music could be coming out of a house like that. But it was, it was.

The mat in front of the house said WELCOME upon it. Alan stood to one side of it, he didn't want to be accused of accepting even the smallest part of their hospitality. He knocked on the door – gently, very gently, because he didn't want to wake the household up. Then he realised how stupid that was; he lifted the knocker high, he let it swing.

He knocked like this for a little while. There was no answer. He felt like an idiot, knocking away, in the middle of the night, dressed like he was going to a business seminar and no one paying him any attention. He stooped down to the letterbox, lifted the flap, called through. He felt a cold draught from it – they must have had their air conditioning on.

'Hello?' he called. 'Hello? Is there anyone there?' He hated how weak and anxious his voice sounded. 'Hello? Could you turn the music down a little? Hello?' You idiot.

He tried knocking again. He then tried knocking whilst calling through the letterbox at the same time. 'Please!' he cried. 'I've got a family and they can't sleep! Really, you're being a little selfish! And, and. And if you don't quieten down, I'll . . .'

Alan had no idea how to finish that sentence, so it was just as well that at that very moment the music switched off. The sudden silence was numbing. He blinked in it.

'Oh,' he said. 'Well, thank you. Thank you, that's very kind!

Sorry to be a nuisance, we don't want to be . . . But it was past midnight and I . . . Well. Well, welcome to the neighbourhood!'

With that he eased the letterbox back into position, gently teasing it closed with his fingers so it wouldn't make any unwelcome sound. And he left their porch, walked up their driveway. He turned around, and the house was still so dark and the curtains still drawn – and he doubted anyone could see him, but nevertheless he gave a friendly neighbourly wave.

The sound that burst out of that house a few seconds later almost knocked him off his feet. It couldn't have been loud enough to have done that – not really – that was silly – but the sudden blast of it frightened him, and he did stagger, he did, he nearly toppled to the ground. It took his brain a few precious moments to realise it was just music, maybe music ten times louder than before – and a few moments longer to identify the song as 'Auld Lang Syne'. But in even that little time he was overcome with an almost primal terror, that this was the roar of a monster, that this was the roar of *death*, that he should run from this inhuman scream wrenched so *impossibly* out of the perfect silence, that he should run away fast whilst he still could.

And he very nearly did; he suddenly knew with absolute cold certainty how very small and useless he was before that wall of noise, and how very quickly the night had become very dark indeed, he could be lost within that pitch darkness, and within the battle cry the pitch was shrieking out, he *knew* that he'd drown in that noise and be lost forever . . .

And instead he found a rage within him he'd long forgotten, or never even guessed he had.

He stood his ground.

'*Should auld acquaintance be forgot, and never—*'

'You *fucks*!' he screamed at the music. 'You selfish *fucks*! I've got work in the morning! And a wife, and a son, and a dog – we've all got work in the morning!'

And up on the first floor he saw a curtain twitch – a little chink of light, then gone.

'I see you!' he raged. 'I see you up there! Do you think I can't see you?' He picked up a loose piece of crazy paving, he ran towards the house, towards that noise, he hurled it up at the window. It struck. For a moment he thought he'd broken the glass, terrified he had – then he *hoped* he had, hoped he'd smashed the whole fucking pane in – and was disappointed when the paving bounced back harmlessly.

'I'm coming to get you!' Alan screamed.

'*We'll take a cup of kindness yet, for the sake of auld lang syne . . . !*'

He raced out of their garden and into his own. He scrabbled at the door of his garage. He pulled out a metal stepladder; it clanked in his grasp. He felt his jacket rip under the strain, but that was too bad, *fuck* Alice for making him wear a jacket in the first place. For a terrible moment as he lugged the ladder out into the darkness he thought the song might have stopped, and he didn't want that, then what would he do? – but no, it was back on for another bout, 'Auld Lang Syne' was ringing in another new year, just so loud, just so selfish, just so fucking festive.

He dragged the ladder out of his garden, first pulling on one side then on the other, it looked as if the two of them were dancing together to the music.

And now he was leaning the ladder against their house – no, *slamming* it against the house, and up he went, the metal rungs creaking under his weight – 'I'm coming to get you!' he shouted again, but perhaps less confidently than before, and he knew his rage was still powering him on, but maybe it was starting to ebb away, who knows, just a little?

And he looked down once, and he wished he hadn't, because the night was so black now, everything was so *black*, and he couldn't see the ground below. But still he climbed and cried, 'I'm coming to get you,' but almost softly now, like it was a secret, and suddenly there were no more rungs to climb, he was at the top, and – look! happy coincidence! – he was right by the window. And there was no light behind, the curtain was closed tight.

'Hey!' He banged upon the glass. 'Hey! Open up! Open up!' And this close to the music he thought it was buffeting him, that the force might knock him from the ladder, but he was strong, he was holding firm – nothing could stop him now, and any terror he might be feeling in his gut, that was just a *private* terror no one could see, right? Right? 'Open up! One last chance!' And he banged again—

And the curtains opened.

And the music stopped.

Later on, he would doubt what he saw in that room. He would suspect that he'd misunderstood it at some fundamental level. Alice would ask him about what had happened that night, and he'd lie, he'd just say he never got a glimpse inside the house at all. That the neighbours had resolutely refused to show themselves, that he still had no idea who their enemies were. It was so much easier that way. He almost began to believe it himself.

The curtains pulled back all the way, they opened wide and he was blinded for a moment in the light of the room. So maybe that's why he couldn't see who had opened them, because someone had to have, surely, they couldn't open themselves? But there was no one in the room – no one – Alan thought there was at first – he gasped when he saw those figures, they looked so human – so lifelike – but . . .

But they were dummies. Dummies, the sort you'd get in clothes shops, modelling the latest fashions. There was a child wearing sports gear, and he was lying on his back, his body splayed out over cardboard boxes. The child looked dead in that position, or wounded, that wasn't a natural way for a body to lie – so why then was he smiling so widely?

There was a man, and he was in a business suit (and, Alan noted, not a suit as good as his, this dummy didn't have someone like Alice to dress him, quite clearly!) – and he was almost standing, propped in the corner of the room, head swivelled towards the window, almost facing Alan but not quite, almost grinning at Alan, almost grinning *because* of Alan, but not really, not quite.

And the third figure – the closest figure – oh – she was naked, and Alan felt such guilt suddenly, here he was staring at her, like she wasn't a woman at all, just an object, a slab of meat – but wait, she *was* just an object, just a dummy, what was the problem? And her breasts were perfect symmetrical mounds, and they looked quite inhuman, so why did Alan want to look anyway? – and her legs were long and smooth and had no trace of hair on them, the (frankly) pretty face locked into a smile too, but it was a cautious smile, a demure smile – it made her look so innocent, as if she needed protecting – or, wait, did it just make her look stupid?

She was bending over, her arse in the air, one hand dangling towards the floor as if in a painful yoga position – and now it looked to Alan as if the man in the corner was *inspecting* that arse, as if he were examining it critically, and his grin was because he had that job, who wouldn't grin if their job was arse-examiner? – and the little boy in the sports clothes was rolling around on the floor laughing at the fun of it.

And all three of them wore Santa hats, little red Santa hats, as if they weren't just part of some Christmas revelry but were Christmas decorations their very selves.

And that's when the dog began to bark, and it was loud, and it was fierce, and it was the fury of a dog defending its territory and its family from attack – and in a moment the curtains pulled back shut, impossibly fast – and Alan was lost again in the darkness, and suddenly the stepladder was falling one way and he felt himself falling another.

'I'm going to die,' he thought, quite clearly, 'I'm falling back into the black,' and down he crashed, and he wondered whether death would hurt. And he wasn't bothered, and he wondered *why* he wasn't bothered, and his brain said to him, 'God, Alan, just how depressed *are* you?', but he put that out of his head quickly, he always put it from his head, he had no time for depression, and besides, he didn't want that to be his final thought as he died.

But he wasn't dead – that fact now dawned on him – he hadn't fallen that far after all – and he was lying in the little flowerbed that only so recently Barbara and Eric had worked at hard to make look pretty.

There was still barking, but it was definitely inside, so he was safe – but what if the beast burst through the door? And he hadn't got time to pick up the stepladder, they could *keep* the stepladder – he stumbled to his feet, ran from the garden, so fast that it wasn't until he reached his own bedroom he realised how bruised he must be and how much those bruises hurt.

'You got them to turn down the music,' said Alice, in the dark. She sounded snug and cosy beneath the duvet. 'Well done.'

'Yes,' said Alan. 'But I think I woke up their dog.'

That night Alan dreamed of the woman dummy. He couldn't help it. He dreamed of her breasts and decided quite formally that they were a lot firmer than Alice's – from what he could remember of Alice's breasts, that is. The dummy's were too perfect to be human, too round, too sculpted – but inhuman was better than nothing, surely. He dreamed that there *had* been hair on that too-smooth plastic skin, something soft there after all. He dreamed that the dummy was smiling at him.

And the next morning Alan woke up, and was surprised at how refreshed he felt. He was in a good mood. A cloud had lifted – he'd known the cloud would just go away if he didn't think about it, and now he could be happy again, couldn't he? – he couldn't even remember why he'd been unhappy in the first place. He thought of the breasts and he smiled – and he looked across at the still-sleeping Alice and he smiled at her too, oh, bless. He felt he could face the day with equanimity. And next door was quiet, no music, no barking, everything back to normal.

He went to his car. The stepladder was propped against the garage door. The neighbours had brought it back. That was kind of them. The neighbours had brought it back. The neighbours had been around and brought it back. All smiles, how kind of them, all smiles and breasts. The neighbours had been around, they had left that still dead house, they had stolen into his garden in the night, they had come on to his property, they could have come up to his very front door, they could have been leaving their foot-prints all over his welcome mat, they could have been wiping their plastic hands all over his door knocker. How kind. The neighbours – they'd been around – in the dark, whilst he slept, whilst his family slept, whilst they slept and would never have known. They'd brought the stepladder back. He could have it back. He could use the stepladder again. He was welcome. He was welcome. He could come over with his stepladder, and climb up, and look through their windows whenever he wanted. He was welcome.

Alan felt a pain in his chest, and had to sit down to catch his breath.

At work, sales continued to slump. Alan called a meeting for his staff. He told them to buck their ideas up. That everyone was counting on them. That he was trying his best to be harsh but fair, everyone could see him being harsh but fair, right? Some of them smiled, and promised Alan that they would indeed buck up, and a couple of them even seemed convincing.

At home Alice would tell him that the barking was at its loudest in the afternoons. It'd start a little after lunchtime usually, and would continue throughout the day. The worst of it was that Bobby's dog was incensed by it. He'd run around the house, yipping back in pointless fury. Alice said she could cope with one dog barking, maybe, at a pinch. But to have two in stereo was beyond her.

The dog next door would settle down each evening. That was when the music came on. It was always Christmas music, but you could only ever tell which song it was by standing out in the front garden. That way you heard not only the beat, but could get the full benefit of the sleigh bells, the choir, the dulcet tones of Bing Crosby, the odd comical parp from Rudolf the Reindeer's shiny red nose.

They tried calling the police. The police took down their details. Said they'd drive by and see for themselves.

One evening the neighbours played 'O Little Town of Bethlehem' seventy-four times straight in succession. Bing Crosby sang it. Bing sounded angry. Bing hated them and wanted them to suffer. When the song eventually segued into 'Once in Royal David's City' Alan and Alice felt so relieved they almost cried.

And in the daytime, Alice would tell Alan, when Bobby came home from school, as he did his homework and his chores, he'd be humming Christmas carols under his breath. She asked him to stop. She screamed at him to shut the hell up.

At work, Alan was forced to call an emergency meeting. He had to use that word in the memo, 'emergency'. He told his sales force to work harder. He begged them. Or else he'd be obliged to take punitive measures. He had to use that phrase in the follow-up memo, 'punitive measures'. One or two openly laughed at him.

Alice said she'd called the police again, and that they'd just said the same thing as before. So Alan called them. He explained the situation very calmly. The police took down his details. Said they'd drive by. Said they'd see for themselves.

The neighbours were at last unpacking their belongings. Their front lawn was littered with cardboard boxes, sheets of plastic wrapping. The breeze would blow them over the fence. And each morning

Alan would leave for work and walk through a flurry of Styrofoam and polystyrene balls.

The dog continued to bark. Bobby's dog stopped. Bobby's dog couldn't take it any more. He'd hide in the kitchen when the barking started and he'd whimper. He'd piss on the floor in fear. He'd throw up.

Alice told Alan that he had to speak to the neighbours again. To go over there, knock on their door, demand an answer. He suggested they should do it together, that as a family they would more represent a united front. Bobby asked if he could come too, Bobby got very excited, and his parents said no, and Bobby got disappointed and a little cross.

Alan and Alice walked to the neighbours' house. The music playing was 'O Little Town of Bethlehem' again, but it wasn't Bing this time, it was some other version, so that was good, that was all right.

The welcome mat read WELCOME – WELCOME TO OUR HOME SWEET HOME! Neither Alan nor Alice wanted to tread on it. They stood in the porch and knocked and called through the letterbox. There was no reply. 'We're not giving in,' Alice told Alan, and he agreed. 'We're not going home until we've got this straightened out.'

But some hours later they had to.

The police told them they should stop phoning them. What they were doing, they said, was harassment. Not only to the neighbours, but to the police receptionist. Their neighbours were fine, good people; they shouldn't hate them just because they were different. 'But different in what way?' asked Alan, and he wasn't angry, and he clearly wasn't shouting, so he didn't think he deserved the subsequent warning. 'Just different.'

Alan and Alice tried knocking on the doors of other people in the street. Neighbours they'd never said hello to, not in all those years. But no one was ever in.

One evening Alan came home to find Bobby was in the front garden. He was playing in all the bubble wrap. 'Look, Daddy,' he said, 'I can make it go pop!' He was jumping on it, rolling around in it, setting off a thousand tiny explosions. He was laughing so much. Alan told him to get away from it, get inside the house. It wasn't theirs, it was rubbish, get away. Bobby looked so hurt – but couldn't he play in it, couldn't he and Daddy play in it together? 'It's not safe,' said Alan. 'You stupid boy, you idiot. It isn't *clean*.'

And Bobby still looked hurt. His mouth hung down in a sad little pout. But then the pout became a scowl. His face contorted. It actually contorted. And slowly, Bobby raised his hand, he raised a single finger. He held it out defiantly at his father.

That night Bobby wasn't allowed to play golf on the Xbox.

Alan and Alice slept wearing earplugs. But Alan thought he could still hear the music. He couldn't be sure whether the thumping was the bass beat or his own heart.

And he dreamed about the mannequin next door with her fake plastic body and tits and her fake plastic smile. 'Oh, Barbara,' he grunted one night, as he took her from behind, bending over like that, arse pointing up to the heavens, just asking for it. He liked to call her Barbara. With his heart thumping away like the drums of 'Winter Wonderland'.

Bobby still played in the garden. Alan would watch him from the window, catching pieces of polystyrene on his tongue like snow. He'd knock on the glass, try to get him to stop, but Bobby couldn't hear, or wouldn't hear, and he looked so happy, like an eight-year-old on Christmas morning. Tilting back his head, mouth wide open, the white specks of packaging floating down on to his face. Spitting them out, or swallowing them down, whichever way the fancy took him.

Alice worked out that the barking next door stopped if no one made a sound. So they tried not to provoke the dog, they trod gently, tried not to walk on floorboard creaks, they kept the television on mute. They talked in whispers, if they talked at all.

'Do you fancy a game of golf, champ?' whispered Alan to Bobby one evening. 'We haven't played golf in ages.' And Bobby shrugged. 'You can be Tiger Woods if you like,' said Alan. And so they played golf together, one last time, and Bobby didn't try very hard, and still won anyway. 'We can play real golf one day, if you like,' said Alan. 'Real golf, not just this fake version, the real one in the fresh air. We can go and have a pint together in a pub. We can be friends.'

At work, Old Man Ellis summoned Alan to a meeting. It was just the two of them, in that airless little office. Ellis told Alan that if he couldn't handle his staff, he'd find someone who could.

One night Alan came home with a good idea. The idea had been buzzing around his head all afternoon, it had kept him happy. 'Let's give them a taste of their own medicine!' he cried, and he didn't even bother to whisper, let's see what they make of *that*! And he and Alice got together all their favourite CDs, and they played them in the hi-fi and turned the volume up as far as it would go. Alice played her Abba, Alan his Pink Floyd. And next door went crazy – the dog began barking like nobody's business, the retaliatory Christmas music was deafening. But it didn't matter, it was *fun*, Alan and Alice rocking out to 'Voulez-Vous' and 'Comfortably Numb'.

Even Bobby joined in, and Bobby was grinning, and Alan hadn't seen Bobby smile for such a long time, and his heart melted, it did. 'Can I play some music too?' asked Bobby, and Alan laughed, and said, 'Sure!' And Bobby played something his parents didn't recognise, and it had a few too many swear words in it for either to approve – but they were all jumping up and down to it, and Alan said, 'I'm not sure you can dance to it, Bobby, but it's got a good beat!' And for some reason they all found that simply hilarious.

At last, of course, they had to give up; they had no more music to play; they were exhausted. And it hadn't done any good, Bing

Crosby was screaming out apoplectic rage, and their own dog was a quivering wreck of piss and sick. But as they got into bed that night, Alice said to Alan, 'Did you recognise it? That was *our* song. Do you remember? That was the song we used to play, back when we first met.' And Alan didn't think they'd ever had a song, they'd never been that romantic, had they? But she kissed him, and it was on the lips – it was very brief, but it was sweet – and then turned over and went to sleep. Alan lay there in the dark and wondered which song she had been referring to. Probably one of the ones by Abba.

The next morning, beneath the sea of cardboard and plastic and bubble wrap crap, Alan saw that there were now holes in the lawn. Craters even. It was like a battlefield. And he supposed that last night the neighbours had let the dog out. And that afternoon, at work, he sacked three of his team force. He called an emergency meeting, and sacked them at random. One of them even cried. 'But I've got a family,' she said. 'Tough,' said Alan. 'We've all got fucking families.'

Alice phoned Alan at work. She never did that. 'Are you coming home soon?' she asked.

'What's the matter?'

'It's the dog. He's very ill.'

'Well, he's always a bit ill, isn't he?'

'This is different. Oh God, he got out of the house. I don't know how, but he escaped, and he's just crawled his way back and . . . Come home soon.'

Alan explained he was really very busy, and that he didn't know much about dogs, and there was nothing he could do to help. But he still left work early, he drove back as quickly as he could.

By now Bobby was home from school. He was crying. 'Oh, Sparky,' he said. 'Sparky, please don't die.' And all at once he was an eight year old again, Alan's special little boy, and he loved him so much, and he pulled him into a hug. And Bobby clung to him, and sobbed all over his suit. 'Please, Daddy, don't let Sparky die.'

'I won't,' said Alan. 'I won't. What did the vet say? You have called the vet?' And both Alice and Bobby looked at him blankly. Alan felt cross. 'Well, why not?'

'Look at him,' said Alice.

The dog was doing its best to stand on all fours, but the paws kept sliding beneath him. At first Alan thought it was simple weakness – but no, it was odder than that, the paws themselves looked so shiny and slippery, they couldn't get purchase on the kitchen tiles. The dog was trying hard not to look at anyone, it almost seemed to be frowning with human irritation – I know how to stand, don't worry, I'll puzzle it out in a moment. Around him lay clumps of fur, big handfuls of it. There was a pool of liquid that looked a bit like cream but smelled much worse.

Then the dog sneezed – a peculiar little squeak like a broken toy, and it almost made Alan laugh. And it was too much for the dog, its legs shot out from underneath him, his belly slumped to the floor in one big hilarious pratfall. And the dog opened its mouth, as if to give some punchline to the gag, and instead retched out a little more of that cream.

'They did this to him,' said Alice. 'They poisoned him.'

'We can't know that.'

'Fuckers,' said Bobby. 'Dirty shitty little fuckers, they did this. Pesky nasty motherfucks.' And he glared at his parents, and that eight-year-old innocence was lost again, and Alan thought it was probably lost for good.

'Hey, boy,' said Alan, bending down towards the dog. 'Hey, champ. How are you doing? Don't you worry, champ, everything will be fine.'

And the dog's eyes bulged wide, in utter confusion, and it retched again. But this time there was no mere trickle of cream. It *poured* out, thick and fast, as if some hose inside had just been turned on. No wonder the eyes bulged – there was more liquid here than there was room inside the dog's body, surely! – it was as if each and every one of his innards had been diluted into one same sticky mulch and were now being pumped out of him on to the floor, coming out now in waves, lapping against the dog's head and getting stuck in the remaining scraps of fur, lapping against the open eyes that stared on beadily in vague disinterest, the contents of his entire body swimming lazily past him and his not even showing the inclination to care.

There was a pinkish quality to the cream now, and Alan thought that might be the blood – but the creamy beige flattened the pink out, it became a beige so lurid it was hardly beige at all. And oh God, it wasn't even liquid, not really, it was like a syrup, soft and smooth, and the dog was now quivering in it, seemed to be supported by it and floating upon it, this syrup so thick you could stand a dessert spoon up in it. Clean, and pure, and hard like plastic.

The dog gave one last shudder, as if trying to shake out the last of its body's contents; a few last drops out, all done? Good.

'Sparky,' said Bobby.

'Now, we have to be brave,' said Alan.

'Fuckers,' said Bobby.

'Now, now.'

'Yes,' said Alice. 'Fuckers.'

Alan opened his mouth. He wasn't sure why, to say something, what? Something conciliatory possibly, or just some sort of eulogy for a dead pet, something suitably touching for the circumstances. His family looked at him expectantly. 'What,' he asked, 'do you want to do?'

'Revenge,' said Bobby. 'We'll get revenge. We'll poison *them*, we'll poison *their* dog. We'll . . . we'll put shit through their letterbox.'

'Right,' said Alan, 'right, or we could . . .'

Alice looked at him. Stared at him, in fact. 'What, Alan?' she said, and it was so soft, that was the dangerous thing. 'Well? Well, tell us. What can we do?'

He tried to think of an answer to that. She waited. Give her her due, she waited. Then she tutted with exasperation and stormed out of the room.

Alan and Bobby watched the dog for a little while. Even now the fur was still falling from its body, each hair a rat deserting a ship that had already sunk. Alan thought he should close the dog's eyes, if only for Bobby's sake, but he didn't. Instead, 'Come on,' he said, awkwardly, reaching out to put his arm around his son, then thinking better of it. 'Come on, let's leave poor old Sparky in peace.' They left the kitchen, and Alan closed the door behind them.

Alice was waiting for them both in the sitting room. 'Here,' she said.

She handed Alan a little cellophane bag, the same she'd use to pack his lunch for work and Bobby's lunch for school. Inside nestled what looked like three sausages, small and thin, with knobbles on – and they were three turds, Alice's turds, and they looked so dainty, they looked like polite little lady turds.

'Oh God,' said Alan.

And Bobby grinned at that, a wolfish grin that showed his teeth. 'Yeah, all right!' he said, and left the room. He returned a minute or two later, still all smiles, his dog was dead but everything was okay now because they had a plan. And he was carrying his own offering in his bare hands, proud, like a hunter, like a child who had now proved himself a man – look upon the fruits of my labours! – and it was a big greasy hot dog of a turd, and Alan realised that Bobby was really no longer just a little boy.

'You expect me to put these through their letterbox, just like that?'

'Not at all,' said Alice. 'We need to tell them why. We need them to know *we know*.' She went to her desk, found an envelope, a nice big padded one. She wrote on it in bold felt tip: DOG KILLERS.

She took her bag of chipolatas dangling from Alan's still outstretched hand, dropped it inside; Bobby dropped his inside as well.

'Now we're just waiting for your contribution,' said Alice.

'Don't you think we've got enough?'

'This is a present from the entire family.'

So Alan went to the toilet. He took the envelope with him. He thought of his wife and son outside the door waiting for him. It was too much pressure. He couldn't perform like that. He strained and strained, he honestly tried. But nothing popped out. He opened the envelope, looked at the turds inside for moral support, at the pioneering turds that would be forebears to his own turds. It did no good.

He flushed away an empty bowl.

'All done?' asked Alice as he emerged.

'Yes,' he lied.

And his family nodded at him grimly. 'Then,' said Bobby, 'it's time.'

The neighbours' house was actually quiet when he stepped outside. It was too early for the Christmas music, and the dog was taking a break from barking. It was peaceful, and Alan almost believed this was a joke, that nothing really had happened, that Barbara and Eric still lived there, and all was well.

He wondered if he were being watched as he walked up the driveway. By *them*, his enemies – and by *them*, his family – both sides watching his progress secretly from behind curtains. He tried to hold the envelope as nonchalantly as possible, as if it wasn't the sole reason for his paying a visit, as if, with his pet dog dead, he now wanted to take his pet envelope for walkies instead.

The sun was already setting as Alan reached the front door, and that was peculiar.

For once he didn't want to attract attention. One simple delivery, and he was done. Gently, very gently, he pushed open the flap of the letterbox. He bent down to it, he peered through into the house

– but there was nothing to see, it was dark. Pitch-dark, and Alan
got the sudden thought that it was from inside the house that the
night was leaking.

He felt a slight draught from it. He shivered, looked back. The
light was almost gone already, get it over with. He measured the
envelope against the letterbox, and it was a perfect fit, the right
size exactly, and he balanced it there, began to feed it in.

And then from the other end he felt a tug.

At first he thought he'd just hit an obstruction, he prepared to
adjust the angle so he could push it through more easily – but
then he felt it again, a definite *tug* – there was something waiting
behind that door, and it'd taken hold of the envelope, it was pulling
it in.

Instinctively Alan pulled back, and he didn't know why – he
wanted this delivered, didn't he? But from inside the house he
heard a growl, something thwarted, something angry, and he knew
then he mustn't let this envelope go inside that house, he mustn't
let any part of his wife or his son go in there, not even the worst
part of them, not even their shit. And he pulled back harder, and
the growler was *shocked* by that, at the sheer nerve of it, there was
a gnashing of teeth too, Alan was sure of it. And he set his feet
upon the welcome mat to try to get a better grip, and he looked
down at it, and that was a mistake, because there was nothing now
on the welcome mat, no wording at all – and more than that, there
was really nothing there, it was smooth and soft and oh so slippery, and Alan couldn't stop himself, Alan fell backwards, Alan let
go.

The envelope was snatched away; the letterbox slammed shut;
the jaws of the house, they slammed shut. And Alan cried out in
frustration and fear, and suddenly realised how very dark the night
was.

When he got home, Alice was in the bedroom waiting for him.
She was wearing her underwear. She never showed that. He could

see her breasts peeking out, saying hello. 'But where's Bobby?' he asked.

'Bobby went to bed hours ago,' said Alice. 'Hey. You did it. You big, bad, bold man. You've been husband to me, and father to our boy. You've protected your family, you've kept us safe.'

And for only the second time since he'd known her, she tore into him. She ripped off his tie, his jacket, her hands were all over him, her lips too. 'I want you so much,' she said, 'I *love* you so much,' and she pulled him down on to the bed – 'Oh, okay,' said Alan – and, oh God, she was everywhere, how was she doing that, when she only had two hands, and she was in him and now he was in her and that last bit was pretty unexpected – 'I love you!' she shouted, and he wanted her to hush, Bobby would hear, the neighbours would hear – and it was all so silent out there, there was no music at all, and Alan could picture them maybe as a family sitting around the contents of the envelope soberly, 'Well, I guess we learned our lesson,' – and Alan wished the music was back, just a bit of it, just to give him a bit of rhythm, it had been a long time since he'd done anything like this. 'I love you,' cried Alice, 'Alan, why did we ever stop? Why did we ever stop loving each other?' And Alan didn't know.

Alan was woken by Alice with a kiss.

'I have to go to work,' he said.

'Couldn't you just stay here with me?'

'Not really,' he said.

'Okay.'

There was still no sound from next door, and Alan supposed that was a good thing.

Alan phoned Alice from work. He never did that.

It was late morning, he wanted to hear her voice.

'I love you,' he said.

'That's nice,' she replied. 'Will you be home at the usual time?'

'I think so. I hope so.'

'Good.'

He phoned her again later in the afternoon, but this time there was no answer.

When he got home at last he was surprised to see the dog was waiting for him.

The fur had fallen out, every last hair of it. But the dog didn't seem too distressed by this. His face was etched into one big doggy grin, tongue lolling out. He waddled towards Alan on those shiny smooth paws of his.

'Hey,' he said. 'Hey. Good dog. Good boy.'

He stroked at his off-beige skin, and it was a little sticky to the touch.

Bobby was playing on his Xbox.

'Hello, champ,' said Alan. 'What about Sparky, then? Sparky pulled through!'

Bobby didn't look up; he was too absorbed in his game. Alice came in from the kitchen.

'Bobby,' she said. 'That dog of yours needs feeding.' Bobby's body twitched in irritation. 'Now, come on,' she said. 'He's your responsibility.'

'Hello,' said Alan. 'I love you.'

'Now, Bobby,' insisted Alice.

So Bobby tottered to his feet. Then tottered to the kitchen, fetched a can of dog food. He tottered back to the dog, who all this time had gazed after his young master in utter adoration. Bobby scooped some of the food out of the tin with his fingers. He bent down towards his dog. And then, very carefully, he smeared it all over the dog's face. He smeared it in good and hard, so that the jellied meat stuck there firm – some of it went into the mouth, and a little on to that hanging tongue, but the majority hung off the face and gave Sparky an impromptu beard.

Then Bobby sat down again, picked up his Xbox joystick. He squeezed the controls hard, and the remains of dog food oozed out from his fist.

Alan watched, appalled. 'What's wrong with Bobby?'

'Nothing's wrong with Bobby,' said his wife. 'Bobby's got his dog back. Bobby's happy, the dog's happy, everybody's happy.'

'Are you happy?'

'Of course I'm happy. Come into the kitchen. I want to talk to you privately.' He followed her, and she smiled as she closed the door.

'What is it?'

'You should sit down.'

He did.

'I'm having an affair,' smiled Alice.

Alan didn't know what to say. 'What?' And then, 'Why?' And, 'But you said you were happy . . .'

'I am happy. I'm happy *because* I'm having an affair.'

'Oh,' said Alan. He supposed he ought to have felt angry. Was that what she wanted? But he had no anger left. He'd used it all up, wasted it on loud music and garden rubbish.

'Don't look glum, Alan. I'm not glum. We're going to sort this out. Let me explain how.'

'Okay.' And Alan felt strangely reassured, actually; Alice always sorted everything out.

She explained how she could keep everything she wanted. And how he could get the same thing in return. That way everything would carry on as normal. It'd just be a *different* normal. A better normal.

He said, very quietly, 'Can I have time to think?'

She was very polite. 'Of course you can, darling.' He'd been staring down at the kitchen table as she coolly told him what she wanted from him, how she saw their marriage surviving, what her conditions were. And now he looked up at her. She was staring at him closely, and there was still that smile, and her head was fixed to one side for the best angle, and he shuddered for the briefest moment. 'Oh, Alan,' she said. 'When we first met, I remember. Trying to work out whether we ought to have just been friends. I think, darling, that we lost our way. I think we could have been such good friends.'

'And last night?'

Alice turned her head to the other side, narrowed her eyes, frowned. 'What about it?'

That night Alan stayed on the sofa. He played on Bobby's Xbox. He played as Tiger Woods. He beat the computer once.

He went to work. The roads were filled with motorists who'd found love. Old Man Ellis called him in for another emergency meeting, and this time Ellis told him he was a disgrace, and threatened him with redundancy, and Ellis was a short ugly man and body odour clung to him like a limpet, but he'd found love, he'd found Mrs Ellis, he'd made it work, and Alan wanted to ask him what the secret was. Waiting on his desk when Alan came out was an unsigned note calling him 'Wanker'. The man who'd called him a wanker was probably in love too.

He thought about calling Alice. He didn't dare.

He didn't go straight home. He went to the pub. He sat on his own. He drank lager and ate crisps.

By the time he reached the house, Alice was already in bed. He undressed in the dark, and climbed in beside her. She didn't move, not a muscle. He couldn't tell whether she were asleep or awake. Alive or dead. Human or. Or. He wanted to rub against her. In the moonlight her skin looked so smooth.

There was still no sound from next door, and the silence, the desperate silence, began to hurt.

'All right,' he said, out loud. 'I'll do what you want.'

*

Alan hadn't been on a date in years, and didn't know how to dress. So Alice took him to the wardrobe and picked out a tie, a jacket, a shirt, shoes. She inspected the results critically. 'You look good enough to eat.' Alice herself was immaculate, she'd never lost the knack, who'd have thought?

'Maybe we don't have to do this then,' said Alan. 'If this is what you like.'

She chewed her lip, just for a second, then laughed. 'Come on,' she said, and plucked him by the sleeve, and took him downstairs.

Bobby was playing golf with his new friend. 'Hello, champ,' said Alan. 'Hello, *champs*.' He thought the boy on the right was Bobby, because that was Tiger Woods.

'Don't wait up!' Alice told the two children gaily.

They stood on the welcome mat. The mat read, NOSTRA CASA and A VERY HAPPY FAMILY LIVES HERE! and HOME SWEET HOME SWEET HOME SWEET HOME SWEET HOME. Alan raised the knocker, but at his touch the door swung open.

'We're expected,' Alice assured him.

The house was pretty. Everything was clean and ordered and there was the smell of recent polish – or was it something besides? On a shelf with the telephone directory Alan saw his padded envelope, still sealed. DOG KILLER, it said, and that accusation seemed so spiteful now. We're all good neighbours, aren't we, good friends. Next to it, he saw, there were other envelopes, similarly sized – CAT POISONER read one. MURDERER said another. Still more: CHILD ABUSER. RAPIST. KILLER. RAPIST. KILLER.

On a shelf beneath, a cup filled to the very brim with sugar.

'But where are they?' said Alan.

'They'll be in the dining room,' said Alice. Her eyes were shining with excitement. 'Let's see what they've got for us!'

They'd cooked pasta. Lasagne, fettuccini.

Barbara had really made an effort. Alan had never seen her with her clothes on before, and she looked beautiful, she'd done a really good job. Barbara smiled, a little demurely, Alan thought. 'Doesn't she look wonderful, Alan?' Alice cooed. 'Good enough to eat!'

Eric's smile had no shyness to it, and he flashed it throughout the whole meal. He was wearing a suit. His tie was pure black. Alan thought it made his own striped one look wrong and silly. Eric looked so good he could have got away with a striped tie; even the Santa hat perched on the side of his head looked smart and chic.

The small talk was very small, but Alice laughed a lot at it, and Alan had almost forgotten what her laughter sounded like. In the background, playing very subtly, was a selection of festive favourites. But there was nothing cheesy about them, they were performed by famous opera singers, and the orchestra was one of the Philharmonics.

It was time for the dessert. 'Allow me,' said Alice, 'you two have worked so hard already,' and she fetched it from the brand-new refrigerator. 'Tiramisu!' she said. 'It's my favourite! Oh, how did you know?' And she sat down, kissed Eric gratefully upon the lips.

'Tiramisu, yum yum,' said Alan.

Alice scooped a fistful of tiramisu from the bowl. She looked straight at Alan. And her eyes never leaving his, she smeared it slowly over her face. She massaged it into her cheeks, her lips and chin – then rubbing lower, down on to the neck, thick cream and chocolate peeping over the top of her cleavage.

Alan winced.

Alice's eyes flashed for a moment. 'If you don't like it,' she said, 'why don't you come over here and wipe it off me? Come on. Lick it off. Lick it off me, if you dare.'

Eric grinned at that, Barbara smiled so demurely. Alan didn't move.

And Alice smiled such a polite smile from beneath her mask of soft dessert. 'I think it's time we left you two lovebirds alone.' And so saying, she got to her feet. She picked up Eric from the waist, she tucked him under her arm. And they left the room.

Alan couldn't be sure, but he thought as he left that Eric may have winked at him.

'Well,' said Alan. He looked at Barbara, who was still smiling, but was it really demure, was she perhaps just as embarrassed as he was? 'Well,' said Alan. 'What do we do now? Just the two of us.'

He reached across the table, and took hold of Barbara's hand. It felt like the skin of his dead dog.

Alan said, 'I hope we can be friends.'

He closed his eyes. He concentrated hard. As if through thought alone he could make that hand warm to his touch, make it take hold of his in turn. As if, by wanting it enough, he could make Barbara love him.

He heard the sound of bedsprings, of his wife shrill and noisy, her screams of pleasure as she reached orgasm. He kept his eyes squeezed tight and tried to block out all the noise, all the noise there was in the world.

ROBERT SHEARMAN is an award-winning writer for stage, television and radio. He was resident playwright at the Northcott Theatre in Exeter, and regular writer for Alan Ayckbourn at the Stephen Joseph Theatre in Scarborough. He is the winner of the Sunday Times Playwriting Award, the Sophie Winter Memorial Trust Award and the Guinness Award for Ingenuity in association with the Royal National Theatre. Many of his plays are collected in *Caustic Comedies*, published by Big Finish Productions.

For BBC Radio he is a regular contributor to the Afternoon Play slot, produced by Martin Jarvis, and his series *The Chain Gang* has won two Sony Awards, and he is acclaimed for his work on *Doctor Who*, bringing the Daleks back to the screen in the BAFTA-winning first series of the revival in an episode nominated for a Hugo Award.

Shearman's first collection of short stories, *Tiny Deaths*, was published by Comma Press in 2007. It won the World Fantasy Award for Best Collection, and was also short-listed for the Edge Hill Short Story Prize and nominated for the Frank O'Connor International Short Story Prize. His second collection, *Love Songs for the Shy and Cynical*, published by Big Finish, won the British Fantasy Award and the Edge Hill Readers' Prize, while his third collection, *Everyone's Just So So Special*, appeared in 2011, again published by Big Finish.

'I have noisy neighbours,' reveals the author. 'They talk too loud. They stamp up and down the stairs. And once in a while, if they're being insufferably happy, they play their music at full volume. They're doing it at this very moment. Bastards.

'My way of dealing with them is to be passive aggressive. I grit my teeth whenever I leave the house and they wave hello to me – oh, I wave back all right, I *smile*, but I'm being ironic. Behind closed doors I shake my fists silently at the walls, and tell them (in hushed tones, in the unlikely event they'd hear me over the decibels) to shut up, shut up, *shut up!*

'The reason I wrote this story is in the hope that one day one of my neighbours will be in a bookshop. They'll be browsing the shelves. They'll recognise my name in this anthology, maybe, and buy it. And then they'll find out. They'll find out exactly how cross I was. And I'll have my passive aggressive revenge.

'If you're reading this in the future, and you are my neighbours, I'm not joking. *Turn the music down!*'

The Man in the Ditch

—LISA TUTTLE—

THERE WAS NOTHING to look at once they were away from the town, only a long road stretching ahead, bare fields on either side, beneath a lowering grey sky. It was very flat and empty out here on the edge of the fens, and dull winter light leeched all colour from the uninspiring landscape. Occasionally there was a ruined windmill in the distance, a knackered old horse gazing sadly over a fence, a few recumbent cows, a dead man in a ditch—

Linzi screamed when she saw it, an ear-piercing screech that might, had J.D. been a less-practised driver, caused a nasty accident. If there was nothing else out here, there were still plenty of vehicles travelling fast and close, both front and back.

'What the fuck?'

She saw how red his face had gone, the vein that throbbed in his temple, and felt bad, but she hadn't screamed for nothing. 'Jay, there was a dead body in the ditch back there – a person!'

'Don't be stupid.' His hands tightened on the wheel and his eyes darted between the mirror and the road, not sparing her a glance.

'I saw it! We have to—'

'What? What do we have to do?'

'I— I don't know. Go back?'

With every passing second the distance grew.

'And why should we do that? Do you see anywhere to turn? And then, even if you could tell me where to stop, there's nowhere to pull over without going right into the ditch. And why? So you can see that what you thought was a dead body was really a load of fly-tipped rubbish?'

She worried at her lip as she tried to recall precise details of what she had seen – a withered, brownish, naked man, lying curled on his side – but she didn't believe it had been an optical illusion. 'It was a man's body. I'm sorry I startled you, but anyone would've yelled, to see a corpse like that.'

J.D. sighed and moved his head around, easing the tension in his neck. 'All right, my lovely. It's over now. A dead body doesn't need our help.'

'But – we ought to tell someone?'

'Tell who?'

'The police?'

He flinched and she shut her eyes, as if his response to the word had been a slap in the face. She opened them again when she heard him put on the indicator.

'If you really saw it, other people did too,' he said calmly. Then he turned left, onto a signposted road, and then, very soon, took another left onto an unmarked road, a narrow, single-track lane. They were now travelling parallel to the main road, back in the direction from which they had come. With a nervous flutter of anticipation low in her belly, Linzi realised he must be responding to her request, taking her back to the spot where she'd seen the body. From here, the main road was easily visible as a steady stream of traffic; only a short stretch of empty land separated the track they were on from the drainage ditch, even though she couldn't see it. But then, she hadn't noticed this road from the other side. She couldn't guess how far they'd gone after her sighting, but she had faith that J.D. knew: he was a professional driver.

Linzi caught hold of her elbows and gave herself a small hug.

Wasn't it just *like* him to grumble and pretend he wasn't doing what she wanted? Not that she *wanted* to see the horrible old dead thing again . . . and, in fact, as the car slowed and then stopped when the track ran out, she prayed to whatever powers there might be that J.D. was right, and she'd been scared by an abandoned stolen shop-window mannequin or a crash-test dummy.

'Here we are,' he said. 'What do you think?'

She looked at his proud smile and remembered what the dead man had pushed out of her mind.

'Come on,' he said, not waiting for her reply. 'Let me show you round our new home.' He hopped out and, with the courtliness that had won her heart, opened her door for her.

She fixed a pleased smile on her face, but he must have picked up a hint of her true feelings because he said, sounding defensive, 'Of course it doesn't look like much now, but use your imagination. Think of all the stuff you can plant. Landscape the holy shit out of it. Whatever you like; I'll pay.'

Tentatively, she tried to explain her unease: 'I thought we'd have neighbours . . .'

'Who the fuck wants neighbours? You said you wanted a house in the country.'

'Yes, yes, I did; I *do*. But I didn't think it would be so far away from everything—'

'It's the *country*. And it's *not* far – what, twenty minutes from Norwich? You must have seen the village signposted, two miles that way for post office, pub and primary school.'

At that reminder of the children they'd have someday she melted against him. 'Oh, honey, I'm not complaining! How could I, when I've got you? I was just surprised. I was imagining a new development.'

'You know I hate those ticky-tacky estates.' He relaxed in her embrace. 'Would Madam like the grand tour?'

They walked over land that was rough but not boggy, as the

fields had appeared from the car window. She saw the boundary markers – poles sporting fluorescent orange plastic tags – and then came upon a pile of rubble and a concrete slab.

'What's this?'

'What's left of the house that used to be here. Why'd you think we've got planning permission to build a new one?'

'What happened to the old house?'

'I think it burnt down, I don't know, twenty years ago. Before that there were cottages. People have always lived here. You might not think to look at it, but it's actually on a rise, higher than the marshes out there. And the soil is a different composition, not marshy, so we can plant what we like. And we're never going to have to worry about other houses going up either side, because who'd build on a bog? We won't have noisy neighbours, or nosy ones popping over every five minutes, complaining that our *leylandii* is blocking their view, wanting to borrow the hedge-trimmer, giving you the eye . . .'

As he worked himself up into a rant she had heard before, staring out at the bleak, blank, featureless plain where the only other life to be seen was in the cars and lorries thundering past, Linzi felt a tremor of doubt. Those things he complained about were leftovers from his past in the suburbs with 'that cheating bitch'. Did their life have to be defined always in reaction to his first marriage?

'Are you cold?' Noticing her sadness, J.D. became tender. He took his coat off and wrapped it around her. 'That wind has teeth. We'll have to plant a line of trees over there as a wind-break, and a hedge on that side, to screen us from nosy buggers staring out of their windows as they drive past. Come on, back to the car now.'

Going back, she couldn't see anything unusual in the ditch. There was nothing in the local news the next day about a body being found, and the next time they drove out east on the A47 she couldn't even identify the spot where she'd thought she'd seen it.

Building soon got started, and a few weeks later, J.D. stopped by the property one evening and took pictures with his phone, sharing them with Linzi when he got home. She made admiring noises until the final picture, when the sound stuck in her throat.

'What— What's that?'

'A side view—'

'I mean down in front, the left-hand corner, that thing.'

He peered at the screen. 'What are you talking about?'

'It looks like—' But she found she didn't want to say it looked like a dead body, a wizened naked man lying on his side, so she just pointed. 'There.'

'Oh. Not sure. Pile of sticks and some weeds, maybe. The light was going. Waste of space, that one.' With the touch of a button, he deleted it.

A few days later, Linzi accompanied her husband to the building site. She was surprised at how quickly everything had changed, how different the space looked now that there was the frame of a house at the centre of it. She was also a little taken aback by how much clutter there was everywhere. Much of it was equipment and building materials, or the discarded packaging for those things, but there were also food wrappings, plastic bottles, beer cans, even the odd item of clothing – a white T-shirt, a single shoe – suggesting the workers considered the space outside the house a general dumping ground. It was easy to imagine some accumulation of trash appearing in dim light like a body, and she abandoned her plan to search for the object that had created such a disturbing impression in the picture and instead clung to her husband's arm and listened to his description of how the work was progressing.

At one time Linzi had made good money dancing in a club – it was where she had met J.D. – but he couldn't stand the thought of other men seeing her naked, so now she worked at Tesco. It wouldn't be too bad as a part-time job when her kids were in school, she thought, but a year into her marriage she still wasn't pregnant and she was getting impatient. The doctor said there was no obvious reason why she shouldn't conceive in due course, but if she wasn't content to wait and see, the next step would be to check her husband's sperm count. Well able to imagine how J.D. would respond to that suggestion, Linzi decided to explore other options first.

She'd heard there was a woman in Lowestoft who had studied all the old traditional ways to increase fertility. First, she read your cards, then she'd advise on the most propitious times for conception and would make up a special herbal tea or a list of vitamin and mineral food supplements based on what the cards revealed. So Linzi made an appointment, and drove down there on her next afternoon off.

The address was in one of the rundown terraced houses across the road from the big parking lot on the seafront. The woman's name was Maeve, and she had a blousy, sun-tanned, gypsyish look: Celtic motif tattoos, hennaed hair, big silver jewellery. She took twenty quid off Linzi before leading her in to a cramped, over-furnished sitting room that smelled of cats and sandalwood incense, where they sat facing each other across a small table.

'You want a baby,' Maeve announced. 'You have been trying and failing to fall pregnant. Your husband . . . no, don't tell me, darling . . . is older than you. You are his second . . . third . . . wife. Don't tell me, I will tell you. You are very keen to start a family, but he, perhaps . . . no, he is also keen. But his children . . . no, no, of course, he has no children. I see that. But the reason . . . Let's see what the cards have to say.'

She opened a wooden box, removed a velvet bag from it, and a deck of cards from that, which she shuffled. She told Linzi to take three cards from the deck and lay them out face-up.

These were not the brightly coloured tarot cards Linzi had expected. Instead, each one offered a murky black and white image like a bad reproduction of a very old photograph, and it was hard to make any sense of them at first glance.

One card showed a dancer, a man who was naked except for a belt tied loosely around his waist and a close-fitting cap on his head, caught mid-pirouette, balancing on one pointed foot, the other leg bent at the knee, arms folded behind his back. His eyes were closed and he was calmly smiling.

The second card had a picture of a woman with a dog's body – or a pregnant bitch with a woman's head. The female face was fixed in a blank, upwards stare, mouth gaping open as if to swallow the object of her gaze, a large silver egg suspended just above her head.

The third card involved a great number of knives and a bleeding body. Before she could make out anything more, Maeve had scooped up all three and returned them to the deck which she cut and shuffled feverishly, muttering, 'That's bad. Very bad.'

'Shall I try again?' Linzi asked meekly.

The woman shot her a venomous glare. 'He won't give you a baby.'

'You mean J.D.?'

'Don't let him trick you.'

'Are you talking about my husband?'

'You shouldn't have married him if you weren't prepared to be faithful.'

'I *am* faithful!' She stared at the fortune-teller, outraged. 'I haven't slept with anyone but J.D., not since our very first date!'

'"Slept with". So oral sex doesn't count.' The woman sneered at her. 'You can't lie to me. You've been unfaithful to your man once, and the cards show it happening again.'

She felt the blood drain from her head and saw little starry spots in the darkness. The bad thing. How did she know? 'I didn't . . . I wasn't . . . I wasn't *cheating* on him. Do the cards tell you *why*?'

Maeve put the cards away. 'I don't care why. That's *your* problem. But I see what's coming, and it's not good. It would be very bad for you to cheat on your husband, especially with that one.'

'I'm not going to cheat on J.D. – I love him! I came here because I thought you were going to help us have a baby. Can't you make me some tea, prescribe some herbs and vitamins?'

Maeve stood up and began to move towards the door. 'I won't help you with fertility until you sort out this problem with your husband. You'll have to decide what you want: this marriage, or something else.'

Linzi remained stubbornly in her seat, twisting around to face the other woman. 'I want this marriage. And a baby. Are you saying I can't? Not have J.D.'s baby? That he's sterile? Please, you have to tell me. I have a right to know.'

Maeve sighed and stopped in the doorway, playing with one of the heavy silver chains hanging from her neck. 'Your husband won't give you a baby. And the other one can't.'

'What "other one"? There is no man in my life but J.D. I swear.'

The woman responded with a hard, contemptuous stare. 'You have to leave now.'

Linzi's feeling of shock had faded, and now she just felt indignant. Twenty quid for that! Not a proper reading, one little incident, taken out of context, misunderstood . . . it was an insult. Maeve might have some kind of psychic talent, to have picked up something, but she'd got it completely wrong.

The bad thing. She thought about it again as she waited for a gap in the traffic that would allow her to cross the street. They never talked about it, but it had cast a shadow over their relationship, and it haunted J.D., a ghost roused every time he had a flash of jealousy over some harmless incident.

But he had no right to feel jealous. Maeve had misunderstood, but J.D. knew perfectly well she hadn't been cheating on him – she'd only sucked that cop's dick so J.D. wouldn't lose his licence.

She'd felt his desperation; she knew as well as he what it would mean. So, a quick, wordless transaction: I'll do you, and you won't do him.

He could have stopped it with a word or a look, but he hadn't. And he had been grateful, at least until his gratitude had soured into resentment. She didn't expect thanks – she would have preferred they pretend it never happened – but why couldn't he understand that when you loved someone as she loved him, no sacrifice was too great?

In her dream Linzi plaited narrow strips of leather into a strong, flexible cord, which became a noose around the tanned and weathered neck of a man who wore nothing else except a soft cap made of animal hide and a flat leather belt loose around his middle. She woke up with the image vivid in her mind, understanding that the 'dancer' she'd seen on the fortune-teller's card was the hanged man.

As the house drew closer to completion, Linzi felt more and more unhappy about the prospect of moving into it. Although the house itself was not the problem – that was turning out to be even better than she'd dared to imagine; you'd have to be crazy to prefer any of the flats she'd ever occupied, or the small end-of-terrace ex-council house that she'd grown up in. She didn't think she was crazy. She hadn't seen anything that looked like a dead body for months, but the creepy black and white picture on the fortune teller's card had merged in her memory with the body she'd seen in the ditch and become an ominous presence that she sensed lying in wait for her, just out of sight, every time they took the turning off the A47 and headed for what J.D. already called their home.

It was impossible to tell him she didn't want to live there, especially not when he was looking forward to it so much, and had put so much money and effort into it. So they moved in, and she told herself she would soon get used to it.

The first week in the new house was something like a second honeymoon. J.D. took a week off work so they could take their time settling in. They hardly went anywhere, except to the village for supplies, or meals in the pub; the days passed in a pleasurable round of companionable work as they sanded and painted and moved things around, and their nights were filled with sex both vigorous and tender. Linzi had never seen her husband so completely happy. He thought she was nervy only because pregnancy still eluded her, and kept encouraging her to relax.

Mostly, as long as J.D. was around, Linzi did manage to relax. She felt safe enough in their new house, looking inwards, happiest when the curtains shut out any sight of the featureless marshes that surrounded them, and she left all the outdoor chores to her husband, having found that no matter what direction she was facing, she was plagued by the uncomfortable sensation that someone was creeping up on her from behind.

And at night, she dreamed about the hanged man.

Sometimes she was plaiting the noose; sometimes she fitted it around his unresisting neck, before or after bestowing a kiss upon his motionless mouth. At other times she was not so immediately involved but stood huddled at the back of a solemn crowd and watched him die, his legs kicking, feet dancing on air, semen spurting a final blessing on the barren ground below.

After J.D. had gone back to work, Linzi invited her mother over for lunch. It was her first visit to the new house.

'So much light in this room,' said her mother, approvingly. 'In all the rooms, in fact. I love the big windows. What a great view.'

Standing slightly behind her mother, Linzi peeked over her shoulder at the long, flat treeless expanse stretching away beneath the blue sky. Although more attractive now in summer colours, she still found it a sinister sight. 'You think so?'

'You don't?' Her mother turned to give her a searching look. 'Is something wrong, Linz?'

She shrugged. 'I just think it's sort of bleak. Come outside,' she added quickly, 'into the garden. Not that it is anything like a garden yet, but . . . I'd like to know what you think.'

Her mother took the request seriously and examined the land from every side. She even got down on her knees and dug into the soil with her hands. Linzi, meanwhile, put her back against a wall of the house and watched her mother closely for any signs that she felt an invasive, invisible presence, but if she did nothing showed.

They went back inside and ate quiche and salad while Linzi's mother made a list of plants her daughter might want to consider and sketched out two possible plans for landscaping. 'It won't look so bleak once you've planted a few shrubs. Maybe, while you're waiting for things to take hold, you could put out a few pots, and some garden furniture, just things for your eye to rest on.' She put her pencil down. 'Now why don't you tell me what you really wanted to talk to me about.'

'Did you feel anything . . . anything *wrong* . . . out there?'

'No, I told you, the soil looks very rich and good; not boggy as I'd expected. Whoever lived here in the past must have tended it well.'

'I don't mean that.' Linzi drew a deep breath. 'Do you remember, when I was really little, you were going to leave me and Tilda with a child-minder, and we went to her house – and then walked straight out again? You said there was no way . . . you felt something wrong in the place, and weren't surprised at all when we heard a few months later that her boyfriend was arrested for being a paedo?'

'Of course I remember.'

'You sensed something wrong in her house. Something bad,

dangerous, even though there was nothing to see. I want to know if you sense anything *here*.'

Alarm flickered in her mother's eyes. 'Linzi, honey, you can come home with me now, stay as long as you like, if you decide—'

'What? No!' Tears sprang to her eyes and she stared, open-mouthed. 'Why would you think—? You want me to leave J.D., don't you? I knew it! You never liked him.'

Her mother threw up her hands. 'I didn't say anything! You're the one who brought up that horrible—'

'I was talking about the way you *sensed* something wrong. That's what you said, that as soon as you walked through the door, you just knew. So I wondered—'

'—if I sensed something here? No. But why should you expect me to, if everything's rosy?'

'I've felt something – not about J.D. This place is haunted. The land.' It all came tumbling out: the dead man in the ditch, the deleted photograph, her feelings, her dreams . . . 'I think – no, I'm *sure* – a man was killed here a long time ago, hanged and then buried as some kind of sacrifice. I think it's his spirit I sense.'

Her mother sighed, shifted in her chair, shot a glance at the clock on the oven. 'Why ask me about it? I've never seen a ghost in my life.'

'But you're sensitive to atmospheres. You knew Tilda and I wouldn't be safe with that woman – you sensed *evil* – you even said so, later!'

'Yes, I did. She seemed all right on the phone, and she had good references, but the moment I walked into her house—' She stopped. 'There was just something about her. But she was a person; alive. How can a dead man hurt you? Whether he was good or evil in his life, after he's dead, he can't *do* anything.'

'You don't believe in ghosts?'

It was a challenge her mother deflected. 'I'm not saying that. I don't know what you saw. I will say this: I never heard of anyone being killed by a ghost. I'd be more afraid of the living.'

'So you think it's safe to stay here?'

'What does J.D. think?'

She turned to look at the clock. 'He never saw it.'

Her mother stood up, and Linzi rose too, saying half-heartedly, 'You should stay . . . and say hello to J.D.'

'No, I have to get back. I've got a meeting this evening. Linzi, whatever you're worried about—'

'I just told you.'

'Well, share it with J.D. That's my advice. I know neither of my marriages worked out, but I do know that what troubles one partner is bound to affect the other. You'll only make things worse if you keep it to yourself.'

Although she ignored her advice to tell J.D., Linzi took heart from her mother's remark that the dead couldn't hurt the living. She didn't want J.D. to feel haunted as she did. His obliviousness was her bulwark. One evening as she passed the kitchen window she caught sight of an unpleasantly familiar shape on the ground, just behind a pile of gravel waiting to be spread, and the shock brought her to a halt and made her lean towards the glass, peering out intently, just as J.D. came up behind her.

'What are you looking at?'

'Oh! I don't know what it is – there, behind the gravel, can you see it?'

'What sort of something? Big or little?'

She opened her arms. 'Big.'

'I don't see anything.'

And as he spoke, it was gone.

But the sense of a sinister, lurking presence remained, and intensified as the days began to grow shorter. She was aware of it, like an assassin waiting to jump out at her, every time she came home, from the moment she stepped out of her car until, nerves taut and vibrating with fear, she managed to scurry into the house and shut the door. Only then did she dare to relax, a little.

That her husband was unable to see the dead man, that he was seemingly immune to any sense of its presence, reassured her. She thought his blindness kept her safe when he was home. The one thing she was dreading was the first time she'd have to spend the night alone.

It would happen very soon. Once a fortnight his scheduled delivery rounds included an overnight stay – mandatory, whenever further driving would push him over the safety limits for hours behind the wheel. Drivers broke those limits all the time, of course, including J.D., but after a recent high-profile fatal accident his company was cracking down.

She was trying to be cool about it, but knew that he'd picked up on her nervousness. The day before he was to leave, she was coming back from shopping and as she glanced across the emptiness to their house, she saw his van, at least an hour before she'd expected him, and called to let him know she was on her way.

'I've been shopping, too,' he said. 'I bought a surprise – well, it's for the house, but I think it will make you happy.'

She felt happy as she pulled in to park beside his van, until she saw something that gripped her heart with a nameless dread: the front door to the house was wide open.

Leaving her purse, phone, bags, everything in the car, she galloped inside, calling his name in blind panic.

'What's wrong?' He was in the kitchen, a carton, packaging, tools on the counter.

'You left the door open!'

'Jesus, Linz, so what? We can't let a little air in? I heard you slam it hard enough!'

She stood with jaw clenched, hands in fists, and tried to regain control.

He came over and held her. 'What's wrong? You didn't bash into my van?'

'No, no, it's fine. I'm fine. I just— I just saw the door and thought— thought someone might— might be inside.'

'So? You knew I was here; I talked to you a minute ago.'

She could think of no plausible explanation and was determined not to speak her fear aloud, her terror that the dead man she had seen in the ditch and then closer on the ground outside was now inside the house with them. But she knew it was true. She could feel that the tenuous safety of their home had been breached by that old ghost.

'Are you going to tell me what happened?' His voice was gentle; he didn't sound angry at all.

'I don't know,' she said, her voice tiny as she clung to him. 'But when I saw the door hanging open, I got scared.'

'Wow. I definitely made the right choice of what to buy you today.'

She was still trying to summon sufficient interest to ask what it was when he said, 'But I'll show you after we've searched the house and you can see we're alone here.'

It was obvious as they walked through the large, light and still sparsely furnished rooms that there were few places a man might hide, but Linzi knew the intruder she feared could hide in plain sight. She didn't know why she'd been cursed with the ability to see him and found herself wishing J.D. *would* see the dead man, just once. Then he'd know what she'd been going through, and they could talk about how they were going to deal with the fact that the ghost of an ancient sacrifice now inhabited their home.

But neither of them saw anything that did not belong, and Linzi had to pretend to be comforted by J.D.'s present to her of a CCTV system. With the cameras mounted outside, she could monitor the property, all approaches to the house, from the TV set in the bedroom. Thus, if she heard spooky noises from outside while he was away, she could check them out without even having to show herself at the window, and find out if it was a fox, or a gust of wind, or even a couple of kids from the village looking for somewhere to take drugs and have sex. She thanked him as ardently as she could, because he had meant well; he couldn't know modern technology was utterly useless against the thing she feared.

But he must have picked up the fact that she was not as reassured as she pretended, because he suggested she invite her mother to stay over while he was away. Considering his prickly relationship with her, the suggestion was staggeringly generous. But she turned it down.

'And then go through this whole rigmarole again in two weeks? No, I have to get used to a night on my own some time. Might as well be tonight,' she told him before she hugged and kissed him goodbye.

The day passed peacefully enough, soundtrack supplied by Radio One as she painted the upstairs room they'd designated as the nursery. The light, buttery yellow would be a good choice for a child of either sex, although she still thought about wallpaper for one wall, pattern to be chosen when she knew she was expecting.

She talked to J.D. around eight, assured him she was coping. He said he'd try to phone her back later, but if he hadn't, she should phone him at bedtime. She agreed, although she wasn't sure what counted as bedtime when they were apart. She was quite tired by ten, but the thought of going to bed alone made her linger downstairs, drinking the rest of a bottle of wine and watching some rubbish film until she nearly fell asleep on the couch. Then she staggered upstairs and fell into bed and into a light, woozy sleep.

A sound, something her sleeping mind recognised without alarm, brought her awake, not frightened, but utterly bewildered. What time was it, and what night? She could feel the still, solid presence of the man sleeping beside her. But if J.D. was home, whose was the key in the door downstairs?

Laying one hand on a sheeted shoulder she whispered, 'J.D.! Honey, wake up!'

From downstairs came the familiar sequence of beeps that meant the alarm system was being disarmed. But who else knew their code? Maybe somebody from the security company, but—

'Honey?' Still more confused than frightened, she fumbled for the light-switch on the hanging cord, and heard someone mounting the stairs.

'J.D.!' She said his name, loud and urgent, as the light came on, and she sat up, shutting her eyes briefly against the flare of light as she tugged at the sheet which he'd pulled up over his head. 'Honey, wake *up*.'

Then she saw what was lying next to her, curled on his side in an almost foetal position, naked brown skin like ancient leather, face beneath the close-fitting cap serenely smiling in death, and the terrified scream that rose in her throat strangled her, cutting off not only sound but breath. In the instant before she blacked out, she saw her husband standing in the doorway, staring at the bed – but not at her.

Mere seconds later, when she came to, she screamed again, out loud this time. Recoiling in horror, she jerked convulsively up and out of the bed before she noticed that it was empty.

She stopped in the doorway, clutching at the doorframe for support, and looked again. Not only was the bed empty, the bedclothes were disturbed only on the side where she had been. There was no depression to indicate that any other head had rested on J.D.'s pillows since she'd plumped them up after making the bed that morning. But J.D. had seen him – she had seen the direction of his gaze and, more importantly, the look on his face; a look she knew she would never forget.

'J.D.?' She tried to call, but her voice was little more than a whisper.

Where was he? Her husband had disappeared as utterly as the ghastly corpse. She had to ask herself if the whole experience had been a nightmare from which she had only now awakened.

Stepping into the dark hall, she felt an unexpected draught. Putting on the light, she looked down the stairs and saw the front door was wide open. Descending, she heard the sound of a motor starting, the easily recognisable, throaty note of J.D.'s van, shifting hard into reverse, flinging up gravel, then driving off at speed.

Uselessly she called her husband's name, ran down the stairs and then back up again for her phone, seeing in her mind's eye the dark, angry flush on his face, the vein throbbing in his temple, tears in his fixed, furious eyes as he pressed harder on the accelerator, as if by going faster he could outpace his own jealous rage.

He thought he'd seen another man in bed with her. Why hadn't he stayed to be sure, stayed to curse her, stayed to fight? She had to reach him, had to tell him the truth, had to make him understand . . .

But his phone went straight to voicemail. She was listening impatiently to the mechanical instructions for leaving a message when she heard the scream of tortured brakes, the slam of metal against metal, the final, shattering sound of a car crash up on the main road. Heart in her throat, she grabbed her keys and ran for her own car, barefoot and in her nightgown, unable to think of anything but the necessity of reaching him, imagining there must be something she could do to help him, to save him; clinging to that belief right up to the moment when she reached the site of the accident and saw her husband lying where he'd been thrown through the windscreen when his van went off the road, half curled on his side, neck broken, already dead in the ditch.

LISA TUTTLE made her first professional sale forty years ago with the short story 'Stranger in the House' – now the opening entry in *Stranger in the House*, Volume One of her Collected Supernatural Fiction, published by Ash-Tree Press.

Perhaps best known for her short fiction, which includes the International Horror Guild Award-winning tale 'Closet Dreams', she is also the author of several novels, including *The Pillow Friend*, *The Mysteries* and *The Silver Bough*, as well as books for children and non-fiction works.

Although born and raised in America, she has been a British resident for the past three decades, and currently lives with her family in Scotland.

As the author explains, '"The Man in the Ditch" was inspired by *The Bog People* by P.V. Glob – or at least by the photograph on the cover. (I don't think I ever actually read that book.)

'I'm not sure when I began to write the first draft, but it must have been when I was still living in Texas, in the days before personal computers, because it was typed on my old IBM Selectric. Fast-forward three decades, travelling through the bleak midwinter to a funeral in Norfolk, gazing out the car window across the fens, I realised *this* was the proper setting for that long-unfinished story . . . As soon as I got back home to Scotland, I wrote it.

'If short fiction was paid by the hour, instead of the word, I should be rich by now. Fortunately, most of my short stories aren't *quite* so long in the making.'

A Child's Problem

—REGGIE OLIVER—

*O*n 28th August 1843 a rising young artist called Richard Dadd
(1817–1886) attacked his father with a razor and killed him
in Cobham Park near Gravesend, Kent. At his trial Dadd was found
guilty but insane, and spent the rest of his life in secure institu-
tions, firstly Bedlam (Bethlem Hospital, now the Imperial War
Museum), then Broadmoor, where he died. While there, Dadd
painted the works for which he is now famous. One of the most
disturbing and enigmatic of these is 'The Child's Problem' (1857),
which hangs in the Tate Gallery collection. It shows a child fearfully reaching up to move a chess piece on a table, while, close by,
a sinister figure, head half-covered by a cloth, appears to be sleeping.
No one has been able to discover the origin or meaning of this
haunting image, but it is known that during the 1850s Dadd was
frequently visited in Broadmoor by Sir George St Maur MP Bart.
(1802–1883), a social reformer who took a great interest in the
treatment of the insane, and of Dadd in particular. It may have
been at the instigation of Sir George that Dadd conceived 'The
Child's Problem'.

I

ONE AFTERNOON IN JULY of the year 1811 a carriage drew up on the drive in front of Tankerton Abbey in the county of Suffolk. It was a clear bright day with a slight breeze, and high white clouds. Deep black shadows lurked among the elms in the park and around the ancient masonry of the house. For a moment nothing happened, then the Abbey's great Gothic portals opened and out ran a liveried footman to let down the steps and open the door of the waiting vehicle.

From it emerged a woman and a man, both in their thirties, followed by a boy of nine. The boy, whose name was George, wore a plum-coloured velvet suit and white shirt with wide ruffled collar such as one sees in fashionable portraits of children by Lawrence and Hoppner. George might have been thought a pretty child, if a little inclined to plumpness, were it not for his sullen expression. The man and woman, his parents, were a well-nourished, undistinguished looking pair, and both of them, particularly the woman, appeared anxious. Their names were Julius and Amelia St Maur, and the house they were visiting belonged to Julius' elder brother, Sir Augustus St Maur, Baronet.

Tankerton Abbey no longer exists, but in those days it was a curious structure. It had been acquired by the St Maur family shortly after its dissolution by Henry VIII, and parts of it had been successively destroyed and built up as the fortunes of the family varied. In the late 18th century it was restored by the late Sir Hercules St Maur, father to Augustus and Julius, employing the fashionable Gothic style in imitation of his friend Horace Walpole at Strawberry Hill. Being half-ruin, half-imitation Gothic, it had about it a curious air of incompleteness, as if its owner had never quite made up his mind whether to live in it or contemplate it in thoughtful melancholy as a *memento mori*. It was finely situated, though, in the heart of a wide shallow valley and the park had been laid out in Humphry Repton's best manner.

Sir Augustus did not meet his relatives at the door; instead they were greeted by Hargreave, the baronet's butler, accompanied by a posse of footmen who took some boxes and other baggage from the carriage. Hargreave was a tall, thin man with prematurely white hair. In a manner that was notably formal and unwelcoming he told the family that Sir Augustus would see them shortly in the library.

Though the two brothers had corresponded regularly, they had barely seen one another since their father's death over a decade ago, for they lived very different lives. In accordance with family tradition, Augustus, being the elder son, had inherited not only the title but the entire Suffolk estate and the sugar plantations in Antigua, from which the bulk of his considerable wealth was derived. Julius, the younger son, had been left a small annuity which was not enough to keep himself and his family in the manner to which he felt entitled. He had entered the medical profession and, by dint of some industry and good family connections, had risen to become a Lecturer in Anatomy at the Royal College of Surgeons in London.

As both he and his wife were somewhat extravagant in their habits, his salary had never been enough and when, again through family influence, he was offered a post as the Principal of a new medical school in Calcutta at a considerably higher salary than the one he enjoyed in London, Julius, with his wife's wholehearted agreement, accepted.

There was, however, one problem: their son George. He was a child of what they called in those days 'a delicate constitution', and his mother believed the Indian climate might do him irreparable damage. Besides, George was approaching the age when he must be sent to school in England, and the long journeys by sea to and from India would be deleterious to both health and purse. A correspondence ensued between the two brothers, which resulted in the agreement that young George should stay with his uncle at Tankerton and be schooled there by tutors until it was time to send him to Eton; in those days boys as young as eight were being entered as Oppidans at that school.

It had not escaped Julius's attention that his brother was a childless widower who had shown no inclination to marry after the early death, some seven years previously, of his wife. Both Julius and Amelia thought that it might be as well for young George to become acquainted with the estate he might one day be master of, and the man from whom, in all probability, he would inherit.

Standing on the drive, George contemplated the Abbey with some dismay. It was quite as large as he had expected it to be, but not nearly as well ordered. He had become used to the neat and disciplined modern houses of the London squares, with their sash windows and their doorways set in the middle of each classically symmetrical façade. What he saw here was a confusion of old and new tumbled together, in parts crumbling, in parts overgrown with ivy and other predatory plants.

Stone gargoyles retched from the guttering; crocketed pinnacles and finials thrust upwards from the battlements like threatening fists (the word 'romantic' was not yet part of the boy's vocabulary). Moreover, for someone used to the bustle of London – the rattle of carriages, the clip of horses, the cry of street hawkers – it was all far too quiet. The faint twitter of bird song barely impinged on his unaccustomed ears.

George was a stubborn, spoilt child. He had decided that he was going to be unhappy at Tankerton and that he would make his parents feel as uncomfortable as possible about deserting him.

The family was now in the entrance hall, a vast, uncomfortable vaulted space that must once have been a refectory or some other public chamber in its days as a monastery. The flagstones were grey and worn. There was a slight draught from somewhere which, even in the depths of June, made them shiver. Hargreave passed them without a glance in their direction and made his way towards an elaborate doorway surmounted by an ogival arch. He knocked and, upon hearing a faint reply from within, entered.

Some time elapsed. Amelia tugged at her husband's sleeve and suggested he go himself to see what was happening, but Julius was reluctant. George passed the time by stamping on the stone floor as loudly as possible to test the echo of the hall until his mother told him to stop.

Hargreave finally emerged from the room beyond the doorway to announce: 'Sir Augustus will see you now in the library.' The door was opened and the three of them went in without so much as a look in Hargreave's direction, which is why they did not notice the mocking smile on his face.

The library they entered had also been constructed in the Gothic style. Its walls were almost entirely covered by bookcases of mahogany and surmounted by shallow perpendicular arches, their shelves protected by framed glass doors. The lower parts were composed of cupboards for keeping albums of prints and draw- ings. Two large leaded casement windows lit the room from the west. Opposite the windows, over the fireplace, hung Gainsborough's portrait of Sir Hercules St Maur in his youthful pride, leaning against an oak tree, a black spaniel at his feet, fowling piece tipped gracefully over one arm, the Abbey adumbrated in the blue distance behind him.

In the middle of the room was a great oak table covered with papers and, at one end, a chessboard with what looked like a game in progress. Behind it sat Sir Augustus. He was barely five years his brother's senior, but he looked considerably older. He was thin and frail, an emaciated version of Julius, with a longer nose and more pronouncedly saturnine features. When he stood up to greet his visitors, George could see that his uncle was almost half a foot taller than his father. A tight white stock pushed up his chin and exaggerated the aspect of superiority. His pale skin had a waxy look to it. He wore a tight-fitting pale blue coat that came down to his feet. George could not tell if it was an overcoat or a dressing gown, but decided on the latter as it appeared to be made of silk.

Sir Augustus, moving slowly with the assistance of an ebony cane, limped out from behind the table and advanced on his sister-in-law whose hand he kissed with formal courtesy. Then he fixed his eyes on her son.

'So! This is young Master George.'

George was conscious of two pale blue eyes staring at him with detached curiosity as if he were a flea under a microscope.

'And you are to spend the next eighteen months or so in my charge until you are fit for Eton. You must be made robust. I hear that the new head man there, Dr Keate, is a great flogger. Have you ever been flogged, Master George? You have not tasted the birch?' George shook his head indignantly. 'I see you are no disciplinarian, Brother Julius. But, as I recall, the worst of it was not the floggings but the fights between boys. Did you know that in my time at Eton there was a boy killed in a fight? I witnessed some of it, but wearied long before the end. Thirty-three rounds. The boy who won was in almost as bad a way as his victim. He came back the following term though, you know. I wonder what became of him? I heard a rumour that he went into the Army and was killed in the Peninsula.'

During this speech Sir Augustus kept his eyes on George, looking for a reaction. George felt some alarm, but the events that his uncle was describing were so remote from his experience that it dulled any terror he might have felt. Eton was more than a year away. Perhaps before then he could contrive to escape its embrace.

'I have secured the services of an excellent tutor for young George,' said Sir Augustus, now addressing George's parents. 'A Mr Vereker. He is our curate at Tankerton Parva. My rector, as

you know, is Dr Bulstrode and he spends all his time in the metrop-
olis conducting antiquarian researches. He pays Mr Vereker a
pittance to take the services and carry out parochial duties. Mr
Vereker is also burdened, as these wretched curates so often are,
with a wife and no fewer than four young children, so extra remu-
neration is much needed. He is a fair scholar. A Balliol man, I
believe.'

'We are very grateful to you for taking such pains on George's
behalf, Brother Gus,' said Julius.

'So I should hope, Brother Julius,' said Sir Augustus, turning his
back on him and studying the chessboard on his table. He picked
up a white piece, contemplated a move, then returned it to its original position on the board. 'And now, if you will excuse me, madam,
gentlemen, I have some estate business to attend to. We meet at
dinner, which is taken here at half-past five o'clock. Hargreave will
show you to your rooms.'

They were dismissed.

The hours that followed were among the most miserable and
unsatisfactory of George's young life. He had hoped, at the very
least, that the prospect of parting from her child would provoke
his mother to extreme tenderness and attention towards him.
George would have welcomed her tears, so that he too could have
an excuse to cry, but none came. Amelia St Maur was kindly, but
brisk. It was as if she were already distancing herself from her son,
so that the break, when it came, would be less agonising. George
tried to do the same, but he would have preferred to show and be
shown grief.

His room was large and luxurious. There was a four-poster bed
with rich damask hangings of blue, faded almost to grey. There
were great presses and cupboards with panels of exquisite
marquetry. A painting on the wall depicted masked revellers in
Venice. The grandeur did not console him. George saw nothing
but a great space in which to be lonely. The one slight consola-

tion that he could find in his misery was in the view from his window.

He looked down onto the balustraded terrace at the back of the house. A few wide, shallow steps led down to a lawn dotted with trees, a great oak tree to his right, several elms to his left, and, in the centre, a magnificent Cedar of Lebanon, not yet in its prime. Beyond this was a lake with a grassy peninsula jutting into its swan-haunted waters, on which stood a square, domed temple with an Ionic portico.

Conversation at dinner that evening was awkward. Mrs St Maur attempted to regale her brother-in-law with the latest society gossip from London, but her efforts were greeted by raised eyebrows and a cold stare from Sir Augustus, and embarrassment from her husband and son. It was the first time in his life that George had been ashamed of his mother, a new and puzzling sensation. He felt pity for her, an emotion which enhanced rather than dissipated his longing to stay with her. That night in his vast bedroom he wept himself to sleep and no one heard him.

II

George saw his parents off dry-eyed the following morning after breakfast. Sir Augustus did not come out to say farewell from the drive, but contented himself with waving a large white cambric handkerchief from behind the library window. When they had gone, George found himself completely alone for the first time in his life, with no one to tell him what to do. He did not have the courage to go to his uncle in the library, as he was already very much afraid of him. The servants, who all seemed to be male, were elusive. George encountered Hargreave once in the hall and was coolly ignored. The boy had been fond of teasing and bullying his parents' servants in London, but they had been female for the most part, and he had been 'Young Master George'. At Tankerton Abbey he did not know quite who he was. He stamped his foot and once more heard that rather satisfying echo.

Eventually, he decided that he must perforce amuse himself, so he set out to explore the Abbey that might one day be his. The exploration was not as satisfying as he had hoped. The Abbey was large and rambling, with two floors, above which were a series of attics inhabited by the servants. However, most of its many rooms were locked. Those that were not were either empty or full of uninteresting lumber.

Only one of the unlocked rooms contained an item of interest. This was a hexagonal chamber at one end of the Abbey's west wing, at the junction of a right-angle and flanked by locked rooms on both sides. The room had a bay window looking out on the park. The room was bare and curtainless, its dusty boards bleached by the sun. No pictures hung on its walls, but in the centre was a large statue. It was plain white and considerably chipped, made not from marble, as George had at first thought, but of plaster. Its base was about a foot high and had lettering incised on it.

It showed a life-sized naked boy, perhaps a little older than George, kneeling on a rough piece of ground, looking upwards, his hands raised and clasped together as if in supplication. Around the wrists were manacles connected by a hanging chain. Though the whole statue was white, George saw from the features of the face and the tight curly hair that the boy was a Negro.

The legend on the base read: AM I NOT A MAN AND A BROTHER?

George walked all around the object, as if some aspect of it might offer an explanation. He had heard his parents occasionally refer to the slave trade; they would speak of 'abolitionists' with vague disapproval. He had even seen prints in shop windows with images not dissimilar to the statue. Once at a tea party to which his mother had taken him, he saw a sugar bowl with AM I NOT

A MAN AND A BROTHER? printed on it, together with: NO SLAVE SUGAR FOUND IN ME. When his mother saw George eyeing the bowl she had tut-tutted, and soon after they had left the party.

'Did anyone tell you that you might enter this room?'

The words which came from behind him struck George like a blow in the back. His Uncle Augustus stood in the doorway, leaning on his cane, wearing his blue coat that came down to the ground. George noted that he wore Turkish slippers, exotically embroidered, with toes that curled upwards to a point. In his eyes, they contributed something dangerous, even mad to his uncle's appearance.

'Nobody told me that I might not, sir,' said George.

Sir Augustus sniffed to express his displeasure and turned on his heel.

George stood shivering with fear in the room with the statue for some minutes. He began to understand that it was not so much Sir Augustus that he feared as the knowledge that he could no longer be a child. That, he realised, was why he mourned the departure of his parents. He felt a vague affection for them, as they did for him; what he missed most, though, was that they had bestowed on him the privilege of innocence.

George felt like stamping his foot, but he did not. He simply waited until he felt his fear and anger drain away into the silence, to be replaced by a small, cold resolve. Suddenly he felt very hungry. No one had summoned him to luncheon. He left the room and came down the front stairs.

In the hall he encountered Hargreave, who pretended not to see him. This was not to be borne.

'Hargreave!' Hargreave turned slowly to face George who was on the stairs a few feet above him.

'Master George?'

'Why was I not informed about luncheon?'

'Sir Augustus does not take luncheon.'

'Never?'

'Never, Master George.' Having given this answer, Hargreave moved swiftly in the direction of the servants' quarters as if to forestall any further interrogations.

George descended the stairs and stood perfectly still in the hall. The silent breezes chilled him. Outside the sun shone. Its slanted rays pierced the armorial window on the landing of the grand staircase, dappling the grey stone floor with soft paw marks of gold and blue light. As he was waiting for his will to return to him, George studied these evanescent colours, vestiges of the St Maur arms painted in light: azure, a gryphon or passant.

To his right was the door to the library where George, with the intuitive faith of the young, was sure he would find his uncle. He knocked on the door, but received no reply. After a moment's hesitation he entered. The room was hot, bright and drowsy, but it was not empty. In the chair behind the table sat Sir Augustus with a large white handkerchief draped over his long, waxy features, hiding his eyes from the glare of the sun. Motes of dust turned slowly in its beams. Sir Augustus, evidently asleep, took long breaths whose expulsion slightly disturbed the white cambric, like an irregular heartbeat.

George gazed in wonder at his sleeping uncle. The sight pleased him, as the sight of all figures of authority in a vulnerable state pleases. On the table were as usual the papers and the chessboard. George had begun to learn chess from his father and had shown some promise. He came closer to the table while his uncle slept on.

For some minutes George studied the chessboard. There were five white pieces on the board and three black. It did not take George long to see that white could checkmate in two moves. It was a comparatively simple problem, a child's problem. He began to feel an irresistible urge to make the White Queen's move which would secure victory. If he could make the move while his uncle slept, he could baffle the man, become almost his equal. For a moment or two fear contended with ambition. He could not reach the chess piece from where he stood. He had to creep around to the side of the table on which his uncle sat and reach up from there.

He made the journey soundlessly. Now his eyes were only on the White Queen. He was reaching up to move it three squares along the board when he found his wrist suddenly gripped by something cold and hard. The sleeping figure reared up, the cambric falling from his uncle's face. The long, stern features were immobile, the eyes were fixed on him, the strong cold grip held him immobile.

'Who told you it was your move?' said Sir Augustus.

After a pause George replied, 'It didn't matter. Even if it was black's turn, he'd have been mated in two moves.'

'Who said you could be white?'

Very slowly Sir Augustus released his hold on George's wrist while at the same time lifting the index finger of his right hand to command him to stay.

'I wanted to know about luncheon, sir,' said George, fully conscious of the inadequacy of his reply.

'I never take luncheon,' said Sir Augustus.

'Hargreave told me.'

'Did he, by God! Then why are you troubling me?'

'I am not used to being without it, sir.'

'Then you should grow accustomed to it. Heaven knows you're plump enough. I suspect your mother of making a mollycoddle of you, sir.'

George blushed. His plumpness was the one subject about which he felt deeply sensitive.

'However, if you must fill your belly, go down to the kitchens and find Mrs Mace, the housekeeper. Say that I sent you. No doubt she will find you some cold beef or bread and milk, or whatever takes your fancy.'

'Where are the kitchens, Uncle?'

'Find them yourself, sir. You have a habit of going where you're not wanted. This will present you with no difficulty.' George began to walk away. 'Hold hard, Master George! I've not finished with you yet. My condition for allowing you to gorge yourself at my expense is this: this afternoon you are to go into my park to find the hanged man and bring him back to me. Do you understand?'

George nodded.

'No, you do not understand, but you may in time. When you have found it you will bring it to me here, half an hour before dinner at five o'clock. Now be off with you!'

George was a little ashamed of himself at having to go in search of Mrs Mace and the kitchens, but he did. They and she were easy to find, and they were both warm. Mrs Mace, a large, motherly soul who was prepared to make a pet of George, gave him some bread and cold beef and pickles. The occasion was somewhat marred by Hargreave, who stood and stared at George as he ate. When he had gone, George asked Mrs Mace whether she was the only woman in the house and she replied that she was. He then asked if Sir Augustus was a good man.

'He's Sir Augustus, Master George, but I don't hardly ever see him. Not since the mistress passed away.'

'How did Lady St Maur die, Mrs Mace?'

'The Lady Circe, that was her name, she came from the West Indies, where your uncle has plantations, but England didn't suit her. Sir Augustus may not have been wise to bring such a woman into the country. They say she wasted away. There's some say that she was no better than she should have been. That's all I know about that, Master George. Now, you finish that beef and them pickles and go out and play like a good boy.'

George wanted to ask Mrs Mace about the hanged man, but

thought on reflection he had better keep that business to himself.

As he left the Abbey, it occurred to George that he was walking out alone for the first time in his life. In London he had always been accompanied by his mother or a governess, or a servant who had been assigned to him. In this place, he might be the heir presumptive, but he had no servants. A clear sky was menaced by heavy accumulations of grey cloud. Beneath were trees and open ground and serpentine paths shaped by a master gardener to furnish ways where he might walk. Everything was available to him, but he had no directions, and no one would take his hand. He began again to feel indignant about his abandonment, but before the tears started, as they so easily had done until now, he realised that he must move or perish. The fall from Eden had already taken place without his consent.

The decision he made was a rational one. The only part of the park he knew was what he had seen from the window of his room, which was at the back of the house. The park was deserted. George could not see any living inhabitants: no people, no deer, not so much as a squirrel. If there were birds, then the wind was too high for him to hear their song. It made a sound in the trees like the distant crash of waves. The clouds were beginning to blow high and fast across the sky; the sun shone with fitful brilliance.

George walked around to the back of the house where the shallow stone steps led down to the lawn that sloped towards the lake. He stared at the view as if it were hostile territory. Nearly all of it had been planted and landscaped deliberately and this somehow increased the threat, though he could not tell why. There was one tree, however, which looked older, and not quite part of the Repton scheme. It was the oak, and it seemed oddly familiar. It was only as he approached the tree that George recognised it as the one against which Sir Hercules had been leaning in the Gainsborough portrait, a black hunting dog at his feet.

The more he looked at the oak the more it seemed to him that this tree was less real than the one in the painting. It looked like a bloated imitation of Gainsborough's oak, a dissolute elder brother. Something black flickered behind it, which might have been a dog's tail. George looked all around the tree but could find nothing.

A gust of wind ruffled the lake, turning it from mirror-glass to hammered pewter; a few spots of rain from a passing cloud stung him. It was a moment of decision. George could have returned to the safety and shelter of the house, but he knew he would find nothing for his delight but empty rooms and the threatening presence of his uncle.

The nearest shelter, if it could be called that, was the little classical temple on the promontory in the lake. George viewed it with some favour only because it bore a resemblance to the classical architecture he was used to in London. Its domed roof of verdigris'd copper looked sickly in the dull light. The Ionic marble portico was reached by a short flight of steps. George ran down towards it, the wind blowing in his face.

To get to the portico he had to walk around the temple. He tried to look in at the window in its side but the glass was misted over with dust and cobwebs. Evidently it had not been entered for some time. He felt a little tremor of excitement and fear.

When he reached the steps to the portico, he saw that the entrance to the body of the temple was to be made through two tall coffered bronze doors, almost black, but streaked with verdigris. He wondered if the great handles could be turned, and if he would have the strength to use them.

He pulled at one handle. The bronze door swung outwards easily, groaning loudly as it did so. George was startled by the noise, a hollow sound with screeching overtones that had an almost human quality about it.

The interior was lit by a window in each of the side walls and

a lantern at the apex of the dome. It was all white and undecor-
ated, save for a marble panel in bas-relief on the back wall. This
showed a naked man standing before a creature half-woman, half-
crouching beast. The two were staring at each other intently:
Oedipus and the Sphinx, perhaps.

In the middle of the interior space of the temple was a wooden
table painted in the French manner, and three oval-backed chairs
similarly decorated around it. On the table was a tea service of
white china engraved in black. The cups were empty, but there
were still a few pale brown crystals of sugar in the bowl. The scenes
depicted were from a West Indian sugar plantation: Negro slaves
cutting cane, overseen by a man in a wide-brimmed hat carrying
a whip; a white man and his wife at their ease on a verandah overlooking the cane fields; a slave settlement with children and chickens
playing in the dirt before a wooden shack.

The sugar bowl was decorated with the most interesting scenes.
One side showed what looked like a slave revolt, with Negroes
setting fire to a field and attacking the man with the whip and the
broad-brimmed hat. One of the Negroes was pinning a white
woman to the ground, her skirts already in disarray. The other
side showed a number of British regimental soldiers clustered under
a tree from whose branches hung a slave with a placard around
his neck. Several other slaves, their arms bound behind their backs,
were being made to watch the spectacle. Whether they were being
shown the hanged man as an example or whether they too were
destined to be the tree's fruit was not clear.

George heard a low moan behind him. He turned and saw the
bronze door slowly beginning to blow shut in the breeze. George ran
towards it. He had a great fear of the door banging to and of being
unable to escape. He managed to reach it in time and then spent
some minutes looking for an object to keep the door ajar. A fallen
branch from the ancient oak served. Having secured his exit, he went
back into the temple, picked up the sugar bowl and left with it.

When he was outside again, George carefully removed the oak branch and allowed the bronze door of the temple to swing shut. It did so with a bang and he heard the faint resonance of the sound echoing inside the building. It surprised him a little that the door had not groaned on its hinges as before. The wind had picked up and the sky was clearing of cloud.

As George passed under the oak he heard a sound which could have been its elderly branches creaking in the wind. To his ears, though, it sounded more like a heavy object on a rope swinging to and fro, though nothing like that was to be seen. He ran back to the Abbey.

At the appointed time, before dinner, George knocked on the library door. There was a pause before there came the peremptory command: 'Enter!'

Sir Augustus was seated as usual behind the table. On it, beside papers, was the chessboard, this time set up for the beginning of a game. Sir Augustus appeared to be studying it, but when he saw his nephew he started.

'Damn you, sir! What do you want here?'

'You told me to come to you half-an-hour before dinner.'

'Ah, yes! I did indeed, Master George, and I gave you a task to perform, did I not?'

'You did, sir! And I have found it.'

'What?'

'I have found the hanged man, as you asked me, Sir Augustus.'

'Have you, by God!'

George was puzzled by his uncle's evident surprise. Did he think so little of his abilities? He showed him the sugar bowl.

Sir Augustus turned it over in his hands. 'Where did you get this?'

George told him.

'Did I say you might enter the Temple of the Sphinx?'

George shook his head.

'Very well. Did you see anything else?'

George shook his head again.

'In God's name, sir, will you stop wagging your head and answer "yes" or "no" like a gentleman!'

'What else might I have seen, Sir Augustus?' There was a silence, and when it became clear to George that his uncle was not going to answer him he said, indicating the chessboard, 'Would you care for a game of chess, sir?'

'No I would not, damn your infernal impertinence, you young jackanapes. Get out, and go to blazes!'

George left the library without a word. When his heart had stopped beating hard and he was breathing freely again, he began to feel a kind of consolation, though of a cold grey sort. He now knew that he was not the only person at the Abbey who felt fear.

III

That evening Mr Vereker, the curate who was coming to tutor George the following morning, came to dine at the Abbey with George and Sir Augustus. He was a moonfaced young man, as thin as his host, though more from malnutrition, it would seem, than from asceticism. George knew very little about carnal matters; nevertheless it amazed him that such a feeble specimen should have managed to sire four children.

Sir Augustus sat at the head of the table with George and Mr Vereker on either side of him. The dinner served was excellent, with several dishes to each course, but Sir Augustus ate sparingly. He drank more than he ate, refilling his glass from a decanter of port which had been placed at his side and which he never passed to the others. George and the curate were given the beer which was also drunk in the servants' hall. There was very little conversation until the main dishes were cleared away, and then it was Sir Augustus who turned to Mr Vereker.

'I understand, sir, that your Christian name is Hamlet. The Reverend Hamlet Vereker?'

'It is, Sir Augustus,' replied Mr Vereker.

'And how does it come about that you are named for a Prince of Denmark, sir?'

'My father, Sir Augustus, was a bookseller, and a great lover of literature. He had a particular fondness for the Swan of Avon.'

'Shakespeare, man! Call him Shakespeare like a plain-speaking gentleman! We'll have none of your namby-pamby pseudo-poetical epithets here. So your father was a bookseller, eh? A lowly trade, but an honest one in the main, I doubt not. And why did not you follow it? What made you aspire to holy orders?'

'It was my own father's dearest wish, and it was to this end that he laboured hard to pay for me to go to Oxford. Besides, I believed myself to have a calling to the ministry.'

'You did, did you? Gad, what a presumptuous fellow you are, sir! So you would claim yourself to be a passable theologian?'

'I flatter myself that—'

'Doubtless you do, young Hamlet the Dane, but we'll have no flattery here. So you know your theology. Very well. I will ask you this. Do you believe in Hell?'

Mr Vereker seemed startled by the question. He shrank from Sir Augustus's unblinking gaze. 'Hell, Sir Augustus?'

'Hell, Mr Vereker. Let us have your opinion on the matter. I presume that you have one?'

'In Scripture it is said—'

'No, no, sir! Do not hide behind Scripture, like a young miss behind a curtain at her first ball. Let us have your own view on the matter. Well?'

'I believe that for some there is eternal damnation, Sir Augustus. It is a canonical belief of the Church of England.'

'Eternal damnation, eh? And you think that to be just, do you?'

'God is just, Sir Augustus.'

'I was not asking you whether God was just, sir. I was asking whether it was just, as you appear to believe, that a man – or woman – should pay everlastingly for a finite series of misdeeds on this earth. Well, Mr Vereker?'

'It is believed that all actions in time possess an eternal reverberation.'

'Do they, by God? And why should that be so? Is it not the truth that all things pass, the good and the bad, and that in life this is both our consolation and our torment?'

Mr Vereker was silent and, soon after the dessert was on the table, he made his excuses and left. George wondered whether this was the moment when Sir Augustus and he might begin to talk together as uncle and nephew, but it was not to be.

Sir Augustus merely stared at George for a few moments as if expecting something from him, then said: 'Well, then, boy, cut along! Cut along and leave me to my port.'

George was becoming accustomed to the silence of the Abbey and of the faint twitter of bird song that announced the morning from behind his heavy damask bedroom curtains. That night he felt no immediate inclination to sleep, and so looked around his bedroom. Apart from his bedroom door, there were two other doors in the walls that stood at right angles to the window. Both were locked. The fact gave George a curious satisfaction; it meant that he knew where he was, that his course was set and his only duty was to react appropriately to an inevitable destiny.

When he got into bed he listened appreciatively to the silence. Perhaps he slept for a while, and when he woke it was not because of a noise but a light, a thin steely blade of light which came from between the window curtains, cutting across his face. The moon was full.

George went to the window, hoping to see for the first time a moon not above rooftops but across trees and grass and water. He opened the curtains and looked out. There were the familiar sights, but transformed into muted shades of grey by the moon. The grass, the dully-silvered mirror of the water, the temple which he now knew to be dedicated to the Sphinx, and the familiar trees, including the oak, now painted in grisaille. The shadows were deep and impenetrable, but seemed to him fuller of life than the illumined landscape which was as still and as drained of colour as a vampire's victim.

While he stared he wondered if the shadows moved, in particular the bulbous ones that gathered like strange fungoid growths around the oak. He thought he caught again the flicker of a dog's tail, as if the animal had darted behind the tree. There was a little clutch of fear at George's heart. He breathed deeply. No dog, living or dead, seen from a window could do anything to him. The thought, as he repeated it to himself, began to give him strength so that he was partly protected from the strangeness of what happened next.

As he gazed at the shadows in the oak tree he thought he saw something within them stir that was darker even than their blackness. It was beginning to emerge from the protection of the tree, vaguely outlined as if it were a mist, but still intensely dark. Then it was standing before him, the figure of a man, or possibly a boy – the scale was so hard to determine – and, though not a single feature could be discerned from this silhouette, George knew it was looking up to him. The figure might have been naked. One arm detached itself and lifted itself up as if to demonstrate something. It was holding a length of rope or chain which had a loop in it. The outline of the man was now clearly etched so that George could see that the top of the head was covered by dense woolly hair.

The man lifted the looped rope in the air. At that moment George was startled by a faint cry from within the house – his uncle perhaps? – then silence. The figure turned and walked back into the density of the oak's shade.

For half an hour George waited in silence for the man or the dog to emerge again, but nothing came. Besides, George had a feeling that there had been a performance, which was now over. He got into bed and fell asleep almost at once. When the faint twitter of birds woke him the next day a part of him confined his experience of the previous night to the status of a dream, but a part of him did not.

Mr Vereker came that morning and unlocked another room in the Abbey which had hitherto been inaccessible to George, the schoolroom. Mr Vereker stared at the dusty shelves of books and the cobwebs that festooned the globes and the orrery in a kind of dismay. George noted his apparent helplessness with satisfaction; it could be used. As if to assert his dominance, George went to one of the tables and, having wiped away its thin patina of dust, sat down at it, smiling eagerly at his new tutor. Mr Vereker seemed relieved and began to recover his spirits.

The rest of the morning passed smoothly. They began with a little Latin, and Mr Vereker was relieved to find that George was a quick learner. Over the following days the curate, acquiring some confidence and even pleasure in his pupil's progress, was bold enough to instruct him in the rudiments of Greek. George consented to be taught out of boredom and the instinctive understanding that knowledge, any knowledge, even apparently useless knowledge, is power. He also wanted to see how far he could control Mr Vereker without his knowing it; Mr Vereker, who appeared so fearful of everything and everybody in life.

With the exception of Sundays, there were lessons till one o'clock, when George would saunter down to Mrs Mace, who was always ready with his bread and meat and pickles. One morning Mr Vereker finished earlier than usual, and so George stayed behind in the schoolroom to see if there was anything there that might amuse him. All the books proved to be worn editions of Eutropius, Virgil and the like, so of no interest, but he did find, at the back of the cupboard a chess set, an inlaid wooden board and, in addition, a battered volume, its calf boards beginning to part from the cracked spine. There was no title on the binding, so George turned to the title page and read: *Chess Analysed, or Instructions Whereby a Perfect Knowledge of this Noble Game May in a Short Time be Acquired*, a translation from the French of Philidor's classic work published in London in 1762. George decided to make this his study outside of school hours.

He came down a little later for his luncheon, only to be stopped in the hall by Hargreave. George had taken a great dislike to Hargreave, even though in the week or so that they had known each other they had barely exchanged a word. It was the man's glacial disdain that George could not stand. He seemed to look on the boy as a mere nuisance, an uncalled-for and probably tempor-ary intrusion into life at the Abbey. All this was expressed by Hargreave not through passion, but by inscrutable blankness. The man was a walking block of ice.

'Sir Augustus wishes to see you in the library, Master George. At once.' Those last two words had the inflexion of a command.

George tried to return the servant's frigid stare with one of his own. 'Very well, Hargreave, that will be all. You may go.'

It was absurd of course; George knew that. His order was super-fluous, but he felt he needed to establish an ascendancy. Hargreave did not indicate by the flicker of an eyebrow that he had been offended by George, or even that he had heard him. His pale blue eyes wandered up for a moment to the armorial window at the top of the stairs, then down to the floor again, avoiding George altogether, before he glided off.

He found his uncle, seated behind the table as usual. The chess-board was there as before, except that a few pieces had been moved, though none had been taken by either side.

'Ah, there you are, Nephew. I have been receiving very poor reports of you. They tell me that you are eating my servant Mrs Mace out of house and home with your greed, filling your plump little face with beef and bread as if we had an inexhaustible supply.'

'Who told you this, sir? Hargreave, I suppose?'

'Damn your impudence, sir! Never mind who told me, it is a fact. Do you not think it a most ungentlemanly thing for an overfed little pudding like yourself to be taking the bread out of the very mouths of my servants? Well, sir?'

'I did not think—'

'No, Nephew, you did not. Henceforth you are to be allowed bread and milk only to break your fast, and bread and cheese for luncheon. It will do you no harm, sir. You shall not starve. And when you dine at my table of an evening, you may have only what I prescribe. Do I make myself clear?'

'Perfectly, Sir Augustus.'

'And there are to be no sweetmeats or puddings until further notice unless—' he hesitated a moment. 'Since you have shown yourself so apt at solving the problem I gave you, I shall offer you another. You must find Cynossema.' He scribbled the word on a piece of paper and handed it to George. 'And tell me its name.'

George stared at the alien word. He refused to show his weakness by asking any questions on the subject. Instead he pointed to the chessboard. 'Would you care for a game, Sir Augustus?'

'No, I would not, damn your impudence. Now, cut along!'

IV

The following morning, having completed a Latin exercise without error and put Mr Vereker in a good frame of mind, George asked him about the word.

'Well, Master George,' said Mr Vereker, 'Cynossema was a naval battle in the Peloponnesian War. You will find it in the very last book of Thucydides, but I doubt that you are ready for him yet, apt though you are. Very shortly, I may try you with a little Xenophon, perhaps even Herodotus. Why do you wish to know?'

'Was Cynossema a place?'

'It was a headland at the entrance of the Hellespont in the Aegean.'

'What does it mean?'

'Master George, I think you may work that out for yourself. It is a portmanteau consisting of two separate words, the first being "cynos", a genitive form of "cyon" meaning—?'

'A dog.'

'The second word is "sema". Well, you remember how I told you that the Pythagoreans – early Gnostics in many ways – had a chant which was "soma sema" – the body is a—?'

'Tomb!'

'Excellent! And so we have—?'

'The dog's tomb. Thank you, Mr Vereker.'

'Why do you wish to know, young sir?'

'You know, Mr Vereker, you really are a most excellent teacher. It is a wonder to me, sir, why you are not a schoolmaster at a famous school.'

Mr Vereker was not one to suspect that he was being deliberately distracted by flattery; guile of that kind was beyond the scope of his understanding. When he spoke, it was to unburden himself of a long unexpressed preoccupation.

'I was elected to a Fellowship of Balliol when I obtained my degree. But Fellows of Oxford colleges may not be married. My wife Clarissa was the daughter of an Oxford apothecary. I suffered from boils and the only relief from them I could obtain was a penny ointment from Clarissa's father. I became very attached to this young lady whom I met in the shop and the depth of our attachment became such that I was—' He hesitated, then finished,

'—obliged to marry her and resign my Fellowship.

'I had already taken Holy Orders, so I was launched on the world as a poor clergyman with no influence, obliged to take what curacy I could to save my growing family from destitution. I have applied for teaching posts at some schools, but the conditions under which most masters labour is little short of slavery and they frown upon persons who are as heavily engaged in matrimony, as I.'

During the Reverend Hamlet Vereker's account George had caught a fleeting glimpse of an adult world of poverty and uncomfortable choices. It was interesting, of course, but not something he wished to dwell on. It made him decide there and then, however, that he would never marry.

That afternoon he wandered the grounds in search of the dog's tomb. Having been at some pains to discover the meaning of the name, George had thought that the rest would be easy. He only had to look for a monument in the park with a statue of a dog on it, but there was none. He did, however, discover many other curious features in the grounds. There was a small Palladian bridge across the canal which supplied the main lake, but the bridge was not a bridge, because one could not cross it: both ends of it were blocked by solid walls of rusticated masonry. There was an obelisk inscribed with hieroglyphs on a plinth at the end of an avenue of yews. There was a shell grotto which housed the statue of a naked old man, a river god, probably, with a long beard, crouching over a scallop-shaped basin of granite. The stone of the statue was a mottled grey colour, but from his open mouth the dark green stain of some kind of lichen extended the length of his beard, as if he had been vomiting bile. It had been a fountain: water had once poured endlessly from the river god's mouth.

Behind the Abbey the grand design of Humphry Repton, the landscape architect, was bordered by a great wood which had been permitted its wildness in order to harbour game, but even here George found evidence of classical incursion.

There was a slight clearing in the trees out of sight of the Abbey in which stood a severe Doric temple of dark stone. In the triangular pediment above the portico a single grinning head dominated the central space of the tympanum, while under the portico and above the temple's doors were carved the words:

MORS IANVA MORTIS

'Death is the gate of Death,' George muttered to himself. But surely that was wrong. Shouldn't it be *Mors Ianua Vitae*: Death is the Gate of Life? He noticed that the bronze doors of this little building were very similar, albeit on a smaller scale, to those of the Temple of the Sphinx.

As he pondered these things, George heard a noise from the trees beyond. Someone was walking through the undergrowth. George crouched behind one of the Doric columns to observe. A man in a much-stained bottle-green velveteen jacket and leggings emerged from behind a belt of trees. He walked furtively but purposefully, examining the ground as he did so, clearing it slightly with a walking stick. Over his shoulder he carried a large canvas bag. Suddenly, emitting a little grunt of satisfaction, he bent down to pick something up. It was a rabbit caught in a snare and it was still struggling. The man gave it a smart tap on the head with the knobbed end of his stick and the creature went limp.

'I say, you! What are you doing?' said George.

The stranger turned suddenly and George could see that the man was afraid. A few seconds passed before his expression was replaced by one of cunning when he realised that it was only a boy that he faced.

'Good afternoon, young sir,' said the man tipping back the

battered moleskin cap that rested on his head. 'And what might you be doing in these woods, if I might make so bold?'

'No, you may not make so bold,' replied George. 'You, sir, are trespassing and I've a good mind to tell my uncle, Sir Augustus, and have you taken in charge.' George observed the effect his words had. 'What is your name?'

'Now why should I tell you that, young sir?'

'Because if you don't, curse you, I'll fetch some men from the Abbey and have you hunted down like a dog, you damned poaching rascal.'

'Fine language you use for a young gentleman, I must say.'

'Damn your impertinence! Your name!'

'Jem Mace. And I was once gamekeeper here.'

'Mace? Are you married to Mrs Mace, our housekeeper, then?'

'Bless you no, young sir. She is my sister. She was never married. The "Mrs" is by way of being what they call a "honorabilic" title, sir, in accordance with her position.'

'You know this park well, then?'

'As well as my own hand, sir.'

'And why are you no longer our gamekeeper?'

'That I will not say, sir.'

George paused and considered whether he should threaten Mace again, but decided not to. He was going to be gracious.

'Very well, then, Mace. I will say nothing about what you were doing. But you must tell me one thing in return. Where is the dog's tomb?'

Mace looked at him in puzzlement for some time, scratching his head. 'Who told you about that?' he said eventually.

'Never you mind that, Mace.'

'There *was* a dog, had a kind of tomb, coal-black he was. A spaniel, good hunting dog, too—'

'What was his name?'

'Don't rightly remember, but you'll find that when you find the tomb, so-called. As I was saying, he was Sir Augustus's favourite dog. Then Sir Augustus goes off to the West Indies and brings back his bride, the Lady Circe, her name was – strange name. Well this here dog, he takes to her something wonderful so he would hardly go near Sir Augustus no more. Some said she had a way with creatures, according to the customs of her people. All I know is that this dog would follow the Lady Circe everywhere and lost all his taste for hunting with the master. Then one day, not long it must have been before the Lady Circe's own death, that dog was found dead. I don't know how he died, but his neck was broken, that's for sure. He was found by the oak and the Lady Circe, she wept hard for him. The oak had a hollow in it and so they made that his tomb, and she had a stone cut to close up the entrance to the hollow and had his name carved on it. I expect you may see it even now if it is not overgrown.'

'How did the Lady Circe die?'

'Well, young master, I've told you my answer to your question and I must be gone. As long as you don't tell a living soul about me, you may find me hereabouts of an afternoon.'

'And if I do tell on you?'

'Then, young master, I won't answer for what may happen.' He lifted his moleskin cap in a perfunctory salute and was gone.

The next minute George was running at full pelt towards the oak. He felt curiously exhilarated, as if a veil was slowly being lifted from his eyes, but he was afraid, too.

It took some time to find the tomb. The lower reaches of the oak tree were overgrown with ivy and George had a hard time tearing it away, even with the help of his pocket knife. While he was doing this, he thought for a moment he heard the sound of panting, like that of a dog. He looked around, but there was nothing. It must have been his own hard breathing from his unaccustomed exertions. A cool breeze fanned his cheek and shook the leaves above him gently.

He had removed nearly all the ivy from the base of the oak before he found a smooth triangular piece of granite jammed into a gap between two great knotted roots. On the stone had been carved in capitals a single three-letter word: DIS.

Shortly before dinner George knocked on the door of the library. He was not beginning to feel easier about making these visits; quite the reverse. He would always find Sir Augustus in the same position, in his chair behind the desk. Sometimes he seemed in a trance, half-asleep, but never fully unconscious, his long saturnine features tense and alert even when the rest of his body appeared relaxed. George always had the impression that his uncle was waiting for him, or someone, or something.

Then there was the chessboard. Sometimes it was set up for a game, and often the pieces had been moved as if a game were in progress, but George had never seen Sir Augustus playing with anyone. Nor had Sir Augustus ever moved a piece in his presence.

George heard Sir Augustus's sharp 'Come!' and entered.

'Well?'

'I have found Cynossema, Sir Augustus.'

His uncle's features assumed an aspect of wary scorn. 'Oh, really, Nephew? And how did you do that?'

'I found it beneath the oak.'

Sir Augustus started violently. 'By God, who told you to look there?' But George had his answer prepared.

'No one, sir. Unless it was Mr Gainsborough.'

'Eh?'

George, assuming his most innocent expression, pointed to the painting of Sir Hercules and his dog above the mantelpiece. 'I assumed that any dog of yours might have been entombed where the painter had shown Sir Hercules's animal, by the oak, so I looked there.'

'And the name? I asked for a name.' Sir Augustus was searching George's face hard for signs of deceit.

'The name, sir, is "Dis". Though whether that is the name of the dog or the name of the tomb I do not know, for Mr Vereker tells me that Dis is an ancient name for the land of the dead, and also of the god of the dead.'

'I know that, damn you! Don't presume to lecture me, you insolent puppy!'

'So may I tell Mrs Mace that my dietary regimen is to be relaxed, Sir Augustus?'

'While you were searching round the oak, did you see or hear anything?'

'See or hear what, Sir Augustus?'

'Did anything untoward occur?'

'Nothing, Uncle. It has been a fine day, has it not? And now may I tell Mrs Mace—?'

'You may go to the Devil, for all I care. Leave me be!'

George obeyed and left the scene of his victory. But he was beginning to learn that all victories have consequences. He had been left with a greater mystery and a greater darkness than before.

That night something woke George. A noise from within the Abbey was penetrating its usually silent vastness. George left his room and went to the top of the staircase that led down into the main hall. Looking down, he saw that a faint light was coming from the library, whose door stood ajar. It was from there too that a sound emanated. It must have been a human sound, but it did not quite seem human. It was a groan, followed by a sobbing exhalation of breath. The groan was strangely like the noise the bronze doors had made when he opened the Temple of the Sphinx.

Then there was another light accompanied by echoing footsteps on the flagstones. From the door to the servants' hall came Hargreave carrying a lighted candelabrum. He walked slowly towards the library. When he was in the middle of the hall, he stopped, as if alerted to something, and slowly turned his head to look up to where George was watching. George retreated quickly into the shadows and then to his room.

He was restless and could not sleep. Once he went to the window to look out. It was a clear night, but the moon was on the wane. By the oak he thought he saw two figures in shadow. One looked like the Negro with the noose that he had seen before, the other was a dog. No movement came from the human figure, but the dog flicked his tail twice. George blinked and withdrew from the window, but when he returned to it a moment or so later they were gone.

V

A few days later, the Reverend Hamlet Vereker was once again invited to dine at Sir Augustus's table. George had gathered from Mrs Mace that Sir Augustus was not a naturally hospitable man, though in the days before his marriage he had been more sociable.

Mr Vereker was no conversationalist – a few quiet platitudes about the weather was his normal limit – so it was not quite clear why Sir Augustus had invited the curate, unless it was to torment him on doctrinal matters. His assault began, as before, at the dessert stage, when the port decanter was already half-empty. This time Sir Augustus turned to the subject of atonement.

'Now then, young Hamlet, tell me: what are your views on the forgiveness of sins? Do you believe in it?'

'Unquestionably, Sir Augustus.'

'Come come, sir, we must have no "unquestionably" here. Questions are all we have on this earth. If we cannot question we die. But let that be. We take the forgiveness of sins as your belief. And yet you have told us that eternal damnation is also in your creed. Now, how can that be, sir?'

'Why, Sir Augustus, that is surely a simple thing that any child knowing his catechism might tell you. God's mercy is infinite, but there is no forgiveness except the sinner repent of his sins.'

'I see. So whatever the sin, if I repent, I will be forgiven.'

'That is so.'

'So I may tell myself, I am to commit a murder, but all is well. I shall repent thereafter and make myself again as white as snow . . . Well, Mr Vereker?'

There was a pause. The curate seemed more than usually nervous and when he spoke he stammered. He said, 'B-but that would not be true repentance.'

'And who are you to judge such a thing? No, don't answer that. Tell me this. In your creed, it is said that Christ died for the sins of all mankind?'

'That is so.'

'Then there is no need for repentance. Our transgressions have been atoned for already by the crucifixion of the Nazarene.'

'The sins of all that truly turn to him are forgiven.'

'Ah! So it is not for all mankind after all. And if a poor sinner is born in Africa and dies there without ever having heard word of our Saviour then he is not redeemed. It might be better had he been taken for a slave, for at least then some canting plantation pastor might have had him baptised.'

'Sir Augustus, what do these questions of yours signify?'

'I am testing your mettle, young Hamlet. I am trying to find the core of your being. Is the blood of truth running in your veins sir, or are you a mere mouthpiece of acceptable cant? I wish to know. I own the living of Tankerton as you are aware; it is a solemn duty to look to the integrity of my clergy.'

Mr Vereker sat still and did not flinch.

George wondered if this was because, as he himself suspected, Sir Augustus's answer had not been the whole truth. George, even at his young age, could tell bluster when he heard it.

Mr Vereker said, 'I can only speak from my own experience, Sir Augustus. I know myself to be a sinner, and I know myself to be redeemed by the blood of Christ. I know this firstly from my own heart, secondly from the confirmation of Scripture, thirdly from the wisdom of saints who have gone before.'

This time it was Sir Augustus's turn to be silent. Eventually he said, half to himself, 'So you call yourself a sinner, noble Hamlet. I wonder if you know what sinner means. What is this sin? You believe that sin was committed by the first man and the first woman?'

'We are all sons and daughters of Adam.'

'And so that sin is inherent in us from birth?'

'That is so.'

'But if there had been no sin of Adam and Eve, might we all still be running about naked, like savages in the jungle?'

'These are vain speculations, Sir Augustus.'

'Indeed, sir! And who are you to say that my speculations are vain? Let me put it to you thus: that the fruit of the tree of the knowledge of good and evil was good fruit, and without it there might be no great nations, no mighty victories, no music, no statued temples and high places. Sin and its knowledge unites us in one bond. Innocence is well lost. Does not the philosopher Diderot say that we are compensated for loss of innocence by loss of prejudice?'

'Diderot was an atheistical Frenchman, Sir Augustus.'

'He may have been both, but he may also be right, Hamlet. There are more things in Heaven and earth than are dreamt of in your philosophy. And what is sin, if by it came wisdom and then salvation? Tell me, if sin is forgiven, is it forgotten, or does it not remain and become our strength?'

'It binds us, Sir Augustus. We may not be free until we are absolved of sin.'

'And only Christ may do this?'

'Man may act as intermediary for this atonement. Absolution is a sacrament of the priesthood.'

'Or a goat.'

'Sir Augustus?'

'Does not Aaron in the book of Leviticus offer a scapegoat as atonement for the sins of the tribes of Israel?'

'That may have been so in the Old Covenant, but not the New.'

'So no goats in our brave New Covenant. That is a pity. It must be a man – such as you Reverend Hamlet – or perhaps a boy.'

Sir Augustus rested his cold glance on George for some moments. George shivered; Mr Vereker half-rose from his seat. Sir Augustus laughed.

'Yes, yes, Mr Vereker! You are released! Or should I say absolved? You may return to your quiverful. The fruit of your loins and your sins no doubt. Stand not upon the order of your going, sir!'

Mr Vereker stood up and very deliberately turned to George.

'We will begin tomorrow morning with Virgil, Master George. The passage that commences: "*facilis descensus Averno*".' Then he bowed to Sir Augustus and was gone.

'I almost begin to like the fellow,' said Sir Augustus. 'Well, Master George, cut along! Cut along!'

Sir Augustus very rarely left the Abbey and, when he did, Hargreave was always particularly vigilant about George's movements in the house. George fancied that this had stemmed from his discovery of the plaster statue of the slave. One day, however, Sir Augustus had to go to London. George, who still hankered after his old home, wondered if his uncle might take him with him. He even hinted as much at dinner the night before his uncle's departure, but the suggestion was ignored. When Sir Augustus left the following morning he took Hargreave with him and offered no reason for his going.

George decided that this was an opportunity to make some discoveries about his uncle. He knew that the library would be locked, but he also knew that a spare key was kept on a hook in Hargeave's pantry. This was not kept locked. Shortly after his lunch on the day of his uncle's departure for London, he went into the pantry and removed the key.

Making sure that there was no one in the hall, he opened the door to the library and slipped inside. His first impression was one of discomfort and unease. This was easily explained. Whenever George had been in there before, a fire had always been burning in the grate, regardless of the weather. Sometimes Sir Augustus had actually had his window open while the fire burned. Today there was no fire and the room had a feeling of dampness about it as well as cold, despite the mild weather.

Once he was in the library, George had to decide exactly what he was looking for. He first studied the bookcases. Behind their glass the condition of the books was pristine, as if they had barely been touched. There were gilded calf-bound editions of Voltaire, Diderot, Racine and other French classics, besides Shakespeare and the poets. George delighted in their elegance, but felt no inclination to sample them.

The cupboards below the glass-fronted cases revealed volumes that were more to his taste. There were great folios of engravings lying on their side, heavy to lift out but wonderful to open. In them were pictures, often hand-coloured, of strange places, exotic beasts and birds, flowers and fruit, so vividly yet delicately painted you could almost smell their perfume.

Other, older and untinted volumes revealed even greater excitements. Here was Callot's *Les Misères et Malheurs de la Guerre*, full of exquisitely elegant depictions of battles, rapes, tortures, hangings and burnings at the stake, all done in the name of War. Another volume from two centuries before was entitled: *Popish Abominations, or Sundrie Tortures and Murthers of the Inquisition Reveal'd*. In it, the ingenuities of those who inflict pain and misery in the name of God were depicted in minutely etched detail. George could see from the roughened edges of the pages that this volume had been pored over.

He was particularly struck by one depiction of a Spanish street scene. A solemn procession of priests and monks is passing by, while, lying in the street, an emaciated woman with a sickly child clinging to one withered breast is stretching out her hand to them in supplication. Not one of the clerics is giving the woman so much as a glance. It was clear that the procession is going to an *auto-da-fé* because behind the priests you could just see a group of penitents, in their conical hats and *sambenitos*, roped together and on their way to execution, or worse. George felt a kind of guilty surprise at the fascination he felt.

A sound disturbed him. He looked up to find that the casement window had somehow opened itself and a sharp breeze had entered the room. He went over to the window and closed it. As he did so, George paused to look at the chessboard which as usual adorned one corner of Sir Augustus's table. A game was in progress, both black and white had about seven or eight pieces left, but white had lost its Queen. George studied the situation intently for several minutes and concluded that black could mate in half a dozen moves. He then went to replace the albums of engravings in their cupboards.

As he was doing this, he noticed a slim folio bound in red leather that he had not looked into. On its spine in gilt lettering were the words ST MAUR. The book contained a dozen hand-painted sheets in watercolour, with a handwritten title page on which, in an elaborate rococo cartouche, was written:

Views of the Abbey of Tankerton and its park
executed in water-colour by Thomas Henry Graine
for Sir Augustus and Lady St Maur,
MDCCCIII

Mr Graine, whoever he may have been, was more than a mere journeyman painter. He had a feeling for the dramatic. His skies were not always serene, and he liked the effects of light and shade that a clouded sky could achieve. Though the views were clearly identifiable, they were not entirely realistic. There was something visionary about them, as if the painter were trying to represent Tankerton as a kind of rural paradise, but a paradise in which a snake lurked, half-hidden.

One of the views was of the Abbey by moonlight with a full moon emerging from behind a cloud laced with silver. Some windows on the ground floor were alight – those of the library. The artist had shown a thin figure standing at one of the casements and looking out: it could only be Sir Augustus. There were views of the Temple of the Sphinx, by the lake, of the Palladian Bridge, the oak tree, and one of the curious Doric temple in the woods where George had encountered Jem Mace.

All the paintings contained at least one figure, human or animal, in them. A black spaniel, Dis perhaps, was snuffling round the oak; a gamekeeper with a cocked fowling piece who could have been Jem Mace was shown patrolling the woods. A Negro, wearing nothing but a pair of white breeches, was seated on the balustrade of the Palladian Bridge and fishing in the waters beneath it. In the painting of the Doric temple, much less thickly surrounded by undergrowth and trees than it now was, a child was shown, its back to the viewer, running away from the scene under a threatening sky. One of the bronze doors to the temple had opened a crack.

The final picture of the series was bathed in sunlight. It showed three figures standing on the crest of a hill looking down into the valley with the Abbey in the distance. Trees and wooded hills curled around it in a serene embrace. It seemed to George somewhat contrived, because he knew of no spot where such a view could be had. The three figures had their backs to the spectator, but the artist had managed to give them each an individual character. To the left was the Negro, shown in the picture of the Palladian Bridge, in his white breeches, carrying in his right hand what looked like a slender length of chain or a dog's leash. To the right was the black spaniel, Dis, one front leg lifted off the ground as if he had just scented prey.

The most striking figure stood between these two. It was that of a fashionably dressed lady, her tallness and slenderness accentuated by the multicoloured turban topped by an ostrich feather that she wore on her head. George could only vaguely remember when they were fashionable. The lady's arms and long, slender neck were a pale golden brown, the colour of satinwood. George had no doubt that he was staring at the back of the late Lady Circe St Maur. Down in the park in front of the Abbey the tiny figure of a gentleman leaning on a cane seemed to be staring up at them, returning their gaze.

George examined the scene for a long time. He felt that it was trying to tell him a story. He would have looked longer, only he was beginning to feel cold again. Had the window come open once more?

Just as he was turning around to confirm this, he heard a clatter and saw that one of the chess pieces, the white King, had fallen on its side and was swaying to and fro on the edge of its circular base. Standing close to it, as if over a defeated enemy, was the black Queen. The pieces had moved; black had mated.

George's heart began to beat wildly; the blood buzzed in his head. With icy fingers he put the albums back into the cupboard and went to the door of the library. Looking out briefly to make sure he was unobserved, he left the library, locked the door behind him and returned the key to the pantry. The rest of the afternoon he spent studying Philidor on chess in the schoolroom.

VI

Sir Augustus returned one morning two days later. As Mr Vereker was finishing his session with George in the schoolroom, a footman entered to summon them both to the library. George was troubled. He felt guilty, even though he did not regard his explorations as a sin. The two of them could be going to see his uncle for a quite different reason, but George's fears were confirmed when he saw, on entering the library, that the chess pieces had been arranged as for the beginning of a new game. George began to tremble uncontrollably.

Sir Augustus had his back to George and his tutor and before he turned he said, 'And what, pray, have you been doing in my library, Nephew?'

George was silent. All his energies were vainly concentrated on preventing himself from shaking.

Sir Augustus turned and scrutinised him minutely. 'And there is no need to deny it, sir. Mrs Mace saw you take the key from Hargreave's pantry.'

'I didn't touch the chessboard, Uncle,' was all George could say.

Sir Augustus's pale face flushed red. 'That's a damned lie, sir! A damned lie!' He almost shrieked the last two words. If George felt fear, then so for some reason did Sir Augustus; but it was small consolation. Sir Augustus went to a window seat, opened it, took out a riding crop and threw it at Mr Vereker.

'Mr Vereker, I hope you know how to use one of these, for if you don't you are out of gainful employment. Take the boy up to the schoolroom and flog the young devil for being a thief and a liar. And do your business thoroughly or I shall know of it. Go!'

George hoped that Mr Vereker might employ some restraint in the exercise of his task, but he did not. George could not see Mr Vereker's face as he inflicted the punishment, but he heard him. The little curate seemed to be in a passion of tears and rage; he sobbed as he performed the act, but his strength was terrible. When the business was done, George did not wait. He immediately ran from the schoolroom and even though he vaguely heard Mr Vereker calling him back, he went on running out of the Abbey and into the grounds. Outside a wind was blowing; overhead a few heavy clouds spat at him as he ran.

He found himself going towards the little Doric temple in the woods. He did not quite know why, but as he ran, the certainty that this was the place to go grew on him. While he was being flogged, shame and rage had to some extent masked the pain that was being inflicted; now he was beginning to taste the physical agony in its fullness. Movement alleviated the pain slightly, but he felt a warm trickle of blood course down the back of his leg.

When he finally halted, panting, under the Doric portico, his cheeks were wet with tears, yet he refused to cry out. Looking up again at the inscription MORS IANVA MORTIS it occurred to him that the 'temple' in whose shelter he stood was most likely a mausoleum, a place perhaps where the St Maurs were buried, where he might lie some day when death claimed him. At that moment he could have been happy to die. He tried the bronze doors, but they were firmly shut.

Then he heard a whistle in the woods behind him. He whistled back and presently a lively liver-coloured spaniel came bounding up to him, followed presently by Jem Mace. In his overwrought state George made much of the spaniel, who began eagerly licking the salt tears from his face.

'You made a friend,' said Jem.

'What's he called?'

'*She* is called Dido.'

'After the Queen of Carthage?'

'Don't know about that, sir. The Lady Circe gave her to me as a pup a short while afore she died. She it was who named her.'

'Did you know the Lady Circe well?'

Then Jem gave George the story. He was not a natural tale-teller. He tended to go backwards and forwards and from side to side, like a hound trying to pick up a scent, but George kept him to his subject by hints and gentle questioning.

Shortly after the death of Sir Hercules in 1798, his heir Sir Augustus had sailed to the West Indies to inspect his sugar plantations. There his eye was caught by the natural daughter of his estate manager by one of the slaves: she was a half-caste girl and her name was Circe. She was tall, slender, outstandingly beautiful, with a skin that shone like dark gold, but she had first attracted Sir Augustus's attention because of her excellence at chess. Every evening she would come to him at the estate mansion and they would play well into the sultry West Indian night. Sir Augustus became infatuated and was determined to bring her back as his bride. She agreed, but insisted on taking her black half-brother Brutus with her to England. Brutus was a slave, but he must be given his liberty when they touched English soil.

So it was, and for the first few years Sir Augustus and the Lady Circe were happy. Brutus stayed at the Abbey, ostensibly as one of the servants, though he was allowed to do pretty much as he pleased, which not unnaturally caused some resentment among the other domestics.

The Lady Circe was a woman of exceptional charm and intelligence as well as beauty, but, in spite of this, she was never fully accepted as an equal by the surrounding gentry. This at first only irritated Sir Augustus who, in any case, wanted no company but hers, but in time he came to resent their ostracism from society and the anger he felt turned him in upon himself.

He began to be suspicious. He resented the way his wife could charm even his dog away from him. He heard his other servants' complaints against Brutus. In his isolation he came to believe that even his wife was conspiring against him. He started to suspect her of illicit relations with her half-brother, and this was reinforced by the way that she would often wander about the park accompanied only by Brutus and Dis, the black spaniel. Some suspected that Sir Augustus was going mad with jealousy as he brooded in his library; but if it was madness, then it was madness of a very cold and calculating kind.

One day the Lady Circe went missing. For a few days nothing was really done about it because Sir Augustus was up in London and it was believed that his wife had gone up to join him, but on his return Sir Augustus instituted a search. Suspicion fell on Brutus, who had been acting strangely.

Then some time later the Lady Circe was found wandering in the grounds, half-distracted, in a terribly emaciated state. From what could be gathered from her distracted ramblings, she had been captured by an unknown masked assailant and taken to the Doric temple (which was indeed a mausoleum) and there locked in, without food or drink, gagged and shackled to Sir Hercules' coffin. The chains by which she had been bound were the same that had once been the sign of Brutus's slavery. He had brought his shackles to England and, after his manumission, had kept them as a grim memorial of his former state.

Every effort was made to restore the Lady Circe to health, but the combination of shock, starvation and dehydration had fatally damaged her system. She lived for only a few days more and then died. Sir Augustus mourned her loss with great pomp and had her coffin placed in the family mausoleum beside Sir Hercules.

Brutus was suspected of being complicit in the Lady Circe's fate, despite the absence of motive and his strong protestations of innocence. He was taken off to Ipswich Gaol, but before he could be tried he hanged himself in his cell.

Shortly afterwards Jem Mace was dismissed from his post as gamekeeper, ostensibly for the misdemeanour of having sold in Beccles Market some hares shot on the estate without having had permission to do so. The real reason, he claimed, was the fact that he had been a favourite of the Lady Circe's and had spoken up for Brutus when he fell under suspicion.

George listened carefully to Jem's story and formed his own

conclusion. That evening he dined alone with Sir Augustus. Part of him wanted to stay hidden in his room until the agony and shame of the flogging had subsided, but a combination of defiance and sheer hunger made him take his place at the dining table.

Most of the meal was consumed in silence, which George felt no inclination to break. At last, at the dessert stage, when Sir Augustus was already more than halfway through his decanter of port, he spoke.

'No doubt you consider yourself very ill-used, Nephew.'

George was silent; he flattered himself that this was the gentlemanly thing to do.

'Do not imagine that I have forgiven you for your transgression. This world is not a forgiving place. We must learn its rules and forget any cant about justice. Some are born rich; others are born to be slaves; some are clever, most are fools. Do not blame human beings for that. If there is injustice in the world, then it is the injustice of God, not of man.'

There was a pause, then George said, 'Will you play chess with me, Uncle Augustus?'

Sir Augustus's pale face flushed red. A pulse at his temple began to quiver. He took a pull at his port. 'Damn your impudence, sir,' he said in a low trembling voice.

'Very well then, Uncle. Set me another challenge. A puzzle. The last two were too easy.'

This time Sir Augustus did not look at him. He stared at his cut-glass decanter, and the red eye of light in its depths that winked in the candle's glare.

'Do you know what you are asking, boy?'

'What will you do in return if I solve the puzzle?'

'If you bring me this, then I will play you at chess. Is that enough?'

'It is enough, Uncle Augustus.'

'Very well. I have warned you, have I not?'

'You have, sir.'

'Good. Then—' A long silence before '—find me the chain that binds beyond the gate of death. And now get out of my sight. Your very presence offends me.'

When he looked out of his bedroom window that evening George saw in the gathering dusk three shadowy figures: the Negro, the dog, and, between them a tall, slender woman with a plumed turban. Three times the feather nodded, but all else was motionless.

The following morning Mr Vereker conducted his lessons without looking at his pupil. George knew that his teacher must be ashamed of having lost control of himself the day before, but he made nothing of it and bided his time. Had not the great Philidor himself written in his manual on chess that *Next to knowing when to seize an opportunity, the most important skill in this game, as in life, is to know when to forgo an advantage.*

When he went down to Mrs Mace for his lunch, George asked her quietly why she had told Sir Augustus that she had seen him take the library key. Mrs Mace was confused. She said she had done no such thing; Sir Augustus had guessed and then forced her into a betrayal. She began to apologise in a most abject way, but George cut her short with a smile and a gesture of absolution. Outside the kitchen window clouds hung heavy over the park. It threatened rain.

VII

Despite this, George knew he must make his journey that afternoon. After he had eaten, and while Mrs Mace was occupied, George took a lantern, a tinderbox and several candle ends from the pantry and slipped through the scullery door.

It was not yet raining, but the air felt heavy and damp. Its moist warmth pricked his skin. George looked around to confirm, as far as possible, that no one was following or observing him, then he set a course for the Doric mausoleum in the woods. Having not yet learned to distrust his own arrogance, he was quite confident that he would find what he wanted there.

As he arrived under the mausoleum's portico it began to rain, at first a few portentously heavy drops, then a steady fall, finally an all-embracing shower that cut out all other sound. George studied the bronze doors. They had neither handle nor keyhole and, when pushed against, they felt solidly immovable. He felt a sudden wave of indignation against Mr Graine, the watercolourist, who had shown one of the doors ajar.

'You'll never open them.'

George started and looked around. Standing in the portico was Hargreave, Sir Augustus's butler. His white face and hair glistened from the rain and there were shiny patches of dampness all over his black clothes. He stood quite still, his pale blue eyes unblinking, a slight sneer on his lips.

George thought he was making a little too much of his dramatic appearance. 'Why not, Hargreave?'

'Because they are false doors, Master George. They are there for show only. The real entrance to the tomb is elsewhere.'

'Then you had better show it to me, Hargreave.'

'And why should I do that, young sir?'

'Because Sir Augustus wishes me to see inside my own family mausoleum, Hargreave, damn your impudence!'

Hargreave smiled but said nothing. He looked up at the sky and sniffed as if he were scenting the air like an animal. Then he said, 'The rain seems to have abated somewhat. If you would follow me, Master George.'

Hargreave led the way around to the back of the mausoleum, where he spent some time clearing away earth and undergrowth from an area directly adjoining the centre of the back wall. Revealed at last was a stone slab with an iron ring, somewhat rusted, set into it. As he crouched over the slab, Hargreave glanced up at

George. Something about the very blankness of his look alerted the boy. Hargreave took hold of the iron ring and pulled away the slab to disclose a narrow flight of stone steps leading down into blackness.

'The St Maur family vault,' said Hargreave wiping his hands carefully on his breaches. George leaned against the back wall of the mausoleum while he lit the candle in the lantern, glancing occasionally at Hargreave as he did so. George noticed that the man seemed impatient about something. He tried not to show the fear he felt. Deliberately he took his time with the lantern.

When it was lit he handed it to Hargreave. 'There you are, Hargreave – you lead the way.'

Hargreave looked perturbed. 'After you, Master George,' he said trying to hand back the lantern to him. George put his hands behind his back and stared at Hargreave. How old was he? Fifty? Sixty? At any rate still strong enough to overwhelm a boy not yet eight years old.

Suddenly Hargreave seemed to lose all control. He threw away the lantern and made a lunge at George, who turned to run from him but slipped in the wet grass. He fell, and Hargreave came down on top of him. George felt his foul panting breath on the back of his neck. The man was whispering curses into his ear, as if willing him to give up all resistance. George went on struggling, but now he found himself being dragged by the legs towards the black entrance of the tomb. He cried out with all the force of his lungs, then, prompted by some strange instinct, he let out a piercing whistle.

There was an answering bark and Hargreave, in his surprise, released his grip on George's legs for a moment. The boy struggled to his feet, but Hargreave was on him again, this time wrapping his long thin arms around George's arms and body and lifting him off the ground. George did his best to kick back at Hargreave's shins, but without much effect. He was swung around and was once again being propelled feet first towards the hole in the ground and the steps leading downwards. George knew that once he was thrown down those steps he would be dead one way or another.

'My uncle will hear of this, you dog!'

'He will, Master George, sir. It was he who gave me the order!'

Now George was being held directly over the black hole. In a frantic effort to save himself, he jerked his head backwards and made contact with Hargreave's mouth. He heard a rattle like dice on a wooden table as he felt the back of his head break the butler's teeth from their rotten moorings.

Hargreave staggered for a moment and let out a yell. At the same time George heard a bark, this time nearer. He twisted in the man's grip, but still he was held fast. Then he sensed rather than felt a thud and found himself crashing to the ground on top of Hargreave. The grip was released and he rolled free.

Lying on the grass, George saw Jem Mace standing over the unconscious Hargreave, holding his fowling piece by the barrel. He must have used its stock as a club on the back of the man's neck. Dido was industriously licking a trickle of blood from Hargreave's mouth.

'Thank you, Jem,' said George as he got to his feet. It was the light-headedness that made his voice sound shrill. 'Your arrival was most timely.' Then he almost laughed at the absurd expression he had just used.

'It was Dido as heard you, Master George.' He glanced down at Hargreave and kicked him with his foot. 'He were the one who betrayed me to Sir Augustus about selling them hares in Beccles Market. What do we do about him?'

George delicately shifted Hargreave's head with the toe of his shoe. It lolled uselessly. 'He doesn't appear to me to be in the land of the living,' he said. Once again George had the strange impression that it was not his voice at all coming from his mouth, but that someone calm and fastidiously detached was speaking through him. 'We must bury him some fathoms deep with my ancestors.' He pointed at the steps leading down into the earth.

With great difficulty the boy and the poacher manhandled the body down the steps. (Dido refused to accompany them.) When they reached the bottom, George's lantern revealed an extraordinary sight. They were in a high, narrow space. On either side of them on shelves were coffins reaching up into a black obscurity where the light did not penetrate.

Jem was for dropping the corpse on the floor of the vault and getting out as soon as possible, but George forbade it. He now had command of the situation. He told Jem that Hargreave was to be put into one of the coffins. They opened several, which George pronounced either too rotten or too small to sustain the dead butler. As each one was opened, George steeled himself to look inside, holding up his lantern to stare on grey and rotted winding sheets, parchment skin stretched across eyeless skulls.

George pointed to one of the largest and newest coffins. Jem opened it and stood back. George took the lantern and peered inside. In the coffin lay the collapsed remains of what had once been a tall, broad-framed man. George recognised the suit of plum-coloured velvet, now stained and faded, from the Gainsborough portrait in the library. It was Sir Hercules.

'We'll put him in there,' he said.

Together they managed to lift Hargreave into the coffin on top of Sir Hercules and replaced the lid. There was one more thing to do.

George identified the coffin at last because it was the newest and its wood was covered in green baize pinned down with brass tacks, almost untarnished. Jem would not look, so George lifted the lid and peered in by himself.

The figure in its winding sheet was slender and still retained the vestiges of her beautiful shape. The features, too, were almost intact, though the eye sockets were empty. Black lustrous coils of hair hung down on each side of a face whose exquisite bone structure was covered by a delicate membrane of golden skin. Over the folded skeletal hands, on one finger of which a sapphire ring still sparkled, had been laid a pair of common iron slave manacles. George picked them up, then gently closed the coffin lid on the Lady Circe's remains.

He signalled to Jem that their task was done and, carrying the lantern, he followed the poacher out of the vault and up the stairway.

Halfway up the steps, George thought he heard a noise like a tapping from one of the coffins. Jem, ahead of him and almost in the open air, had heard nothing. The boy played with the possibility that Hargreave had, after all, survived the blow from Jem's gun stock and was feebly trying to attract attention. He considered whether he could live with the possibility that he might have imprisoned a man alive in a coffin with a corpse. It did not take him long to decide that he could, but he stamped heavily up the last few steps to the vault so as to drown out any lesser noises.

When he and Jem were both above ground again, George said, 'When my time comes, I shall not be buried in that vault.' They replaced the slab and covered it with grass and leaves.

George returned to the Abbey, but he did not show himself until half-past five, when he walked calmly into the dining room, one hand behind his back holding the manacles. Sir Augustus was already seated at the head of the table, and when he saw George his pale skin became greyer.

'Good evening, Uncle Augustus,' said George.

'Where is Hargreave?' said Sir Augustus.

'I do not know, sir,' answered George with only metaphysical truthfulness. He seated himself and dropped the manacles onto the floor beside his chair.

Soup was eaten in silence. When one of the footmen came in with the entrée, a fricassée of rabbit, Sir Augustus asked again.

'Where is Hargreave?'

'I could not say, Sir Augustus,' answered the footman. 'We saw him leave the Abbey at about two of the clock. Since then he has not been seen.'

'In which direction was he going?' asked Sir Augustus.

'I am not sure, Sir Augustus. I will make enquiries of the other servants.'

The rabbit and other dishes were eaten again in silence. Sir Augustus finished his decanter of port and called for another.

When the servants had left the boy and his uncle with the dessert, George said, 'Will you play chess with me this evening, Uncle?'

Sir Augustus, who had fallen almost into a trance over his second decanter of port, started violently.

'What was that?'

George repeated the question.

Sir Augustus smiled thinly. 'I thought I had set you a task to perform before you might have the temerity to make such a request of me.'

'I have performed it, Uncle,' said George, picking the shackles off the floor where he had concealed them and placing them on the dining table.

Sir Augustus stared at them for a long minute, then he said quietly, almost to himself, 'Are you a boy, or are you the devil incarnate?'

'Shall we play after dinner, sir?'

Sir Augustus rose slowly and, supported heavily by his stick, came to stand over his nephew. George saw a man who was putting out the last remnants of his power and authority.

'Where is Hargreave?' said Sir Augustus.

'I do not know, Uncle.'

He picked up the manacles. 'How did you find these?'

'By finding the entrance of the mausoleum. It was a matter of observation and calculation. Like a game.'

'If I find you have been lying to me, I'll have young Hamlet flog you to within an inch of your life.'

George reached out for a walnut and broke open its skull between the silver jaws of a nutcracker.

Sir Augustus left the room.

George was in possession of the field.

It must have been near to midnight when a noise woke George from a deep sleep in his bedroom. It sounded like a groan, or perhaps a heavy door opening. He went to the window and looked out. The clouds and rain were gone, leaving behind an intensely clear night lit by stars and a diminishing moon. Almost without emotion, George saw the three figures on the lawn beside the faintly glittering lake. The central figure beckoned to him. George nodded and left the window. Curiosity had mastered almost all his fear. He must know the end of it all.

He slipped out of his room and down the main staircase, pausing in the hall to note the faint thread of light under the library door that indicated Sir Augustus's presence there. He lifted the latch of the front door and went out onto the drive. For a few moments he looked from left to right. The grounds were bare and silent. He decided to wait concealed in the deep shadow of a buttress that supported the entrance to the Abbey. There he felt secure. It was a warm night. Not an owl hooted; not a leaf stirred. His mind strayed over the events of the day.

Presently he looked out from his vantage point, and this time he saw something.

A thin shadow in a long gown, wearing a turban with a great nodding plume, was crawling towards the faintly glowing library window. It was such an unnatural apparition. George was reminded of a giant doll, a puppet, perhaps, whose head lolled and wagged as if there were no bones or muscles in the long neck. At first it moved slowly, then, as it found its ability, it began to proceed rapidly on all fours, to scuttle almost, like a spider up a wall.

Some way behind it on the lawn stood the dog and Brutus with his rope, motionless.

When the creature reached the window it reached up with its long arms and pulled itself almost to a standing position, the thin trailing legs supporting the body crookedly. With a suddenness that shook George out of his fascinated trance, the thing threw back its turbaned head and smashed it like a hammer through the glass of the library window. Then, with her strong forearms, the Lady Circe pulled her long body and her crooked stick legs through the shattered casement. It looked as if the Abbey were swallowing her, like a lizard devouring a grasshopper.

George heard a cry – high, piercing, full of animal terror and human despair. It could have been anybody's voice – a man's, a woman's, or a child's – but George knew it to be Sir Augustus. He waited for further sounds for a minute, but none came. He turned to see that Dis and Brutus still stood motionless on the lawn in front of the Abbey. George half-raised a hand in greeting to them, then went back into the hall. No sound came from the library. He walked up the main stairs and back to his bedroom. It was only when he was in bed that George felt stunned and a little ashamed at his lack of fear and absence of compassion. Something had separated him from the agony; by it he had both gained and lost.

The following morning he lay in bed listening to the sounds of the Abbey waking up and the inevitable agitations following the discovery of Sir Augustus's body in the library. George heard Mrs Mace weeping. He rose, dressed himself and went to the top of the stairs where he could half-hear a whispered conversation about what they should tell the young Master. He liked the phrase 'young Master'.

It was some days later that he heard from Jem what had happened. Some kind of savage beast of unknown origin must have leapt through the library window in the night. Sir Augustus was found in his chair with half his face torn away and the lower part of his body disembowelled; his heart and other organs were nowhere to be found. It was remarked as strange that, despite the violence of the attack, the chessboard on the table remained intact, a game apparently in progress.

That morning, when George came down into the hall, he was treated with a new deference and solicitude. The body was spirited away to be examined and for the coroner to pronounce a verdict. Strenuous efforts had been made to prevent George from seeing it. He was to be protected at all costs, so he spent much of the day in the company of Mrs Mace, whose kindness and solicitude bored him. Towards evening, when at last he was left to his own devices, he sauntered into the library, which had been left unlocked. There he studied the game in progress on the chessboard. Black could mate in three moves. He moved a black knight, then the white King, then the black Queen.

'Checkmate,' he said out loud, and the sound of his own voice in that lonely place frightened him a little. A cold breeze blew in from the open casement.

In the Michaelmas of 1811, George St Maur, now heir apparent to the Baronetcy of St Maur, was entered for Eton at Hexter's House. He was given his own room and seemed to the other boys a self-possessed creature, despite his comparative youth. It was not long, however, before his mettle was tried by a boy called Damer. Damer was by no means the most senior boy in the house, but was known as 'the Cock of Hexter's' by virtue of his good looks, sporting prowess and general daring. One afternoon he wandered into George's room.

That morning George had received a packing case from Tankerton Abbey containing some books he had requested from its library. He was in the process of taking the volumes from the case and placing them neatly on his shelves. On the table by the window was a chessboard. There were five white pieces on the board and three black: white could checkmate in two moves. It was a child's problem.

'Hullo, St Maur,' said Damer. 'I've decided that you're to be my slave this half.'

'Oh, have you indeed, Damer?' said George, continuing to arrange his books.

Damer came up and stood over the younger boy. 'Well, you're a cool customer, I'll say that, young 'un, but you won't be so damned cool when I've finished with you.'

He made a grab for George's left arm and twisted it round behind his back in a half-nelson. George dropped the books he had been carrying, stepped back and stamped hard with his heel on Damer's foot. Damer was so startled that he let go of George's arm, crying out with pain as he did so.

'By God, you'll pay for this, you young jackanapes!'

'No doubt,' said George, calmly picking up his books from the floor as Damer sat down heavily in a chair to nurse his bruised foot. 'I'll tell you what, Damer. You see that chessboard there by the window. There's a problem on it, a simple one. White mates in two moves. Solve it and I will be your slave – at least until the end of the half.'

Damer stared at him for a while in silent astonishment, then he burst out: 'You dare to play games with me, boy? Do you think I can't torment you to within an inch of your life, you little devil?'

'You may of course hurt me, Damer, though not without hurting yourself in the course of so doing. I have learned to disregard pain to a very large extent. I suggest that you address yourself to the chess problem – it really is quite elementary – rather than indulge in any further bluster. I gave you fair terms.'

Damer stared at George for a full fifteen seconds. Once again he had been baffled by the younger boy's unexpected behaviour. Finally he said, 'You're mad, St Maur. You're crackbrained. They ought to have sent you to Bedlam, not Eton.' Then he left the room, slamming the door behind him.

Almost before he had gone, George St Maur had turned his attention once again to his packing case and had begun to take out the set of Diderot which he had particularly requested from the Tankerton library. With deliberation, he began to place the gilded calf volumes in the glass-fronted bookcase above his bureau.

REGGIE OLIVER has been a professional playwright, actor and theatre director since 1975. His biography of Stella Gibbons, *Out of the Woodshed,* was published by Bloomsbury in 1998.

Besides plays, his publications include four volumes of horror stories, with a fifth collection, *Dances in the Dark,* due from Tartarus Press. An omnibus edition of his stories entitled *Dramas from the Depths* is published by Centipede, as part of its 'Masters of the Weird Tale' series.

The author's novel, *The Dracula Papers I – The Scholar's Tale,* the first of a projected four, was published in January 2011 – the same time as his farce, *Once Bitten,* was a Christmas season sell-out hit at the Orange Tree Theatre, Richmond.

'The painter Richard Dadd has long fascinated me,' Oliver explains, 'and images from his work have been an inspiration for several stories of mine.

'One picture of his in particular, "The Child's Problem", with its strange atmosphere of enigmatic menace, haunted me. It took me many years before I worked out the story behind it – a tale of guilt, power games, childhood and the loss of innocence.'

Sad, Dark Thing

—MICHAEL MARSHALL SMITH—

AIMLESS. A SHORT, simple word. It means 'without aim', where 'aim' derives from the idea of calculation with a view to action. Without purpose or direction, therefore, lacking a considered goal or future that you can see. People mainly use the word in a blunt, softened fashion. They walk 'aimlessly' down a street, not sure whether to have a coffee or if they should check out the new magazines in the bookstore or maybe sit on that bench and watch the world go by. It's not a big deal, this aimlessness. It's a temporary state and often comes with a side order of ease. An hour without something hanging over you, with no great need to do or achieve anything in particular? In this world of busy lives and do-this and do-that, it sounds pretty good.

But being wholly without purpose? With no direction home? That is not such a good deal. Being truly aimless is like being dead. It may even be the same thing, or worse. It is the aimless who find the wrong roads, and drive down them, simply because they have nowhere else to go.

Miller usually found himself driving on Saturday afternoons. He could make the morning go away by staying in bed an extra half-hour, tidying away stray emails, spending time on the deck, looking out over the forest with a magazine or the iPad and a succession of coffees. He made the coffees in a machine that sat on the kitchen counter and cost nearly eight hundred dollars. It made a very good cup of coffee. It should. It had cost nearly eight hundred dollars.

By noon a combination of caffeine and other factors would mean that he wasn't very hungry. He would go back indoors nonetheless, and put together a plate from the fridge. The ingredients would be things he'd gathered from delis up in San Francisco during the week, or else from the New Leaf markets in Santa Cruz or Felton as he returned home on Friday afternoon. The idea was that this would constitute a treat, and remind him of the good things in life. That was the idea. He would also pour some juice into one of the only two glasses in the cabinet that got any use. The other was his scotch glass, the one with the faded white logo on it, but that only came out in the evenings. He was very firm about that.

He would bring the plate and glass back out and eat at the table which stood further along the deck from the chair in which he'd spent most of the morning. By then the sun would have moved around, and the table got shade, which he preferred when he was eating. The change in position was also supposed to make it feel like he was doing something different to what he'd done all morning, though it did not, especially. He was still a man sitting in silence on a raised deck, within view of many trees, eating expensive foods that tasted like cardboard.

Afterward he took the plate indoors and washed it in the sink. He had a dishwasher, naturally. Dishwashers are there to save time. He washed the plate and silverware by hand, watching the water swirl away and then drying everything and putting it to one side. He was down a wife and a child, now living three hundred miles away. He was short on women and children, therefore, but in their place, from the hollows they had left behind, he had time. Time crawled in an endless parade of minutes from between those cracks, arriving like an army of little black ants, crawling up over his skin, up his face, and into his mouth, ears and eyes.

So why not wash the plate. And the knife, and the fork, and the glass. Hold back the ants, for a few minutes, at least.

He never left the house with a goal. On those afternoons he was, truly, aimless. From where the house stood, high in the Santa Cruz Mountains, he could have reached a number of diverting places within an hour or two. San Jose. Saratoga. Los Gatos. Santa Cruz itself, then south to Monterey, Carmel and Big Sur. Even way down to Los Angeles, if he felt like making a weekend of it.

And then what?

Instead he simply drove.

There are only so many major routes you can take through the area's mountains and redwood forests. Highways 17 and 9, or the road out over to Bonny Doon, Route 1 north or south. Of these, only 17 is of any real size. In between the main thoroughfares, however, there are other options. Roads that don't do much except connect one minor two-lane highway to another. Roads that used to count for something before modern alternatives came along to supplant or supersede or negate them.

Side roads, old roads, forgotten roads.

Usually there wasn't much to see down these. Stretches of forest, maybe a stream, eventually a house, well back from the road. Rural, mountainous backwoods where the tree and poison oak reigned supreme. Chains across tracks which led down or up into the woods, some gentle inclines, others pretty steep, meandering off towards some house which stood even further from the through-lines, back in a twenty- or fifty-acre lot. Every now and then you'd pass one of the area's very few tourist traps, like the 'Mystery Spot', an old-fashioned affair which claimed to honour a site of 'Unfathomable Weirdness' but in fact paid cheerful homage to geometry, and to man's willingness to be deceived.

He'd seen all of these long ago. The local attractions with his wife and child, the shadowed roads and tracks on his own solitary excursions over the last few months. At least, you might have thought he would have seen them all. Every Saturday he drove, however, and every time he found a road he had never seen before.

Today the road was off Branciforte Drive, the long, old highway which heads off through largely uncolonised regions of the mountains and forests to the southeast of Scott's Valley. As he drove north along it, mind elsewhere and nowhere, he noticed a turning. A glance in the rear-view mirror showed no one behind and so he slowed to peer along the turn.

A two-lane road, overhung with tall trees, including some redwoods. It gave no indication of leading anywhere at all.

Fine by him.

He made the turn and drove on. The trees were tall and thick, cutting off much of the light from above. The road passed smoothly up and down, riding the natural contours, curving abruptly once in a while to avoid the trunk of an especially big tree or to skirt a small canyon carved out over millennia by some small and bloody-minded stream. There were no houses or other signs of habitation. Could be public land, he was beginning to think, though he didn't recall there being any around here and hadn't seen any indication of a park boundary, and then he saw a sign by the road up ahead.

STOP

That's all it said. Despite himself, he found he was doing just that, pulling over towards it. When the car was stationary, he looked at the sign curiously. It had been hand-lettered, some time ago, in black marker on a panel cut from a cardboard box and nailed to a tree.

He looked back the way he'd come, and then up the road once more. He saw no traffic in either direction, and also no indication of why the sign would be here. Sure, the road curved again about forty yards ahead, but no more markedly than it had ten or fifteen times since he'd left Branciforte Drive. There had been no warning signs on those bends. If you simply wanted people to observe the speed limit then you'd be more likely to advise them to 'Slow', and anyway, it didn't look at all like an official sign.

Then he realised that, further on, there was in fact a turning off the road.

He took his foot off the brake and let the car roll forward down the slope, crunching over twigs and gravel. A driveway, it looked like, though a long one, bending off into the trees. Single lane, roughly made up. Maybe five yards down it was another sign, evidently the work of the same craftsman as the previous.

TOURISTS WELCOME

He grunted, in something like a laugh. If you had yourself some kind of attraction, of course tourists were welcome. What would be the point otherwise? It was a strange way of putting it.

An odd way of advertising it, too. No indication of what was in store or why a busy family should turn off what was already a pretty minor road and head off into the woods. No lure except those two words.

They were working on him, though, he had to admit. He eased his foot gently back on the gas and carefully directed the car along the track, between the trees.

After about a quarter of a mile he saw a building ahead – a couple of them, in fact, arranged in a loose compound, one a ramshackle two-storey farmhouse, the other a disused barn. There was also something that was or had been a garage, with a broken-down truck/tractor parked diagonally in front of it. It was parked insofar as it was not moving, at least, not in the sense that whoever had last driven the thing had made any effort, when abandoning it, to align its form with anything. The surfaces of the vehicle were dusty and rusted and liberally covered in old leaves and specks of bark. A wooden crate, about four feet square, stood rotting in the back. The near-front tyre was flat.

The track ended in a widened parking area, big enough for four or five cars. It was empty. There was no sign of life at all, in fact, but something – he wasn't sure what – said this habitation was a going concern, rather than a collection of ruins that someone had walked away from at some point in the last few years.

Nailed to a tree in front of the main house was another cardboard sign.

WELCOME

He parked, turned off the engine, and got out. It was very quiet. It usually is in those mountains, when you're away from the road. Sometimes you'll hear the faint roar of an airplane, way up above, but apart from that it's just the occasional tweet of some winged creature or an indistinct rustle as something small and furry or scaly makes its way through the bushes.

He stood for a few minutes, flapping his hand to discourage a noisy fly which appeared from nowhere, bothered his face and then zipped chaotically off.

Eventually he called out, 'Hello?'

You'd think that – on what was evidently a very slow day for this attraction, whatever it was – the sound of an arriving vehicle would have someone bustling into sight, eager to make a few bucks, to pitch their wares. He stood a few minutes more, however, without seeing or hearing any sign of life. It figured. Aimless people find aimless things, and it didn't seem like much was going to happen here. You find what you're looking for, and he hadn't been looking for anything at all.

He turned back towards the car, aware that he wasn't even feeling disappointment. He hadn't expected much, and that's exactly what he'd got.

As he held up his hand to press the button to unlock the doors, however, he heard a creaking sound.

He turned back to see there was now a man on the tilting porch that ran along half of the front of the wooden house. He was dressed in canvas jeans and a vest that had probably once been white. The man had probably once been clean, too, though he looked now like he'd spent most of the morning trying to fix the underside of a car. Perhaps he had.

'What you want?' His voice was flat and unwelcoming. He looked to be in his mid-late fifties. Hair once black was now half grey, and also none too clean. He did not look like he'd been either expecting or desirous of company.

'What have you got?'

The man on the porch leant on the rail and kept looking at him, but said nothing.

'It says "Tourists Welcome",' Miller said, when it became clear the local had nothing to offer. 'I'm not feeling especially welcome, to be honest.'

The man on the porch looked weary. 'Christ. The boy was supposed to take down those damned signs. They still up?'

'Yes.'

'Even the one out on the road, says "Stop"?'

'Yes,' Miller said. 'Otherwise I wouldn't have stopped.'

The other man swore and shook his head. 'Told the boy weeks ago. Told him I don't know how many times.'

Miller frowned. 'You don't notice, when you drive in and out? That the signs are still there?'

'Haven't been to town in a while.'

'Well, look. I turned down your road because it looked like there was something to see.'

'Nope. Doesn't say anything like that.'

'It's implied, though, wouldn't you say?'

The man lifted his chin a little. 'You a lawyer?'

'No. I'm a businessman. With time on my hands. Is there something to see here, or not?'

After a moment the man on the porch straightened and came walking down the steps.

'One dollar,' he said. 'As you're here.'

'For what? The parking?'

The man stared at him as if he was crazy. 'No. To see.'

'One dollar?' It seemed inconceivable that in this day and age there would be anything under the sun for a dollar, especially if it was trying to present as something worth experiencing. 'Really?'

'That's cheap,' the man said, misunderstanding.

'It is what it is,' Miller said, getting his wallet out and pulling a dollar bill from it.

The other man laughed, a short, sour sound. 'You got that right.'

After he'd taken the dollar and stuffed it into one of the pockets of his jeans, the man walked away. Miller took this to mean that he should follow, and so he did. It looked for a moment as if they were headed towards the house, but then the path – such as it was – took an abrupt right onto a course that led them between the house and the tilting barn. The house was large and gabled and must once have been quite something. Lord knows what it was doing out here, lost by itself in a patch of forest that had never been near a major road or town or anyplace else that people with money might wish to be. Its glory days were long behind it anyway. Looking up at it, you'd give it about another five years standing, unless someone got onto rebuilding or at least shoring it right away.

The man led the way through slender trunks into an area around the back of the barn. Though the land in front of the house and around the side had barely been what you'd think of as tamed, here the forest abruptly came into its own. Trees of significant size shot up all around, looking – as redwoods do – like they'd been there since the dawn of time. A sharp, rocky incline led down towards a stream about thirty yards away. The stream was perhaps eight feet across, with steep sides. A rickety bridge of old, grey wood lay across it. The man led him to the near side of this, and then stopped.

'What?'

'This is it.'

Miller looked again at the bridge. 'A dollar, to look at a bridge some guy threw up fifty years ago?' Suddenly it wasn't seeming so dumb a pricing system after all.

The man handed him a small tarnished key and raised his other arm to point. Between the trees on the other side of the creek was a small hut.

'It's in there.'

'What is?'

The man shrugged. 'A sad, dark thing.'

The water which trickled below the bridge smelled fresh and clean. Miller got a better look at the hut, shed, whatever, when he reached the other side. It was about half the size of a log cabin, but made of grey, battered planks instead of logs. The patterns of lichen over the sides and the moss-covered roof said it had been here, and in this form, for a good long time – far longer than the house, most likely. Could be an original settler's cabin, the home of whichever long-ago pioneer had first arrived here, driven west by hope or desperation. It looked about contemporary with the rickety bridge, certainly.

There was a small padlock on the door.

He looked back.

The other man was still standing at the far end of the bridge, looking up at the canopy of leaves above. It wasn't clear what he was looking at, but it didn't seem like he was waiting for the right moment to rush over, bang the other guy on the head and steal his wallet. If he'd wanted to do that he could have done it back up at the house. There was no sign of anyone else around – this boy he'd mentioned, for example – and he looked like he was waiting patiently for the conclusion of whatever needed to happen for him to have earned his dollar.

Miller turned back and fitted the key in the lock. It was stiff, but it turned. He opened the door. Inside was total dark. He hesitated, looked back across the bridge, but the man had gone.

He opened the door further, and stepped inside.

The interior of the cabin was cooler than it had been outside, but also stuffy. There was a faint smell. Not a bad smell, particularly. It was like old, damp leaves. It was like the back of a closet where you store things you do not need. It was like a corner of the attic of a house not much loved, in the night, after rain.

The only light was that which managed to get past him from the door behind. The cabin had no windows, or if it had, they had been covered over. The door he'd entered by was right at one end of the building, which meant the rest of the interior led ahead. It could only have been ten, twelve feet. It seemed longer, because it was so dark. The man stood there, not sure what happened next.

The door slowly swung closed behind him, not all the way, but leaving a gap of a couple of inches. No one came and shut it on him or turned the lock or started hollering about he'd have to pay a thousand bucks to get back out again. The man waited.

In a while, there was a quiet sound.

It was a rustling. Not quite a shuffling. A sense of something moving a little at the far end, turning away from the wall, perhaps. Just after the sound, there was a low waft of a new odour, as if the movement had caused something to change its relationship to the environment, as if a body long held curled or crouched in a particular shape or position had realigned enough for hidden sweat to be released into the unmoving air.

Miller froze.

In all his life, he'd never felt the hairs on the back of his neck rise. You read about it, hear about it. You knew they were supposed to do it, but he'd never felt it, not his own hairs, on his own neck. They did it then, though, and the peculiar thing was that he was not afraid, or not only that.

He was in there with something, that was for certain. It was not a known thing, either. It was . . . he didn't know. He wasn't sure. He just knew that there was *something* over there in the darkness. Something about the size of a man, he thought, maybe a little smaller.

He wasn't sure it was male, though. Something said to him it was female. He couldn't imagine where this impression might be coming from, as he couldn't see it and he couldn't hear anything, either – after the initial movement, it had been still. There was just something in the air that told him things about it, that said underneath the shadows it wrapped around itself like a pair of dark angel's wings, it knew despair, bitter madness and melancholy better even than he did. He knew that beneath those shadows it was naked, and not male.

He knew also that it was this, and not fear, that was making his breathing come ragged and forced.

He stayed in there with it for half-an-hour, doing nothing, just listening, staring into the darkness but not seeing anything. That's how long it seemed like it had been, anyway, when he eventually emerged back into the forest. It was hard to tell.

He closed the cabin door behind him but he did not lock it because he saw that the man was back, standing once more at the far end of the bridge. Miller clasped the key firmly in his fist and walked over towards him.

'How much?' he said.

'For what? You already paid.'

'No,' Miller said. 'I want to buy it.'

*

It was eight by the time Miller got back to his house. He didn't know how that could be unless he'd spent longer in the cabin than he realised. It didn't matter a whole lot, and in fact there were good things about it. The light had begun to fade. In twenty minutes it would be gone entirely. He spent those minutes sitting in the front seat of the car, waiting for darkness, his mind as close to a comfortable blank as it had been in a long time.

When it was finally dark he got out of the car and went over to the house. He dealt with the security system, unlocked the front door and left it hanging open.

He walked back to the vehicle and went around to the trunk. He rested his hand on the metal there for a moment, and it felt cold. He unlocked the back and turned away, not fast but naturally, and walked towards the wooden steps which led to the smaller of the two raised decks. He walked up them and stood there for a few minutes, looking out into the dark stand of trees, and then turned and headed back down the steps towards the car.

The trunk was empty now, and so he shut it and walked slowly towards the open door of his house and went inside, and shut and locked that door behind him too.

It was night, and it was dark, and they·were both inside and that felt right.

He poured a small Scotch in a large glass. He took it out through the sliding glass doors to the chair on the main deck where he'd spent the morning and sat there cradling the drink, taking a sip once in a while. He found himself remembering, as he often did at this time, the first time he'd met his wife. He'd been living down on East Cliff then, in a house which was much smaller than this one but only a couple of minutes' walk from the beach. Late one Saturday afternoon, bored and restless, he'd taken a walk to the Crow's Nest, the big restaurant that was the only place to eat or drink along that stretch. He'd bought a similar Scotch at the upstairs bar and taken it out onto the balcony to watch the sun go down over the harbour. After a while he noticed that amongst the family groups of sunburned tourists and knots of tattooed locals there was a woman sitting at a table by herself. She had a tall glass of beer and seemed to be doing the same thing he was, and he wondered why. Not why she was doing that, but why he was – why they both were. He did not know then, and he did not know now, why people sit and look out into the distance by themselves, or what they hope to see.

After a couple more drinks he went over and introduced himself. Her name was Catherine and she worked at the university. They got married eighteen months later and though by then – his business having taken off in the meantime – he could have afforded anywhere in town, they hired the Crow's Nest and had the wedding party there. A year after that their daughter was born and they called her Matilde, after Catherine's mother, who was French. Business was still good and they moved out of his place on East Cliff and into the big house he had built in the mountains and for seven years all was good, and then, for some reason, it was no longer good any more. He didn't think it had been his fault, though it could have been. He didn't think it was her fault either, though that too was possible. It had simply stopped working. They'd been two people, and then one, but then two again, facing different ways. There had been a view to share together, then there was not, and if you look with only one eye then there is no depth of field. There had been no infidelity. In some ways that might have been easier. It would have been something to react to, to blame, to hide behind. Far worse, in fact, to sit on opposite sides of the breakfast table and wonder who the other person was, and why they were there, and when they would go.

Six months later, she did. Matilde went with her, of course. He didn't think there was much more that could be said or understood on the subject. When first he'd sat out on this deck alone, trying to work it all through in his head, the recounting could take hours. As time went on, the story seemed to get shorter and shorter. As they said around these parts, it is what it is.

Or it was what it was.

Time passed and then it was late. The Scotch was long gone but he didn't feel the desire for any more. He took the glass indoors and washed it in the sink, putting it on the draining board next to the plate and the knife and the fork from lunch. No lights were on. He hadn't bothered to flick any switches when he came in, and – having sat for so long out on the deck – his eyes were accustomed, and he felt no need to turn any on now.

He dried his hands on a cloth and walked around the house, aimlessly at first. He had done this many times in the last few months, hearing echoes. When he got to the area which had been Catherine's study, he stopped. There was nothing left in the space now bar the empty desk and the empty bookshelves. He could tell that the chair had been moved, however. He didn't recall precisely how it had been, or when he'd last listlessly walked this way, but he knew that it had been moved, somehow.

He went back to walking, and eventually fetched up outside the room that had been Matilde's. The door was slightly ajar. The space beyond was dark.

He could feel a warmth coming out of it, though, and heard a sound in there, something quiet, and he turned and walked slowly away.

He took a shower in the dark. Afterward he padded back to the kitchen in his bare feet and a gown and picked his Scotch glass up from the draining board. Even after many, many trips through the dishwasher you could see the ghost of the restaurant logo that had once been stamped on it, the remains of a mast and a crow's nest. Catherine had slipped it into her purse one long-ago night, without him knowing about it, and then given the glass to him as an anniversary present. How did a person who would do that change into the person now living half the state away? He didn't know, any more than he knew why he had so little to say on the phone to his daughter, or why people sat and looked at views, or why they drove to nowhere on Saturday afternoons. Our heads turn and point at things. Light comes into our eyes. Words come out of our mouths.

And then? And so?

Carefully, he brought the edge of the glass down upon the edge of the counter. It broke pretty much as he'd hoped it would, the base remaining in one piece, the sides shattering into several jagged points.

He padded back through into the bedroom, put the broken glass on the nightstand, took off the robe and lay back on the bed. That's how they'd always done it, when they'd wanted to signal that tonight didn't have to just be about going to sleep. Under the covers with a book, then probably not tonight, Josephine.

Naked and on top, on the other hand . . .

A shorthand. A shared language. There is little sadder, however, than a tongue for which only one speaker remains. He closed his eyes and after a while, for the first time since he'd stood stunned in the driveway and watched his family leave, he cried.

Afterward he lay and waited.

She came in the night.

Three days later, in the late afternoon, a battered truck pulled down into the driveway and parked alongside the car that was there. It was the first time the truck had been on the road in nearly two years, and the driver left the engine running when he got out because he wasn't all that sure it would start up again. The patched front tyre was holding up, though, for now.

He went around the back and opened up the wooden crate,

propping the flap with a stick. Then he walked over to the big front door and rang on the bell. Waited a while, and did it again. No answer. Of course.

He rubbed his face in his hands, wearily, took a step back. The door looked solid. No way a kick would get it open. He looked around and saw the steps up to the side deck.

When he got around to the back of the house he picked up the chair that sat by itself, hefted it to judge the weight, and threw it through the big glass door. When he'd satisfied himself that the hole in the smashed glass was big enough, he walked back along the deck and around the front and then up the driveway to stand on the road for a while, out of view of the house.

He smoked a cigarette, and then another to be sure, and when he came back down the driveway he was relieved to see that the flap on the crate on the back of his truck was now closed.

He climbed into the cab and sat a moment, looking at the big house. Then he put the truck into reverse, got back up to the highway and drove slowly home.

When he made the turn into his own drive later, he saw the STOP sign was still there. Didn't matter how many times he told the boy, the sign was still there.

He drove along the track to the house, parked the truck. He opened the crate without looking at it and went inside.

Later, sitting on his porch in the darkness, he listened to the sound of the wind moving through the tops of the trees all around. He drank a warm beer, and then another. He looked at the grime on his hands. He wondered what it was that made some people catch sight of the sign, what it was in their eyes, what it was in the way they looked, that made them see. He wondered how the man in the big house had done it, and hoped he had not suffered much. He wondered why he had never attempted the same thing. He wondered why it was only on nights like these that he was able to remember that his boy had been dead twenty years.

Finally he went indoors and lay in bed staring at the ceiling. He did this every night, even though there was never anything there to see: nothing, unless it is that sad, dark thing that eventually takes us in its arms and makes us sleep.

MICHAEL MARSHALL SMITH is a novelist and screenwriter. Under that name he has published seventy short stories and three novels: *Only Forward*, *Spares* and *One of Us*, winning the Philip K. Dick Award, International Horror Guild Award, August Derleth Award and the Prix Bob Morane in France. He has won the British Fantasy Award for Best Short Fiction four times, more than any other author.

Writing as 'Michael Marshall', he has also published five international best-selling thrillers, including *The Straw Men*, *The Intruders*, *Bad Things* and, most recently, *Killer Move*. *The Intruders* is under series development with BBC Television.

He is currently involved in several screenwriting projects, including a television pilot set in New York and an animated horror movie for children. The author lives in North London with his wife, son and two cats.

'This story came directly out of a locale and its atmosphere,' reveals Smith. 'The Santa Cruz Mountains are stunning, with picturesque creeks and as many redwoods as you could shake a stick at, but drive up or down some of those shadowy country side-roads and you'll soon find yourself in the kind of woods that are very quiet and very still and announce on some inaudible wavelength that you're here under sufferance, and that you should not push your luck.

'This particular story probably wouldn't have been written had not a friend emailed me one day with three words he'd seen somewhere, saying it sounded like a great title for something.

'He was right, and it's the title I've used. The story fell straight into my head – I love it when they do that.'

Near Zennor

—ELIZABETH HAND—

H E FOUND THE LETTERS inside a round metal candy tin, at the bottom of a plastic storage box in the garage, alongside strings of outdoor Christmas lights and various oddments his wife had saved for the yard sale she'd never managed to organise in almost thirty years of marriage. She'd died suddenly, shockingly, of a brain aneurysm, while planting daffodil bulbs the previous September.

Now everything was going to Goodwill. The house in New Canaan had been listed with a realtor; despite the terrible market, she'd reassured Jeffrey that it should sell relatively quickly, and for something close to his asking price.

'It's a beautiful house, Jeffrey,' she said, 'not that I'm surprised.' Jeffrey was a noted architect: she glanced at him as she stepped carefully along a flagstone path in her Louboutin heels. 'And these gardens are incredible.'

'That was all Anthea.' He paused beside a stone wall, surveying an emerald swathe of new grass, small exposed hillocks of black earth, piles of neatly-raked leaves left by the crew he'd hired to do the work that Anthea had always done on her own. In the distance, birch trees glowed spectral white against a leaden February sky that gave a twilit cast to midday. 'She always said that if I'd had to pay her for all this, I wouldn't have been able to afford her. She was right.'

He signed the final sheaf of contracts and returned them to the realtor. 'You're in Brooklyn now?' she asked, turning back towards the house.

'Yes. Green Park. A colleague of mine is in Singapore for a few months; he's letting me stay there till I get my bearings.'

'Well, good luck. I'll be in touch soon.' She opened the door of her Prius and hesitated. 'I know how hard this is for you. I lost my father two years ago. Nothing helps, really.'

Jeffrey nodded. 'Thanks. I know.'

He'd spent the last five months cycling through wordless, imageless night terrors from which he awoke gasping; dreams in which Anthea lay beside him, breathing softly then smiling as he touched her face; nightmares in which the neuro-electrical storm that had killed her raged inside his own head, a flaring nova that engulfed the world around him and left him floating in an endless black space, the stars expiring one by one as he drifted past them.

He knew that grief had no target demographic, that all around him versions of this cosmic reshuffling took place every day. He and Anthea had had their own shared experience years before, when they had lost their first and only daughter to sudden infant death syndrome. They were both in their late thirties at the time. They never tried to have another child, on their own or through adoption. It was as though some psychic house fire had consumed them both: it was a year before Jeffrey could enter the room that had been Julia's, and for months after her death neither he nor Anthea could bear to sit at the dining table and finish a meal together, or sleep in the same bed. The thought of being that close to another human being, of having one's hand or foot graze another's and wake however fleetingly to the realisation that this too could be lost – it left both of them with a terror that they had never been able to articulate, even to each other.

Now, as then, he kept busy with work at his office in the city and dutifully accepted invitations for lunch and dinner there and in New Canaan. Nights were a prolonged torment: he was haunted by the realisation that Anthea had been extinguished, a spent match pinched between one's fingers. He thought of Houdini, arch-rationalist of another century, who desired proof of a spirit world he desperately wanted to believe in. Jeffrey believed in nothing, yet if there had been a drug to twist his neurons into some synaptic impersonation of faith, he would have taken it.

For the past month he'd devoted most of his time to packing up the house, donating Anthea's clothes to various charity shops, deciding what to store and what to sell, what to divvy up among nieces and nephews, Anthea's sister, a few close friends. Throughout he experienced grief as a sort of low-grade flu, a persistent, inescapable ache that suffused not just his thoughts but his bones and tendons: a throbbing in his temples, black sparks that distorted his vision; an acrid chemical taste in the back of his throat, as though he'd bitten into one of the pills his doctor had given him to help him sleep.

He watched as the realtor drove off soundlessly, returned to the garage and transferred the plastic bin of Christmas lights into his own car, to drop off at a neighbour's the following weekend. He put the tin box with the letters on the seat beside him. As he pulled out of the driveway, it began to snow.

That night, he sat at the dining table in the Brooklyn loft and opened the candy tin. Inside were five letters, each bearing the same stamp: RETURN TO SENDER. At the bottom of the tin was a locket on a chain, cheap gold-coloured metal and chipped red enamel circled by tiny fake pearls. He opened it: it was empty. He examined it for an engraved inscription, initials, a name, but there was nothing. He set it aside and turned to the letters.

All were postmarked 1971 – February, March, April, July, end of August – all addressed to the same person at the same address, carefully spelled out in Anthea's swooping schoolgirl's hand.

Mr Robert Bennington,
Golovenna Farm,
Padwithiel,
Cornwall

Love letters? He didn't recognise the name Robert Bennington. Anthea would have been thirteen in February; her birthday was in May. He moved the envelopes across the table, as though performing a card trick. His heart pounded, which was ridiculous. He and Anthea had told each other about everything – three-ways at university, coke-fuelled orgies during the 1980s, affairs and flirtations throughout their marriage.

None of that mattered now; little of it had mattered then. Still his hands shook as he opened the first envelope. A single sheet of onionskin was inside. He unfolded it gingerly and smoothed it on the table.

His wife's handwriting hadn't changed much in forty years. The same cramped cursive, each *i* so heavily dotted in black ink that the pen had almost poked through the thin paper. Anthea had been English, born and raised in North London. They'd met at the University of London, where they were both studying, and moved to New Canaan after they'd married. It was an area that Anthea had often said reminded her of the English countryside, though Jeffrey had never ventured outside London, other than a few excursions to Kent and Brighton. Where was Padwithiel?

21 February, 1971
Dear Mr Bennington,
    My name is Anthea Ryson . . .

And would a thirteen-year-old girl address her boyfriend as 'Mr', even forty years ago?

    . . . I am thirteen years old and live in London. Last year my friend Evelyn let me read *Still the Seasons* for the first time and since then I have read it two more

times, also Black Clouds Over Bragmoor and The Second
Sun. They are my favourite books! I keep looking for
more but the library here doesn't have them. I have asked
and they said I should try the shops but that is expen-
sive. My teacher said that sometimes you come to
schools and speak, I hope some day you'll come to
Islington Day School. Are you writing more books about
Tisha and the great Battle? I hope so, please write back!
My address is 42 Highbury Fields, London NW1.
  Very truly yours,
  Anthea Ryson

Jeffrey set aside the letter and gazed at the remaining four
envelopes. *What a prick*, he thought. He never even wrote her back.
He turned to his laptop and Googled Robert Bennington.

*Robert Bennington (1932–), British author of a popular series of chil-
dren's fantasy novels published during the 1960s known as 'The Sun
Battles'. Bennington's books rode the literary tidal wave generated by
J.R.R. Tolkien's work, but his commercial and critical standing were
irrevocably shaken in the late 1990s when he became the centre of a
drawn-out court case involving charges of paedophilia and sexual assault,
with accusations lodged against him by several girl fans, now adults.
One of the alleged victims later changed her account and the case was
eventually dismissed amidst much controversy by child advocates and
women's rights groups. Bennington's reputation never recovered: school
libraries refused to keep his books on their shelves. All of his novels are
now out of print, although digital editions (illegal) can be found, along
with used copies of the four books in the 'Battles' sequence . . .*

Jeffrey's neck prickled. The court case didn't ring a bell, but the
books did. Anthea had thrust one upon him shortly after they first
met.

'These were my *favourites*.' She rolled over in bed and pulled a yellowed paperback from a shelf crowded with textbooks and Penguin editions of the mystery novels she loved. 'I must have read this twenty times.'

'Twenty?' Jeffrey raised an eyebrow.

'Well, maybe seven. A *lot*. Did you ever read them?'

'I never even heard of them.'

'You have to read it. Right now.' She nudged him with her bare foot. 'You can't leave here till you do.'

'Who says I want to leave?' He tried to kiss her, but she pushed him away.

'Uh uh. Not till you read it. I'm serious!'

So he'd read it, staying up till 3:00 a.m., intermittently dozing off before waking with a start to pick up the book again.

'It gave me bad dreams,' he said as grey morning light leaked through the narrow window of Anthea's flat. 'I don't like it.'

'I know.' Anthea laughed. 'That's what I liked about them – they always made me feel sort of sick.'

Jeffrey shook his head adamantly. 'I don't like it,' he repeated.

Anthea frowned, finally shrugged, picked up the book and dropped it onto the floor. 'Well, nobody's perfect,' she said, and rolled on top of him.

A year or so later he did read *Still the Seasons*, when a virus kept him in bed for several days and Anthea was caught up with research at the British Library. The book unsettled him deeply. There were no monsters *per se*, no dragons or Nazgûl or witches, just two sets of cousins, two boys and two girls, trapped in a portal between one of those grim post-war English cities, Manchester or Birmingham, and a magical land that wasn't really magical at all but even bleaker and more threatening than the council flats where the children lived.

Jeffrey remembered unseen hands tapping at a window, and one of the boys fighting off something invisible that crawled under the bedcovers and attacked in a flapping wave of sheets and blankets. Worst of all was the last chapter, which he read late one night and could never recall clearly, save for the vague, enveloping dread it engendered, something he had never encountered before or since.

Anthea had been right – the book had a weirdly visceral power, more like the effect of a low-budget black-and-white horror movie than a children's fantasy novel. How many of those grown-up kids now knew their hero had been a paedophile?

Jeffrey spent a half-hour scanning articles on Bennington's trial, none of them very informative. It had happened over a decade ago; since then there'd been a few dozen blog posts, pretty equally divided between *Whatever happened to . . . ?* and excoriations by women who had themselves been sexually abused, though not by Bennington.

He couldn't imagine that had happened to Anthea. She'd certainly never mentioned it, and she'd always been dismissive, even slightly callous, about friends who underwent counselling or psychotherapy for childhood traumas. As for the books themselves, he didn't recall seeing them when he'd sorted through their shelves to pack everything up. Probably they'd been donated to a library book sale years ago, if they'd even made the crossing from London.

He picked up the second envelope. It was postmarked 'March 18, 1971'. He opened it and withdrew a sheet of lined paper torn from a school notebook.

Dear Rob,

Well, we all got back on the train, Evelyn was in a lot of trouble for being out all night and of course we couldn't tell her aunt why, her mother said she can't talk to me on the phone but I see her at school anyway so it doesn't matter. I still can't believe it all happened. Evelyn's mother said she was going to call my mother and Moira's but so far she didn't. Thank you so much

for talking to us. You signed Evelyn's book but you
forgot to sign mine. Next time!!!
    Yours sincerely your friend,
    Anthea

Jeffrey felt a flash of cold through his chest. *Dear Rob, I still
can't believe it all happened.* He quickly opened the remaining
envelopes, read first one then the next and finally the last.

12 April 1971
Dear Rob,
    Maybe I wrote down your address wrong because the
last letter I sent was returned. But I asked Moira and
she had the same address and she said her letter wasn't
returned. Evelyn didn't write yet but says she will. It
was such a really, really great time to see you! Thank
you again for the books, I thanked you in the last letter
but thank you again. I hope you'll write back this time,
we still want to come again on holiday in July! I can't
believe it was exactly one month ago we were there.
    Your friend,
    Anthea Ryson

July 20, 1971
Dear Rob,
    Well I still haven't heard from you so I guess you're
mad maybe or just forgot about me, ha ha. School is out
now and I was wondering if you still wanted us to come
and stay? Evelyn says we never could and her aunt
would tell her mother but we could hitch-hike, also
Evelyn's brother Martin has a caravan and he and his
girlfriend are going to Wales for a festival and we
thought they might give us a ride partway, he said

maybe they would. Then we could hitch-hike the rest. The big news is Moira ran away from home and they called the POLICE. Evelyn said she went without us to see you and she's really mad. Moira's boyfriend Peter is mad too.

If she is there with you is it okay if I come too? I could come alone without Evelyn, her mother is a BITCH.

Please please write!

Anthea (Ryson)

Dear Rob,

I hate you. I wrote FIVE LETTERS including this one and I know it is the RIGHT address. I think Moira went to your house without us. FUCK YOU. Tell her I hate her too and so does Evelyn. We never told anyone if she says we did she is a LIAR.

FUCK YOU FUCK YOU FUCK YOU

Where a signature should have been, the page was ripped and blotched with blue ink – Anthea had scribbled something so many times the pen tore through the lined paper. Unlike the other four, this sheet was badly crumpled, as though she'd thrown it away then retrieved it. Jeffrey glanced at the envelope. The postmark read 'August 28'. She'd gone back to school for the fall term, and presumably that had been the end of it.

Except, perhaps, for Moira, whoever she was. Evelyn would be Evelyn Thurlow, Anthea's closest friend from her school days in Islington. Jeffrey had met her several times while at university, and Evelyn had stayed with them for a weekend in the early 1990s, when she was attending a conference in Manhattan. She was a flight-test engineer for a British defence contractor, living outside Cheltenham; she and Anthea would have hour-long conversations on their birthdays, planning a dream vacation together to some-place warm – Greece or Turkey or the Caribbean.

Jeffrey had emailed her about Anthea's death, and they had spoken on the phone – Evelyn wanted to fly over for the funeral but was on deadline for a major government contract and couldn't take the time off.

'I so wish I could be there,' she'd said, her voice breaking. 'Everything's just so crazed at the moment. I hope you understand . . .'

'It's okay. She knew how much you loved her. She was always so happy to hear from you.'

'I know,' Evelyn choked. 'I just wish – I just wish I'd been able to see her again.'

Now he sat and stared at the five letters. The sight made him feel lightheaded and slightly queasy: as though he'd opened his closet door and found himself at the edge of a precipice, gazing down some impossible distance to a world made tiny and unreal. Why had she never mentioned any of this? Had she hidden the letters for all these years, or simply forgotten she had them? He knew it wasn't rational; knew his response derived from his compulsive sense of order, what Anthea had always called his architect's left brain.

'Jeffrey would never even try to put a square peg into a round hole,' she'd said once at a dinner party. 'He'd just design a new hole to fit it.'

He could think of no place he could fit the five letters written to Robert Bennington. After a few minutes, he replaced each in its proper envelope and stacked them atop each other. Then he turned back to his laptop, and wrote an email to Evelyn.

He arrived in Cheltenham two weeks later. Evelyn picked him up at the train station early Monday afternoon. He'd told her he was in London on business, spent the preceding weekend at a hotel in Bloomsbury and wandered the city, walking past the building where he and Anthea had lived right after university, before they moved to the US.

It was a relief to board the train and stare out the window at an unfamiliar landscape, suburbs giving way to farms and the gently rolling outskirts of the Cotswolds.

Evelyn's husband, Chris, worked for one of the high-tech corporations in Cheltenham; their house was a rambling, expensively renovated cottage twenty minutes from the congested city centre.

'Anthea would have loved these gardens,' Jeffrey said, surveying swathes of narcissus already in bloom, alongside yellow primroses and a carpet of crocuses beneath an ancient beech. 'Everything at home is still brown. We had snow a few weeks ago.'

'It must be very hard, giving up the house.' Evelyn poured him a glass of Medoc and sat across from him in the slate-floored conservatory.

'Not as hard as staying would have been,' Jeffrey raised his glass. 'To old friends and old times.'

'To Anthea,' said Evelyn.

They talked into the evening, polishing off the Medoc and starting on a second bottle long before Chris arrived home from work. Evelyn was florid and heavyset, her unruly raven hair long as ever and braided into a single plait, thick and grey-streaked. She'd met her contract deadline just days ago and her dark eyes still looked hollowed from lack of sleep. Chris prepared dinner, lamb with mint and peas; their children were both off at university, so Jeffrey and Chris and Evelyn lingered over the table until almost midnight.

'Leave the dishes,' Chris said, rising. 'I'll get them in the morning.' He bent to kiss the top of his wife's head, then nodded at Jeffrey. 'Good to see you, Jeffrey.'

'Come on.' Evelyn grabbed a bottle of Armagnac and headed for the conservatory. 'Get those glasses, Jeffrey. I'm not going in till noon. Project's done, and the mice will play.'

Jeffrey followed her, settling onto the worn sofa and placing two glasses on the side-table. Evelyn filled both, flopped into an armchair and smiled. 'It *is* good to see you.'

'And you.'

He sipped his Armagnac. For several minutes they sat in silence, staring out of the window at the garden, the narcissus and primroses faint gleams in the darkness. Jeffrey finished his glass, poured another and asked, 'Do you remember someone named Robert Bennington?'

Evelyn cradled her glass against her chest. She gazed at Jeffrey for a long moment before answering. 'The writer? Yes. I read his books when I was a girl. Both of us did – me and Anthea.'

'But – you knew him. You met him, when you were thirteen. On vacation or something.'

Evelyn turned, her profile silhouetted against the window. 'We did,' she said at last, and turned back to him. 'Why are you asking?'

'I found some letters that Anthea wrote to him, back in 1971, after you and she and a girl named Moira saw him in Cornwall. Did you know he was a paedophile? He was arrested about fifteen years ago.'

'Yes, I read about that. It was a big scandal.' Evelyn finished her Armagnac and set her glass on the table. 'Well, a medium-sized scandal. I don't think many people even remembered who he was by then. He was a cult writer, really. The books were rather dark for children's books.'

She hesitated. 'Anthea wasn't molested by him, if that's what you're asking about. None of us were. He invited us to tea – we invited ourselves, actually – he was very nice and let us come in and gave us Nutella sandwiches and tangerines.'

'Three little teenyboppers show up at his door, I bet he was very nice,' said Jeffrey. 'What about Moira? What happened to her?'

'I don't know.' Evelyn sighed. 'No one ever knew. She ran away from home that summer. We never heard from her again.'

'Did they question him? Was he even taken into custody?'

'Of course they did!' Evelyn said, exasperated. 'I mean, I don't know for sure, but I'm certain they did. Moira had a difficult home life; her parents were Irish and the father drank. And a lot of kids ran away back then, you know that – all us little hippies. What did the letters say, Jeffrey?'

He removed them from his pocket and handed them to her. 'You can read them. He never did – they all came back to Anthea. Where's Padwithiel?'

'Near Zennor. My aunt and uncle lived there. We went and stayed with them during our school holidays one spring.' She sorted through the envelopes, pulled out one and opened it, unfolding the letter with care. 'February twenty-first. This was right before we knew we'd be going there for the holidays. It was my idea. I remember when she wrote this – she got the address somehow, and that's how we realised he lived near my uncle's farm. Padwithiel.'

She leaned into the lamp and read the first letter, set it down and continued to read each of the others. When she was finished, she placed the last one on the table, sank back into her chair and gazed at Jeffrey.

'She never told you about what happened.'

'You just said that nothing happened.'

'I don't mean with Robert. She called me every year on the anniversary. March 12.' She looked away. 'Next week, that is. I never told Chris. It wasn't a secret, we just— Well, I'll just tell you.

'We went to school together, the three of us, and after Anthea sent that letter to Robert Bennington, she and I cooked up the idea of going to see him. Moira never read his books – she wasn't much of a reader. But she heard us talking about his books all the time, and we'd all play these games where we'd be the ones who fought the Sun Battles. She just did whatever we told her to, though for some reason she always wanted prisoners to be boiled in oil. She must've seen it in a movie.

'Even though we were older now, we still wanted to believe that magic could happen like in those books – probably we wanted to believe it even more. And all that New Agey, hippie stuff, Tarot cards and Biba and "Ride a White Swan" – it all just seemed like it could be real. My aunt and uncle had a farm near Zennor. My mother asked if we three could stay there for the holidays and Aunt Becca said that would be fine. My cousins are older, and they were already off at university. So we took the train to Penzance and Aunt Becca picked us up.

'They were turning one of the outbuildings into a pottery studio for her, and that's where we stayed. There was no electricity yet, but we had a kerosene heater and we could stay up as late as we wanted. I think we got maybe five hours' sleep the whole time we were there.' She laughed. 'We'd be up all night, but then Uncle Ray would start in with the tractors at dawn. We'd end up going into the house and napping in one of my cousin's beds for half the afternoon whenever we could. We were very grumpy houseguests.

'It rained the first few days we were there, just pissing down. Finally one morning we got up and the sun was shining. It was cold, but we didn't care – we were just so happy we could get outside for a while. At first we just walked along the road, but it was so muddy from all the rain that we ended up heading across the moor. Technically it's not really open moorland – there are old stone walls crisscrossing everything, ancient field systems. Some of them are thousands of years old, and farmers still keep them up and use them. These had not been kept up. The land was completely overgrown, though you could still see the walls and climb them. Which is what we did.

'We weren't that far from the house – we could still see it, and I'm pretty sure we were still on my uncle's land. We found a place where the walls were higher than elsewhere, more like proper hedgerows. There was no break in the wall like there usually is, no gate or old entryway. So we found a spot that was relatively untangled and we all climbed up and then jumped to the other side. The walls were completely overgrown with blackthorn and all these viney things. It was like Sleeping Beauty's castle – the thorns hurt like shit. I remember I was wearing new boots and they got ruined, just scratched everywhere. And Moira tore her jacket and we knew she'd catch grief for that. But we thought there must be something wonderful on the other side – that was the game we were playing, that we'd find some amazing place. Do you know *The Secret Garden*? We thought it might be like that. At least I did.'

'And was it?'

Evelyn shook her head. 'It wasn't a garden. It was just this big overgrown field. Dead grass and stones. But it was rather beautiful in a bleak way. Ant laughed and started yelling "Heathcliff, Heathcliff!" And it was warmer – the walls were high enough to keep out the wind, and there were some trees that had grown up on top of the walls as well. They weren't in leaf yet, but they formed a bit of a windbreak.

'We ended up staying there all day – completely lost track of the time. I thought only an hour had gone by, but Ant had a watch; at one point she said it was past three and I was shocked – I mean, really shocked. It was like we'd gone to sleep and woken up, only we weren't asleep at all.'

'What were you doing?'

Evelyn shrugged. 'Playing. The sort of let's-pretend game we always did when we were younger and hadn't done for a while. Moira had a boyfriend, Ant and I really *wanted* boyfriends – mostly that's what we talked about whenever we got together. But for some reason, that day Ant said "Let's do Sun Battles," and we all agreed. So that's what we did. Now of course I can see why – I've seen it with my own kids when they were that age, you're on the cusp of everything, and you just want to hold on to being young for as long as you can.

'I don't remember much of what we did that day, except how strange it all felt. As though something was about to happen. I felt like that a lot, it was all tied in with being a teenager; but this was different. It was like being high, or tripping, only none of us had ever done any drugs at that stage. And we were stone-cold sober. Really all we did was wander around the moor and clamber up and down the walls and hedgerows and among the trees, pretending we were in Gearnzath. That was the world in *The Sun Battles* – like Narnia, only much scarier. We were mostly just wandering around and making things up, until Ant told us it was after three o'clock.

'I think it was her idea that we should do some kind of ritual. I know it wouldn't have been Moira's, and I don't think it was mine. But I knew there was going to be a full moon that night – I'd heard my uncle mention it – and so we decided that we would each sacrifice a sacred thing, and then retrieve them all before moonrise. We turned our pockets inside out, looking for what we could use. I had a comb – just a red plastic thing – so that was mine. Ant had a locket on a chain from Woolworths, cheap, but the locket part opened.

'And Moira had a pencil. It said RAVENWOOD on the side, so we called the field Ravenwood. We climbed up on the wall and stood facing the sun and made up some sort of chant. I don't remember what we said. Then we tossed our things onto the moor. None of us threw them far, and Ant barely tossed hers – she didn't want to lose the locket. I didn't care about the comb, but it was so light it just fell a few yards from where we stood. Same with the pencil. We all marked where they fell – I remember mine very clearly, it came down right on top of this big flat stone.

'Then we left. It was getting late and cold, and we were all starving – we'd had nothing to eat since breakfast. We went back to the house and hung out in the barn for a while, and then we had dinner. We didn't talk much. Moira hid her jacket so they couldn't see she'd torn it, and I took my boots off so no one would see how I'd got them all mauled by the thorns. I remember my aunt wondering if we were up to something, and my uncle saying what the hell could we possibly be up to in Zennor? After dinner we sat in the living room and waited for the sun to go down, and when we saw the moon start to rise above the hills, we went back outside.

'It was bright enough that we could find our way without a torch – a flashlight. I think that must have been one of the rules, that we had to retrieve our things by moonlight. It was cold out, and none of us had dressed very warmly, so we ran. It didn't take long. We climbed back over the wall and then down onto the field, at the exact spot where we'd thrown our things.

'They weren't there. I knew exactly where the rock was where my comb had landed – the rock was there, but not the comb. Ant's locket had landed only a few feet past it, and it wasn't there either. And Moira's pencil was gone, too.'

'The wind could have moved them,' said Jeffrey. 'Or an animal.'

'Maybe the wind,' said Evelyn. 'Though the whole reason we'd stayed there all day was that there was no wind – it was protected, and warm.'

'Maybe a bird took it? Don't some birds like shiny things?'

'What would a bird do with a pencil? Or a plastic comb?'

Jeffrey made a face. 'Probably you just didn't see where they fell. You thought you did, in daylight, but everything looks different at night. Especially in moonlight.'

'I knew where they were.' Evelyn shook her head and reached for the bottle of Armagnac. 'Especially my comb. I have that engineer's eye, I can look at things and keep a very precise picture in my mind. The comb wasn't where it should have been. And there was no reason for it to be gone, unless . . .'

'Unless some other kids had seen you and found everything after you left,' said Jeffrey.

'No.' Evelyn sipped her drink. 'We started looking. The moon was coming up – it rose above the hill, and it was very bright. Because it was so cold there was hoarfrost on the grass, and ice in places where the rain had frozen. So all that reflected the moonlight. Everything glittered. It was beautiful, but it was no longer fun – it was scary. None of us was even talking; we just split up and crisscrossed the field, looking for our things.

'And then Moira said, "There's someone there," and pointed. I thought it was someone on the track that led back to the farm-house – it's not a proper road, just a rutted path that runs along-side one edge of that old field system. I looked up and yes, there were three people there – three torches, anyway. Flashlights. You couldn't see who was carrying them, but they were walking slowly along the path. I thought maybe it was my uncle and two of the men who worked with him, coming to tell us it was time to go home. They were walking from the wrong direction, across the moor, but I thought maybe they'd gone out to work on some-thing. So I ran to the left edge of the field and climbed up on the wall.'

She stopped, glancing out the window at the black garden, and finally turned back. 'I could see the three lights from there,' she said. 'But the angle was all wrong. They weren't on the road at all – they were in the next field, up above Ravenwood. And they weren't flashlights. They were high up in the air, like this—'

She set down her glass and got to her feet, a bit unsteadily, extended both her arms and mimed holding something in her hands. 'Like someone was carrying a pole eight or ten feet high, and there was a light on top of it. Not a flame. Like a ball of light . . .'

She cupped her hands around an invisible globe the size of a soccer ball. 'Like that. White light, sort of foggy. The lights bobbed as they were walking.'

'Did you see who it was?'

'No. We couldn't see anything. And, this is the part that I can't explain – it just felt bad. Like, horrible. Terrifying.'

'You thought you'd summoned up whatever it was you'd been playing at.' Jeffrey nodded sympathetically and finished his drink.

'It was just marsh gas, Ev. You know that. Will o' the wisp, or what-ever you call it here. They must get it all the time out there in the country. Or fog. Or someone just out walking in the moonlight.'

Evelyn settled back into her armchair. 'It wasn't,' she said. 'I've seen marsh gas. There was no fog. The moon was so bright you could see every single rock in that field. Whatever it was, we all saw it. And you couldn't hear anything – there were no voices, no footsteps, nothing. They were just there, moving closer to us – slowly,' she repeated, and moved her hand up and down, as though calming a cranky child. 'That was the creepiest thing, how slowly they just kept coming.'

'Why didn't you just run?'

'Because we couldn't. You know how kids will all know about something horrible, but they'll never tell a grown-up? It was like that. We knew we had to find our things before we could go.

'I found my comb first. It was way over – maybe twenty feet from where I'd seen it fall. I grabbed it and began to run across the turf, looking for the locket and Moira's pencil. The whole time the moon was rising, and that was horrible too – it was a beau-tiful clear night, no clouds at all. And the moon was so beautiful, but it just terrified me. I can't explain it.'

Jeffrey smiled wryly. 'Yeah? How about this: three thirteen-year-old girls in the dark under a full moon, with a very active im-agination?'

'Hush. A few minutes later Moira yelled: she'd found her pencil. She turned and started running back towards the wall, I screamed after her that she had to help us find the locket. She wouldn't come back. She didn't go over the wall without us, but she wouldn't help. I ran over to Ant, but she yelled at me to keep searching where I was. I did, I even started heading for the far end of the field, towards the other wall – where the lights were.

'They were very close now, close to the far wall I mean. You could see how high up they were, taller than a person. I could hear

Moira crying. I looked back and suddenly I saw Ant dive to the ground. She screamed "I found it!" and I could see the chain shining in her hand.

'And we just turned and hightailed it. I've never run so fast in my life. I grabbed Ant's arm, and by the time we got to the wall Moira was already on top and jumping down the other side. I fell and Ant had to help me up, Moira grabbed her and we ran all the way back to the farm and locked the door when we got inside.

'We looked out the window and the lights were still there. They were there for hours. My uncle had a Border Collie; we cracked the door to see if she'd hear something and bark, but she didn't. She wouldn't go outside – we tried to get her to look and she wouldn't budge.'

'Did you tell your aunt and uncle?'

Evelyn shook her head. 'No. We stayed in the house that night, in my cousin's room. It overlooked the moor, so we could watch the lights. After about two hours they began to move back the way they'd come – slowly; it was about another hour before they were gone completely. We went out next morning to see if there was anything there – we took the dog to protect us.'

'And?'

'There was nothing. The grass was all beaten down, as though someone had been walking over it, but probably that was just us.'

She fell silent.

'Well,' Jeffrey said after a long moment. 'It's certainly a good story.'

'It's a true story. Here, wait.'

She stood and went into the other room, and Jeffrey heard her go upstairs. He crossed to the window and stared out into the night, the dark garden occluded by shadow and runnels of mist, blueish in the dim light cast from the conservatory.

'Look. I still have it.'

He turned to see Evelyn holding a small round tin. She withdrew a small object and stared at it, placed it back inside and handed him the tin. 'My comb. There's some pictures here too.'

'That tin.' He stared at the lid, blue enamel with the words ST AUSTELL SWEETS: FUDGE FROM REAL CORNISH CREAM stamped in gold above the silhouette of what looked like a lighthouse beacon. 'It's just like the one I found with Anthea's letters in it.'

Evelyn nodded. 'That's right. Aunt Becca gave one to each of us the day we arrived. The fudge was supposed to last the entire two weeks, and I think we ate it all that first night.'

He opened the tin and gazed at a bright-red plastic comb sitting atop several snapshots; he dug into his pocket and pulled out Anthea's locket.

'There it is,' said Evelyn wonderingly. She took the locket and dangled it in front of her, clicked it open and shut then returned it to Jeffrey. 'She never had anything in it that I knew. Here, look at these.'

She took back the tin. He sat waiting as she sorted through the snapshots then passed him six small black-and-white photos, each with OCTOBER 1971 written on the back.

'That was my camera.' Evelyn sank back into the armchair. 'I didn't finish shooting the roll till we went back to school.'

There were two girls in most of the photos. One was Anthea, apple-cheeked, her face still rounded with puppy fat and her brown hair longer than he'd ever seen it; eyebrows unplucked, wearing baggy bell-bottom jeans and a white peasant shirt. The other girl was taller, sturdy but long-limbed, with long straight blonde hair and a broad smooth forehead, elongated eyes and a wide mouth bared in a grin.

'That's Moira,' said Evelyn.

'She's beautiful.'

'She was. We were the ugly ducklings, Ant and me. Fortunately

I was taking most of the photos, so you don't see me except in the ones Aunt Becca took.'

'You were adorable.' Jeffrey flipped to a photo of all three girls laughing and feeding each other something with their hands, Evelyn still in braces, her hair cut in a severe black bob. 'You were all adorable. She's just—'

He scrutinised a photo of Moira by herself, slightly out of focus so all you saw was a blurred wave of blonde hair and her smile, a flash of narrowed eyes. 'She's beautiful. Photogenic.'

Evelyn laughed. 'Is that what you call it? No, Moira was very pretty, all the boys liked her. But she was a tomboy, like us. Ant was the one who was boy-crazy. Me and Moira, not so much.'

'What about when you saw Robert Bennington? When was that?'

'The next day. Nothing happened – I mean, he was very nice, but there was nothing strange like that night. Nothing *untoward*,' she added, lips pursed. 'My aunt knew who he was – she didn't *know* him, except to say hello to at the post office, and she'd never read his books. But she knew he was the children's writer, and she knew which house was supposed to be his. We told her we were going to see him, she told us to be polite and not be a nuisance and not stay long.

'So we were polite and not nuisances, and we stayed for two hours. Maybe three. We trekked over to his house, and that took almost an hour. A big old stone house. There was a standing stone and an old barrow nearby, it looked like a hayrick. A fogou. He was very proud that there was a fogou on his land – like a cave, but man-made. He said it was three thousand years old. He took us out to see it, and then we walked back to his house and he made us Nutella sandwiches and tangerines and orange squash. We just walked up to his door and knocked – *I* knocked, Ant was too nervous and Moira was just embarrassed. Ant and I had our copies of *The Second Sun*, and he was very sweet and invited us in and said he'd sign them before we left.'

'Oh, sure – "Come up and see my fogou, girls".'

'No – he wanted us to see it because it gave him an idea for his book. It was like a portal, he said. He wasn't a dirty old man, Jeffrey! He wasn't even that old – maybe forty? He had long hair, longish, anyway – to his shoulders – and he had cool clothes, an embroidered shirt and corduroy flares. And pointy-toed boots – blue boot, bright sky-blue, very pointy toes. That was the only thing about him I thought was odd. I wondered how his toes fit into them – if he had long pointy toes to go along with the shoes.' She laughed. 'Really, he was very charming, talked to us about the books but wouldn't reveal any secrets – he said there would be another in the series but it never appeared. He signed our books – well, he signed mine, Moira didn't have one and for some reason he forgot Ant's. And eventually we left.'

'Did you tell him about the lights?'

'We did. He said he'd heard of things like that happening before. That part of Cornwall is ancient, there are all kinds of stone circles and menhirs, cromlechs, things like that.'

'What's a cromlech?'

'You know – a dolmen.' At Jeffrey's frown she picked up several of the snapshots and arranged them on the side-table, a simple house of cards: three photos supporting a fourth laid atop them. 'Like that. It's a kind of prehistoric grave, made of big flat stones. Stonehenge, only small. The fogou was a bit like that. They're all over West Penwith – that's where Zennor is. Aleister Crowley lived there, and D.H. Lawrence and his wife. That was years before Robert's time, but he said there were always stories about odd things happening. I don't know what kind of things – it was always pretty boring when I visited as a girl, except for that one time.'

Jeffrey made a face. 'He was out there with a flashlight, Ev, leading you girls on.'

'He didn't even know we were there!' protested Evelyn, so vehemently that the makeshift house of photos collapsed. 'He looked genuinely startled when we knocked on his door – I was afraid he'd yell at us to leave. Or, I don't know, have us arrested. He said that field had a name. It was a funny word, Cornish. It meant something, though of course I don't remember what.'

She stopped and leaned towards Jeffrey. 'Why do you care about this, Jeffrey? *Did* Anthea say something?'

'No. I just found those letters, and—'

He laid his hands atop his knees, turned to stare past Evelyn into the darkness, so that she wouldn't see his eyes welling. 'I just wanted to know. And I can't ask her.'

Evelyn sighed. 'Well, there's nothing to know, except what I told you. We went back once more – we took torches this time, and walking sticks and the dog. We stayed out till 3:00 a.m. Nothing happened except we caught hell from my aunt and uncle because they heard the dog barking and looked in the barn and we were gone.

'And that was the end of it. I still have the book he signed for me. Ant must have kept her copy – she was always mad he didn't sign it. Did she still have that?'

'I don't know. Maybe. I couldn't find it. Your friend Moira, you're not in touch with her?'

Evelyn shook her head. 'I told you, she disappeared – she ran away that summer. There were problems at home, the father was a drunk and maybe the mother, too. We never went over there – it wasn't a welcoming place. She had an older sister, but I never knew her. Look, if you're thinking Robert Bennington killed her, that's ridiculous. I'm sure her name came up during the trial, if anything had happened we would have heard about it. An investigation.'

'Did you tell them about Moira?'

'Of course not. Look, Jeffrey – I think you should forget about all that. It's nothing to do with you, and it was all a long time ago. Ant never cared about it – I told her about the trial, I'd read about it in the *Guardian*, but she was even less curious about it than I was. I don't even know if Robert Bennington is still alive. He'd be an old man now.'

She leaned over to take his hand. 'I can see you're tired, Jeffrey. This has all been so awful for you, you must be totally exhausted. Do you want to just stay here for a few days? Or come back after your meeting in London?'

'No – I mean, probably not. Probably I need to get back to Brooklyn. I have some projects I backburnered, I need to get to them in the next few weeks. I'm sorry, Ev.'

He rubbed his eyes and stood. 'I didn't mean to hammer you about this stuff. You're right – I'm just beat. All this—' He sorted the snapshots into a small stack, and asked, 'Could I have one of these? It doesn't matter which one.'

'Of course. Whichever, take your pick.'

He chose a photo of the three girls, Moira and Evelyn doubled over laughing as Anthea stared at them, smiling and slightly puzzled.

'Thank you, Ev,' he said. He replaced each of Anthea's letters into its envelope, slid the photo into the last one, then stared at the sheaf in his hand, as though wondering how it got there. 'It's just, I dunno. Meaningless, I guess; but I want it to mean some-thing. I want *something* to mean something.'

'Anthea meant something.' Evelyn stood and put her arms around him. 'Your life together meant something. And your life now means something.'

'I know.' He kissed the top of her head. 'I keep telling myself that.'

Evelyn dropped him off at the station next morning. He felt guilty, lying that he had meetings back in London, but he sensed both her relief and regret that he was leaving.

'I'm sorry about last night,' he said as Evelyn turned into the parking lot. 'I feel like the Bad Fairy at the christening, bringing up all that stuff.'

'No, it was interesting.' Evelyn squinted into the sun. 'I hadn't thought about any of that for awhile. Not since Ant called me last March.'

Jeffrey hesitated, then asked, 'What do you think happened? I mean, you're the one with the advanced degree in structural engineering.'

Evelyn laughed. 'Yes – and see where it's got me. I have no idea, Jeffrey. If you ask me, logically, what do I think? Well, I think it's just one of those things that we'll never know what happened. Maybe two different dimensions overlapped – in superstring theory, something like that is theoretically possible, a sort of duality.'

She shook her head. 'I know it's crazy. Probably it's just one of those things that don't make any sense and never will. Like how did Bush stay in office for so long?'

'That I could explain.' Jeffrey smiled. 'But it's depressing and would take too long. Thanks again, Ev.'

They hopped out of the car and hugged on the curb. 'You should come back soon,' said Ev, wiping her eyes. 'This is stupid, that it took so long for us all to get together again.'

'I know. I will – soon, I promise. And you and Chris, come to New York. Once I have a place, it would be great.'

He watched her drive off, waving as she turned back onto the main road; went into the station and walked to a ticket window.

'Can I get to Penzance from here?'

'What time?'

'Now.'

The station agent looked at her computer. 'There's a train in about half an hour. Change trains in Plymouth, arrive at Penzance a little before four.'

He bought a first-class, one-way ticket to Penzance, found a seat in the waiting area, took out his phone and looked online for a place to stay near Zennor. There wasn't much – a few farmhouses designed for summer rentals, all still closed for the winter. An inn that had in recent years been turned into a popular gastropub was open; but even now, the first week of March, they were fully booked. Finally he came upon a B&B called Cliff Cottage. There were only two rooms, and the official opening date was not until the following weekend, but he called anyway.

'A room?' The woman who answered sounded tired but friendly. 'We're not really ready yet, we've been doing some renovations and—'

'All I need is a bed,' Jeffrey broke in. He took a deep breath. 'The truth is, my wife died recently. I just need some time to be away from the rest of the world and . . .' His voice trailed off.

He felt a pang of self-loathing, playing the pity card; listened to a long silence on the line before the woman said, 'Oh, dear, I'm so sorry. Well, yes, if you don't mind that we're really not up and running. The grout's not even dry yet in the new bath. Do you have a good head for heights?'

'Heights?'

'Yes. Vertigo? Some people have a very hard time with the driveway. There's a two-night minimum for a stay.'

Jeffrey assured her he'd never had any issues with vertigo. He gave her his credit card info, rang off and called to reserve a car in Penzance.

He slept most of the way to Plymouth, exhausted and faintly hung-over. The train from Plymouth to Penzance was nearly empty. He bought a beer and a sandwich in the buffet car and went to his seat. He'd bought a novel in London at Waterstone's, but instead of reading, gazed out at a landscape that was a dream of books he'd read as a child – granite farmhouses, woolly-coated ponies in stone paddocks; fields improbably green against lowering grey sky, graphite clouds broken by blades of golden sun, a rainbow that pierced a thunderhead then faded as though erased by some unseen hand. Ringnecked pheasants, a running fox. More fields planted with something that shone a startling goldfinch-yellow. A silvery coastline hemmed by arches of russet stone. Children wrestling in the middle of an empty road. A woman walking with head bowed against the wind, hands extended before her like a diviner.

Abandoned mineshafts and slagheaps; ruins glimpsed in an eyeflash before the train dove into a tunnel; black birds wheeling above a dun-coloured tor surrounded by scorched heath.

And, again and again, groves of gnarled oaks that underscored the absence of great forests in a landscape that had been scoured of trees thousands of years ago. It was beautiful yet also slightly disturbing, like watching an underpopulated, narratively fractured silent movie that played across the train window.

The trees were what most unsettled Jeffrey: the thought that men had so thoroughly occupied this countryside for so long that they had flensed it of everything – rocks, trees, shrubs all put to some human use so that only the abraded land remained. He felt relieved when the train at last reached Penzance, with the beach-front promenade to one side, glassy waves breaking on the sand and the dark towers of St Michael's Mount suspended between water and pearly sky.

He grabbed his bag and walked through the station, outside to where people waited on the curb with luggage or headed to the parking lot. The clouds had lifted: a chill steady wind blew from off the water, bringing the smell of salt and sea-wrack. He shivered and pulled on his woollen overcoat, looking around for the vehicle from the rental car company that was supposed to meet him.

He finally spotted it, a small white car parked along the sidewalk. A man in a dark blazer leaned against the car, smoking and talking to a teenage boy with dreadlocks and rainbow-knit cap and a woman with matted dark-blonde hair.

'You my ride?' Jeffrey said, smiling.

The man took a drag from his cigarette and passed it to the woman. She was older than Jeffrey had first thought, in her early thirties, face seamed and sun-weathered and her eyes bloodshot. She wore tight flared jeans and a fuzzy sky-blue sweater beneath a stained Arsenal windbreaker.

'Spare anything?' she said as he stopped alongside the car. She reeked of sweat and marijuana smoke.

'Go on now, Erthy,' the man said, scowling. He turned to Jeffrey. 'Mr Kearin?'

'That's me,' said Jeffrey.

'Gotta 'nother rollie, Evan?' the woman prodded.

'Come on, Erthy,' said the rainbow-hatted boy. He spun and began walking towards the station. 'Peace, Evan.'

'I apologise for that,' Evan said as he opened the passenger door for Jeffrey. 'I know the boy, his family's neighbours of my sister's.'

'Bit old for him, isn't she?' Jeffrey glanced to where the two huddled against the station wall, smoke welling from their cupped hands.

'Yeah, Erthy's a tough nut. She used to sleep rough by the St Erth train station. Only this last winter she's taken up in Penzance. Every summer we get the smackhead hippies here; there's always some poor souls who stay and take up on the street. Not that you want to hear about that,' he added, laughing as he swung into the driver's seat. 'On vacation?'

Jeffrey nodded. 'Just a few days.'

'Staying here in Penzance?'

'Cardu. Near Zennor.'

'Might see some sun, but probably not till the weekend.'

He ended up with the same small white car. 'Only one we have, this last minute,' Evan said, tapping at the computer in the rental office. 'But it's better really for driving out there in the countryside. Roads are extremely narrow. Have you driven around here before? No? I would strongly recommend the extra damages policy . . .'

It had been decades since Jeffrey had been behind the wheel of a car in the UK. He began to sweat as soon as he left the rental car lot, eyes darting between the map Evan had given him and the GPS on his iPhone. In minutes the busy roundabout was behind him; the car crept up a narrow, winding hillside, with high stone walls on either side that swiftly gave way to hedgerows bordering open farmland. A brilliant yellow field proved to be planted with daffodils, their constricted yellow throats not quite in bloom. After several more minutes, he came to a crossroads.

Almost immediately he got lost. The distances between villages and roads were deceptive: what appeared on the map to be a mile or more instead contracted into a few hundred yards, or else expanded into a series of zigzags and switchbacks that appeared to point him back towards Penzance. The GPS directions made no sense, advising him to turn directly into stone walls or gated driveways or fields where cows grazed on young spring grass. The roads were only wide enough for one car to pass, with tiny turnouts every fifty feet or so where one could pull over, but the high hedgerows and labyrinthine turns made it difficult to spot oncoming vehicles.

His destination, a village called Cardu, was roughly seven miles from Penzance; after half an hour the odometer registered that he'd gone fifteen miles and he had no idea where he was. There was no cell phone reception. The sun dangled a hand's-span above the western horizon, staining ragged stone outcroppings and a bleak expanse of moor an ominous reddish-bronze, and throwing the black fretwork of stone walls into stark relief. He finally parked in one of the narrow turnouts, sat for a few minutes staring into the sullen blood-red eye of the sun, and at last got out.

The hedgerows offered little protection from the harsh wind that raked across the moor. Jeffrey pulled at the collar of his coat, turning his back to the wind, and noticed a small sign that read PUBLIC FOOTPATH. He walked over and saw a narrow gap in the hedgerow, three steps formed of wide flat stones. He took the three in one long stride and found himself at the edge of an overgrown field, similar to what Evelyn had described in her account of the lights near Zennor. An ancient-looking stone wall bounded the far edge of the field, with a wider gap that opened to the next field and what looked like another sign. He squinted, but couldn't make out what it read, and began to pick his way across the turf.

It was treacherous going – the countless hummocks hid deep holes, and more than once he barely kept himself from wrenching his ankle. The air smelled strongly of raw earth and cow manure. As the sun dipped lower, a wedge of shadow was driven between him and the swiftly darkening sky, making it still more difficult to see his way. But after a few minutes he reached the far wall, and bent to read the sign beside the gap into the next field.

CAS CIRCLE.

He glanced back, saw a glint of white where the rental car was parked, straightened and walked on. There was a footpath here – hardly a path, really; just a trail where turf and bracken had been flattened by the passage of not-many feet. He followed it, stopping when he came to a large upright stone that came up to his waist. He looked to one side then the other, and saw more stones, forming a group more ovoid than circular, perhaps thirty feet in diameter. He ran his hand across the first stone – rough granite, ridged with lichen and friable bits of moss that crumbled at his touch.

The reek of manure was fainter here: he could smell something fresh and sweet, and when he looked down saw a silvery gleam at the base of the rock. He crouched and dipped his fingers into a tiny pool, no bigger than his shoe. The water was icy-cold, and even after he withdrew his hand, the surface trembled.

A spring. He dipped his cupped palm into it and sniffed warily, expecting a foetid whiff of cow muck.

But the water smelled clean, of rock and rain. Without thinking he drew his hand to his mouth and sipped, immediately flicked his fingers to send glinting droplets into the night.

That was stupid, he thought, hastily wiping his hand on his trousers. *Now I'll get dysentery. Or whatever one gets from cows.*

He stood there for another minute, then turned and retraced his steps to the rental car. He saw a pair of headlights approaching and flagged down a white delivery van.

'I'm lost,' he said, and showed the driver the map that Evan had given him.

'Not too lost.' The driver perused the map, then gave him directions. 'Once you see the inn you're almost there.'

Jeffrey thanked him, got back into the car and started to drive. In ten minutes he reached the inn, a rambling stucco structure with half a dozen cars out front. There was no sign identifying Cardu, and no indication that there was anything more to the village than the inn and a deeply rutted road flanked by a handful of granite cottages in varying states of disrepair. He eased the rental car by the mottled grey buildings to where what passed for a road ended; bore right and headed down a cobblestoned, hairpin drive that zigzagged along the cliff-edge.

He could hear but could not see the ocean, waves crashing against rocks hundreds of feet below. Now and then he got a skin-crawling glimpse of immense cliffs like congealed flames – ruddy stone, apricot-yellow gorse, lurid flares of orange lichen all burned to ash as afterglow faded from the western sky.

He wrenched his gaze back to the narrow strip of road immediately in front of him. Gorse and brambles tore at the doors; once he bottomed out, then nosed the car across a water-filled gulley that widened into a stream that cascaded down the cliff to the sea below.

'Holy fucking Christ,' he said, and kept in first gear. In another five minutes he was safely parked beside the cottage, alongside a small coupé.

'We thought maybe you weren't coming,' someone called as Jeffrey stepped shakily out onto a cobblestone drive. Straggly rosebushes grew between a row of granite slabs that resembled headstones. These were presumably to keep cars from veering down an incline that led to a ruined outbuilding, a few faint stars already framed in its gaping windows. 'Some people, they start down here and just give up and turn back.'

Jeffrey looked around, finally spotted a slight man in his early sixties standing in the doorway of a grey stone cottage tucked into the lee of the cliff. 'Oh, hi. No, I made it.'

Jeffrey ducked back into the car, grabbed his bag and headed for the cottage.

'Harry,' the man said, and held the door for him.

'Jeffrey. I spoke to your wife this afternoon.'

The man's brow furrowed. 'Wife?' He was a head shorter than Jeffrey, clean-shaven, with a sun-weathered face and sleek grey-flecked dark brown hair to his shoulders. A ropey old cable-knit sweater hung from his lank frame.

'Well, someone. A woman.'

'Oh, that was Thomsa. My sister.' The man nodded, as though this confusion had never occurred before. 'We're still trying to get unpacked. We don't really open till this weekend, but . . .'

He held the door so Jeffrey could pass inside. 'Thomsa told me of your loss. My condolences.'

Inside was a small room with slate floors and plastered walls, sparely furnished with a plain wooden table and four chairs intricately carved with Celtic knots; a sideboard holding books and maps and artfully mismatched crockery; large gas stove and a side-table covered with notepads and pens, unopened bills and a laptop. A modern cast-iron wood-stove had been fitted into a wide, old-fashioned hearth. The stove radiated warmth and an acrid, not unpleasant scent, redolent of coal-smoke and burning sage. Peat, Jeffrey realised with surprise. There was a closed door on the other side of the room, and from behind this came the sound of a television. Harry looked at Jeffrey, cocking an eyebrow.

'It's beautiful,' said Jeffrey.

Harry nodded. 'I'll take you to your room.'

Jeffrey followed him up a narrow stair beneath the eaves, into a short hallway flanked by two doors. 'Your room's here. Bath's down there, you'll have it all to yourself. What time would you like breakfast?'

'Seven, maybe?'

'How about seven-thirty?'

Jeffrey smiled wanly. 'Sure.'

The room was small, white plaster walls and a window-seat overlooking the sea, a big bed heaped with a white duvet and myriad pillows, corner wardrobe carved with the same Celtic knots as the chairs below. No TV or radio or telephone, not even a clock. Jeffrey unpacked his bag and checked his phone for service: none.

He closed the wardrobe, looked in his backpack and swore. He'd left his book on the train. He ran a hand through his hair, stepped to the window-seat and stared out.

It was too dark now to see much, though light from windows on the floor below illuminated a small, winding patch of garden, bound on the cliff side by a stone wall. Beyond that there was only rock and, far below, the sea. Waves thundered against the unseen shore, a muted roar like a jet turbine. He could feel the house around him shake.

And not just the house, he thought; it felt as though the ground and everything around him trembled without ceasing. He paced to the other window, which overlooked the drive, and stared at his rental car and the coupé beside it through a frieze of branches, a tree so contorted by wind and salt that its limbs only grew in one direction. He turned off the room's single light, waited for his eyes to adjust; stared back out through one window, and then the other.

For as far as he could see, there was only night. Ghostly light seeped from a room downstairs onto the sliver of lawn. Starlight touched on the endless sweep of moor, like another sea unrolling from the line of cliffs brooding above black waves and distant headlands. There was no sign of human habitation: no distant lights, no street-lamps, no cars, no ships or lighthouse beacons: nothing.

He sank onto the window seat, dread knotting his chest. He had never seen anything like this – even hiking in the Mojave Desert with Anthea ten years earlier, there had been a scattering of lights sifted across the horizon and satellites moving slowly through the constellations. He grabbed his phone, fighting a cold black solitary horror. There was still no reception.

He put the phone aside and stared at a framed sepia-tinted photograph on the wall: a three-masted schooner wrecked on the rocks beneath a cliff he suspected was the same one where the cottage stood. Why was he even here? He felt as he had once in college, waking in a strange room after a night of heavy drinking, surrounded by people he didn't know in a squalid flat used as a shooting gallery. The same sense that he'd been engaged in some kind of psychic somnambulism, walking perilously close to a precipice.

Here, of course he actually *was* perched on the edge of a precipice. He stood and went into the hall, switching on the light; walked into the bathroom and turned on all the lights there as well.

It was almost as large as his bedroom, cheerfully appointed with yellow and blue towels piled atop a wooden chair, a massive porcelain tub, hand-woven yellow rugs and a fistful of daffodils in a cobalt glass vase on a wide windowsill. He moved the towels and sat on the chair for a few minutes, then crossed to pick up the vase and drew it to his face.

The daffodils smelled sweetly, of overturned earth warming in the sunlight. Anthea had loved daffodils, planting a hundred new bulbs every autumn; daffodils and jonquil and narcissus and crocuses, all the harbingers of spring. He inhaled again, deeply, and replaced the flowers on the sill. He left a light on beside the sink, returned to his room and went to bed.

He woke before 7:00. Thin sunlight filtered through the white curtains he'd drawn the night before and for several minutes he lay in bed, listening to the rhythmic boom of surf on the rocks. He finally got up, pulled aside the curtain and looked out.

A line of clouds hung above the western horizon, but over the headland the sky was pale blue, shot with gold where the sun rose above the moor. Hundreds of feet below Jeffrey's bedroom navy swells crashed against the base of the cliffs and swirled around ragged granite pinnacles that rose from the sea, surrounded by clouds of white seabirds. There was a crescent of white sand, and a black cavern-mouth gouged into one of the cliffs where a vortex rose and subsided with the waves.

The memory of last night's horror faded: sunlight and wheeling birds, the vast expanse of air and sea and all-but-treeless moor made him feel exhilarated. For the first time since Anthea's death he had a premonition not of dread but of the sort of exultation he felt as a teenager, waking in his boyhood room in early spring.

He dressed and shaved – there was no shower, only that dinghy-sized tub, so he'd forgo bathing till later. He waited until he was certain he heard movement in the kitchen, and went downstairs.

'Good morning.' A woman who might have been Harry's twin leaned against the slate sink. Slender, small-boned, with straight dark hair held back with two combs from a narrow face, brown-eyed and weathered as her brother's. 'I'm Thomsa.'

He shook her hand, glanced around for signs of coffee then peered out the window. 'This is an amazing place.'

'Yes, it is,' Thomsa said evenly. She spooned coffee into a glass cafetière, picked up a steaming kettle and poured hot water over the grounds. 'Coffee, right? I have tea if you prefer. Would you like eggs? Some people have all sorts of food allergies. Vegans, how do you feed them?' She stared at him in consternation, turned back to the sink, glancing at a bowl of eggs. 'How many?'

The cottage was silent, save for the drone of a television behind the closed door and the thunder of waves beating against the cliffs. Jeffrey sat at a table set for one, poured himself coffee and stared out to where the moor rose behind them. 'Does the sound of the ocean ever bother you?' he asked.

Thomsa laughed. 'No. We've been here thirty-five years; we're used to that. But we're building a house in Greece, in Hydra, that's where we just returned from. There's a church in the village and every afternoon the bells ring, I don't know why. At first I thought, isn't that lovely, church bells! Now I'm sick of them and just wish they'd shut up.'

She set a plate of fried eggs and thick-cut bacon in front of him, along with slabs of toasted brown bread and glass bowls of jam, picked up a mug and settled at the table. 'So, are you here on holiday?'

'Mmm, yes.' Jeffrey nodded, his mouth full. 'My wife died last fall. I just needed to get away for a bit.'

'Yes, of course. I'm very sorry.'

'She visited here once when she was a girl – not here, but at a farm nearby, in Zennor. I don't know the last name of the family, but the woman was named Becca.'

'Becca? Mmmm, no, I don't think so. Maybe Harry will know.'

'This would have been 1971.'

'Ah – no, we didn't move here till '75. Summer, us and all the other hippie types from back then.' She sipped her tea. 'No tourists around this time of year. Usually we don't open till the second week in March. But we don't have anyone scheduled yet, so.' She shrugged, pushing back a wisp of dark hair. 'It's quiet this time of year. No German tour buses. Do you paint?'

'Paint?' Jeffrey blinked. 'No. I'm an architect, so I draw, but mostly just for work. I sketch sometimes.'

'We get a lot of artists. There's the Tate in St Ives, if you like modern architecture. And of course there are all the prehistoric ruins – standing stones, and Zennor Quoit. There are all sorts of legends about them, fairy tales. People disappearing. They're very interesting, if you don't mind the walk.'

'Are there places to eat?'

'The inn here, though you might want to stop in and make a booking. There's the pub in Zennor, and St Ives of course, though it can be hard to park. And Penzance.'

Jeffrey winced. 'Not sure I want to get back on the road again immediately.'

'Yes, the drive here's a bit tricky, isn't it? But Zennor's only two miles, if you don't mind walking – lots of people do, we get hikers from all over on the coastal footpath. And Harry might be going out later, he could drop you off in Zennor if you like.'

'Thanks. Not sure what I'll do yet. But thank you.'

He ate his breakfast, making small talk with Thomsa and nodding at Harry when he emerged and darted through the kitchen, raising a hand as he slipped outside. Minutes later, Jeffrey glimpsed him pushing a wheelbarrow full of gardening equipment.

'I think the rain's supposed to hold off,' Thomsa said, staring out the window. 'I hope so. We want to finish that wall. Would you like me to make more coffee?'

'If you don't mind.'

Jeffrey dabbed a crust into the blackcurrant jam. He wanted to ask if Thomsa or her brother knew Robert Bennington, but was afraid he might be stirring up memories of some local scandal, or that he'd be taken for a journalist or some other busybody. He finished the toast, thanked Thomsa when she poured him more coffee, then reached for one of the brochures on the sideboard.

'So does this show where those ruins are?'

'Yes. You'll want the Ordnance Survey map. Here—'

She cleared the dishes, gathered a map and unfolded it. She tapped the outline of a tiny cove between two spurs of land. 'We're here.'

She traced one of the spurs, lifted her head to stare out the window to a grey-green spine of rock stretching directly to the south. 'That's Gurnard's Head. And there's Zennor Head—'

She turned and pointed in the opposite direction, to a looming promontory a few miles distant, and looked back down at the map. 'You can see where everything's marked.'

Jeffrey squinted to make out words printed in a tiny, Gothic font. TUMULI, STANDING STONE, HUT CIRCLE, CAIRN. 'Is there a fogou around here?'

'A fogou?' She frowned slightly. 'Yes, there is – out towards Zennor, across the moor. It's a bit of a walk.'

'Could you give me directions? Just sort of point the way? I might try and find it – give me something to do.'

Thomsa stepped to the window. 'The coastal path is there – see? If you follow it up to the ridge, you'll see a trail veer off. There's an old road there, the farmers use it sometimes. All those old fields run alongside it. The fogou's on the Golovenna Farm; I don't know how many fields back that is. It would be faster if you drove towards Zennor then hiked over the moor, but you could probably do it from here. You'll have to find an opening in the stone walls or climb over – do you have hiking shoes?' She looked dubiously at his sneakers. 'Well, they'll probably be all right.'

'I'll give it a shot. Can I take that map?'

'Yes, of course. It's not the best map – there's a more detailed Ordnance Survey one, I think.'

He thanked her and downed the rest of his coffee, went upstairs and pulled a heavy woollen sweater over his flannel shirt, grabbed his cell phone and returned downstairs. He retrieved the map and stuck it in his coat pocket, said goodbye to Thomsa, rinsing dishes in the sink, and walked outside.

The air was warmer, almost balmy despite a stiff wind that had torn the line of clouds into grey shreds. Harry knelt beside a stone wall, poking at the ground with a small spade. Jeffrey paused to watch him, then turned to survey clusters of daffodils and jonquils, scores of them, scattered across the terraced slopes among rocks and apple trees. The flowers were not yet in bloom, but he could glimpse sunlit yellow and orange and saffron petals swelling within the green buds atop each slender stalk.

'Going out?' Harry called.

'Yes.' Jeffrey stooped to brush his fingers across one of the flowers. 'My wife loved daffodils. She must have planted thousands of them.'

Harry nodded. 'Should open in the next few days. If we get some sun.'

Jeffrey waved farewell and turned to walk up the drive.

In a few minutes, the cottage was lost to sight. The cobblestones briefly gave way to cracked concrete, then a deep rut that marked a makeshift path that led uphill, towards the half-dozen buildings that made up the village. He stayed on the driveway, and after another hundred feet reached a spot where a narrow footpath meandered off to the left, marked by a sign. This would be the path that Thomsa had pointed out.

He shaded his eyes and looked back. He could just make out Cliff Cottage, its windows a flare of gold in the sun. He stepped onto the trail, walking with care across loose stones and channels where water raced downhill, fed by the early spring rains. To one side, the land sheared away to cliffs and crashing waves; he could see where the coastal path wound along the headland, fading into the emerald crown of Zennor Head. Above him, the ground rose steeply, overgrown with coiled ferns, newly sprung grass, thickets of gorse in brilliant sun-yellow bloom where bees and tiny orange butterflies fed. At the top of the incline, he could see the dark rim of a line of stone walls. He stayed on the footpath until it began to bear towards the cliffs, then looked for a place where he could break away and make for the ancient fields. He saw what looked like a path left by some kind of animal and scrambled up, dodging gorse, his sneakers sliding on loose scree, until he reached the top of the headland.

The wind here was so strong he nearly lost his balance as he hopped down into a grassy lane. The lane ran parallel to a long ridge of stone walls perhaps four feet high, braided with strands of rusted barbed wire. On the other side, endless intersections of yet more walls divided the moor into a dizzyingly ragged patchwork: jade-green, beryl, creamy yellow; ochre and golden amber. Here and there, twisted trees grew within sheltered corners, or rose from atop the walls themselves, gnarled branches scraping at the sky. High overhead, a bird arrowed towards the sea, and its plaintive cry rose above the roar of wind in his ears.

He pulled out the map, struggling to open it in the wind, finally gave up and shoved it back into his pocket. He tried to count back four fields, but it was hopeless – he couldn't make out where one field ended and another began.

And he had no idea what field to start with. He walked alongside the lane, away from the cottage and the village of Cardu, hoping he might find a gate or opening. He finally settled on a spot where the barbed wire had become engulfed by a protective thatch of dead vegetation. He clambered over the rocks, clutching desperately at dried leaves as the wall gave way beneath his feet and nearly falling onto a lethal-looking knot of barbed wire. Gasping, he reached the top of the wall, flailed as wind buffeted him then crouched until he could catch his breath.

The top of the wall was covered with vines, grey and leafless, as thick as his fingers and unpleasantly reminiscent of veins and arteries. This serpentine mass seemed to hold the stones together, though when he tried to step down the other side, the rocks once again gave way and he fell into a patch of whip-like vines studded with thorns the length of his thumbnail. Cursing, he extricated himself, his chinos torn and hands gouged and bloody, and staggered into the field.

Here at least there was some protection from the wind. The field sloped slightly uphill to the next wall. There was so sign of a gate or breach. He shoved his hands into his pockets and strode through knee-high grass, pale green and starred with minute yellow flowers. He reached the wall and walked alongside it. In one corner several large rocks had fallen. He hoisted himself up until he could see into the next field. It was no different from the one he'd just traversed, save for a single massive evergreen in its centre.

Other than the tree, the field seemed devoid of any vegetation larger than a tussock. He tried to peer into the field beyond, and the ones after that, but the countryside dissolved into a glitter of green and topaz beneath the morning sun, with a few stone pinnacles stark against the horizon where moor gave way to sky.

He turned and walked back, head down against the wind; climbed into the first field and crossed it, searching until he spied what looked like a safe place to gain access to the lane once more. Another tangle of blackthorn snagged him as he jumped down and landed hard, grimacing as a thorn tore at his neck. He glared at the wall, then headed back to the cottage, picking thorns from his overcoat and jeans.

He was starving by the time he arrived at the cottage, also filthy. It had grown too warm for his coat; he slung it over his shoulder, wiping sweat from his cheeks. Thomsa was outside, removing a shovel from the trunk of the car.

'Oh, hello! You're back quickly!'

He stopped, grateful for the wind on his overheated face. 'Quickly?'

'I thought you'd be off till lunchtime. A few hours, anyway?'

'I thought it *was* lunchtime.' He looked at his watch and frowned. 'That can't be right. It's not even ten.'

Thomsa nodded, setting the shovel beside the car. 'I thought maybe you forgot something.' She glanced at him, startled. 'Oh my – you're bleeding – did you fall?'

He shook his head. 'No, well, yes,' he said sheepishly. 'I tried to find that fogou. Didn't get very far. Are you sure it's just ten? I thought I was out there for hours – I figured it must be noon, at least. What time did I leave?'

'Half-past nine, I think.'

He started to argue, instead shrugged. 'I might try again. You said there's a better Ordnance Survey map? Something with more details?'

'Yes. You could probably get it in Penzance – call the bookshop there if you like, phone book's on the table.'

He found the phone book in the kitchen and rang the book-store. They had a copy of the map and would hold it for him. He rummaged on the table for a brochure with a map of Penzance, went upstairs to spend a few minutes washing up from his trek, and hurried outside. Thomsa and Harry were lugging stones across the grass to repair the wall. Jeffrey waved, ducked into the rental car and crept back up the drive towards Cardu.

In broad daylight it still took almost ten minutes. He glanced out to where the coastal footpath wound across the top of the cliffs, could barely discern a darker trail leading to the old field systems, and, beyond that, the erratic cross-stitch of stone walls fading into the eastern sky. Even if he'd only gone as far as the second field, it seemed impossible that he could have hiked all the way there and back to the cottage in half an hour.

The drive to Penzance took less time than that; barely long enough for Jeffrey to reflect how unusual it was for him to act like this, impulsively. Everything an architect did was according to plan. Out on the moor and gorse-covered cliffs the strangeness of the immense, dour landscape had temporarily banished the near-constant presence of his dead wife. Now, in the confines of the cramped rental car, images of other vehicles and other trips returned, all with Anthea beside him. He pushed them away, tried to focus on the fact that here at last was a place where he'd managed to escape her; and remembered that was not true at all.

Anthea had been here, too. Not the Anthea he had loved, but her mayfly self, the girl he'd never known; the Anthea who'd contained an entire secret world he'd never known existed. It seemed absurd, but he desperately wished she had confided in him about her visit to Bennington's house, and the strange night that had preceded it. Evelyn's talk of superstring theory was silly – he found himself sympathising with Moira, content to let someone else read the creepy books and tell her what to do. He believed in none of it, of course. Yet it didn't matter what he believed, but whether Anthea had, and why.

Penzance was surprisingly crowded for a weekday morning in early March. He circled the town's winding streets twice before he found a parking space, several blocks from the bookstore. He walked past shops and restaurants featuring variations on themes involving pirates, fish, pixies, sailing ships. As he passed a tattoo parlour, he glanced into the adjoining alley and saw the same rainbow-hatted boy from the train station, holding a skateboard and standing with several other teenagers who were passing around a joint. The boy looked up, saw Jeffrey and smiled. Jeffrey lifted his hand and smiled back. The boy called out to him, his words garbled by the wind, put down his skateboard and did a headstand alongside it. Jeffrey laughed and kept going.

There was only one other customer in the shop when he arrived, a man in a business suit talking to two women behind the register.

'Can I help you?' The older of the two women smiled. She had close-cropped red hair and fashionable eyeglasses, and set aside an iPad as Jeffrey approached.

'I called about an Ordnance Survey map?'

'Yes. It's right here.'

She handed it to him, and he unfolded it enough to see that

it showed the same area of West Penwith as the other map, enlarged and far more detailed.

The woman with the glasses cocked her head. 'Shall I ring that up?'

Jeffrey closed the map and set it onto the counter. 'Sure, in a minute. I'm going to look around a bit first.'

She returned to chatting. Jeffrey wandered the shop. It was small but crowded with neatly stacked shelves and tables, racks of maps and postcards, with an extensive section of books about Cornwall – guidebooks, tributes to Daphne du Maurier and Barbara Hepworth, DVDs of *The Pirates of Penzance* and *Rebecca*, histories of the mines and glossy photo volumes about surfing in Newquay. He spent a few minutes flipping through one of these, then continued to the back of the store. There was an entire wall of children's books, picture books near the floor, books for older children arranged alphabetically above them. He scanned the Bs, and looked aside as the younger woman approached, carrying an armful of calendars.

'Are you looking for something in particular?'

He glanced back at the shelves. 'Do you have anything by Robert Bennington?'

The young woman set the calendars down, ran a hand along the shelf housing the Bs; frowned and looked back to the counter. 'Rose, do we have anything by Robert Bennington? It rings a bell, but I don't see anything here. Children's writer, is he?' she added, turning to Jeffrey.

'Yes. *The Sun Battles*, I think that's one of them.'

The other customer nodded goodbye as Rose joined the others in the back.

'Robert Bennington?' She halted, straightening a stack of coffee table books, tapped her lower lip then quickly nodded. 'Oh yes! The fantasy writer. We did have his books – he's fallen out of favour.' She cast a knowing look at the younger clerk. 'He was the child molester.'

'Oh, right.' The younger woman made a face. 'I don't think his books are even in print now, are they?'

'I don't think so,' said Rose. 'I'll check. We could order something for you, if they are.'

'That's okay – I'm only here for a few days.'

Jeffrey followed her to the counter and waited as she searched online.

'No, nothing's available.' Rose shook her head. 'Sad bit of business, wasn't it? I heard something recently; he had a stroke I think. He might even have died, I can't recall now who told me. He must be quite elderly, if he's still alive.'

'He lived around here, didn't he?' said Jeffrey.

'Out near Zennor, I think. He bought the old Golovenna Farm, years ago. We used to sell quite a lot of his books – he was very popular. Like the *Harry Potter* books now. Well, not that popular.' She smiled. 'But he did very well. He came in here once or twice, it must be twenty years at least. A very handsome man. Theatrical. He wore a long scarf, like Doctor Who. I'm sure you could find used copies online, or there's a second-hand bookshop just round the corner – they might well have something.'

'That's all right. But thank you for checking.'

He paid for the map and went back out onto the sidewalk. It was getting on to noon. He wandered the streets for several minutes looking for a place to eat, settled on a small, airy Italian restaurant where he had grilled sardines and spaghetti and a glass of wine. Not very Cornish, perhaps, but he promised himself to check on the pub in Zennor later.

The Ordnance map was too large and unwieldy to open at his little table, so he stared out the window, watching tourists and women with small children in tow as they popped in and out of the shops across the street. The rainbow-hatted boy and his cronies loped by, skateboards in hand. Dropouts or burnouts, Jeffrey thought; the local constabulary must spend half its time chasing them from place to place. He finished his wine and ordered a cup of coffee, gulped it down, paid the check, and left.

A few high white clouds scudded high overhead, borne on a steady wind that sent up flurries of grit and petals blown from ornamental cherry trees. Here in the heart of Penzance, the midday sun was almost hot: Jeffrey hooked his coat over his shoulder and ambled back to his car. He paused to glance at postcards and souvenirs in a shop window, but could think of no one to send a card to. Evelyn? She'd rather have something from Zennor, another reason to visit the pub.

He turned the corner, had almost reached the tattoo parlour when a plaintive cry rang out.

'*Have you seen him?*'

Jeffrey halted. In the same alley where he'd glimpsed the boys earlier, a forlorn figure sat on the broken asphalt, twitchy fingers toying with an unlit cigarette. Erthy, the thirtyish woman who'd been at the station the day before. As Jeffrey hesitated she lifted her head, swiped a fringe of dirty hair from her eyes and stumbled to her feet. His heart sank as she hurried towards him, but before he could flee she was already in his face, her breath warm and beery. 'Gotta light?'

'No, sorry,' he said, and began to step away.

'Wait – you're London, right?'

'No, I'm just visiting.'

'No – I saw you.'

He paused, thrown off-balance by a ridiculous jolt of unease. Her eyes were bloodshot, the irises a peculiar marbled blue like flawed bottle-glass, and there was a vivid crimson splotch in one eye, as though a capillary had burst. It made it seem as though she looked at him sideways, even though she was staring at him straight on.

'You're on the London train!' She nodded in excitement. 'I need to get back.'

'I'm sorry.' He spun and walked off as quickly as he could without breaking into a run. Behind him he heard footsteps, and again the same wrenching cry.

'*Have you seen him?*'

He did run then, as the woman screamed expletives and a shower of gravel pelted his back.

He reached his rental car, his heart pounding. He looked over his shoulder, jumped inside and locked the doors before pulling out into the street. As he drove off, he caught a flash in the rear-view mirror of the woman sidling in the other direction, unlit cigarette still twitching between her fingers.

When he arrived back at the cottage, he found Thomsa and Harry sitting at the kitchen table, surrounded by the remains of lunch, sandwich crusts and apple cores.

'Oh, hello.' Thomsa looked up, smiling, and patted the chair beside her. 'Did you go to The Tinners for lunch?'

'Penzance.' Jeffrey sat and dropped his map onto the table. 'I think I'll head out again, then maybe have dinner at the pub.'

'He wants to see the fogou,' said Thomsa. 'He went earlier but couldn't find it. There is a fogou, isn't there, Harry? Out by Zennor Hill?'

Jeffrey hesitated, then said, 'A friend of mine told me about it – she and my wife saw it when they were girls.'

'Yes,' said Harry after a moment. 'Where the children's writer lived. Some sort of ruins there, anyway.'

Jeffrey kept his tone casual. 'A writer?'

'I believe so,' said Thomsa. 'We didn't know him. Someone who stayed here once went looking for him, but he wasn't home – this was years ago. The old Golovenna Farm.'

Jeffrey pointed to the seemingly random network of lines that covered the map, like crazing on a piece of old pottery. 'What's all this mean?'

Harry pulled his chair closer and traced the boundaries of Cardu with a dirt-stained finger. 'Those are the field systems – the stone walls.'

'You're kidding.' Jeffrey laughed. 'That must've driven someone nuts, getting all that down.'

'Oh, it's all GPS and satellite photos now,' said Thomsa. 'I'm sorry I didn't have this map earlier, before you went for your walk.'

Harry angled the map so the sunlight illuminated the area surrounding Cardu. 'This is our cove, here . . .'

They pored over the map. Jeffrey pointed at markers for hut circles and cairns, standing stones and tumuli, all within a hand's-span of Cardu, as Harry continued to shake his head.

'It's this one, I think,' Harry said at last, and glanced at his sister. He scored a square half-inch of the page with a blackened finger-nail, minute Gothic letters trapped within the web of field systems.

CHAMBERED CAIRN

'That looks right,' said Thomsa. 'But it's a ways off the road. I'm not certain where the house is – the woman who went looking for it said she roamed the moor for hours before she came on it.'

Jeffrey ran his finger along the line marking the main road. 'It looks like I can drive to here. If there's a place to park, I can just hike in. It doesn't look that far. As long as I don't get towed.'

'You shouldn't get towed,' said Thomsa. 'All that land's part of Golovenna, and no one's there. He never farmed it, just let it all go back to the moor. You'd only be a mile or so from Zennor if you left your car. They have musicians on Thursday nights, some of the locals come in and play after dinner.'

Jeffrey refolded the map. When he looked up, Harry was gone. Thomsa handed him an apple.

'Watch for the bogs,' she said. 'Marsh grass, it looks sturdy, but when you put your foot down it gives way and you can sink under.

Like quicksand. They found a girl's body ten years back. Horses and sheep, too.' Jeffrey grimaced and she laughed. 'You'll be all right – just stay on the footpaths.'

He thanked her, went upstairs to exchange his overcoat for a windbreaker, and returned to his car. The clouds were gone: the sun shone high in a sky the summer blue of gentians. He felt the same surge of exultation he'd experienced that morning, the sea-fresh wind tangling the stems of daffodils and narcissus, white gulls crying overhead. He kept the window down as he drove up the twisting way to Cardu and the honeyed scent of gorse filled the car.

The road to Zennor coiled between hedgerows misted green with new growth and emerald fields where brown-and-white cattle grazed. In the distance a single tractor moved so slowly across a black furrow that Jeffrey could track its progress only by the skein of crows that followed it, the birds dipping then rising like a black thread drawn through blue cloth.

Twice he pulled over to consult the map. His phone didn't work here – he couldn't even get the time, let alone directions. The car's clock read 14:21. He saw no other roads, only deeply-rutted tracks protected by stiles, some metal, most of weathered wood. He tried counting stone walls to determine which marked the fields Harry had said belonged to Golovenna Farm, and stopped a third time before deciding the map was all but useless. He drove another hundred feet until he found a swathe of gravel between two tumble-down stone walls, a rusted gate sagging between them. Beyond it stretched an overgrown field bisected by a stone-strewn path.

He was less than a mile from Zennor. He folded the map and jammed it into his windbreaker pocket along with the apple, and stepped out of the car.

The dark height before him would be Zennor Hill. Golovenna Farm was somewhere between there and where he stood. He turned slowly, scanning everything around him to fix it in his memory: the winding road, intermittently visible between walls and hedgerows; the ridge of cliffs falling down to the sea, bookended by the dark bulk of Gurnards Head in the southwest and Zennor Head to the northeast. On the horizon were scattered outcroppings that might have been tors or ruins or even buildings. He locked the car, checked that he had his phone, climbed over the metal gate and began to walk.

The afternoon sun beat down fiercely. He wished he'd brought a hat, or sunglasses. He crossed the first field in a few minutes, and was relieved to find a break in the next wall, an opening formed by a pair of tall, broad stones. The path narrowed here but was still clearly discernible where it bore straight in front of him, an arrow of new green grass flashing through ankle-high turf overgrown with daisies and fronds of young bracken.

The ground felt springy beneath his feet. He remembered Thomsa's warning about the bogs and glanced around for something he might use as a walking stick. There were no trees in sight, only wicked-looking thickets of blackthorn clustered along the perimeter of the field.

He found another gap in the next wall, guarded like the first by two broad stones nearly as tall as he was. He clambered onto the wall, fighting to open his map in the brisk wind, and examined it, trying to find some affinity between the fields around him and the crazed pattern on the page. At last he shoved the map back into his pocket, set his back to the wind and shaded his eyes with his hand.

It was hard to see – he was staring due west, into the sun – but he thought he glimpsed a black bulge some three or four fields off, a dark blister within the haze of green and yellow. It might be a ruin, or just as likely a farm or outbuildings. He clambered down into the next field, crushing dead bracken and shoots of heather; picked his way through a breach where stones had fallen and hurried until he reached yet another wall.

There were the remnants of a gate here, a rusted latch and iron pins protruding from the granite. Jeffrey crouched beside the wall to catch his breath. After a few minutes he scrambled to his feet and walked through the gap, letting one hand rest for an instant upon the stone. Despite the hot afternoon sun it felt cold beneath his palm, more like metal than granite. He glanced aside to make sure he hadn't touched a bit of rusted hardware, but saw only a boulder seamed with moss.

The fields he'd already passed through had seemed rank and overgrown, as though claimed by the wilderness decades ago. Yet there was no mistaking what stretched before him as anything but open moor. Clumps of gorse sprang everywhere, starbursts of yellow blossom shadowing pale-green ferns and tufts of dogtooth violets. He walked cautiously – he couldn't see the earth underfoot for all the new growth – but the ground felt solid beneath mats of dead bracken that gave off a spicy October scent. He was so intent on watching his step that he nearly walked into a standing stone.

He sucked his breath in sharply and stumbled backward. For a fraction of a second he'd perceived a figure there, but it was only a stone, twice his height and leaning at a forty-five degree angle, so that it pointed towards the sea. He circled it, then ran his hand across its granite flank, sun-warmed and furred with lichen and dried moss. He kicked at the thatch of ferns and ivy that surrounded its base, stooped and dug his hand through the vegetation, until his fingers dug into raw earth.

He withdrew his hand and backed away, staring at the ancient monument, at once minatory and banal. He could recall no indication of a standing stone between Cardu and Zennor, and when he checked the map he saw nothing there.

But something else loomed up from the moor a short distance away – a house. He headed towards it, slowing his steps in case someone saw him, so that they might have time to come outside.

No one appeared. After five minutes he stood in a rutted drive beside a long, one-storey building of grey stone similar to those he'd passed on the main road; slate-roofed, with deep small windows and a wizened tree beside the door, its branches rattling in the wind. A worn hand-lettered sign hung beneath the low eaves: GOLOVENNA FARM.

Jeffrey looked around. He saw no car, only a large plastic trash bin that had blown over. He rapped at the door, waited, then knocked again, calling out a greeting. When no one answered he tried the knob, but the door was locked.

He stepped away to peer in through the window. There were no curtains. Inside looked dark and empty, no furniture or signs that someone lived here, or indeed if anyone had for years. He walked round the house, stopping to look inside each window and half-heartedly trying to open them, without success. When he'd completed this circuit, he wandered over to the trash bin and looked inside. It too was empty.

He righted it, then stood and surveyed the land around him. The rutted path joined a narrow, rock-strewn drive that led off into the moor to the west. He saw what looked like another structure not far from where the two tracks joined, a collapsed building of some sort.

He headed towards it. A flock of little birds flittered from a gorse bush, making a sweet high-pitched song as they soared past him, close enough that he could see their speckled breasts and hear their wings beat against the wind. They settled on the ruined building, twittering companionably as he approached, then took flight once more.

It wasn't a building but a mound, roughly rectangular but with rounded corners, maybe twenty feet long and half again as wide; as tall as he was, and so overgrown with ferns and blackthorn that he might have mistaken it for a hillock. He kicked through brambles and clinging thorns until he reached one end, where the mound's curve had been sheared off.

Erosion, he thought at first; then realised that he was gazing into an entryway. He glanced behind him before drawing closer, until he stood knee-deep in dried bracken and whip-like black-thorn.

In front of him was a simple doorway of upright stones, man-high, with a larger stone laid across the tops to form a lintel. Three more stones were set into the ground as steps, descending to a passage choked with young ferns and ivy mottled black and green as malachite.

Jeffrey ducked his head beneath the lintel and peered down into the tunnel. He could see nothing but vague outlines of more stones and straggling vines. He reached to thump the ceiling to see if anything moved.

Nothing did. He checked his phone – still no signal – turned to stare up into the sky, trying to guess what time it was. He'd left the car around 2:30, and he couldn't have been walking for more than an hour. Say it was four o'clock, to be safe. He still had a good hour-and-a-half to get back to the road before dark.

He took out the apple Thomsa had given him and ate it, dropped the core beside the top step; zipped his windbreaker and descended into the passage.

He couldn't see how long it was, but he counted thirty paces, pausing every few steps to look back at the entrance, before the light faded enough that he needed to use his cell phone for illu-mination. The walls glittered faintly where broken crystals were embedded in the granite, and there was a moist, earthy smell, like a damp cellar. He could stand upright with his arms outstretched, his fingertips grazing the walls to either side. The vegetation disap-peared after the first ten paces, except for moss, and after a few more steps there was nothing beneath his feet but bare earth. The walls were of stone, dirt packed between them and hardened by the centuries so that it was almost indistinguishable from the granite.

He kept going, glancing back as the entryway diminished to a bright mouth, then a glowing eye, and finally a hole no larger than that left by a finger thrust through a piece of black cloth.

A few steps more and even that was gone. He stopped, his breath coming faster, then walked another five paces, the glow from his cell phone a blue moth flickering in his hand. Once again he stopped to look back.

He could see nothing behind him. He shut off the cell phone's light, experimentally moved his hand swiftly up and down before his face; closed his eyes then opened them. There was no difference.

His mouth went dry. He turned his phone on, took a few more steps deeper into the passage before halting again. The phone's periwinkle glow was insubstantial as a breath of vapour: he could see neither the ground beneath him nor the walls to either side. He raised his arms and extended them, expecting to feel cold stone beneath his fingertips.

The walls were gone. He stepped backwards, counting five paces, and again extended his arms. Still nothing. He dropped his hands and began to walk forward, counting each step – five, six, seven, ten, thirteen – stopped and slowly turned in a circle, holding the phone at arm's-length as he strove to discern some feature in the encroaching darkness. The pallid blue gleam flared then went out.

He swore furiously, fighting panic. He turned the phone on and off, to no avail; finally shoved it into his pocket and stood, trying to calm himself.

It was impossible that he could be lost. The mound above him wasn't that large, and even if the fogou's passage continued for some distance underground, he would eventually reach the end, at which point he could turn around and painstakingly wend his way back out again. He tried to recall something he'd read once, about navigating the maze at Hampton Court – always keep your hand on the left-hand side of the hedge. All he had to do was locate a wall, and walk back into daylight.

He was fairly certain that he was still facing the same way as when he had first entered. He turned, so that he was now facing where the doorway should be, and walked, counting aloud as he did. When he reached one hundred he stopped.

There was no way he had walked more than a hundred paces into the tunnel. Somehow, he had got turned around. He wiped his face, slick and chill with sweat, and breathed deeply, trying to slow his racing heart. He heard nothing, saw nothing save that impenetrable darkness. Everything he had ever read about getting lost advised staying put and waiting for help; but that involved being lost above ground, where someone would eventually find you. At some point Thomsa and Harry would notice he hadn't returned, but that might not be till morning.

And who knew how long it might be before they located him? The thought of spending another twelve hours or more here, motionless, unable to see or hear, or touch anything save the ground beneath his feet, filled Jeffrey with such overwhelming horror that he felt dizzy.

And that was worst of all: if he fell, would he even touch the ground? He crouched, felt an absurd wash of relief as he pressed his palms against the floor. He straightened, took another deep breath and began to walk.

He tried counting his steps, as a means to keep track of time, but before long a preternatural stillness came over him, a sense that he was no longer awake but dreaming. He pinched the back of his hand, hard enough that he gasped. Yet still the feeling remained, that he'd somehow fallen into a recurring dream, the horror deadened somewhat by a strange familiarity. As though he'd stepped into an icy pool, he stopped, shivering, and realised the source of his apprehension.

It had been in the last chapter of Robert Bennington's book, *Still the Seasons*; the chapter that he'd never been able to recall clearly. Even now it was like remembering something that had happened *to* him, not something he'd read: the last of the novel's four children passing through a portal between one world and another, surrounded by utter darkness and the growing realisation that with each step the world around her was disintegrating and that she herself was disintegrating as well, until the book ended with her isolated consciousness fragmented into incalculable motes within an endless, starless void.

The terror of that memory jarred him. He jammed his hands into his pockets and felt his cell phone and the map, his car keys, some change. He walked more quickly, gazing straight ahead, focused on finding the spark within the passage that would resolve into the entrance.

After some time his heart jumped – it was there, so small he might have imagined it, a wink of light faint as a clouded star.

But when he ran a few paces he realised it was his mind playing tricks on him. A phantom light floated in the air, like the luminous blobs behind one's knuckled eyelids. He blinked and rubbed his eyes: the light remained.

'Hello?' he called, hesitating. There was no reply.

He started to walk, but slowly, calling out several times into the silence. The light gradually grew brighter. A few more minutes and a second light appeared, and then a third. They cast no glow upon the tunnel, nor shadows: he could see neither walls nor ceiling, nor any sign of those who carried the lights. All three seemed suspended in the air, perhaps ten feet above the floor, and all bobbed slowly up and down, as though each was borne upon a pole.

Jeffrey froze. The lights were closer now, perhaps thirty feet from where he stood.

'Who is it?' he whispered.

He heard the slightest of sounds, a susurrus as of escaping air. With a cry he turned and fled, his footsteps echoing through the passage. He heard no sounds of pursuit, but when he looked back, the lights were still there, moving slowly towards him. With a gasp he ran harder, his chest aching, until one foot skidded on something and he fell. As he scrambled back up, his hand touched a flat smooth object; he grabbed it and without thinking jammed it into his pocket, and raced on down the tunnel.

And now, impossibly, in the vast darkness before him he saw a jot of light that might have been reflected from a spider's eye. He kept going. Whenever he glanced back, he saw the trio of lights behind him.

They seemed to be more distant now. And there was no doubt that the light in front of him spilled from the fogou's entrance – he could see the outlines of the doorway, and the dim glister of quartz and mica in the walls to either side. With a gasp he reached the steps, stumbled up them and back out into the blinding light of afternoon. He stopped, coughing and covering his eyes until he could see, then staggered back across first one field and then the next, hoisting himself over rocks heedless of blackthorns tearing his palms and clothing, until at last he reached the final overgrown tract of heather and bracken, and saw the white roof of his rental car shining in the sun.

He ran up to it, jammed the key into the lock and with a gasp fell into the driver's seat. He locked the doors, flinching as another car drove past, and finally looked out the window.

To one side was the gate he'd scaled, with field after field beyond; to the other side the silhouettes of Gurnard's Head and its sister promontory. Beyond the fields, the sun hung well above the lowering mass of Zennor Hill. The car's clock read 15:23.

He shook his head in disbelief: it was impossible he'd been gone for scarcely an hour. He reached for his cell phone and felt something in the pocket beside it – the object he'd skidded on inside the fogou.

He pulled it out. A blue metal disc, slightly flattened where he'd stepped on it, with gold-stamped words above a beacon.

ST AUSTELL SWEETS: FUDGE FROM REAL CORNISH CREAM

He turned it over in his hands and ran a finger across the raised lettering.

Aunt Becca gave one to each of us the day we arrived. The fudge was supposed to last the entire two weeks, and I think we ate it all that first night.

The same kind of candy tin where Evelyn had kept her comb and Anthea her locket and chain. He stared at it, the tin bright and enamel glossy-blue as though it had been painted yesterday. Anyone could have a candy tin, especially one from a local company that catered to tourists.

After a minute he set it down, took out his wallet and removed the photo Evelyn had given him: Evelyn and Moira doubled-up with laughter as Anthea stared at them, slightly puzzled, a half-smile on her face as though trying to determine if they were laughing at her.

He gazed at the photo for a long time, returned it to his wallet, then slid the candy lid back into his pocket. He still had no service on his phone.

He drove very slowly back to Cardu, nauseated from sunstroke and his terror at being underground. He knew he'd never been seriously lost – a backwards glance as he fled the mound reassured him that it hadn't been large enough for that.

Yet he was profoundly unnerved by his reaction to the darkness, the way his sight had betrayed him and his imagination reflexively dredged up the images from Evelyn's story. He was purged of any desire to remain another night at the cottage, or even in England, and considered checking to see if there was an evening train back to London.

But by the time he edged the car down the long drive to the cottage, his disquiet had ebbed somewhat. Thomsa and Harry's car was gone. A stretch of wall had been newly repaired, and many more daffodils and narcissus had opened, their sweet fragrance following him as he trudged to the front door.

Inside he found a plate with a loaf of freshly baked bread and some local blue cheese, beside it several pamphlets with a yellow Post-It note.

> *Jeffrey —*
> *Gone to see a play in Penzance. Please turn off lights downstairs. I found these books today and thought you might be interested in them.*
> *Thomsa*

He glanced at the pamphlets – another map, a flyer about a music night at the pub in Zennor, a small paperback with a green cover – crossed to the refrigerator and foraged until he found two bottles of beer. Probably not proper B&B etiquette, but he'd apologise in the morning.

He grabbed the plate and book and went upstairs to his room. He kicked off his shoes, groaning with exhaustion, removed his torn windbreaker and regarded himself in the mirror, his face scratched and flecked with bits of greenery.

'What a mess,' he murmured, and collapsed onto the bed.

He downed one of the bottles of beer and most of the bread and cheese. Outside, light leaked from a sky deepening to ultramarine. He heard the boom and sigh of waves, and for a long while he reclined in the window-seat and stared out at the cliffs, watching as shadows slipped down them like black paint. At last he stood and got some clean clothes from his bag. He hooked a finger around the remaining bottle, picked up the book Thomsa had left for him and retired to the bathroom.

The immense tub took ages to fill, but there seemed to be unlimited hot water. He put all the lights on and undressed, sank into the tub and gave himself over to the mindless luxury of hot water and steam and the scent of daffodils on the windowsill.

Finally he turned the water off. He reached for the bottle he'd set on the floor and opened it, dried his hands and picked up the book, a worn paperback, its creased cover showing a sweep of green hills topped by a massive tor, with a glimpse of sea in the distance.

OLD TALES FOR NEW DAYS
BY ROBERT BENNINGTON

Jeffrey whistled softly, took a long swallow of beer and opened the book. It was not a novel but a collection of stories, published in 1970 – Cornish folktales, according to a brief preface, 'told anew for today's generation'. He scanned the table of contents – 'Pisky-Led', 'Tregeagle and the Devil', 'Jack the Giant Killer' – then sat up quickly in the tub, spilling water as he gazed at a title underlined with red ink: 'Cherry of Zennor'. He flipped through the pages until he found it.

Sixteen-year-old Cherry was the prettiest girl in Zennor, not that she knew it. One day while walking on the moor she met a young man as handsome as she was lovely.

'Will you come with me?' he asked, and held out a beautiful lace handkerchief to entice her. 'I'm a widower with an infant son who needs tending. I'll pay you better wages than any man or woman earns from here to Kenidjack Castle, and give you dresses that will be the envy of every girl at Morvah Fair.'

Now, Cherry had never had a penny in her pocket in her entire young life, so she let the young man take her arm and lead her across the moor . . .

There were no echoes here of *The Sun Battles*, no vertiginous terrors of darkness and the abyss; just a folk tale that reminded Jeffrey a bit of *Rip Van Winkle*, with Cherry caring for the young son and, as the weeks passed, falling in love with the mysterious man.

Each day she put ointment on the boy's eyes, warned by his

father never to let a drop fall upon her own, until of course one day she couldn't resist doing so, and saw an entire host of gorgeously-dressed men and women moving through the house around her, including her mysterious employer and a beautiful woman who was obviously his wife. Bereft and betrayed, Cherry fled; her lover caught up with her on the moor and pressed some coins into her hand.

'You must go now and forget what you have seen,' he said sadly, and touched the corner of her eye. When she returned home she found her parents dead and gone, along with everyone she knew, and her cottage a ruin open to the sky. Some say it is still a good idea to avoid the moors near Zennor.

Jeffrey closed the book and dropped it on the floor beside the tub. When he at last headed back down the corridor, he heard voices from the kitchen, and Thomsa's voice raised in laughter. He didn't go downstairs; only returned to his room and locked the door behind him.

He left early the next morning, after sharing breakfast with Thomsa at the kitchen table.

'Harry's had to go to St Ives to pick up some tools he had repaired.' She poured Jeffrey more coffee and pushed the cream across the table towards him. 'Did you have a nice ramble yesterday and go to the Tinners?'

Jeffrey smiled but said nothing. He was halfway up the winding driveway back to Cardu before he realised he'd forgotten to mention the two bottles of beer.

He returned the rental car and got a ride to the station from Evan, the same man who'd picked him up two days earlier.

'Have a good time in Zennor?'

'Very nice,' said Jeffrey.

'Quiet this time of year.' Evan pulled the car to the curb. 'Looks like your train's here already.'

Jeffrey got out, slung his bag over his shoulder and started for the station entrance. His heart sank when he saw two figures arguing on the sidewalk a few yards away, one a policeman.

'Come on now, Erthy,' he was saying, glancing up as Jeffrey drew closer. 'You know better than this.'

'Fuck you!' she shouted, and kicked at him. 'Not my fucking name!'

'That's it.'

The policeman grabbed her wrist and bent his head to speak into a walkie-talkie. Jeffrey began to hurry past. The woman screamed after him, shaking her clenched fist. Her eye with its bloody starburst glowed crimson in the morning sun.

'London!' Her voice rose desperately as she fought to pull away from the cop. 'London, please, take me—'

Jeffrey shook his head. As he did, the woman raised her fist and flung something at him. He gasped as it stung his cheek, clapping a hand to his face as the policeman shouted and began to drag the woman away from the station.

'London! *London!*'

As her shrieks echoed across the plaza, Jeffrey stared at a speck of blood on his finger. Then he stooped to pick up what she'd thrown at him: a yellow pencil worn with toothmarks, its graphite tip blunted but the tiny, embossed black letters still clearly readable above the ferrule.

RAVENWOOD.

ELIZABETH HAND is the author of numerous multiple-award-winning, genre-spanning novels and collections of short fiction, as well as a long-time reviewer and critic for many publications.

She has two novels coming out in 2012: *Available Dark*, a psychological thriller and follow-up to her Shirley Jackson Award-winner *Generation Loss*, and *Radiant Days*, a YA novel about the French poet Arthur Rimbaud.

She lives on the coast of Maine, where she is at work on *Wylding Hall*, a YA suspense novel inspired by Daphne du Maurier's *Rebecca*.

'I have a complicated relationship with West Penwith,' explains Hand, 'my favourite part of the UK (except, of course, for London). In 2000, I had to cancel an overseas journey at the last minute, the highlight of which was to be my third trip to West Penwith. Crushed by not being able to visit, I spent those three weeks home in Maine, writing "Cleopatra Brimstone".

'My next trip coincided with 2001's devastating foot-and-mouth epidemic, which curtailed much of the research I'd intended to do – no tromping across the moors and open fields. A few years later, I once again had to cancel a trip to the countryside near Zennor. And, while in London in March 2011, two days before my now much-delayed return to Cornwall, I learned that my oldest and closest friend had suffered a brain aneurysm, was in a coma and not expected to recover. Eerily, just days before my friend was stricken, I'd begun a story – this one – with the protagonist's beloved wife dying of a brain aneurysm. I did go to West Penwith, though the trip was inevitably overshadowed by grief. My friend died the day I returned to the US.

'All of the events recounted by Evelyn, involving an impromptu ritual and subsequent appearance of three spectral lights, actually occurred on March 12, 1971, to myself and two friends in Pound

Ridge, New York. I have no more explanation for what happened than Jeffrey does in the story – less, in fact, because as far as I know there are no burial mounds off Long Ridge Road. Unless, of course, there are.'

Last Words

—RICHARD CHRISTIAN MATHESON—

I SAVOUR a good moment of death.

The stumbling exhalations of consciousness as the sufferer lingers and searches for final words; the poignant exit.

Classic stuff.

Demise can come with eyes tightly shut; far less interesting than with them open, spiritually scanning the cosmic path that awaits. Even in filmmaking, a final stare, upon passing, is always more evocative than lids fluttering which produces a lazy, maudlin finish. With eyes open, available light affixes to the unblinking stare and, though the effect is slightly unnerving, allows it to glow with heart-felt drama that approaches the lyrical.

All deaths are different. The end can come via terror or nobility. Mostly it's a trivial detour into eternity which is how most bid dull *adieu*. Still, however it comes, everyone is entitled to their final moment; a fitting segue to consider details:

A simple stabbing, by way of example, doesn't allow much time for reflection, especially if the blade interferes with airways. Too much blood loss. Always worse if awkwardly located for removal by its victim. In a similar way, final words are more manageable when the damage doesn't directly affect cardiac function, vocalisation or mental acuity. Mortal injuries ranging from blunt trauma to partial evisceration can also aid in composing final thoughts. Blood loss is minimal enough to provide focus. Poison, owing to its often delayed effect, is also nicely collaborative, its slower impact inviting moments of review. In some cases it may also trigger eventual seizure in the expiring party, a convulsive response that can produce suffocation, adding unexpected gravitas to final words. In especially theatrical examples, the mouth will froth, which provides visual flourish; a value nearly cinematic.

But crucially, whether by disease, mishap or tragedy, when the time comes, there is no turning back and any negotiation with the heavens is ill-spent energy. Last second desperation that consumes valuable time is no ally. Far more useful, as the pulse wanes, to think of final words. On that subject, some examples are shared here, drawn from quotes, gathered over years of encounters with those who are short on time.

Example one:

'Oh, God, Mother, don't let this happen to me! Please help me! I will always love you!'

Spontaneous and appreciative, although there is a hint of the well-worn. Of course, everyone isn't Shakespeare. When he died, maybe he wasn't either.

Another example:

'It hurts . . . it hurts . . . I can't believe how bad it hurts!'

A triumph of the succinct. Almost musical. According to notes, that was a gunshot to both knees and three into the heart. Postscript: the deceased didn't last long after that. Bled out all over the forest floor. They never found her.

They rarely do.

This next one is memorable:

'. . . In the next world, I will never see such cruelty . . .'

Stirring in its own way, like tormented Irish poetry. It could go well with tea. Minimal emotional indulgence; always notable.

According to notes, he was duct-taped and a drill had been used on his skull.

This one from 2004 is a favourite:

'*What did I do wrong?*'

Was there ever a more existential lament? Worthy of Camus. According to notes, acid was poured into his eyes and rectum. Philosophy flowed as he tried to flee.

Let us take a moment to remind ourselves that most don't think about the final thing they'll say. Certainly, few know how they'll die. But as in all movie death scenes, the telling close-up will come. And with any luck, someone may be near to witness the final utterance. No matter how they depart this deceiving world, most wish to be remembered. It's therefore vital they consider their last words. At the stroke of midnight, it's too late to assemble a worthy farewell and despite any torment they suffer, no matter how afraid, no matter how rapidly their blood empties, they mustn't improvise. Pain is momentary. They have to get past those things. Take my word for it.

To be avoided is the clumsy nonchalance some actors affect on the Oscars, fumbling with notes scribbled on napkins or, far worse, sputtering and hoping the heavens will rain eloquence. But the heavens don't. They never did and never will; they are a fiction. Each person must provide their own finale. All books have an important final line. All movies have one. So should a life.

I do love movies.

A last piece of advice: know thyself. For example, I take lives because I enjoy hearing people suffer. I relish the begging and the sounds of helpless shock. Sometimes I wish I could make them myself.

The best one I ever heard was:

'*You will suffer forever for what you've done.*'

She was a young mother, very pretty and genuine. I won't go into the things I did to her with pliers and bleach, but I will say some people just don't want to die and for the entire weekend she wouldn't stop pleading or screaming. It was heaven.

However, to set the record straight: she was mistaken. As it turns out, to the surprise and dismay of many, I do enjoy my life and look forward to every day, notwithstanding what some figured would happen. Losing my voice when I was two was a bad break. That's all. Despite that animal cutting out my larynx when I wouldn't stop crying, I never sought pity. I wanted to speak like others, but had to get over it. I never looked for sympathy and never from my mother, who was dead inside and let him fucking do it until my soft throat was so sawed-open my head slumped to one side and I couldn't call out for help even though I tried and they just left me to fucking die.

The last words I remember ever saying were 'You hurt me, Dada . . .'

Pathetic.

The day I burned their house down and stood on the sidewalk listening to them beg and die, my life began, again. *'Someone save us! We're burning to death!'* Predictable. Selfish, blameless. So fucking them. It was my first saved quote.

Sometimes when what's left of my throat spasms and I can't easily breathe or sleep, I watch the video recordings of the people I've killed. It's like going to the movies. Tense; filled with twists.

The last words are always the highlight.

RICHARD CHRISTIAN MATHESON is a novelist, short story writer and screenwriter/producer. He is also the president of Matheson Entertainment, a production company he formed with his father, Richard Matheson, which is currently involved with multiple film and television projects.

He has written and co-written feature film and television projects for Richard Donner, Ivan Reitman, Joel Silver, Steven Spielberg, Bryan Singer and many others. To date, Matheson has written and sold fourteen original spec feature scripts, which is considered a record.

His credits include *Sole Survivor*, a four-hour Fox mini-series based on Dean Koontz's best-selling novel; *Delusion*, an original horror suspense film for VH1; *Demons*, an original dark suspense film for Showtime Networks, and the adaptation of Roger Zelazny's *The Chronicles of Amber* as a four-hour mini-series for the Syfy Channel.

Matheson has also recently created and written *Majestic*, a one-hour paranormal series for TNT, based on the work of Whitley Strieber, and he is currently in development on *Dragons*, a six-hour mini-series with director Bryan Singer, which he created. He also recently created *Splatter*, a web-based horror project with Roger Corman, directed by Joe Dante.

Some of his short stories are collected in *Scars and Other Distinguishing Marks*, with an introduction by Stephen King, and *Dystopia*. His debut novel, *Created By*, was a Bram Stoker Award nominee, and his new novella, *The Ritual of Illusion*, is available from PS Publishing.

About 'Last Words', Matheson explains: 'This story blends idealism and a black heart. Its oddly-reasoned crux is that, in the end, we must be heard and remembered.'

STEPHEN JONES lives in London, England. He is the winner of three World Fantasy Awards, four Horror Writers' Association Bram Stoker Awards and three International Horror Guild Awards, as well as being a twenty-one time recipient of the British Fantasy Award and a Hugo Award nominee. A former television producer/director and genre movie publicist and consultant (the first three *Hellraiser* movies, *Nightbreed*, *Split Second* etc.), he has written and edited more than 100 books, including *Coraline: A Visual Companion*, *The Essential Monster Movie Guide*, *Horror: 100 Best Books* and *Horror: Another 100 Best Books* (both with Kim Newman) and the *Dark Terrors*, *Dark Voices* and *The Mammoth Book of Best New Horror* series. He was Guest of Honour at the 2002 World Fantasy Convention in Minneapolis, Minnesota, and the 2004 World Horror Convention in Phoenix, Arizona, and is a guest lecturer at UCLA in California and London's Kingston University and St Mary's University College. You can visit his web site at *www.stephenjoneseditor.com*.

Acknowledgements

I would like to thank Jo Fletcher, Val and Les Edwards, Marlaine Delargy, Chuck Verrill, Mandy Slater and Dorothy Lumley for all their help and support.